Soul Beliefs

The Soul Stone Series

Penelope Coggins

Staten House

Copyright © 2024 by Penelope Coggins

All rights reserved.

No part of this publication may be reproduced, distributed, or transmitted in any form or by any means, including photocopying, recording, or other electronic or mechanical methods, without the prior written permission of the publisher, except as permitted by U.S. copyright law. For permission requests, contact [include publisher/author contact info].

The story, all names, characters, and incidents portrayed in this production are fictitious. No identification with actual persons (living or deceased), places, buildings, and products is intended or should be inferred.

Book Cover by Algart

To my Soulmate,
You are the reason I can be me and not be afraid of it.
And
To Twelve Year Old Me
Who first thought up this story.
You will never understand how much your story has helped me
but I promise I've loved every second of writing it.

Note From The Author

Firstly I want to say thank you for picking up my book. This is my debut novel and no doubt I've gotten some things wrong but that's why I want to make sure I'm being truly transparent about the content with in it.

Soul Beliefs is a romance novel and was written with a New Adult/Adult audience in mind, therefor it does include scenes suitable for readers 18+. I do believe these scenes can be skipped and you'll still get a full picture of the story, but I still understand if you chose to turn around now.

In addition, the book does touch on topics such as anxiety, an on page panic attack, talk of an alcoholic parent, talk of a parent passing away, talk of being abandoned by a parent, divorce and grief. If you know these can be triggers for you, please keep this in mind.

Lastly please bear in mind that the book is written in British English, but that Katherine is from The United States and so some words have been spelt and chosen to reflect this. James is from Australia and so much in the same way certain words are spelt differently to reflect where he is from.

Playlist

Pocketful Of Sunshine - Natasha Bedingfield
Cosmic Love - Florence + The Machine
Unconditionally - Katy Perry
Apple Pie - Lizzy McAlpine
Always Been You - Jessie Murph
Turning Page - Sleeping at last
Fix You - Coldplay
Flicker - Niall Horan
Lover (Taylor's Version) - Taylor Swift
Wondering - Olivia Rodrigo
Bedroom Ceiling - Sody
You & I - One Direction
It'll Be Okay - Shawn Mendes
Hate To Be Lame - Lizzy McAlpine
Like I Can - Sam Smith
Sway - Kacey Musgraves
I Don't Want To Be That Guy - Restless Road
The Only Exception - Paramore

'But love is blind and lovers cannot see.'
William Shakespeare, *The Merchant of Venice*

Soul Stone *(noun)*

Definition:

1. A crystal-like object that everyone finds upon reaching the age of sixteen, designed to assist in finding their true soulmate. The stone initially appears foggy and misty with a crystal look. As the individual is looking at their soulmate, the soul stone emits a radiant glow, normally lasting a few minutes. Once the soulmate has been indicated, the soul stone becomes fully transparent, symbolising the discovery of one's soulmate.

2. Soul stones can be used by certain gifted individuals to tell others the location of their soulmate.

- "As Sarah walked into the room, she made eye contact with a girl in the corner, and her soul stone began to glow strongly, indicating the discovery for her soulmate."

- "When David turned sixteen, he found his soul stone in his room, an ethereal crystal said to guide him to his true soulmate."

Prologue
Katherine

Five years ago

"Hey, Dad, look what I found!" I rush into my father's hospital room and sit down in the chair beside his bed. Excitedly, I fish for his stone that I stored in my pocket to show him.

I hate this room. I hate that it's cold and too white, and that him being here means he's not getting better. Mom and I did our best to make it feel more like home with photos on the table next to his bed, and his favourite blanket on the bed, but nothing really worked.

The stone is clear, unlike the misted one hanging around my neck. It's cold to the touch, too. I don't think mine's ever been that cold; I reach for the one around my neck to make sure.

He takes it in his frail hands, they shake a little. I try not to notice—for his sake, but also my own.

He looks so thin now—everywhere. His face isn't the one I remember, and I try to not let *this* face be the one embedded in my mind forever. Because this isn't him, not really. It's a version of him but not the dad that used to put me on his shoulders when we'd watch the Macy's Thanksgiving Day Parade, or the dad that cheered so loud at my middle school graduation that I tripped across the stage. Those are the memories I try to hold on to.

"Sweetie." His voice is dry.

I scoot my chair closer to the side of his bed, I hold the hand laying next to him, and only slightly, do I pull back when I feel the frigid temperature of his body. But I make myself hold on tighter, letting my warmth sink into him.

He's not looking at me. I think it's because he doesn't want me to see him cry but he's looking at the stone in his other hand as he moves it around. But I see it, a tear races down his face and it takes everything in me not to react.

"Yeah, Dad?" I don't know how many more of these trips I'll get. And it might sound weird, but I voice record them all. I haven't told Mom. I don't want her to think I've completely lost my mind, or make me delete them.

I'm hoping one day she might thank me for it, but right now, I don't think her knowing would help. Right now, I think it would make her think I've given up on him.

He starts out, "I want you to have an amazing full life." He breaks out in a coughing fit, so I hand him some water.

I imagine this is the worst part about being a doctor. Being the patient yourself. Not being able to believe the doctors when they say *it'll be okay* or *we'll try this trial*. Knowing exactly what's happening to you, I can't ever know how that feels.

I might not be a doctor, despite my parents best efforts, but I've been around them enough to not believe them either. I've heard my dad and mom talk about patients in the same condition as him, those stories never end well. I'm running low on believing in miracles.

Dad has been a doctor at this very hospital for twenty-two years, and with that much experience, he knows exactly what's happening. He knew something was wrong when he first got ill, he knew the first time he passed out on shift. And we knew when Dad's doctor, his friend, handed him his test results. My world stopped that day, everything came to a halt.

I hear my mom shuffle and stand in the doorway, but I don't look at her—I keep my sights on Dad.

"Katherine, I want you to live all the life you can, live every minute of it, okay? Don't let any of this stop you, or this." He holds the stone up so I can see it again, and he looks down at the one hanging around my neck.

I've worn it since I got it over a year ago; I don't ever take it off, which I know is strange to some. I've been told enough by the kids at my school that it's all stupid and no one cares anymore, but god, I care so much. It's one of the last bits of hope I have.

One of the last bits of magic I still think exists.

"I love your mom and you more than anything, I'm so lucky to of had this time with you both."

"Dad, don't talk like that," I say, squeezing his hand a little.

"Sweetie." He rests both his hands on mine, and then reaches to wipe my face. I hadn't even noticed I was crying, the tears are hot on my face now but I can't stop them.

I don't sob, I don't make a noise.

"Go to college, get that degree you want. Live your life, find your soulmate if you want... But make sure you have your own life, too. Okay?"

He's looking at me like he wants me to promise, he used to give me that look when I was younger and he'd take me for ice cream just before dinner and make me promise to not tell my mom.

I'm not sure I know what he means. My application for NYU is already in the admissions hands but I don't say anything, I just nod my head.

My mom comes in wiping her own eyes, she's got her own white doctors coat on. She's been a doctor here longer than my dad and I know she can't be lied to either.

"Come on, Kat, I think Dad needs some rest now. Bella is waiting outside for you." She puts an arm around me and we switch places.

"I love you, Dad." I kiss his forehead before walking out the door. When I reach it, I turn to look at him again, him and Mom are holding hands, looking at each other. Their love makes my heart feel warm and full. Even with everything else going on.

My heart hasn't felt full since I walked across the threshold of his hospital room.

Four years ago

I make the three and half hour trip from my home in New York to Washington, D.C.

After months of researching online, I read in a chat room that there's a woman here that can use your stone and her 'spirit powers' to help find your soulmate.

I jumped at the chance to try and get some real answers, to try and narrow down my search to a location I could work with.

After what feels like hours of looking for her home, I finally find it hidden away between two tall modern buildings. Old, red brick; really, it sticks out like a sore thumb.

Taking a deep breath I knock on the front door, ready as I'll ever be.

"Katherine Miller." I blurt out my name right as she opens it.

A smile pulls on her dark purple painted lips, and her eyes sparkle. "Come in, dear," she says, shuffling back into the house. Her long grey cardigan drags on the floor as she lets me pass her.

SOUL BELIEFS

The inside is just what I imagine a fortune teller's house to look like. And all of a sudden, I'm not sure if maybe I'm being ripped off.

Thick velvet curtains are hung up everywhere which make the room dark, the only light are the hundreds of candles on every open space I can see. My mind quickly turns to the fire hazard those curtains and candles impose.

"You seem awfully young to be worrying about your soul stone, dear. The men and women I get visiting me are ones who have searched for years with no luck, so why are you worrying about this now?" The elegant older lady questions me as she sets down a pot of tea and a large world map onto the round table in front of us.

Time.

It's the answer I give her, and it's the answer I've given everyone—not that they understand.

The earlier I can find my soulmate, the longer I have with them. It seems simple to me, and it's simple to the woman sitting across from me, too. She simply nods her head and puts her hand out for my stone.

Carefully, I unclasp the chain around my neck. After I give it to her, she holds it in her left hand and holds my hand in the right. She sits there with her eyes closed for what feels like forever, but is actually two minutes. Once she's given the stone some 'natural energy' from herself—which I don't actually understand, and she didn't really explain—she holds it over the map, letting it hang from the chain.

As we sit there in silence, I can almost hear the candles flickering from behind me and I begin to worry it'll never work. That this might have been a complete waste of my time and that maybe my soulmate isn't even out there.

My anxieties begin to swirl themselves up into a frenzy.

As if my stone can read my worried mind and wants to prove me wrong, it moves.

I'd never seen or heard of anything like it before. No one really knows where the stones come from, and no one knows when it all started, it's just how it's always been. So, no one I know questions it. I certainly never have, but in this moment, I definitely do. In this moment, my mind explodes thinking about how much magic could be in the world that I never knew about.

It swings gently at first, over continents and countries. But then it seems to linger over New York for far too long, the woman keeps her arm still until the stone is pulling hard against her. She only moves it when I think the stone is pulling so hard that it might take her arm clean off.

But then it stops.

The lady leans over the table, keeping the stone still to make sure she doesn't lose where it's landed, and she reads it aloud as if I can't see it myself.

"Sydney, Australia."

Chapter 1
Katherine

Present day

Standing in a dimly lit and over crowded bar was not really how I wanted to spend one of my last nights in New York.

In all fairness, half of the people here are my friends—or at least acquaintances—but still, it feels like too many people. Maybe letting Isabella organise this was a bad idea. But she's the social butterfly in this friendship, these things are more her speed.

People I've only seen in a lecture hall or campus corridors keep coming up to me with drinks I didn't order. But I take them to not be rude. I can practically feel the hangover I'm going to have tomorrow.

I shift my weight from one foot to the other as I wait for my best friend to come back from dancing with some guy. My feet hurt already and I regret my shoe choice, black strappy heels, but Bella insisted.

I can feel my ponytail tickle my shoulder blades as I sway to the music slightly, checking the door every other second. The tight green dress I'm wearing feels like I've been rolled in saran wrap. It keeps riding up every time I move too much, meaning I look ridiculous with one of my hands permanently attached to the hem of it.

It's not even slightly similar to what I would normally wear on a night out, but this is our last night together for god knows how long and I don't want the last thing Bella remembers is us arguing because the dress she brought me is too tight for my liking. It makes her happy to pick things for me and I want her to be happy, even if I don't really look like me.

I see Bella making her way back over to me from the dance floor. When she reaches me, her cheeks are flushed. She takes the glass I've been holding for her and downs it in one gulp. She sends a bright smile my way as she takes my hand, leading me back over to the bar. My eyes land on the door again as we pass it, thinking how easy it would be to slip out and leave.

"So, Sunday," she yells over the obnoxiously loud bass music playing. Bella is not the kind of person to get sad, but I can see the hint of it lingering in the corners of her eyes now.

When I finally made up my mind that I would be going to Australia, I knew I didn't want to leave until the summer was over. It meant I could keep working my waitress job over the busy tourist period. Of course, I've been saving money since I was eighteen for this trip, but the tips were too good to miss.

Waiting until now also meant that as our summer is coming to an end, spring would be in full swing in Australia. I had planned it to a T so that I got even more of my favourite seasons.

My extensive collection of summer dresses have never been so happy.

I feel my fingers reach for the soul stone around my neck. A necklace I've worn since I got it over six years ago. One that matches the ones my mom and Nan made, and still wear.

The thing is, for once, I'm not scared. Or nervous. Or worried.

I've been scared about most things my whole life, I only became more anxious when I lost my dad five years ago. I didn't think that day would be the last time I told him I loved him, I didn't think that would be the last time I got to hold his hand and he would hold it back. But it was; that next day he fell into a coma and a week later he was no longer here.

But going to Australia to find my soulmate is the only thing I'm not nervous about. Because this is what I've been thinking about my whole life.

This is the last miracle I have.

Bella told me I'm setting my expectations too high. That when I find my soulmate, it'll be nothing like I've dreamed. That I'll end up disappointing myself.

She has also tried to change my mind a million times about leaving. Says I'm too young, beautiful, and smart to be wasting my time with 'stupid, ungrateful, unworthy men'—her words.

We've been best friends for as long as I can remember, I can't think of a time she wasn't by my side, helping me fight my battles and being that shoulder to cry on when I needed it. But we are complete opposites. She gave up on finding her soulmate when we were kids. I guess it's because she didn't grow up with soulmates around her all the time like me.

Most people my age don't even believe in them.

My parents didn't get that much time with each other, and I don't want that. Forever might not be real, but I want as long as I can possibly get.

"Will you be coming with me?" I ask in response to her. "To the airport," I clarify. I had asked her months ago when I got my plane ticket if she wanted to come, too, but unlike me, she has an internship at a photography studio starting in a couple of weeks.

If you knew us both, you would think it was the other way around. Bella has always been the wild child of us both. The impulsive one, the 'do almost anything for a good time' one. But she's the one with a real job, and I am the one going off on a crazy adventure.

PENELOPE COGGINS

"Of course, but I still think you're crazy. There are plenty of good guys here that could make you just as happy as any guy in Australia could," she grumbles, gesturing around the over crowded bar as if I would change my mind about the whole matter, about the thing I've been planning for over three years.

I shake my head at her, letting a small laugh fall from my lips. She laughs with me knowing she won't win.

My eyes scan the room as she orders us another round of drinks from the bartender who has been paying her far more attention than anyone else here. I don't blame him, she's gorgeous.

Her dark curly hair falls around her face framing her amazing jaw line and striking features. Her beautiful olive skin is basically glowing under the black dress she's wearing, the girl makes anything look like it should be on a page of Vogue. She's the spitting image of her grandma when she first moved to New York from Spain. The picture of her hanging in Bella's family apartment always brings a smile to my face, especially the ones of both her grandparents together.

As she turns back around while waiting for our drinks, the sad look in her brown eyes has grown bigger. I suspect the amount of alcohol we've had is playing a part in her actually showing her emotions for a change. The girl is one of the most closed books I've ever met, she's my best friend and sometimes I don't even feel like I get the whole picture for what's going on in her head. Considering all the things she's helped me with over the years, I would like to think I've helped her open up a little more. I wear my heart on my fucking forehead—my sleeve is too subtle.

"Come on, Bella, you should be happy I'm finally getting that life you've always told me about, and—" I'm cut off by the feeling of two broad hands landing on my shoulders, a feeling that at any other time in a bar would mean I'm about to get super irritated with a guy, but the familiar scent of bonfire and fall spices fills me.

SOUL BELIEFS

When I turn around there he is, Nick. Or Nicolás, when he's with his family; Bella's twin brother and my other best friend.

Nicolás Sainz—any girl's dream boy. I would know, I was one of them. At eight years old, Nick ran into a seven year old Kat roller skating down the corridor of our apartment building. I kinda loved him right away.

Fast forward to a sixteen year old Kat having her heart broken when her stone didn't glow for him. And that was that. The love I was so sure that I felt was pushed down to the deepest, darkest parts of my heart, but still, it's there in a wistful kind of way.

In the way we sometimes look at each other from across the room, in the way we dance together on a night out, that's just how it is.

Neither Nick nor I have ever said anything or acted on any possible feelings, because sometimes at the end of the day, a best friend is all you actually need. It sounds ridiculous, but I've had six years to come to that conclusion. *Time heals all*, they say. That's true for my heartbreak about Nick, but not for everything.

He is equally as beautiful as his sister. Brown short hair, deep brown eyes I've gazed into a million times before. His skin tone is a little deeper than Bella's that seems to glow even more under the white t-shirt he is currently wearing. And how is it fair for boys to have such long lashes.

Okay, he's not beautiful... he's hot. But I'm not meant to think that.

"I'm sorry I'm late, Katy. My shift ran over, and—" I cut him off by throwing my arms around his neck and bringing him in for a hug. I feel his arms wrap around me, too. The warmth from his chest seeping into my bones, his fingers grazing the bare skin on my back and I feel the goosebumps rise.

I don't care why he's late, I'm just happy he's here.

Apart from Bella, Nick has always been there for me, even when he moved to Kentucky for college. We were always on the other end of the phone for each other. He moved back to New York after graduation, and uncharacteristically for him, he has no idea what he wants to do. So, he's currently working shifts as a bartender.

Before I can think of anything else, he's slipping out of our hug and is holding his hands out to me and Bella. "Fancy a dance, ladies?" On a normal day I'd probably be playing referee to another one of their fights, but every once and a while, they take a break from ripping each other's heads off.

I'm not sure what I expected from being best friends with twins.

I wake up as the sun starts to pour into my room.

The majority of the night is a blur. I remember more drinking, lots of dancing and a very slow and painful stagger back home.

A headache begins to swirl itself around in my brain. Making its way from the front to the back. It's the kind that will sit behind my eyes for the whole day and honestly I don't have time for it.

I lay for a moment longer regretting not drinking the glass of water I left out for myself before I'd gone out.

Lifting my head from my pillow, just enough, I scan my room. My eyes lock on to the mess of clothes and shoes on the floor and I smile in spite of it. Bella and I won't get to do this for a while, I'm almost glad for the mess. Then the two half packed suitcases off in the corner remind me that I am leaving tomorrow, and I'm not ready.

SOUL BELIEFS

Not ready to pack everything up, not ready to move across the world on a crazy search, not ready to actually say goodbye to everyone.

My anxiety for the situation makes me feel sick, or maybe that's the alcohol?

Definitely the tequila, my little voice says. She's right, of course.

I'm wondering if I'll ever feel ready. If I waited another week, a month, even another year.

No you wouldn't be, my brain tells me, and once again, she's right.

I hate her a little.

Feeling under my pillow, I find my phone. The screen reads 10:28 a.m.

One text from Bella at 2 a.m. to say goodnight. But I guess it should have said good morning by the time we got to sleep.

One text from Mom at 5 a.m. to say she was leaving the hospital and she'd probably sleep until lunch time, a reminder to be quiet until then. As if I need one.

And one text from Nick at 10:19 a.m. to say he's on the fire escape.

I smile at that one and finally pull myself out of my bed and climb out my window, grabbing a sweatshirt on my way.

"Well, fancy seeing you here," I say as I climb up the flight of stairs to his fire escape.

"What, on my own fire escape?" he asks sarcastically, handing me a mug of much needed coffee as I sit down next to him looking out over a city that's been up for hours—or that never actually went to sleep.

We've always done this. Bella's not exactly a morning person and I expect she'll be in bed for most of the day. Which I'm totally fine with. Yes, it's my last day but we made a big list of everything we wanted to do over the summer together.

We did every last thing on it.

Mornings are more of a Nick and me thing. Guess that's the best thing about having your best friends live in the apartment above yours.

Bella and Nick moved into the building when I was seven, and the three of us have been inseparable ever since. My dad used to say if you saw one of us, the other two weren't far behind. And nothing was more true.

This is the first time I haven't known what to say to him, which I don't think has happened in the fifteen years I've known him. With Bella, it's like we never stop talking, never thinking about what we're saying. We're always rolling one conversation into another, never too sure how we ended up there. But with Nick, it's a little different, and it's hard to explain. Silence has never bothered us, but this one does.

When Dad died, Bella would come stay over and just let me cry and watch crap TV with me to take my mind off life. But we never really talked about it. When I was ready, it was Nick that I talked to about how I felt. Nick's brain works in a similar way to mine, he understands what I'm trying to say without me having to say too much.

Which just makes this all a little harder.

He's been gone for four years for college. We talked every week—on the phone, over email, FaceTime. He even came home for every holiday. But when I told him about me going to Australia, it came as a shock. He hadn't been there for every late night conversation, every pro-con list until I made the decision. That's not his fault; regardless, this summer has been hard.

I'm startled when he finally speaks. "Just keep me in the loop, yeah?" His voice goes up at the end, a dead giveaway that there's something else he's not saying. His smile is small, and I want more than anything for it to be the big toothy grin I'm used to seeing.

He and Bella have the exact same eyes, and the sad look that she was trying to hide from me last night is prominent in his. I wonder for a minute if they think I'm never coming back, and then I remember that I actually have no idea when I'll be coming back, either.

SOUL BELIEFS

"Of course. Always," I say, smiling. And I mean it; I can't imagine not having him in my life, not sharing everything with him. "Are you going to come to the airport tomorrow?" I ask him.

"Of course, Katy," he finally says, giving me another small smile.

And that's all we really say about it. We sat there for another hour or so. I tell him about the sights I want to see and he tells me about the girl he met at work the other night. I smile at that.

When we were growing up, I always thought how easy it would have been if we'd been each other's soulmates. We were already best friends and he's always been handsome—that's not hard to miss—but when he got his stone and nothing happened between us, I thought maybe I had to wait till I got mine. When I got mine four months later, nothing.

That was hard for sixteen year old Katherine to get over, we never talked about it. I think maybe he'd been hoping the same, too. Much like Bella, he's not all that bothered about the whole soul stone thing.

I think maybe sometimes the universe doesn't want you to have it easy, it wants you to work for the things that are going to be worth it.

Chapter 2
Katherine

After we finish, and Nick goes back home, I remember that I still haven't finished packing, which honestly for me is the hardest part.

I consider overpacking as an Olympic sport and I currently hold the gold. I've always been that way and it's not because I have too many clothes to choose from, well I do, but I like to be prepared for every occasion. I'm the planner kind of anxious person.

Just when I think I'm done, I pull out an outfit to wear for the plane ride, and replace the space I've made with a pair of jeans.

I stand the suitcase right side up and don't hear a thing move, packed tight just how I like it.

There's a knock on my door. "Sweetie?" Mom says as she peaks her head around it.

I gesture for her to come in and beam at the two suitcases. "I finished packing," I tell her as if I've just finished painting the Mona Lisa.

She lets out a tired laugh, the kind that just makes me want to hug her. "I can see that, the kitchen sink in there too?"

"Very funny, only the essentials I promise." But even I don't believe my lie.

"I've heard that before." She has, every vacation we've ever been on.

"Well, if you've forgotten anything, I can bring it at Christmas." She says it so casually, as if we haven't talked about her not coming over a million times.

We came to the conclusion that she shouldn't visit, yet she insists. For one, she's a doctor, it's not easy to get the time off for holidays, even when she's worked there for longer than I've been alive. Also my nan, she comes to our house every year for Christmas, always has. I love my nan too much to let her be alone at Christmas.

And not that I'll ever tell her, but I worry her being in Australia will remind her too much of Dad.

I smile at her almost regretfully; this is the hardest part, leaving her. We've always been close, we were the three musketeers when Dad was still with us. And then when he wasn't, Mom and I just got closer.

When someone dies, it can either push you further apart or pull you together and I was lucky Mom and I were the latter. Days were spent together on the couch watching movies and crying. Keeping each other accountable to make sure we went outside and got some fresh air. That's not to say we didn't have bad days or days when we both wanted to be left alone. We dealt with it in our own ways, but we did it together. Really, she's my best friend and the thought of her being on her own makes me want to cry just looking at her.

"Mom, I've said if you don't want to leave Nan at Christmas, it's okay." I give her a reassuring smile. I mean it, I'll have my Aunt Ella, it's not like I'll be on my own.

"Danny's having her over," she tells me.

I can't hide the surprised look that comes across my face. "Uncle Danny? As in your brother? As in 'burns water' Uncle Danny?"

"Yes, and don't be mean," she says scolding me while also not being able to hold back a laugh of her own.

"Sorry, but wow."

"I know." And I can only laugh louder remembering the time he had us over for dinner and we had to call the fire department because the chicken was on fire. "I was thinking we could go for one last walk around your favourite parts of the city and you could pick up some snacks for your trip. Then we can come back and watch a movie, get Chinese, and then get an early night before the taxi picks us up at 6 a.m. Sounds like a plan?"

"Sounds like a plan." I smile at her.

I wasn't joking when I said this was the hardest part. She's always been my biggest supporter. I know she probably worries about me, but I'm more worried about her.

My mom has never really been on her own. She lived with my nan and grandad while studying, and then with my dad and now with me. When I'm not here, I worry if she'll be okay on her own.

But that's what we do, even with the unshakeable sick feeling in my stomach and the tightness that starts in my chest. We take a walk down past the university I graduated from only a few months ago, I smile thinking about the journalism diploma framed in our living room.

We go past my favourite coffee shop and I get the best soy caramel latte in the city.

Even though it is the most touristy thing about this city, we wander through Time Square because while I might be a local, the best things are the most cliché. But we only stay five minutes, because why is it always so busy?

We take one last subway ride back to the apartment and stop off at the corner shop to get some snacks for my plane ride. I buy a whole box of Twinkies and tell myself I'll definitely be able to fit them in my suitcase, there's no way Australia has anything as good as them. Maybe I can convince Mom to send me some.

By the time we get back, it's 4 p.m. We both shower and get into comfy clothes and Mom orders the Chinese, and by the time it arrives, I'm starving.

We eat while we watch my favourite movie, Dirty Dancing.

I text both Bella and Nick to say the taxi will be outside at 6 a.m.—sharp. I do this separately because I know neither will pass the information along, just to be petty. I'm told that's normal sibling behaviour, but I wouldn't know.

At about 9:30 p.m., Mom and I head to my room so she can watch me struggle to fit the box of Twinkies in my suitcase and then begin to say our goodbyes.

We sit on my bed, she pulls me into her side and I rest my head on her shoulder as she strokes my hair. Mom used to do it every night for about three months after my dad died, it was the only thing that got me to sleep then. I either couldn't fall asleep because my panic-filled thoughts wouldn't stop, or I woke up already crying because I'd had a dream about him.

She'd come into my room or I'd go into hers, and I'd end up crying more because I felt so guilty I was keeping her up. But still, she'd stroke my hair until it stopped or I fell asleep.

"I'm going to miss you so much, honey." There's a strain in her voice like she doesn't want to cry because she knows it'll make me cry, so I stay looking forward just in case.

"I'm going to miss you, too, Mom. Are you sure you'll be okay?" It seems silly to ask now, the flights are booked, my bags are packed, and I'm as ready as I'll ever be. Maybe I'm making it about her to not think about the fact I've never been without her, either. I didn't go away to college, I stayed right here with her. NYU had always been the dream, but after Dad was gone, it wasn't even a conversation about where I'd go.

"Me? Of course, I'll be okay, silly." There's a sad smile on her face I can tell without even looking at her but she continues. "Honey, I got my happy ending." She pauses. "I didn't have that long with your dad, but they were the happiest years of my life. And everyday, I get to look at you and I still get to see my favourite parts of him." She holds me tighter against her. "Your story is only just beginning, so promise you'll still have some fun. You've got your whole life to be in love, make sure you have some adventures, too. Or at least try not to be so strict on yourself. Okay?"

I squeeze her hand that's around my shoulder. "Okay."

After mom heads to bed, I go through my check list one last time. I grab my brown, leather backpack and go though that too just to be safe.

I open my laptop and load my blog up on the screen. I've had this since I was a teenager. My therapist said it would be good to have somewhere to brain dump, and I've never been good at keeping a diary, so this seemed like the best option.

Over the years, it's developed a little but it's still mostly where I go to get everything out of my head to quiet my thoughts. It's completely anonymous, the thought of anyone reading my inner thoughts or mad ramblings makes my skin itch.

Bella is the only one who even knows about it. Only because I made the mistake of keeping my laptop open when she was over. In her defense, she thought it was someone else's blog I was reading until she put two and two together.

She promised she wouldn't go find it on her own and she's never brought it up again since, but I know her, she definitely reads it.

This is it.

I type as if anyone might actually read it.

Tomorrow morning, I'm gone. It feels like only yesterday I booked my ticket and made my plans.

Seeing those words in black and white in front of me almost doesn't feel real. I knew the day would come eventually, I mean I booked the tickets for god sake, but it almost never really felt real.

Am I doing the right thing? This is where the brain dump part comes in.

I don't know if anyone can actually answer that for me and I'm not sure if I can either. I guess you just have to do what you think is right and hope it leads you to the right place or person. I've always felt so at home here but there's always been something missing, something missing within me. I've never felt like a whole piece, a whole person. Maybe it's the feeling of being on edge all the time or maybe it's something completely different.

I wish I had the answers, that I knew what the right thing to do was. I hate not knowing, I hate the uncertainty and I hate the questioning. I like things when there is a right or wrong answer. I like knowing what's going to happen.

But right now, I have no clue what's going to happen and there is nothing I can do about it, not being in control is the scariest thing I've ever felt.

I stare at the blinking cursor and then send the post out into the world.

I slip my laptop into its sleeve and slide it into the back of my backpack, jamming the charger into the bag, too.

My 5 a.m. alarm goes off and I think it's a dream, a terrifying dream where I'm up before the sun has reached the sky.

A knock at my door soon jolts me up again. "Honey, you need to be up."

"Yep, Mom, I'm awake," I say with my face muffled into my pillow.

"I mean it," she says, stepping into my room, placing a mug of coffee down on my bedside table. "You'll have plenty of time to sleep on the planes." She reminds me as if the reminder of being on planes for the next twenty four hours will make me feel better. It doesn't.

"Don't remind me," I say, picking the mug up and bringing it to my lips while taking a long drink.

It takes a minute, but eventually, I pull myself from my bed, and get ready and pack up all the last bits, like my phone changer, and toothbrush.

I pull my suitcases into the hallway and then go back to my room. I look around for a minute, pretending that I'm checking that I haven't left anything important behind but really I'm just drinking in the sight one last time.

It's just a bedroom, little Katherine in my head tells me, I'll have one in Australia, but I know it won't be the same.

My phone buzzes bring me out of my own mind, it's Nick, saying he and a very groggy Bella are at our door. I check the time—5:50 a.m.—I shout to Mom and ask her to let them in. I hear her ask Nick to carry one of the suitcases downstairs.

I let out a long sigh, and close my door behind me ready for my next adventure.

The long taxi drive to the airport is not met without protest. Mostly from Bella, either complaining that it's too early, or insisting that I can still change my mind.

But as I see the first sign for the airport, I have to block her out because I'm scared that if she talks for much longer, I might actually change my mind. I didn't think that was possible but the more she talks it triggers my strongest emotion and it's not love.

It's so strong, it makes my chest feel constricted, and I have to physically make my brain think about anything else to make sure I don't ask the man to turn the car around.

I think about how much I can't wait to see the Sydney Opera house or the Sydney Harbour Bridge.

I think about Ella and how I can't wait to spend time with her after everything. After Dad's death, after not seeing each other for so long.

The sudden jolt of the taxi pulling to a stop brings me back, I look out the window and I know I can't turn back now.

"If you don't give me updates on every guy you meet, I'll take it as a personal attack," Bella tells me as she pulls me in for a tight hug, one I'm worried will break my ribs.

"I'll miss you, too, Bella," I tell her as she releases me and puts her hands either side of my face and just looks at me. Her eyes start to mist and I feel mine do the same, we're the kind of friends that don't need to talk. Who can look at each other and tell the other everything they need to know. Right now I'm telling her *I love you and wish you were coming with me*, she's telling me *don't forget me, I love you*.

Eventually, she lets go and Nick steps in her place bringing me into a hug. I rest my face on his chest and he smells so good, like home. I spend the whole two seconds wishing one last time that my stone would glow.

"Just call me, yeah?" he asks into my hair and I nod against him. He kisses the top of my head and lets me move to my mom.

We've already said our goodbyes, but I still watch as her eyes mist. She doesn't hug me, she knows too well it'll tip us over the edge and we'll both be sobbing. She holds my hands instead and I watch as she takes me in.

"Remember what I said, okay?" she tells me, and I nod at her, too.

I sling my backpack on, and then take a suitcase in each hand and make my way towards the door, struggling. It slides open, but before I go in, I look back at them.

Mom's still keeping it together but I'm not sure I will be able to make it to TSA without falling apart. But I see Bella put her arm around her, and I know that she and Nick will look after her while I'm away.

When I step foot inside, that's when it happens; the realisation. It crashes into me all at once and it's only then that what I'm about to go through feels real.

I'm going to go find my soulmate.

Chapter 3
James

Another day, another dollar, as my dad would say.

I can't complain. Living in Sydney is what most people dream of. It's exciting, full of people and you're never far from the beach. That last one is *my* dream—and reality. Everyday I wake up and get to work right on the beach.

I'm lucky to get to do the one thing I love—surf, and teach other people to surf. I'm around people who understand the rush that comes with catching the best wave of the day, and the water crashing over you.

But people don't get the peace it brings too, they don't understand that it sometimes feels like flying. It's just you, the ocean, and the sun that beats down on you. It's euphoric.

And seeing the look on the kids' faces as they manage to ride their first wave is the highlight of my day.

I finish my last lesson of the day and walk the kids back to the shop so they can be collected by their parents.

Some of the kids in this class could probably move up to the next level but I haven't been able to convince them yet. I think they think they're not ready; I get that, surfing can be dangerous. I don't blame them for being worried. A wind too strong, a wave too big or a dickhead on the waves who doesn't know the rules and etiquette and anything could happen.

The last kid waves to me as he runs to his mum's car. I stack the surfboards up in the rack outside the shop making sure they're secure. Reaching for the zip running down my chest, I unzip my wetsuit half way and pull my arms out of it with great difficulty, and let them hang at my side.

I step through the door, and my boss Ella looks up from her spot behind the counter. She's got a phone wedged between her ear and shoulder. "Can you wax that surfboard?" she whispers as she points to a board resting up against the front of the counter.

I nod, quickly grabbing my work t-shirt from under the till and pull it over my head. I pick up some wax at the same time. I mostly live in a permanent state of being half dressed, being in and out of the sea all day, but it's just weird in the shop.

Ella says she's sure some of the girls that come into the store only come in to see me and she might be right. Like I say I'm surfing everyday, and I'm probably in the best shape of my life, I can't help if other people want to appreciate the hard work I put in. Not that I'm interested after a good flirt and one night together. They all want me to be their soulmate or some bullshit.

I couldn't believe in that stuff any less if I tried. It pulled my family apart, and I've had enough drama to last me a lifetime—and then some.

The bell above the door rings, a warm breeze from the outside slides in and the smell of the salt air sneaks in. Then in strides, Mr. Town Gossip himself, Neil Wides.

He knows everything about everyone, and is always up to date on what's going on around here. It drives any normal person insane, including me and my dad.

I try not to look up from the surfboard I'm waxing long enough to make eye contact with him, for more then one reason, the main being I might 'accidentally' hit him. I'm lucky that I'm not his intended target today; he keeps a straight beeline for Ella. She's off the phone now and fair game for him.

Ella has been good to me for the past eight years while I've worked here at the surf shop, I'm protective over her like I would be with family. So naturally, I keep a well tuned ear on their conversation, ready to provide backup if need be. She's kind and warm hearted, but tough when need be—both of which make me look up to her.

"So, Eleanor, when is that wonderful niece of yours moving in?" he quizzes as his eyes scan her face. And I watch as he rubs his sweaty hands over his shorts.

But she's ready with a well practised smile. "Oh, hello, Neil. It's so nice to see you, too! She'll actually be here tomorrow afternoon." The smile falters, but only for a second, not long enough for any normal person to notice, and I hope not long enough for him to notice.

If he does, he doesn't say anything and he doesn't change his expression as he continues. "Well, won't it be exciting having another American around." He says it like an insult. I mean, we're only half an hour from Sydney, we get a lot of tourists in town. But it's what we thrive off.

Sometimes I forget Ella lived in America or I guess I should say born there because she's lived here for longer than she ever lived there. She moved here like thirty-five years ago, I can't even imagine her being anywhere else. She's one of the most decorated surfers I have the privilege of knowing.

I can only hope her niece has some of the same qualities as her, despite the fact she's here to find her soulmate which already makes me think she's going to be unbearable, everyone that believes in that stuff seems to be. God, I hate romantics.

Ella let slip the other day why she's coming when my best friend Maddie asked how long she'd be staying. I guess she hadn't been planning on telling us, or at least me, by the way her eyes went wide the minute the words left her lips.

It all depends on how long it takes for her to find her soulmate, I guess.

I think I remember her, an image of a red head with a face full of freckles comes to mind, but maybe that's just because the pictures I've seen of Ella in her twenties shows her looking just the same.

They used to visit every other year until Ella's brother died; I think the last time they were here was seven years ago, which means Ella's niece would have been fifteen, or so. I would have only just started at the shop, but back then, it was only really a shack on the beach.

"I'll be sure to stop by once she's adjusted," Neil speaks again, but only when she hasn't said anything. I'm not one hundred percent sure what he wanted to accomplish with this visit. But that's his M.O. I guess, going around annoying people, spreading rumours and lies.

"Looking forward to it," Ella says, and the sickly sweet fake smile on her face changes to a scowl the minute he's left. "God, I hate that man," she expresses running her hands through her hair, a stress tic we both share, then turns to me. "You're still sure you'll be okay running the place tomorrow when I go to get Kat?"

"Yes, I'm sure. And Maddie will be here too, so we'll be fine," I say, reassuring her.

"Well, I'm sure she'll be tired once she gets here, so I'll take her home and I can swing by here to close up." She sends a smile my way, and then is off doing the next job. That woman is always on the move.

I'm not too sure how she actually feels about Katherine coming here. I wonder if it'll be like seeing a ghost of some kind. I think that's how my dad used to look at me when my mum first left. Sometimes being around someone familiar that reminds them of another helps people, and sometimes it ruins them. I'm hoping Ella's stronger than that.

SOUL BELIEFS

It feels like Ella's been in a bit of a slump for a few years now, we've all noticed it. I can only hope that having family around—having Katherine around—helps with that.

We all treat Ella like she's part of ours, but I know it's not always the same even with the life she's made for herself. I wish I could help more but I know it's not the same no matter how much you might want it to be.

I've made a new family with the people here, with Maddie, Ella, my friends. But I know it doesn't completely patch up the hole my mum left.

If Katherine is willing to fly twenty four hours to get here, she must be all kinds of strong—or maybe just crazy. I'm hoping it's a little of both. I think the people round here could do with a little more of both.

Chapter 4
Katherine

I'm thankful for getting through customs and security quickly, because frankly, I'm exhausted. Like if someone knocked into me right now and I fell over, I'd probably just lie down and take a nap.

I never really understood how sitting on a plane can make you feel so tired, but I haven't travelled anywhere in seven years, and my body can tell.

I'm so excited when I lock eyes with Ella beyond the doors in arrivals that I can hardly keep it together. If I wasn't lugging two heavy suitcases behind me, I'd run to her—but I am. I see her let out a little laugh watching me struggle. The nervousness that had been twisting in my stomach for the last five hours of my flight loosens a little.

I throw my suitcases to the side before I reach her, the noise of them hitting the ground are muffled by the sounds of the busy airport. I run into her arms that are already open, welcoming me.

"Honey, I'm so glad to see you," she tells me, and I'm sure that she means it. Any last bit of worry that I had about her not wanting to see me, or that I was imposing on her space, washes away as we share a hug.

She smells like sunshine, she always has—maybe it's this country; I'd like to think that will rub off on me a little. She's got some more wrinkles around her eyes like Mom does, and it's another reminder for how long it's been since I've seen her. The red hair we share is a little duller on her side.

Everyone used to say I was the spitting image of her growing up, and seeing her now, I hope that's true, she's fifty-three now and doesn't look a day over forty. I'll be lucky to look that good.

"Me too," I tell her as I pull away and pick up my two suitcases again.

"You know I already have a kitchen sink right?" She laughs and I wonder for a moment if it's actually her and Mom who are related. She beams her bright smile at me making me feel at home before I'm even out of the airport.

Before we leave the airport, we make a quick stop at one of the stands selling phone sim cards and get me one that I can just renew each month. I change it out and quickly text Mom to tell her that I've landed, and I do the same for Bella and Nick.

It's not long until we're passing the 'Welcome to Gull's Bay' sign and I start to smile as I look out the window. I kinda forgot how charming it is. It's not a huge city but it's not a dinky town either; it's the perfect in-between. It would take you half an hour to drive from one side to the other but would only take about ten minutes to walk through the town centre.

The beach stretches a good while along the coast of the town, that's where Ella's shop is. There's beautiful houses with stairs that lead you down on to the path that runs along the beach. We stayed in one that was a B&B at one point when Ella was having her house renovated.

Gull's Bay is best known for being a tourist location. It's only like half an hour from Sydney so it's easy to guess why. I never noticed all the tourists before because I guess I was one. I wonder if I'll feel like a local eventually?

I had assumed we were going straight to the house so I could unpack and probably sleep for at least two days, but as we take a right, I see the waves crashing onto the sand. When she stops the car next to the shop, I take no time getting out, finally feeling the warm breeze on my skin.

Kicking my shoes off, we walk down a little and sit on the wall ledge.

As we sit there, the amazing Australian sun beating down on my face, the fresh air starts to help with my current state of exhaustion. Ella continues to tell me about life things, things about Gull's Bay, things I should be paying more attention to but my mind is distracted.

Distracted by the hot boy, or maybe I should say man, running across the beach. His blonde hair flows back as the wind moves it, and when it does I can see the smile on his face. And what a smile it is, bright and inviting; I can't see his eyes from this far away but I imagine they light up when he smiles like that. He's laughing as he races in front of a group of teens trailing behind him, all of them with surfboards tucked under their arms.

"And that's James," Ella explains, bringing me out of my own mind.

"What, sorry?" My head spins back to her, knowing I've been caught.

A laugh slips from her lips. "The blonde you're ogling. His name is James, and he works in the shop." He drops his board near the sea and gets them to line up in front of him.

He works for Ella? Surely, I would have met him before. "I was not…ogling." I turn back to look at her, and what I see is a smug smile pulling on her lips, there is a clear view of the hole I've just dug for myself.

"Sure, Kat, whatever you say." Her smile doesn't waver for a second, and despite what we're talking about it's nice to be able to talk to her like this.

But I'm not here to flirt with beautiful blonde surfers, as much as I might like to, and she knows that. "I was not, you know that's not why I'm here, Aunt Ella."

SOUL BELIEFS

Her smile fades just enough for me to know she's going to say the same thing as my mom, they're far too similar for my own good. "Just promise me one thing." *Or maybe she's more like my dad than I think.* "Can you just, how do I say this... have a good time?"

My eyebrows knit together. "What do you mean?"

"Well, I know why you're here, but don't just go running up to every guy you meet and throw your stone at him."

I can't help but laugh, I'm not one hundred percent sure how I'm going to find my soulmate in a city of five million. But I know I will *not* be throwing my stone at every guy I remotely have something in common with.

"I'm being serious," she protests while also laughing.

I take a breath. "I know, Ella." I think for a minute, think about what she's saying, about what Mom said before I left too and about what Dad said to me that last day. Something makes me wonder if maybe they're all right.

Maybe I can't force my soulmate to show up. Maybe I have to just let it happen. I've put myself in the best place for that but maybe it's all part of the big soulmate 'plan'.

"Tell you what," I start as I move my hair out the way and reach behind my neck unclasping the necklace I have on. "You hold on to this." I place the stone and chain in her hand and she wraps her fingers tight around it.

Maybe I do need to just live my life, I've spent so much time being scared of a future I can't control. Anxious about all the things I do or don't do, about every mistake I've made or going to make, about... everything. Grieving for my dad and the future he doesn't get to have, while also selfishly grieving the future I don't get to have with him.

Maybe it is time I just kinda lived. Bella would say I need to step into the spotlight, but that seems a bit bright and scary. Maybe I can try doing things a little differently for a change.

PENELOPE COGGINS

My neck feels odd, naked. I look down and feel where my stone would normally lay. Six years, that's how long it's been sitting there. I feel almost a little cold without it.

"You sure about this, sweetheart?" She moves it around in her hand.

No, would be the honest answer, because I'm not. I haven't taken that thing off to shower or to sleep, ever. I was always too scared of losing it or something happening to it or walking into my soulmate and having no idea it was them because I didn't have it on, it was too much of a risk for me. I just couldn't do it, couldn't trust myself to know it was them. Even thinking about it now, even with it still in my view, my stomach churns and my mouth goes dry. I know this is the right thing to do, but it just feels like a part of me has been taken away.

"Just keep it safe, okay? Until I want it again." I know that she will, but that knot of worry in my chest starts itself up again; it feels like it never really goes away.

"Okay," is all she says, and then wraps her arm around me, pulling me gently so my head leans on her shoulder and we sit like that for what seems like forever.

Eventually, we get up, and walk back to the car. She tells me multiple times on the drive back to her place that it's my house too, but that seems a bit weird right now. Ella, she feels like home, and I feel safe with her, but this isn't my home. My home is back in New York with my mom, home is where Dad was. I have to blink away tears just thinking about it on the drive over.

"And this is your room." She flings the door open to what I remembered was the guest room the last time I was here. As I step in, my eyes grow wide, it's been completely redone and is stunning.

I roll my two suitcases in and abandon them next to the bed, my eyes sticking on what used to be a set of windows that have now been replaced for a charming set of French doors that led to the back garden.

Throwing them open I notice that the decking that used to just run along where Ella's room is, now stretches and runs along the whole back of the house.

Between my set of doors, and the French doors connected to Ella's room, is a cute metal set of blue chairs with a vintage looking table that looked a lot more beat up the last time I saw it. It's a pastel green now that compliments the chairs.

Her garden is as immaculate as ever. The trees that separate her garden from the house behind hers are taller than they were seven years ago, just another reminder of how long it's been.

"I thought that maybe when the weather's warm enough, we could have breakfast out here together. I sorted the table so you could write out here if you wanted." Her voice comes from behind me and I'm in some kind of shock.

"Ella, it's..." I'm at a loss for words as I turn back around to see her standing in the doorway. "Thank you," is all I really know to say as I give her another hug.

Taking me in for god knows how long, and then her doing all these little things for me. To make me feel more at home, more comfortable, it's almost too much for my heart to take but I refuse to get overly emotional about a room and outdoor furniture.

"I'm going to run to the shop and grab some bits for dinner," she says, pulling away from me, putting her hands on my shoulders. "I won't be gone too long. Will you be okay?" The worry in her eyes is sweet but unnecessary.

"Ella, honestly, I'm going to unpack, and then probably nap." I let out a laugh, trying to reassure her.

She looks me over, almost like she's convinced that I might be gone when she gets back. I smile at her with hopes that it lets her know I'll be here. She lets out a little sigh and nods her head. "Okay."

The layout of the room makes me happy in a weird 'I like making the most of a space' kind of way. Truthfully, the room is pretty big, maybe only a little smaller than the one I have in New York. The bed's on the left when you walk into the room, up against the corner, a night stand next to it. Neatly in the space between the door frame and bed.

On the right is the wardrobe and long chest of drawers with nothing on it. I have no doubt that within a couple of weeks I will buy enough knick-knacks to cover the whole thing.

I put the picture of Mom, Dad, and me on my nightstand, and one of Bella, Nick, and me, too.

She's even put a desk in the room, between the wall and where the French doors start. She has truly thought of everything.

I pull my laptop out of my backpack and set it down on it, along with a couple of notepads I brought with me, and of course no trip is complete without a couple of romance novels.

I really hope there are bookstores nearby, I already finished one on the flight here.

I spend the next hour or so unpacking and hanging my things in the wardrobe and folding up the rest to put things into my chest of drawers. Once everything is out of my suitcases, I slide them under the bed and finally fling myself onto my bed and let out a big sigh.

This is it. The start of my big adventure. It's been four years in the making, and I'm finally here. My ever present knot in my stomach squeezes me tightly just to remind me it's still there and to not get too excited or comfortable.

I have no idea what I'm going to do, where I'm going to start or if this whole thing will be a complete waste of time. I pull the blanket up over my head and pretend I'm not over thinking everything for once and eventually I fall asleep for a jet lag nap.

The next day I'm so tired and my body is so jet lagged, all I can bring myself to do is just hang around Ella's house. I nap every now and again, and spend the rest of the time that I'm actually awake reading out on the patio once I decide I need some fresh air.

But as the jet leg lingers, Ella decides to wake me up at 8 a.m. the following day and tells me that I just have to push through it or I'll always be off the clock. She's right but technically I'm in the future and I'm very confused by it all.

"Come on kid, get dressed. I'll make breakfast, and then I'll take you to the shop," she tells me, planting a mug of coffee down on the nightstand. I watch as her face falls seeing the picture of Dad, but it's only for a second. Almost as if I imagined it completely. When she turns back to me, she's wearing a bright smile.

She walks back to the door but before leaving, she notices I haven't moved at all.

"Katherine, up, dress, you can do this." I groan in response and sit up turning and dangling my legs off the bed. She closes the door behind her and I find my body moving all on its own.

My brain is definitely telling my body to stay in bed but instead I'm moving towards the French door throwing the curtains open to see the day ahead.

The sun shines bright, even though it's still early, the clouds are sparse across the sky. I push the doors open and test the temperature outside, the sun warms my skin and then a breeze hits me a second later, bringing goosebumps to the surface on my arms.

Turning, I pull the doors of my wardrobe open. *Okay, Katherine, you can do this. You can make a good impression on these people. You can make friends with these people.*

God, what if they hate me?

What if they think I look terrible or that I'm annoying or that I'm weird?

What does one wear for this occasion?

I scan the items in my wardrobe for help but nothing stands out to me. If Bella was here she'd know exactly what to put me in. Something that makes it seem like I'm nice and like I'm not a total nervous wrack.

You are nice, my brain tries to remind me.

She's right, I am, and I'm sure I'll make a good impression. I just need to pick something to make sure they don't hate me.

A green dress catches my eye. I pull it out and hold it in front of me.

Green, a good colour for my hair. It's sweet looking, with some kind of floral pattern on it, and that surely can't be a bad thing. It's a short dress, but on me, it comes just above my knees. I wonder how much of a tourist I'll look to them in it and decide quite a lot.

But I'm out of time, so I pull it on anyway.

"This is my niece Katherine," Ella tells the pretty blonde girl standing behind the counter at the shop.

I can't quite believe the shop I'm standing in right now is even the same one from seven years ago. I think it's the high ceilings and all the windows, it's so light and welcoming, you feel like you're still outside. I remember when I was a kid and it was just a little shed on the beachfront. Ella sold surfboards and taught lessons to a few people here and there.

Now it's all exposed wood and white walls, surfboards stacked up all over. It's changed so much but still so Ella in every little way. The mismatched countertops, the hand painted sign on the front of the till counter, down to the little 'Ella's Surf Shop' stickers in a bowl in front of me.

SOUL BELIEFS

As far as I know, it's just Ella, the blonde girl in front of me, James, and Gregg. Ella's known Gregg since moving to the town, so he's been here every time we visited.

The girl behind the counter hasn't stopped smiling since we came in and I think it's actually creeping me out a little. Maybe it's because people in New York don't smile this much at strangers, maybe the sunshine makes you happier here?

She could also be one of the most beautiful people I've ever seen in my life. Her skin has a beautiful all-over glowing tan, one that us pale city girls could only dream of, which tells me she was probably born and raised here. Her hair is a dark blonde shade with amazing natural highlights bleached by the sun that makes her features stand out even more as her hair falls around her face. She looks like some kind of goddess. Even in her 'Ella's Surf Shop' work t-shirt and denim shorts, I could only wish to look so beautiful.

As she comes around the counter, I put my hand out to shake hers which she completely ignores bringing me in for a tight hug. Yep, the air must be different on this side of the world.

"It's so nice to meet you, Katherine. I'm Maddie," she tells me, her voice is as bubbly as her appearance. "Ella's told us so much about you."

I like her already, she's like a breath of fresh air quite literally. Maddie is definitely some of the sunshine I've been missing.

As she pulls away from me I hear a bell ring from above the shop door and time kind of stops.

Turning towards the door I see one of the most gorgeous men I've ever seen.

It's the same guy from the other day on the beach, Ella told me he worked in the shop so I knew I'd meet him properly at some point. But standing this close to him, even from across the shop, is a little intoxicating. From far away the other day he looked like any blonde surf guy you'd see.

He's the tallest man I've ever seen, which is probably a bit of over statement. His skin glows with a sun kissed tan, I assume is from all the days spent out on the water. The t-shirt he's wearing clings to his well defined arms, the fabric flexing with every moment as he moves closing the door behind him. Black tattoos snake up his arms, disappearing under his sleeve and peeking out again around the collar. His hair, still damp and curling at the ends, frames his face with the sun bleached strands and stops at his jaw. Which of course just draws my attention to his face.

His eyes pierce into mine as I realise he's doing the exact same thing to me that I've just done to him. It instantly makes me feel self conscious in my dress, in my skin. His eyes rake over me like I'm in my underwear.

"Ogling," Ella whispers in my ear as I notice he's actually walking over to me. "James," she says, her voice high and happy, but also on edge. She moves from me, and brings him in for a hug. His face changes when she's looking at him. He smiles and hugs her back like I would with my mom. He towers over her, as I imagine he does with everyone. "My niece, Katherine, I told you about," she explains, gesturing to me with her hand.

"Hi." My voice comes out small and I don't even recognise it all that much. I can feel my hands sweating in a way they didn't with Maddie. I discreetly wipe them on my dress and then put one out for him. He, just like Maddie, completely ignores it but not to hug, he just looks at it like I've handed him a live bomb.

"Ah, the romantic?" The side of his mouth twists up a little and I don't like it.

I scoff. "Excuse me?" My voice comes out a lot flatter this time, I'm proud of myself for that. No man, no matter how beautiful, talks to me like I'm some book he's judging the shit out of its cover. It's his tone, I know exactly what he means by it, I've heard it a million times before.

"Kat will be working in the shop for..." Ella pauses looking back over at me, not that he breaks eye contact with me at any point.

I finally peel my eyes away from him. "I haven't booked a return ticket yet." Maddie's smile grows bigger and James' frown deepens so much I worry he'll never be able to get it out.

If I had any question about them knowing why I'm here, he's answered them. That's got to be why he's looking at me like he'd love nothing more than for me to leave or maybe it's something else. I haven't known the guy for more than five seconds, I don't think even *I* can make that much of a bad impression on him that quickly.

"James, I need to talk to you about the kids' class tomorrow," Ella says and they both move away from the counter and closer to the front of the store.

She told me James teaches most of the lessons now that she's getting older; apparently he's great with the younger kids but considering the way he just talked to me, I'm not sure he's good with humans in general.

"Don't mind him, he's a bit of a grump," Maddie tells me as she comes to stand in front of me bringing me back. "He's also rubbish with new people, give him a minute." She smiles again and it's like it lights up the whole store. Maybe she's his girlfriend?

I won't say anything to Ella, or my mom, or to Bella for that matter, but god am I scared. Terrified that I've made a mistake or I am rushing this. Nothing is really all that certain when it comes to soulmates and moving across the world to find mine sounds ridiculous to some people. I look at Maddie and wonder if she'll think the same.

Do I tell her? It's not that I'm really one to keep my cards close to my chest but really I'm one to keep them hidden under lock and key.

PENELOPE COGGINS

I grew up with anxiety running my life. When I was little, I guess maybe it was cute in a *Aww little Katherine's worried about the world* kind of way. But then when I hit about twelve years old, it got so much worse. I remember being laughed at on the subway by a group of girls at my school and not being able to leave the apartment for a week. I'd have a panic attack every time I thought someone was talking about me or laughing at me. That's when Dad got me an appointment with a therapist. Turned out he dealt with the same when he was younger, too. He told me he had it under control by the time he was in his twenties but he still had days when he wanted to pull the covers over his head and stop the world.

It was nice in a strange way to have someone who didn't think I'd completely lost my mind because I felt like I had. I felt like every little thing was the end of the world. The panic attacks were the worst when my mind wouldn't or couldn't stop. It felt like having a million little Katherine's in my head shouting and screaming at once and like having a heart attack all at the same time but Dad was there every time. Even now when I feel like it might happen, I listen to one of his old voicemails or videos, and it helps. It's like having him next to me again, reminding me to breathe.

It helped, and Mom was so understanding when things took me longer, or on days when all I wanted to do was cry, even now. When Dad passed, it all spiked back up again; I felt like little twelve year old Katherine again going into that therapist office for the first time. We slept on the couch for days because I just couldn't bear to be on my own. She left me little post-it notes all over the apartment when she started going back to work to remind me to do all kind of basic things that my brain just didn't have space to remind me to do, things like making sure I ate a meal and drank some water.

I'm not nearly as bad now as I used to be but I'm left with the emotional and mental scars of it all. It still affects my everyday decisions;

what I wear, what I say, where I feel like I can go. I still hate big groups of people and I still hate new places but I'm better at pushing myself to do these things even if my heart is pounding out my chest, my hands are sweating and I feel like I might be sick. I can convince myself I'm not in any real danger.

I think I have Nick and Bella to thank for that a bit. Bella's the best at saying, *No, Katherine, this place will not be scary*, and making me believe her. She won't leave me either. If we went to a party I was stressed about, she'd be by my side the whole time until I told her I was okay. Nick's better when I one hundred percent can not leave the house and go out. He makes me laugh when I really want to cry and he'll even put up with watching Disney movies when he's more of a horror movie guy.

I'm lucky really, even with it all.

Even with my anxiety bringing a boat load of self-doubt and low self-esteem.

I'm always worried about what people will think or say, or *not* say, or say to other people.

Maddie's hand landing on my shoulder makes me realise I'm staring at Ella and James and that my eyes have started to water. "Let me show you around the shop a bit more if you're going to be working here." She beams at me, nodding her head towards what I can only assume is the stockroom.

I blink my eyes a couple of times and smile back at her, though I'm sure mine will never be as bright as hers.

Chapter 5
Katherine

"So, do you think you're settling in okay?" Ella asks as she sets her wine glass back down on the table and scans over the menu in her hands.

I look around the small restaurant in town she brought me to; it's calm and people are sipping on wine without a care in the world. The interior looks like someone's gone down to the beach and collected every single shell and discarded piece of wood. It's cute in the rustic beach kind of way. We're sitting on the patio and I can hear the waves crashing in the distance as the sun is close to setting. It would be perfect, if I could get my brain to be completely calm.

Have I settled?

The day after Ella took me to the shop, she got me to work a real shift with Maddie, showing me all the ropes. It's been a week since then and I've worked a total of three shifts. I'm selling surfboards, wetsuits and everything else someone might need for the beach. Ella's also made this little hub in the store now for small businesses in the area to sell things out of her shop, like t-shirts, stickers, candles and I've had to restrain myself from buying everything.

It's not all that different from the store jobs I had back in New York. Smiling at customers, talking to them about what they want or need. When it comes to the more surf specific questions, I have to turn them to Maddie. She's been surfing since she was able to stand, she said no one expects me to know all the answers.

I can tell you one person who does.

James.

He has made it abundantly clear he has no interest in being friends.

I overheard him talking to Maddie the other day. *How naive does she have to be to think she'll really find her soulmate, it's pathetic.* They were both standing in the stockroom, and just as I was about to walk in, his words hit me like a ton of bricks. My cheeks instantly went hot, but I moved closer to the partition curtain so I could hear better.

Because I love torturing myself like that.

James, you're being a dick right now. Give her a break.

Having Maddie stick up for me gave me the courage to actually step into the room but that hasn't stopped me from thinking about it. Like, constantly. I can't even look at him really without feeling embarrassed.

It doesn't help that I'm still waiting for my brain to work correctly around him so that I can actually tell him where to shove it when he's being a dick. But as of right now, my brain either closes up with embarrassment or melts, because yes, he's still ridiculously hot. So, for the foreseeable future, the shop will be filled with awkward silences and weird looks whenever we are left alone. I'm still not sure if they're dating. Aesthetically, it makes sense but Maddie's way too nice to put up with him.

I look up from my own menu at her. "Yeah, I'm loving it here," I tell her smiling as I pick up my drink.

I'm not lying. I went for a walk around the town the other day after working in the morning to get my bearings. I can't always be relying on Ella every time I need something, I hate feeling like I'm a burden on her. The town is beautiful and just how I remember it.

Not a lot has changed which I am happy about. Some of the shops had a revamp, but the cute book/coffee shop is still standing, just with a new lick of paint. All the old knick-knack shops I used to roam are just where I remember them, full of the stuff my mom told me not to buy too much of.

Ella tells me once she's had someone take a look at the old car she has, it's all mine, which terrifies me a little. I got my licence with Bella when we were seventeen because it felt like something we would need in the future but no one drives in New York if you can help it. So it's safe to say I haven't driven in years, and the streets of Gull's Bay will not be safe soon.

"Good." Her eyes travel to the waiter walking over to us. He stops and chats with Ella for a minute before taking our order. When I'm with her, I sometimes feel like I'm with a local celebrity. Everyone knows her.

And now it feels like I am too. Every time we're stopped, they ask why I'm here and I'm always glad that Ella says it's a very long graduation trip.

She says she's noticed what she called 'friction' between me and James. I tell her it was fine, which it is, but she says something cryptic about how she should have known he'd have a problem. I didn't press for more information even though I really wanted to. Either way, I'm glad the whole population of Sydney isn't aware of my soulmate search.

The rest of the night is filled with more catching up and laughter. I feel like I'm getting to know Ella all over again. I don't know how much I've changed on the outside since I've last seen her, but I know that I've changed so much on the inside. I feel like I'm a different person to the one she might remember.

SOUL BELIEFS

"It's been two weeks since you left, and you're telling me you haven't met a single hot guy!?" Bella and I have worked out the time zone difference pretty quickly, even if it's hard for her to fit me into her new busy schedule.

Her internship at the photography studio mostly consists of getting coffee and carrying stupidly heavy equipment around. Good thing my girls never been a quitter because I would have given up after the first day from the sounds of it, but it's her dream and I'm so proud of her.

"Bella, it's not that simple," I try to tell her as I cross the road trying to not get run over.

She laughs. "Yes. Yes, it is. You are currently in a country where most guys walk around topless. You're telling me not a single one has caught your eye?"

I shake my head even though she can't see me, god what I wouldn't do to have her out here with me. Bella always knows the right thing to say to guys, or the right thing to wear to impress them. I'm one hundred percent sure I would not have had a single boyfriend in high school or college if it wasn't for her coaching. "Bella I don't think my soulmate will be someone who wanders around topless." I laugh as the shop comes into view.

"What about that guy you work with?" she quizzes. I swear this girl doesn't miss a beat.

"God, don't remind me." My smile instantly fades as my eyes land on him. He's like the devil. Speak of him and he fucking appears. I'm all but five feet from the shop and he comes running up from the beach, of course topless. I'd love to look into this guys wardrobe because I can bet I wouldn't find a single t-shirt.

"I looked him up. He's hot. Can he be my soulmate if he's not yours?" I have to stop myself from quizzing her about how she found him online, I don't think I want to know.

"He's also a total ass."

"Talking about my ass, are we Katherine?"

Here he is, blocking me from getting to the door.

His body glistens from the sea water, or maybe it's sweat, I'm not sure I mind either way. He's got a crazy amount of tattoos, and because I'm trying not to look at him too much, I can't make out what they are. But as we stand there I see what looks like a squid or octopus on his shoulder, half the tentacles falling down his back and the other half wraps around his chest, one so close to his nipple.

Oh, Jesus.

His hair is pushed back, curly locks are tucked behind his ears. I so badly wish he wasn't hot, because then maybe my brain would work at a reasonable pace around him and my body wouldn't be reacting in a way I wish it wouldn't. I tell myself it's the breeze making my nipples peak, and I just pray he doesn't notice. I think it's a curse in life for guys who are dicks to also be hot, it should be against the law or something. I think Satan might have made him just to torture me.

"Is that him?" I hear Bella in my ear and I try hard to not blush as he stares me down, a smirk twisting at the counter of his lips.

"Yes, Bella. Look, I have to go, I'm at work." I rush out my words, trying to get off the phone as quickly as possible. Before it's too obvious that we were in fact talking about him.

"No wait—" But I cut her off by shoving my phone into my bag.

"Not everything is about you James, or is that just what you're used to?"

Bella's right. I've been here just over two weeks and every time I have the displeasure of being in the shop with him he seems to have at least two or three girls drooling over him. I'm lucky he mostly stays outside teaching lessons because watching these girls fall all over him is second hand embarrassment.

Girls shooting their shot is one thing, and I fully respect a woman going after what she wants, but James clearly has got no interest in them and he basically says that to them and yet here they are. I've seen the same girl come in every shift asking about surfboard wax. I'm no expert but surely you don't go through it that quickly.

He presses a hand to his bare chest over where his heart should be. "Ouch. Didn't know you were so mean, thought you were all about love, Katherine." He pushes the door open and waits for me to walk in front of him. "And anyway, from what I can see, you don't seem to mind the view that much," he tells me, a smirk on his face as his eyes drop to my chest, my white dress doing nothing to disguise how my body seems to be reacting to his.

I feel my cheeks heat as I pass him. Dear god, today is going to be long.

"Tell me what you did in college?" Dom's question is almost drowned out by the noise in the bar and also by the fact that I have not been paying attention to him.

Twenty minutes of him telling me about *him*... I've never known a man to wait a whole half an hour into a date before asking a question about the other person.

I listened for the first ten while he told me about his job, or should I say bragged about. That's red flag one.

Red flag two would be the sports bar he brought me to. He can tell me it's because of the great drinks, I have had three already, but it's definitely because of the ten TV screens dotted around the space. His eyes have flicked to them in-between every sentence. I'm almost impressed that he can tell me so much while checking the score of the Australian football game showing on the TV nearest us.

The guy is a top-class asshole.

This is my fourth date in the three and half weeks I've been here. This is the first time where a guy has taken me for drinks, something about an evening date told me I should dress up, told me that maybe he even liked me. But as I watch his eyes trail down my neck to my chest for the third time, I'm about ready to leave, or knock his teeth out.

My pink silk bodycon dress feels like total overkill right now and I feel like everyone was looking at me as we walked in earlier. My stomach has been in bits since, my worst panic is having people stare at me or me thinking people are looking at me. Judging me. Thinking I look stupid or ugly or anything really. And this is setting me on edge. Maybe if the date was actually going well I'd feel better—but it's not—so my brain has more space to worry.

I try to bring myself back to the conversation now that he's actually including me in it.

"Oh, I did journalism at NYU." I'm about to tell him all about it, but he's already telling me about a friend or someone who did the same thing and I'm tuning him out again.

The guy is good looking, don't get me wrong, but I can't imagine myself spending another hour with him, let alone my whole life. The night is a bust, I know it. I'd rather be back at Ella's in my PJs watching some romcom but I can't tell him that. I'll have to let it play out and hope he'll let me pay half so I don't feel like I've used him for a night out.

And then I think that maybe I have died and I'm in hell.

Burning.

My eyes travel over to the bar hoping for a waitress to see me so at least I can drown myself in another great cocktail, but instead, my eyes lock with him.

James.

He's like a bloody parasite.

He sees me and I give him a small polite smile before turning back and paying plenty of attention to my date. Because even though I'm having one of the worst dates of my life, James does not need to know that.

I can't seem to shake him, he's everywhere I go.

This is the third time he's magically been at the same place as me and I'm starting to think it's not a coincidence. The first time, a coffee shop in town. That was easy to explain away, he didn't say anything to me and I'm not even sure if he saw me that time. He was sat in the corner when we got there.

Date two we went to a breakfast place in Sydney. *Cute*.

Unfortunately, for me, he thought I was Canadian. Let's just say he didn't like Americans and was, in his words, 'insulted' by me being an American. He finished that date pretty quickly. I actually laughed when he said it, I couldn't help it. As Bella would say, it was good for the plot.

Where was James you might ask? Saving my butt, that's where.

My date had driven us to the place and I ended up stranded. I paid for our coffees and took them to go. Then I walked outside to call Ella to see if she could come get me or tell me how to get the ferry back. But before I could, James was just rolling past in his truck and pulled in when he saw me. He didn't really ask what happened but I got in and he took me back to Gull's Bay.

A weirdly nice thing for him to do considering I'm convinced that he hates me. I hadn't seen him in the restaurant but when he passed me a doughnut in a wrapping from said breakfast place, I knew he had to have been there and had seen the whole thing.

Strike two of me being embarrassed around him.

Then for the third date, he wasn't there and I was almost sad about it.

I was stood up.

That one might have hurt the most. Might have.

And that brings us to date number four, going about as well as a root canal.

Maybe I'm just not made for this. I have thought about asking Ella for my necklace back, regardless of only being here for a month. I need to stop being such a baby about this. This is what I have to do, my soulmate is not going to turn up on his own. I need to put myself out there even if it means I have to endure a million bad dates.

But does that mean I actually want to sit though this one any longer? No, and as if on cue, my bag starts to vibrate.

"I'm so sorry, I need to get this," I tell him as I stop him mid long story as I see Bella's name flash up on my screen. I basically fall off my chair trying to step away from the table so quickly.

"Yeah, of course, no worries." He flashes me a smile as I walk towards the door, it's far too loud in there to talk to her and honestly I need the air.

"Thank god," I say as I pick up her call while leaning up against the wall of the bar, happy to not have Dom's voice in my ear.

"That bad?" she questions.

"That bad. He has asked me one question about myself since we got here." After the last terrible date, Bella told me she would call me after half an hour to save me if I needed it, and god do I need it. I don't feel like I'm asking for too much from these guys, am I?

"Christ! What's wrong with the guys on your side of the world, maybe you should come back?" I turn to look through the big window next to me so I can see my date.

"You know I've only been here like a month right? Sadly I think it's going to take longer than that to find my soulmate." My eyes travel as I look into the room from outside. Then, I see something I don't think will end well for me.

The six foot something surfer moving towards my date!

This date might be going as well as the Titanic but he doesn't need to know that. He doesn't need to know anything.

"He's here again," I say quickly knowing she'll know what I'm meaning. "And he's walking towards my date."

"Go!" Bella has now come round to the fact that yes, James is gorgeous, but he is my nemesis and nothing is more true than hating your best friend's nemesis. That's how we are.

I hang up with her, while making up some excuses in my head as to why I must leave and beeline for my date but considering my five steps are the equivalent to James' one, I'm no match and he's here before I can blink and is talking to him.

"Oh, Katherine, I didn't know you were on a date with Dom." The words drip from his mouth as he smiles and I want to die again.

"You never mentioned you worked with James," my date says and he must not realise that's because I haven't had the chance to tell him my last name let alone who I work with.

Then it clicks. You've got to be shitting me!

He knows him! They know each other!

I try my best to not fall right through the floor and right down to my fiery death.

"You guys should come join us," James offers, pointing over to Maddie and a couple of other people sat at the bar. I decide this has got to be another coincidence because he's with other people, and honestly why would he be stalking my dates. It's a ridiculous thought to even cross my mind.

Even if it is, James doesn't realise he's saving me again.

My date must think this is a car crash too because he nods quicker than I've ever seen someone do, he doesn't even look at me until he's picked up his drink and is moving towards the group at the bar.

"Is that okay, Kat?" he finally asks, and as much as I'd like to leave, I'm already dressed up and getting a ride back with one of them wouldn't be the worst thing in the world. Maddie's there too, so what's the worst that could happen?

The cogs in my mind kick in, thinking over everything before I nod and smile at him and he's off again before I can even regroup.

James leans down toward me, the tall bastard. "Search going well then, Katherine?" His smirk is evil and handsome and I'd like to slap it off him and also make out with him, I hate myself for the second one.

I pick my drink up from the table before plastering a perfect smile on my face. "Shut up."

Chapter 6
Katherine

I hear the loud chatter of children before I see them. That may be my favourite part of this job.

I've never been a big kid person. I never had any siblings so I guess maybe it's an only child thing. I didn't have to deal with any babies or little kids at home so I was never great with them as I got older.

This is different, though; the way their faces light up before a lesson with excitement and anticipation or after a class the smiles they have are bigger than anything I've ever seen. I sadly have to say James is great with them and seeing him with the kids only makes him hotter.

Why does the world work like that?

I round the corner and see them all standing next to the stand that holds all the lesson surfboards for the day. A gaggle of eight year olds hand James their boards and then run to parents waiting in parked cars.

As the last girl hands hers to him, I watch him struggle with about six boards at once. Now, I don't want to inflate his ego any more, but he's strong. He looks like he could carry me around all day and never be out of breath.

Why are you picturing that?

But he loses his balance a little as he slips on the puddle of water on the floor from where his wetsuit has been dripping and he loses grip on a couple.

I run forward to catch the couple sliding from his grip. My fingers brush his and he looks up at me.

"I've got this Katherine," he snaps at me and I step back more than happy to watch him struggle to get them all in the stand without dropping them.

"I was just trying to help," I tell him, my voice tight with annoyance now.

"I don't need *your* help," he says, regaining his balance and he manages to get one board in the stand but as he does, the ones already stacked slip forward and he catches them with one foot.

"Do you want a hand now?" I guess again, crossing my arms over my chest as even more boards start to fall. He wraps a finger around the edge of another to stop them from falling completely on the floor; he officially looks like he might fall over now.

I wait and tap my fingers on my arm and keep looking at him, I've got my I hate you smile down to a T now thanks to him and he hates it. He lets out a loud huff and then almost whispers, "Yes."

"I'm sorry, James, what was that? I couldn't hear you," I mock as he has to move his feet quickly to catch another.

"Yes, Katherine I'd love your help," he says so reluctantly.

"Why didn't you just say so," I say, reaching forward and grabbing half of the ones he's holding, letting him put both feet on the floor again.

He puts his half away, and then takes the ones I'm holding and puts them away too.

Once I'm sure he's not going to say thank you, I walk into the shop ready to start my shift with Gregg. I don't get to work with him very often, Ella does the schedule and it would seem that she mostly works with him.

I see what you're doing, Miss Ella.

SOUL BELIEFS

"I'm covering Gregg tonight," James mutters into my ear as he comes up behind me. His breath is far too close to me, and far too warm. My cheeks start to heat from his proximity. I'm lucky he doesn't stick around for too long to see it.

It's faded by the time Ella approaches me as I begin folding t-shirts at the front of the store.

"James will close with you tonight," she says with an airy voice as if the information didn't just make my day terrible, I was hoping James was joking or lying to mess with me.

"Yeah, he mentioned." I don't even look up at her, I don't think she needs to see the sour face I've got to know I'm not too happy about it. Morning shifts with him aren't too bad, he's out on the water most of the time. But during the afternoon ones, he's in the store more.

She laughs.

Laughs!

As if any of this is actually funny.

"I think you just need to get to know each other more," she says in a soft tone, the way you do when you're talking to a child who's about to cry. My aunt has yet to grasp the fact that it was not me who started this, it was her precious James. He hated me first, and it only felt right to follow suit.

"Please, just stop putting us together, he's the worst, he's cocky and treats me like I'm an idiot," I tell her again, it feels like I'm always repeating myself. It is completely beyond me why she keeps putting us together on shifts and then complains when she comes in and sees that we're arguing. It's inevitable. It's like the sun coming up in the morning or the moon appearing at night, unstoppable.

"I heard that!" he shouts from his spot behind the counter, arms crossed and brows pinched.

I put my hand over my heart and plaster a sad frown on my face as I turn towards him. "Oh, thank goodness, I was worried I was talking too quietly." He turns and walks off, hopefully leaving me with some peace.

"You are both literal children," Ella says, bringing my attention back to her.

"I can't help that he's a five year old in a twenty-five year old's body." I smile at her as sweetly as I can.

She rolls her eyes, and then reaches into her pocket, pulling out a set of car keys. "Jeremy dropped these off for me today." She drops them in my hand. "It's parked around the back, think you'll be okay driving home after your shift?"

"Jesus you're letting Katherine out on the open road? I'll start wearing a crash helmet," James says as he passes us, not even looking at me.

"See! I never start it, he does," I tell her, throwing my hands in his direction.

"Literal children," she says, shaking her head as she heads for the front door.

Chapter 7
Katherine

Posted 10th September 2024 22:39

Do you think you've ever been in love?

I don't.

I love my family. I still love my dad and Grandad even though they're gone. I love my best friends. But that's it.

I've never loved anyone else. Never a boyfriend.

What does it feel like?

What does it feel like to have someone there? It surely must be different to anything I've felt before.

Why would thousands of people write songs, movies, and books about it if it wasn't different, if it didn't feel different.

Does a soulmate love feel different to other romantic love? I feel like it doesn't. You feel the love the same as if they were your soulmate, why would people do it otherwise?

Maybe that's a silly observation. Maybe people fall for people who aren't their soulmates because they don't want to search for a love like that. Is it less pressure to love someone else? To just love someone because you can, because you do love them?

I sometimes wonder what it would be like to not have that internalised pressure. To let myself just love because I can. But I don't know how, maybe I've never met someone who made me think it was worth it to give up on looking. Or maybe I just don't know how to love right.

PENELOPE COGGINS

Will I be able to love my soulmate?

Chapter 8

James

She's been here a month.

It feels like so much longer. She's everywhere.

She's at the shop, she's in town, she's friends with my friends now. It's like a thunderstorm ruining a perfect day of surfing. I don't like it.

She dresses like she's a goddamn bouquet.

Every outfit is either florals or pastels, and even when I think she's wearing something a little less like a spring field, there they are. Take her denim shorts for instance. She wore them to work the other day and I was knocked over by how much she looked like the other girls around here. Then I noticed all the little flowers stitched all over them, on the pockets, on the belt loops, or the hems.

She walks around like a botanical garden in the summer, and I want to know why.

Why she feels the need to try and brighten up every space? Why the smile on her face doesn't match her eyes?

Everyone loves her, of course. Ella's a no brainer—I guess she is her niece—but Maddie treats her like she's known her forever. She says, "They just click."

I like things how they were, I like things to stay the same. She's always smiling at everything, everyone, except me of course. I'm not sure they're real smiles, they never look real, and I hate that too. Fake things, fake people. I guess if she were to smile at me, I'd want it to be a real one.

What am I even saying?!

This is what I mean, she's in my head.

She's beautiful, of course, but in the same way that the sky is blue and the ocean is wet. Nothing special, just a fact of life. Not that it matters, my body still seems to react to her in a way I rather it didn't, and hers seems to do the same with me.

The little breaths she takes when I get a little too close to her makes me wonder what they'd sound like in the bedroom.

God, help me.

Today is no different. I'm behind the counter while she helps some customers pick out a new wetsuit. She's good with people, a skill I can't say I have unless they have a surfboard in their hand. I have a class but not for another hour and being in store with her is killing me.

Her laugh rips through me again and honestly nothing the guy she's with is saying can be that funny. Why does she have to try so hard? She's got such a need to people please. I'm tired from just watching her.

I want to rip my eyes out. But when I honestly think it can't get any worse, it does.

Neil.

He strides in and I'm reminded there are people I hate more than Katherine at this moment. I question if I even hate her when he comes up to me.

I'll never forget the things he said about my family, the way he made sixteen year old James' life harder for no reason.

"James, good to see you, boy. I was wondering if Ella's niece was here." He must be losing his touch in his old age if it's taken him a whole month to come in and terrorise her. But honestly, I can't think of anything he can really say to her to do any harm, and messing with her a little might brighten my day.

I nod my head in her direction, she's near the front of the store, and this time, without company.

He walks off in her direction and I make it look like I'm busy while he introduces himself, but I make it a point to discreetly look over at them.

She's still smiling and I don't know how that's possible. But it's definitely wavering, her hands clench beside her legs. She's wearing shorts today, it's different from her usual skirts and dresses. But her legs are still so pale and smooth.

Why am I looking at her legs?!

This girl is trying to kill me, I'm sure of it. We're not even going to talk about her in that pink dress last week.

As much as I try to ignore them, I can't. I hate him for all the things he said about my dad and me when we moved to town, for all the rumours he started about my parents. It was a dick move to let him go talk to her. Ella's like family to me and I'd protect her from him if she needed it, so why should I think it's okay to put Katherine in the lion's den? All areas of my brain fight with each other.

She represents everything that you hate, she's just like your mum. She doesn't care who she hurts while trying to find her soulmate. The little voice inside my head is quick to remind me of where the apprehension even came from.

But then I hear him, and his words, and I can't let her do this. Not here. "I'm sorry about your father, cancer is a cruel thing," he says to her, and she just looks at him.

I've never seen her like this before, she looks human, like a real person, and not a put together version of herself that she parades around. She looks real, and I'm not sure what to do. Her mouth falls open but nothing comes out.

"Shame Ella's been all on her own this whole time, so alone." Okay I'm done, I don't know if he's being a dick for the fun of it, or—actually, I do know. He's being a dick for fun.

Her eyes shift over to me for all of two seconds and she looks like she's about to cry. No matter how much she and I don't get along, how much I might be a dick to her, I've got to save her.

"Okay, that's enough," I say from my spot behind the counter. No one else is in the store now, so I don't care what I say to him, though I never have.

I walk towards them and stand behind her, I'm too close to her, I can feel the heat from her back radiating onto my chest.

He doesn't say anything but I continue, "Get out." I'm not a man of many words and I'm hoping he's smart enough to see the violence in my eyes. Because if he doesn't and pushes me I'm not afraid of knocking all his teeth out right here. I tell myself not for her but for me.

"James, I'm just chatting." He smiles at me over Katherine's head.

"We both know that's not what you're doing." I step around her so she's half behind me.

He looks me up and down again and I can't tell if he's trying to size me up or not. I've got a good foot on him and he doesn't look like he's done any exercising, apart from running his mouth, for five years. I could snap him in half if I wanted, and I want to. But I won't.

"Good to meet you, Katherine." Her name on his lips makes me clench my fists, I've only got so much will power in me and he's putting me right on the edge.

After he's gone, and at least a mile from the store, I notice how quiet it is now. There's the melody on the radio and a faint noise coming from Katherine behind me. I realise it's her trying not to cry and my mind goes blank. I don't deal with people crying well and I can only imagine she'd rather have anyone else here other than me.

When I finally lock eyes with her, my face falls, and my heart is in my throat. Her eyes are glassy and her nose is red but she's not letting herself actually cry.

"Don't, guys like that don't deserve you crying over them. He's a waste of air." I want to touch her, to comfort her, hold her hand, something. Whatever this feeling is, it's overwhelming. But I don't do any of that. "You okay?"

"You didn't have to say anything, I was fine."

My eyes roll on their own and my jaw clenches. "A simple 'thank you' would work, Katherine."

"Thank you." She seems smaller somehow now with her shoulder rolled in, and she won't meet my eyes. Before I can say anything else, she's walking away from me and toward the back room.

"I honestly don't get what your problem is?" Maddie asks while we drive to Ella's the next day.

It's a Sunday, the weather is uncharacteristically hot for the end of September, and Ella's invited us all over for dinner in her garden. She's an amazing cook and anything beats sitting at home with my dad, a pizza, and him shouting about something or another.

I'm all he's got now and I hate to hate him sometimes, so I try my best to remind myself why he's the way he is. But sometimes it's hard looking after someone who should be looking after you. Our worlds collapsed when Mum left. He simply lost it, which left me to step up. It wasn't talked about, never has been, but it's just how things went. I looked after the both of us, kept us both going.

I'm an adult now but I had to start taking care of things when I was sixteen, I owe a lot to Ella for giving me a weekend job then.

I give her a side eye look before setting my eyes back on the road. "Was that a real question?"

I've known Maddie since her first day at the shop when we were seventeen, but I'd seen her around before that. On the beach, around town, but never through our high school years despite our time overlapping. I wasn't in the best place mentally then to be making friends, so I didn't really. I originally lived in Sydney before my family fell apart, and then Dad moved us to Gull's Bay for a new mechanic job at a garage a friend of his owned. I took to spending all my free time at the beach, working out my anger on the waves, and by working at the shop.

Maddie and I are very similar. I'd probably consider her my best friend if that was something you said at the age of twenty-five. I've never loved her in any way other than as a sister, and it's nice to have someone I can share everything with. Our family lives are very different and the way she was brought up was even more different but we both started surfing the minute we could swim and a surfboard fit us, so we get each other. There is one very big difference between us two, she likes Katherine.

"Yes, it was a real question, James." She takes a breath and I can tell she's thinking about what she's going to say. I hate that. I hate people watching what they say because they don't want to hurt someone's feelings. Sometimes you just have to say what you need to say, although in this case I'd like her to just drop the whole thing. "Look I get it, why she's here isn't your favourite thing in the world." I can hear the *but* before she's even thought it. "But, I think you'd like her if you gave her a chance, and besides, all that stuff was nine years ago, some people would say holding a grudge against that much of the planet might be unhealthy."

She said that so quickly, I'm not sure she was breathing.

She has a point.

Sadly, yes, she does have a point, and yet here I am feeling sick when I see Katherine. It's like a mix of sickness and like being hit by a truck. I'm convinced it's got to be the very male, primitive part of my brain reacting to her body.

Yeah that whole thing about her being obviously beautiful might have been a lie, she is gorgeous.

Her ginger hair shines even when the sun has set, I kinda like how it's such a contrast from how calm she comes across, I wonder how much fire she has buried in her. Her skin, very pale for this side of the world, still glows in its own way. Which only makes me notice her curves in every place a man wants to hold, and it doesn't seem to matter what she wears, my eyes still make them out.

But that's completely besides the point. She's not my type and even if she was, she annoys me far too much. Her people pleasing tendencies are like nails on a chalkboard.

I pull into the drive at Ella's and turn to Maddie before we get out. "Maddie, I get what you're doing."

"I don't think you do."

"I think you're trying to replace me with Little Miss Sunshine."

She laughs and I hope that's the end of whatever conversation she was trying to have. I'm not taking the bait and I don't have the strength to fight, or at least disagree, with Maddie, she's relentless. Once the girls got something in her mind, that's it.

"You know I'd never replace you, Mr. Grumpy," she says, getting out of my truck. "Hey, Ella!" Maddie shouts as we walk round to the back of her house and see the side gate is already open.

The smell of her food wafts over from the BBQ and I forget about everything Maddie was just saying. If Ella wasn't my boss and basically a surrogate parent, I'd marry her just for her chicken wing recipe.

Chapter 9
Katherine

Ella's continuing battle to get James and me to be friends continues.

But this time she's taken it too far. She's invited the devil right into my only sanctuary. Her home.

I'm standing at the closed French doors in my room while on the phone with Nick. I wave to Maddie as I see her walk into the garden, ignoring James.

I've found it's the only way forward, if I pretend he doesn't exist, then he can't get on my nerves. It's a foolproof plan if you ask me.

"Bella's been stressed a lot lately. Has she said anything to you?" Nick asks me. He's right, she has been, more than I've ever seen. I don't even remember her being this stressed during our finals or when she was applying for jobs.

"No, but you know what she's like." He lets out a small laugh on the other end of the phone and it only just reminds me of how much I miss him. "But tell me what's going on with you? Any luck with jobs?" Nick and I don't talk on the phone as much as Bella and I do, so I miss more about what's going on with him.

I feel the sigh he lets out in my bones. "I've applied to a few game designer positions but haven't heard anything as of yet." I hate the tone of his voice, like he wants to give up, like he feels like he's not good enough. He's wrong, of course. He's one of the most talented artists I've ever seen, he just doesn't believe in himself.

All he needs is one yes, one person to open a door for him and he could do anything. The dream for him is to design video games but it's a competitive field much like journalism and photography. As a group we really chose some stable jobs to go into.

Not.

"Nick, you'll get one, just gotta have hope. You never know what's around the corner."

He pauses for a minute, it actually feels like an hour. I hate talking on the phone, it feels so impersonal. But it's the closest thing I have with him right now, and at least I get to hear his voice.

"I better let you go," he finally says.

I sigh. "Yeah, cause I'm really looking forward to it," I say, sarcasm laced with every word. But he finally laughs and it's wonderful to hear.

"Speak soon, miss you," he says before hanging up and I feel like I'm even farther away from him than just an ocean. I truly wish I could just forget all this, just love him, it would be so easy. So simple, but I know it would be unfair to him and I can't think of anything worse than hurting him.

"Why so many highlighters?" James asks from behind me and I definitely jump at least five feet in the air and my heart jumps an extra ten.

"What are you doing?" I question trying to get my breathing back to normal making sure he hasn't given me a heart attack. I walk over to where he stands at my desk. I'm not possessive over my things by any means but the things at my desk, my books, and notebooks, that's different, and don't get me started on my laptop.

"Ella asked for you. Why do your books have so many coloured tabs?" He asks again as he picks up the novel I finished last night, flicking the page a little. I get nervous instantly.

Those tabs are for lines I liked so much I want to go back and reread them, or for moments that made me laugh and cry and for those moments when I literally wanted to, or did, throw my book across the room. They're for the moments that made me fall into a different world where I don't have to be my own main character, or I get to be a character with some great power that makes me feel unstoppable. Moments that make me think I can go on. They are not moments for him.

"Would you just—" I say as I take the book out of his hands and put it back down.

His eyes scan my desk even as I'm standing right there like the nosey, insufferable man he is. I tap my foot on the floor and wait for him to look back up at me, but he doesn't.

Instead his eyes move and look at the rest of the room. Moving from the desk, to the wall of pictures, to the chest of drawers with my knick-knacks on. And then he settles on my bed for a second. A second far too long for my liking. I get this feeling all over as if maybe this is okay, him being in my space and even though I'd really like him to leave I also kinda don't. It's odd, maddening even, and I want it to stop.

"Okay that's enough," I say, snapping my fingers near his ear bringing his focus back to my face. I feel my skin start to heat and itch. I need him out of my space within the next minute or I might completely combust.

Or throw him on the bed?

No! God no.

Yes, he needs to be gone, now. Before my brain completely melts out of my ears apparently.

"You said Ella asked for me," I say, hoping if I remind him, his two brain cells might work just long enough to help us both end this interaction.

"Right, yeah, she said food's ready," he says, looking me over like he just did my room. We've been in this weird in-between for a week now since that date in the bar.

The evening I had after he invaded the date was actually okay. It's like, if I hang with him in a group, it turns out he's not that terrible. But then there was yesterday when he stood up for me. I believe I should be able to stand up for myself, deal with my own problems. Yet what is it about a man like James stepping in and telling a guy to fuck off for you?

If only we could actually put our differences aside and be friends. Okay, maybe I don't mean that. Maybe we could at least be civil with each other.

But the way he's looking at me, I don't think that could ever be possible. His eyes have shifted from indifference to something much darker than their usual ocean blue, to a sea storm that could drown me. He blinks as if he can tell they've changed too, but it doesn't do any good. I know what he's thinking, *poor little romantic Katherine* but something much shittier cause it's him.

I try not to be disappointed because why should I be, why should I care, why do I need his approval?

I turn and open up the French doors, letting in the warm breeze, and only turning around to make sure he's following me because I'm not leaving him there in my safe space.

He's already in my head.

Chapter 10

Katherine

Posted 19th September 2024 13:48

'I love you' means that you don't want to change a single thing about me but you'll be happy when I grow as a person, because that means we get to grow together.

It means that you don't expect perfection from me, you simply think I'm perfect the way I am, and in turn, I won't expect perfection from you.

It means that you'll love me through the worst of times and stand by my side through the darkest of times and I will hold your hand through it all.

It means loving me when I don't love myself.

It means loving me when I'm at my lowest and not just when I'm at my happiest, because there is never one without the other.

'I love you' means telling you my deepest darkest secrets and you not judging me for them, and in turn, me listening to your secrets, if you'll let me, and not judging you for yours.

It means caring so much we'll never let go and that I'll fight for what we have everyday.

It means that I'm thinking about you always, dreaming of you every night, only needing and wanting you and knowing that you feel the same way.

SOUL BELIEFS

It means so much more that I'm not able to put into words, but it means I'll try everyday to show you, even if I can't say it.
I hope this is what it means to say 'I love you' to someone.

Chapter 11

James

I slam the front door to my house and jump in my truck before my dad can say another word.

"He's drunk," I tell myself, as if that'll calm me down and not make me want to go back inside and choke him.

Sometimes it's hard to stay here and live in this house with him, but he has no one else; we're all the other has. I can't just leave, leave him, I don't think I'd ever forgive myself if something happened to him while I was gone. His drinking is unpredictable, I don't know what version of him I'll come home to and I don't know what he'll do if I don't come home. I go out and party and hang with friends, but I'm still in the same country, in the same town for god sake.

I rest my head on my steering wheel to calm my breathing before I drive to work.

Things used to be different, I used to be different.

I think that's what hurts the most, that he hasn't always been like this. I wasn't always like this. I remember so vividly what it used to be like. We used to be a happy family. You'd never really think that it'd be love that tears your family apart when it used to be the only thing that made us strong. Now I treat it like the devil.

I tell myself there's no point dwelling on the things you can't change. No point in letting that past control your life—but I'm the biggest hypocrite of them all. Because if that was the case, I wouldn't still hold a grudge against my mum, and I wouldn't be hating on Katherine. But I do, and I am.

Coming to terms with the fact that this is your life and this is what it'll always look like is hard but something I've had ten years to come to terms with. I could change, but I'm not sure in a town like Gull's Bay that that's a possibility. Living in a place where everyone knows you, knows your story, it's hard to break out of the mould they've put you in.

I make the fifteen minute drive to the shop, every minute putting distance between me and my dad, between me and the anger I feel towards this whole situation. By the time I pull up in the car park, I feel like myself again. I grab my surfboard out of the open truck and tuck it under my arm.

When I get to the shop door, I'm stopped in my tracks. I look through the window in the door and see Katherine. She's dancing around the store singing to whatever song is playing on the radio. I can barely hear it but I can hear *her*.

She moves around like she wouldn't care if someone walked in. She looks relaxed, happy. But I have a feeling that would all disappear if she realised I could see her.

I look around the store, no one else is in at the moment. Our lunch time lull.

I can't help looking at her, staring is more like it. I don't think I've seen her look so carefree, as if her brain has let her have a day off from whatever seems to be occupying her thoughts.

I can always see it, the cogs spinning a hundred miles a minute. When I look her in the eyes, I can see it.

Is it weird to feel sorry for her in that way?

Yes.

I wish I had been different that day. That first day we met, I wish I had just said hello with a smile. Taken her hand in a handshake, and showed her, and myself, that we could be friends. But I couldn't do that. I couldn't pretend like the reason she's here makes sense to me or like it's a good idea. Like the idea of soulmates doesn't tear me in half, open me up to old wounds I'd been trying so hard to forget.

In a way I wish Ella had never told me. Had never said why she was coming here. But she did and I can't change that. My heart and my brain knew I couldn't be friends with her before I'd even met her.

Yet I'm still standing here on the other side of the door, hand hovering over the handle watching her.

Her dress clings to her body, and flows with the way of her silhouette. Her hair up in a ponytail whips around as she cleans the shelves. I watch as she brings the polish bottle to her mouth using it as a mic. A laugh works its way up my throat and it's out before I can stop it.

And then the bubble that I've been living in for the last few minutes bursts. She sees me standing rooted to my spot and I can only wonder what she's thinking as she moves to turn the radio down. Then she looks at me, waiting for me to come in.

"Who let you be in charge?" I ask her as I push the door open finally.

Her arms are crossed over her chest as she looks at me mulling over my words, a red blush creeps up her neck just touching her face a little. It might make her stand out round here but I love how pale she still is, I like knowing my words have got to her. Knowing I've made her feel something.

"What do you want?" Katherine finally asks me, the intense look she's sending me is hard to ignore.

"To not have that performance etched in my brain would be a start." I just can't help but give her a hard time.

That blush finally works its way up her face and the line of her lips gets thinner. But she doesn't say a word. Not a single thing—which is odd.

I move across the store towards her, only stopping when I'm beside her. "Aww, you're blushing," I say close to her temple and the red only grows. She must be able to feel my breath along her skin, because I can practically feel the heat radiating off her. She smells like sweet vanilla, mixed with a bit of cinnamon.

"God, you're such a child." *There it is.* There's the Katherine who hates me.

Do I hate her?

Yes.

Do I strangely care about her?

Also, yes.

I have to remind myself that we're not friends because for what feels like a split second—a millisecond, not even a whole breath—when she looks up at me, my chest tightens. Then it's gone, like the feeling was never there. There's a look in her eyes that makes me think she felt it too but it's gone before I can even look for it again.

Stop.

I remind myself why she's here. I think about all the reasons people like her have ruined my life and then I'm okay again.

"I'm here to work, Katherine," I tell her, moving behind the register to pull out the list of classes I have this afternoon from the small filing cabinet.

She scoffs, I hear it from the other end of the shop where she's refolding a t-shirt a hundred times. I think it might fall apart if she's not careful. "You're never early," she tells me.

I look down at my phone as I pull it out my pocket, she's right I'm a whole twenty minutes early. She doesn't need to know why I had to get out of my house, that would be sharing too much. And sharing too much is something friends would do. And she and I are *not* friends.

"It's a thing called 'personal growth' Katherine, I imagine someone as co-dependent as you wouldn't understand."

I tap my fingers against the edge of the counter as I lean on it. The setting sun creates a shadow over the store.

"Katherine, I'm going to lock you in this shop if you don't hurry up!" I shout into the back room.

I should've known it was a lie when she said we could leave soon. Two minutes really means ten in the world of girls getting changed. As much as I may not want to go home to my dad, I also really don't want to be standing in this shop waiting for her.

"It's literally only been like five minutes, will you chill out?" she shouts back as she pushes the curtain back and comes into full view.

Shit.

Everything in me is fighting with itself. The part of my brain that knows soulmate searches are only trouble, and the part that wants to run my fingers over the bare skin on her arms. I'm only human, and as much as I don't like her, I also want to stand here and look at her for a little while longer.

She's now in a pink and red dress that hugs her everywhere it possibly could. One of the straps falls off her shoulder and my hand itches to pull it back up for her, which makes it impossible for me not to look at her neck. Why does her skin look so smooth? I have to physically remember how to breathe as she moves around the counter space picking her stuff up.

Her high ponytail from the day is gone and now falls around her shoulders, all curly and it looks like I need to run my fingers through it. Now she's got, whatever is it girls wear on their eyelids, on and it catches the light, shimmering.

The amount of effort I have to put into not starting to be attracted to her is ungodly.

It's been far too long since I got any female physical contact, because there is no way in any other context I would be this attracted to her.

She must be able to tell I'm looking at her because she leans over the counter to sign off the till, making her ass stick out so much more than it needs to. A groan works its way up my throat and almost slips past my lips, I muffle it before she turns to look at me.

"What?" she asks, eyebrows pulled together and I can't help looking at her lips as she licks them.

"Where are you going all dressed up? Big date?" I barely manage to get the whole sentence out without sounding winded.

A slow smile grows on her face. "Why? Are you going to show up again?"

My nostrils flare.

The first time it was an accident, and then I don't know what happened after that. It just happened, and by happened, I mean I started to show up on purpose. Which I'm so not ready to get into right now.

She smiles at me as she stands and throws her bag over her shoulders. "Good night, James." That's it. She walks out and I watch. I watch her walk away. It's bloody ridiculous and unnerving and I need to get laid. I need something, someone, to take the image of her out of my mind.

Now.

Chapter 12
Katherine

"Katherine, you look insane! That dress is fucking amazing!" Maddie practically yells at me as I walk into The Sydney Siren, the bar she told me to come to tonight. It's busier than I thought it would be, so I'm glad she came to meet me at the door.

I could have told James it was a girls' night but there would be absolutely no fun in that. The fun was watching his face when I stepped out in this ridiculous dress and then told him I knew he's been following my dates. Now that, I should have got a picture of. The guy looked like I'd tried to proposition him and then slapped him, it was wonderful leaving him speechless. I had been debating calling him out on it and I think my new found confidence from the way he was looking at me just pushed me over the edge.

When Maddie texted me this morning, inviting me to girls' night with some of her friends, I had been pretty unsure. New people, new places, two of my literally least favourite things in the world. But anxiety is funny sometimes. Today was a good day and I woke up feeling like all the things I normally think are going to kill me, won't. Anxiety is a confusing mistress.

My mind wanders back to the conversation I had with my mom a couple of days ago. We talked on the phone after she'd had a difficult shift and all I had to tell her about was the shop. She asked me about friends and I could only really talk about Maddie. It made me realize since I've been here all I've done is work, read and be pissed off with James. This was meant to be my big adventure, something I'd look back on and say yeah I did that, all on my own. But it hasn't been that, I want to meet my soulmate more than anything and I want to be able to say I did stuff on the way.

It's a very new idea for me so I found the list I originally made months ago and added a few new things.

> **Kat's Soulmate Search Bucket List**
> - Find Soulmate
> - See the Sydney Opera House and take ridiculous tourist picture on the stairs
> - See Sydney Harbour Bridge
> - Find where Dance Academy was filmed
> - Watch the sunset from Stargaze Perch Lighthouse
> - Go to the Royal Botanical Gardens
> - Learn to surf - ridiculous I work in a surf shop and can't
> - Get first tattoo

It's not exactly groundbreaking and the last one is pretty out there for me but if I can tick them all off it's definitely something I can be proud of.

"Thank you," I tell her, squeezing her in a hug. She takes my hand and leads me over to a booth along one of the sides of the room.

The bar didn't really look like much on the outside. But inside, it's kinda crazy. My eyes take a minute to take it all in as I'm pulled across the space. To call it solely a bar wouldn't be quite right. The bar itself is definitely the main focal point of the space, running along the back wall, it's higher than the rest of the room. Tall shelves run along the wall behind it covered in different bottles of what I can only assume are fancy spirits, with fairy lights woven in-between.

There's a few tall tables near it, mostly taken up by men who look like they would rather be anywhere else. I imagine they're boyfriends being dragged along, or guys trying to look too cool.

Running right through the middle of the room is a dance floor, with disco balls hanging above making the floor glitter. Either side of it are booths with big round tables and plush comfy looking seats.

"Everyone, this is Katherine." Maddie beams at the group in front of me. Thankfully, there's only four other girls and they all smile back at me warmly, melting the last bits of worry I was holding on to about coming out tonight.

Maddie slides into one side of the booth patting the space next to her for me to do the same. "I already got you a cocktail when I went up last, thought you might need it. I know you were on the close with James today." She hands me a pink sparkly drink that smells of bubble gum and I take a long sip from the straw, happy when the strong taste of vodka burns my throat on the way down.

"Maddie was just telling us you're from New York, must be amazing to live there," a girl across from the table tells me, raising her voice to be heard over the music and people. She's just as beautiful as Maddie, with her glowing sun kissed skin and sea salt curly hair. Come to think of it, all the girls round the table are crazy beautiful, I find myself wiping my hands down my thighs. Nervous settling down in my gut again.

SOUL BELIEFS

"Yeah it's great, but I think you guys have got it beat," I say smiling back at her.

My mind goes blank as I watch them all talk back and forth, pulling me into conversation as best as they can in the midst of it all. The confidence I walked in with seems to have caught a ride home without me so I take to the next best thing, liquid confidence.

The cocktail doesn't last long once I've decided this. Soon, Maddie squeezes my forearm bringing me back to the room. "Want another?" she asks, lifting her own empty glass and laughing.

"Yes," I say without hesitation, lifting myself out of the booth and holding a hand out for her to get up too. She doesn't let go of it as we weave across the room navigating a busy bar area before finding a little space on the bar to wait to be served.

Once we reach a spot that isn't too crowded, she turns to me, her eyes studying my face but her own looking worried. "Is everything okay? You're really quiet." *Shit.*

"Oh, yeah. I'm fine, just tired, nothing to worry about." I've gotten good at fake smiles over the years, one only a very few people can see through.

I knew my anxiety still had its claws deep in me but I hoped I'd been hiding the wounds a lot better than this. I'd come to the realisation a long time ago it wouldn't be something that wouldn't go away. It was a part of me, part of my character, something I'd have to learn to live with rather than something I had to fight, because god, was that exhausting. I had to learn its patterns and warning signs. I had to learn ways to make it as small as possible and not add to the big ball of rubber bands collecting in my chest, waiting to snap under pressure. It worked, I learned techniques to help stop it before it got out of hand, I learned ways to calm myself.

But even as my anxiety became smaller and only a distant memory, the self-doubt and low self-esteem never did. For me, no amount of therapy helped with that, it's just something I have to change on my own, it's something that takes so much time because it's something that's so ingrained in my head.

Even looking at Maddie now, no matter how much I think we're friends, my brain is thinking about a hundred things she might hate about me. I don't exactly have a lot of friends back in New York and I guess I'm always scared of opening up to new people. Past experiences told me it was better to keep to myself. I was bullied a lot in middle school, for one thing or another, so eventually, I kinda lost track of the list of things people didn't like about me. My therapist told me that played a big part in my low self-esteem and self-doubt.

"Okay, good." The perfectly curated smile works on Maddie. She blows out a breath as the bartender comes over. "Two of your sweetest and strongest cocktails please." The bartender winks at her as he walks away and it's like déjà vu from my last night with Bella. Then she turns back to me as we wait. "I know it's not easy to make friends here with everything going on, so I thought it might be nice for you to meet some of my girlfriends. I hope you don't mind… " Just another reason why Maddie has a soul of gold.

"Thank you, Maddie." My smile this time reaches my eyes and even more so when she passes me my new cocktail, this time it's yellow and orange and smells of pineapple and rum. As we start to walk back to the table something dawns on me. "Wait, did you pay for this one too? I can get my own." I'm all for a free drink here or there but I don't want Maddie to think she has to buy my friendship.

She waves her free hand in the air. "It's fine, don't worry about it." I go to protest again, getting ready to take some cash out of my bag, but she grabs my hand again before I can.

After the yellow cocktail, there was an orange cocktail, a purple one and a weird blue one. I'm well on my way to being the most unselfconscious version of myself. One of the girls, Becca, has her hand in mine thrown up in the air as we jump around the dance floor to a song I don't really know but it feels good, it helps me feel free a little. To think I could be anything, anyone I wanted in this bar because no one really knows me here.

"Kat, you're the best!" Becca yells in my ear as she pulls me in for a hug as she sways on her feet almost taking us both down in the process. For a bar, this place is pretty club-like, it's midnight now and Sydney Siren could give some of the best clubs in New York a run for their money. There was even some drink throwing going on at one point.

"That guy is definitely checking you out." She points over to the railing near the bar and she's right, I think. My visions not quite on point right now. God, am I happy I stayed in my Nike's before coming out, otherwise I'm sure I'd be falling over like Becca. I drop her off at the booth that some of the girls are still sitting in.

"I'm just going to get her some water," I tell them as I make my way over to the bar, a harder feat than it was a few hours ago. There are a lot more bodies pushed on the dance floor, I'm happy for my small size so I can squeeze pass, but I don't take my eyes off the blonde still watching me. He's got a familiar look but so do most of the guys in this town. There's a couple of guys who seem to be talking to him, or at him. He doesn't look away as his lips move, I assume answering them.

He's cute from what my eyes let me see, broad shoulders and strong arms flex as he moves off the railing. He turns to watch me walk up the stairs to the bar platform. I have to stop looking at him when I reach the stairs just to make sure I don't fall on my face or ass. I don't look back again, not wanting to look like a total creep. I might be here for my soulmate, but I am not opposed to some harmless flirting or making out with a guy at a bar. Hey, for all I know, he could be my soulmate.

"Can I get two bottles of water please?" I ask the girl behind the bar when she comes over to me, nodding her head before walking away.

"No big date then." The voice comes from behind me and I don't need to turn to know who it is. His mouth is so close to my ear so I can hear him over the noise, and I can feel his breath on my face. There is an involuntary shiver that travels down my spine.

"I never said I had one, you just assumed," I tell James as I pay for the bottles and turn to look at him.

God, he's so close, my breasts almost touch his chest when we're face to face. I move slightly out of the way to let someone else get to the bar. Then I roll my eyes at his stupid gorgeous smile on his stupid beautiful face. Has he always been this beautiful?

Then I'm looking at the rest of him, looking down at his shirt. I have a sudden revelation and he watches as I work it out.

It was him.

It was him looking at me, *staring* at me. It was him I fucking considering making out with, I almost want to throw up at the thought.

"So, did you just happen to be here, or did you follow me here too?" The alcohol I've had does wonders for my ability to talk to him like I actually want to, and maybe now he's had a drink as well, he'll actually give me an answer.

Chapter 13
James

She's so close to me, I can bloody smell her. The smell of French pastries floats up between us and I can only assume it's her shampoo. God, is it distracting. I still can't give her an answer as to why I showed up to those dates. And I'm not about to have that conversation with this drunk version of her, either.

"Who's this then, James?" Willie comes up behind me, placing an arm around my shoulder, and I know he's sending her his 'signature' smile and 'fuck me' eyes. He's predictable and almost the same as me. He's a surfer too, but he's more on the competition circuit, so he's not around as much.

When I texted him after my shift to see where he was, it didn't take much to get him to come with me. This time I didn't follow her, not that I followed her on these dates I was just—looking out for her... Yes, that makes sense. She's Ella's niece, I just wanted to make sure nothing happened to her. I'm a good guy, really.

I did know Maddie would be here, because when all else fails, at least I knew I could crash my best friend's night.

She smiles back at him and I'm sure if she didn't have two bottles in her hands she'd be twirling her hair like a love sick school girl, it makes me want to be sick a little, but it's not jealousy.

Willie's not so up front with girls. One minute he's here in Sydney, the next he's in a different time zone and they don't hear from him for months. At least I know how to tell girls they're a one night fling from the start. They think they can change my mind, but I remind them over and over that I am not a relationship guy. And neither is Willie. Maybe he's not the best guy around, but I've known him since I moved here and sometimes those friendships are hard to shake.

"Katherine," she says to him, pretending I'm not here. "James's work nemesis."

He laughs—the bloody bastard. Still, I have to fight the sides of my mouth coming up in a smile from her comment. *Nemesis*. She's so dramatic. It's cute.

No, it's not.

"So, this is the little red head you've been talking about, I can see why she's got you so worked up, she's hot," he says, not at all lowering his voice. I feel my blood start to boil and my hands clench and unclench repeatedly trying not to want to throw him across the dance floor.

"He talks about me?"

"Oh, I can't get him to shut up. *Katherine this, Katherine that.*"

I need to put a stop to this weird exchange between them, he's not flirty with her because—just, no. I'm not jealous, I just know that she won't survive him.

I swear my life was not this complicated before I met her.

I don't think about it, I just move. I take the two bottles out of her hands, handing them to Willie. "Take these over to the booth Maddie is at." He doesn't say anything, just gives me a shit eating grin and a knowing look. I don't like it because that's not what this is, I'm not jealous and I'm not making a move. I just need to talk to her.

Who you trying to convince?

"Nice to meet you, Katherine," he says to her before heading down into the jaws of the dance floor.

When I take her hand in mine, the shocked and horrified look she gives me makes me feel something. But I don't think about it too much. Scanning the room, I see a quiet corner near what looks like a storage room. Pulling her thought the bar is no mean feat, as she drags her steps the whole way.

"What do you want?" she asks, crossing her arms over her chest when we get the spot and it only makes my eyes draw to that area of her body. I came here to get away from the thought of her, the one that hasn't left my mind since she walked out of the shop, and here she is, somehow looking even better. I take her in for a second now that we're alone, her hair is more tousled, and her dress seems to be hugging her even more and her lips look swollen.

Oh, my god.

"For you to fucking leave. You've messing with my head." I need to be mean, because if I'm meaner to her, maybe she'll just stay away from me and I'll have a chance to get over whatever the hell is happening to me.

"Wow."

As I watch the moisture pool in her eyes, I try to keep the straightest face I can, but I didn't mean to make her cry. Okay, maybe that was too far. She blinks it away quickly and turns her face away from me only for a second and when she's looking at me again, it's like I never said anything,

"You're everywhere, this is my place, Katherine." And I don't just mean this bar, I mean... I don't really know what I mean.

"You own the bar? Well, Christ, sorry, I'll go grab my purse," she snarls back at me.

No matter how beautiful she looks, my brain doesn't stop from reminding me of everything. "Fuck off, you know that's not what I meant."

A wicked smile pulls on to her face and once again I want to know how soft her lips are, what it would feel like to feel them on mine. Watching her dance the way she was, hips swaying and body moving to the beat only made me want to run my hands along her waist.

I need to stop.

"No, James, I'm clearly far too stupid to understand. But let me explain something to you." Her face is as fiery as her words sound and this is the Katherine I'm used to, this is okay. "You. Do. Not. Own. Australia. You can't stop me being here. I've dealt with far worse things than you. So, if you think you can scare me off, you'll be sadly mistaken." Her face drops.

Now, all I'm thinking about is what she went through. Who hurt her? She already thinks I'm a monster, so what does she classify as worse than me?

I think of what makes me hate her the most, and I pull at that, bringing that back to the front of my brain. Reminding me of all the pain and crying and drunk fights I'm far too familiar with. "You people just think you can walk it and ruin peoples lives."

Her eyebrows pull together. "Ruin lives? This has literally nothing to do with you!"

"God, you are so insufferable!"

"Then leave me alone!"

"I don't think that's an option."

"What?" she asks but the sound gets lost in my lips as I press mine to hers.

My body jumps into autopilot, and my brain is no longer in the driver's seat. I needed to do this, if just to get it out of my system. Maybe it'll stop me having these weird feelings, I'll learn that we have no physical chemistry and it can all stop. It's a selfish thing to do to her but it's one kiss, that's all.

But as her hands find my hair, pulling me closer, I know that's not the road we're going down. My mouth moves over hers like I've been starved my whole life of this feeling. I'm not sure how to stop, how to pull away from her. I nip at her lower lip and she opens her mouth letting my tongue battle with hers, as if that's something new for us. She tastes like whatever cocktail she's been drinking, something sweet, and it suddenly becomes my favourite drink.

My hands are on her hips pushing her back until she hits the wall. But she doesn't blink, just keeps kissing me like I'm the only guy in the room; I kinda wish I was. She pulls on my hair as our bodies melt into each other as mine pushes into her, a moan from me getting lost in her mouth when her stomach rubs on my cock through my jeans.

"Kat!" Maddie's voice breaks though the loud bass music that I'd almost forgotten was even playing and Katherine pulls away from me so quickly it's like I'm on fire, and I just might very well be.

Every fibre of my body is on fire, like she's lit something inside of me, and I don't know how to put it out, but I want to feel it again and again. I just look down at her like I don't know what on earth has happened to us. Our breathing is laboured and in sync, her eyes are heavy and lips are wet and I'd properly kiss her again if it wasn't for Maddie's voice carrying over the music again.

"Kat!"

"I need to go," she tells me, she looks confused and in a daze, I don't blame her because I feel the same.

I don't say anything, she just walks out of my grip, then she's out of the shadows back into the light of the dance floor finding Maddie. I watch her until she's back with our friend. I watch as she smiles at her and the other girls, telling them some lie I'm sure is more convincing than the truth. I watch as she looks around the room again looking for me, our eyes lock one more time and then I leave.

The fuck just happened and how do we pretend it never did?

The best way to pretend something never happened? Avoidance.

I've always found that's the best way for both parties to have time to completely erase the moment from their minds and forget it ever happened. But when that moment happens to be the best kiss of your life, somehow it's a little hard to just forget and that's exactly what it was.

So what do I do now?

This doesn't happen to me, I've never let it happen. It's got to be a fluke because I don't know what else to tell myself, it seems the most logical answer. The only way to test this theory would be to kiss again and that's not happening! I've never been more sure of something than that, never again.

Back to the idea of avoidance: once again, it's a great idea if I didn't have to work with her and see her like every other day. Avoiding someone becomes a little tricky when you literally can't avoid them.

I'm trying something new, being nice. Maybe if we can just be nice then we won't fight and the weird feeling will stop. The logic is thin, I know, but when we fight, it's like something clicks. That pure raw emotion of hating someone can make you feel something, can make you feel emotional.

Nice. It's such a nothing emotion, it's not strong and fiery enough to make me feel anything. I'm fuelled on impulsive moments and feelings, and nothing is as controlled as being nice.

That brings me to walking to the surf shop for the afternoon shift with a tray of coffee cups. I know the girls have all been working this morning since Ella needed Maddie in earlier to help with a new surf class she's trying out, OAP surfing.

Coffee is something people who are being nice do, right? How have I forgotten what's normal? I have friends. I know how to be nice to them, what to do when they're sad or need someone. I know how to be nice.

But with Katherine, for some reason, I don't know how to be nice; I don't know what to do, what to say, and I know it's because deep down my brain is wired to hate her and it's hard to not do that, but god it shouldn't be this hard.

I shouldn't be rethinking everything.

They're all standing around the till when I get to them looking at something on screen.

"Those are good numbers, Ella. I'll do the class next week, see what happens," Maddie says with a smile finally looking up and seeing me, her smile doesn't change and I only hope that means Katherine hasn't told her about the club. She's probably just as confused or embarrassed as I am so I can only hope she won't say anything.

"Coffee," I say, handing Maddie her iced matcha and then Ella her americano with a dash of milk and then my hand hovers over the last cup. The other two have already started talking again, but Katherine, she's just looking at me.

"I got you your favourite," I say as I hand her the caramel latte with soy milk and slap myself mentally for saying it out loud. I could have just given it to her and not said anything, she could have thought I had just guessed. Remembering someone's coffee order doesn't seem like that big a deal. It's not like I haven't heard her order it before, on those first two dates she went on they got coffee.

Okay, it sounds worse when I think about it like that.

All three of them snap their heads towards me.

Hey, Earth, I'd super appreciate a sink hole right where I'm standing, thanks.

Maddie and Ella share a look and I start wishing to be struck down by lighting as well as the sink hole. I'm never going to live this down.

But Katherine doesn't say anything; she just takes the cup from my outstretched hand and then takes a sip. "Thanks," is all I get before she's walking off into the back room. I should be glad she didn't make a big deal out of it, that she didn't say too much or ask how I knew. I should be glad.

And yet, I'm not.

Chapter 14
Katherine

My list of things I want to do while I'm here is off to a great start.
Surf lessons.

Between Ella and me both working down at the shop, we haven't actually spent all that much time together. So, this is a nice thing for us to do together, a way for me to feel closer to her.

The actual concept of surfing is maybe not as great. After my first lesson with Ella, it's safe to say I'm not exactly a natural but I've got a bit of time to get a grasp on the fundamentals, so I don't feel too defeated when I only manage to stand up on the board with Ella's help, *twice*.

I'm not exactly the most coordinated person on the planet, I'm much more content being sat in one place, behind a desk writing. It's not like you can fall into the unpredictable ocean when your butt is on a chair. I'm in control there.

"I think that's probably enough for today, love," Ella says, sitting down beside me.

"Was I that bad?" I laugh, making her laugh too. "I'm taking that as a yes."

I'm trying this new thing where I'm letting myself be bad things. Being *perfect* at things has been a staple part of my personality since I was a kid. And I remember when Dad died thinking that if I could be perfect at college, be at the top of all my classes, that everything would feel better. They didn't. And it was exhausting, always trying to be great, never doing anything I didn't think I'd be perfect at first try.

We sit for a minute, just looking out at the afternoon sea as my body screams at me. I'm sure I haven't done this much physical exercise since Bella and I did a hot yoga class two years ago.

A group of kids, maybe eleven or twelve years old, with surfboards under their arms, run along the beach and jump in the sea without any hesitation.

Oh, to be that age again, you have no idea of the world then; kids say what they mean, and mean what they say and don't hold back, they don't run from their problems. Everything is unknown and exciting instead of terrifying.

Following after the kids, with a grin only the Cheshire cat could compete with, is the blonde hair maniac I've been doing my best to not be anywhere near.

Apart from his strange behaviour with my coffee order last week, we've done a pretty good job of avoiding each other. I even convinced Gregg to swap a couple of shifts to give me even more time to completely erase the events from the night at the bar from my mind.

For the most part, not being near him is working pretty well to forget all about the kiss. It's been like remembering a distant dream, every time it resurfaces, I'm blanking on little parts more and more, and now it's so far away from my mind, it's like it never happened. And that's where I am now. Until I look at him for longer than I should. Then I remember the feeling of his lips on mine and how soft they were, how it felt to be in his arms. I remember the feeling of his fingers digging into my hips. And the moan he let out when my body moulded into his.

"Ella." I wait for her to look back in my direction before I say anything else. "Did you ever want to find your soulmate?" I ask her, realizing I've never seen her with a partner and that I've never asked her before. I guess it had never really crossed my mind. All I know is she seemed so happy however she was living her life.

Her eyebrows come together as she looks at me. "Me? I guess not really." She looks back over in the direction of the sea as if maybe it'll give her the right words to say. "I moved here when I was only eighteen, on a whim and a wish that I could surf for a living. The idea of love didn't even cross my mind. Don't get me wrong, I've dated and had my fair share of relationships." She smiles at me and I believe she has a happy life but there's a little something in her voice that tells me it crosses her mind now and again. My mind floats to the way Gregg looks at her sometimes.

I can't help myself even though I'm worried I might be about to cross a line somewhere. "And what about now?"

"Now?" She thinks about it for a minute and an even bigger smile creeps onto her face. "Kat, I got to have the one thing I dreamed of my whole life, a career I thought was too far away for me to grab and now I get to share that knowledge with other people who want to feel the same thing I got to."

"And what's that?"

"Free."

Someone walking along the beach stops and starts talking to Ella before I can ask her anything else but god does it make my brain swirl thinking about it.

I think about that for the rest of the day and evening and still when I'm lying in bed that night looking up at the ceiling.

Have I ever felt that?

Free?

Best friends tell each other everything right? And, well, in the two months I've been here, I haven't had a problem with telling Bella anything and everything that's been going on. We've always been like that, sharing every little thing that happens to us.

Except every time I've talked to her the last couple of weeks, I just can't bring myself to tell her about the kiss. It's no big deal and means absolutely nothing to either me or James. Yet every time the conversation turns to me or how my search is going, my throat goes dry and I just can't tell her.

I'm not sure what I'm worried about. Bella would never judge me for anything, if anything I have this feeling that maybe she'd be proud or something. Yet, it just sits on the tip of my tongue every time.

In fairness, I haven't actually told anyone, and considering Maddie still looks at me like I've got one head, I'm guessing he hasn't either which makes it easier. I mean I don't even know what to say. *James kissed me in a dark corner of a bar after his friend flirted with me, I think he was flirting with me, anyway I didn't exactly push him off me and may have kissed him back, and oh yes, it was maybe the best kiss of my whole life.*

Yeah, for some reason, I'm not too sure that's the best way to put it, but it's what happened. The last bit is still confusing me a lot. I've kissed my fair share of guys in my time. Horrible drunk sloppy kisses, passionate and full of passion kisses, kisses that you did when you were fourteen that were the most embarrassing of your life, but James was different. It wasn't sloppy or drunk, at least not on his part, it was passionate but not full of love, full of something else.

SOUL BELIEFS

Thinking about it gives me butterflies and sweaty palms in a non-anxiety way and I find my mind floating back to that dark corner in the bar whenever I start daydreaming.

The possibility that maybe it was because I was so mad at him at that moment has crossed my mind and it's the thing that makes the most sense. Passion can come from more places than just love, I passionately can't stand the guy so that could be a thing. Hates kisses, that's a new one to add to the list.

"God, and then the spawn of Satan took the camera. Kat, you still there?" Bella's voice brings me back to the room, eyes watering from me staring out my doors into the garden.

"Yeah, sorry, I'm still here." I can hear the distance in my own voice as I say it, because really I'm not in this conversation, I'm back in that bar trying to make sense of it.

"I'm sorry, I've been going on about work for like ten minutes." A little laugh slips from her voice and it's even further away than I am. "Tell me what's going on with you?"

What's going on with me?

"Oh, well, you know, um, just the usual."

"Okay, that was a strangely vague answer, even for you." The girl can sniff out deception like a bloodhound. Me, I'm like a wet napkin at this point, secrets eat at me like termites. When I was sixteen I drank one beer at a party and managed to keep it from my mom for a total of twelve hours, and eight of those hours were only because she was on shift at the hospital. The fact I haven't already told her is what I can only call a miracle, or the different time zones.

I feel it rising in me like that beer did five minutes after I drank it. "James kissed me," I tell her knowing I need to tell her, someone, before the termites eat my insides.

Silence.

I check my phone to make sure I haven't been disconnected from her but the phone screen shows I'm still on the line with her.

"Bella?"

Silence.

Maybe she passed out?

"I'm so sorry, I'm just processing that information." I wait for another second. "WHAT!"

I have to peel my phone away from my ear before I'm left with a damaged eardrum, I keep it away from my face while she says a few things in Spanish that I only half understand. That only tends to happen when she's really annoyed or shocked or sometimes super excited. Okay, actually it happens a lot. At this moment, I'm not too sure which one she is.

"Okay," she finally says and I rest the phone back on my ear. "When did this happen? How did this happen? Was it good?" Her questions all seem to come at once and I'm unprepared for every one of them.

"Okay, lets try one question at a time, please?" I ask as I flop down in one of the chairs on the patio outside my room, lucky that Ella is at the shop so I don't have to worry about her overhearing this conversation.

"The most important one, was it good?" The smile on her face carries across oceans and right through my phone. She damn well knows the answer, because lets face it, if it was terrible I wouldn't have been worried to tell her. I would have called her right away to laugh about it.

"Great." It comes out as a whisper, my very being is in pain to even admit it, I'm basically humiliated by how it made me feel.

"I'm sorry, Katherine, but I'm going to need a little more detail."

I'm not happy at all admitting this but I know if I keep the details to a minimum she will only keep poking at me until I tell her and I honestly don't want to talk about it for any longer then I have too. "It was the best kiss I've ever had, are you happy?"

"Even better than that New Year's kiss with Benny?" Oh, Christ, how could I have forgotten the great New Year's kiss of 2019? Nothing ever happened with Benny apart from that beautiful kiss, of course my stone didn't glow so he wasn't the one.

I think it over for probably less then a second because the world hates me and I know the answer. "Yes."

"Jesus, boy kisses as good as he looks. Okay, second, when?"

"Like a week or so ago."

"A WEEK!"

"Jesus, Bella... eardrums," I say pulling the phone away from my face.

"I need all the details so I can forget that my best friend kept this from me for a whole week."

"I went to a bar with Maddie and some other girls, he turned up and the usual back and forth, then his friend was flirting or whatever."

"He was *so* jealous."

"Anyway," I move past that quickly, because the thought had crossed my mind later that night when I was still drunk but what would he be jealous of? "He pulled me over to a corner and started going on about how people like me just think they do whatever they want and then we kissed."

"Angry kissing?" she quizzes.

"Had to be, because I don't know what else it was." It has to be that, because if it's anything else, that only makes it worse and oh so very much confusing.

"And how do you feel about it?"

"Feel about what?" Out of all the questions she could have asked, I didn't think that would be one. "I don't know, weird, I guess. And a little confused, so confused. Not just by him, but by me. I didn't push him off. If anything, I kept that kiss going for way longer than necessary."

"Oh, baby," she says in the motherly tone she has, the one that makes me feel a little safer and like she's about to solve all my problems.

"I know." I pull the phone away from my ear when I feel it buzzing and see my mom's picture flash across the screen. "My mom is calling, can I talk later?"

"Of course, but I want to FaceTime later, I miss you."

"Sounds good, miss you more." I hang up with Bella quickly before I miss my mom's call. "Hey, Mom."

"Hey, my beautiful girl, are you busy?"

Chapter 15

Katherine

P osted 21st October 2024 08:19

Having your birthday in a different country is weird.

Every birthday after Dad died has been weird but there's something different about this one.

When he passed, I didn't really want to celebrate any more, not mine anyway; it just kinda felt off without him. Dad was a big birthday guy. The party, the decorations, the presents, the surprises. Mom tried her best to carry it on but we both knew it just wasn't the same, it wasn't her fault, it was just the way it was.

So after that, we just kept it low-key. Apart from my twenty-first, nothing was going to stop Bella and Nick from taking me out and making a whole thing about it. They had been twenty-one for about four months before me and they both acted like such 'experts' all night.

Birthdays just felt like another thing he was going to miss out on, and I was too. I wouldn't get another home baked cake by him or another birthday breakfast of pancakes full of rainbow sprinkles.

Another year he missed out on, another year of hoping I'm making him proud, another year of wondering where I'd be if he was still here holding my hand.

And this ones no different.

Happy birthday to me.

I miss you, Dad.

I close my laptop and slide to the foot of the bed. I feel weird, I know I should be happy, it's my birthday after all. But for the past seven years, I've felt like there is such pressure put on birthdays like they should be this amazing day and it's never as good as you want it to be. For me, I put on a brave face and pretend it's not the worst day of the year for me. Somehow my birthday makes me feel even worse than the anniversary of his death.

It might sound weird, but I asked Ella if I could work today; she gave me a look but didn't ask why and put me on the schedule for the late shift. I've heard her moving around in the kitchen for about an hour now and I've had a sick feeling building the whole time.

I throw open the curtains that look out into the back yard, strangely it's overcast for a change. I want to put off stepping out of my room for as long as possible but I know Ella wants to go to the shop and I don't want whatever she's done to go to waste. I'm so grateful for her and everything she's done and continues to do.

A knock on my door makes me turn around, Ella standing in my doorway bringing a smile to my face uncontrollably. "Happy Birthday, darling." She sings holding a cake that looks hand iced and with a few candles dotted around. I blink quickly to stop myself from crying in front of her. "Now blow them out before they ruin the cake."

It's super predictable what my birthday wish is every year. It's been the same for most of my life. *I wish to find my soulmate.* There were a few years when I wished for Dad to get better, and one year when I wished I'd be a secret princess, like in The Princess Diaries.

Needless to say, none of my birthday wishes have ever come true but that doesn't stop me closing my eyes and blowing out my candles and wishing all the same.

I wish to find my soulmate.

Except this year when I close my eyes it's James' face that I see and I don't know what to make of that. So I open them as quickly as I closed them to look at the cake Ella made.

It's even cuter up close, she's piped little flowers on it with my name. She pulls me out into the kitchen and it's like I've been kicked in the gut; I've stepped back in time to when Dad was still here. I hang in the doorway for a minute before I can even bring myself to check what's sat on the plate on the breakfast bar.

Balloons scatter the room, a big banner hangs over the window, presents litter the bar but the real icing on top of this birthday cake is the rainbow sprinkle pancakes with strawberries on top looking back at me when I walk forward. A tear slips down my cheek and I don't want to cry when she's clearly put so much work in, but god, she's making it hard to keep it together.

"I know birthdays aren't quite the same any more, I get that, but I still wanted to do something." She's holding a stack of three books with a ribbon around them tied in a bow at the top. I can see their crisp edges and I can't wait to open them up and smell that new book smell. The cute cartoon cover at the top matches all the other romance books I have in my room already.

"Ella, this is…" I'm not sure I have words for it, coming from her it almost feels like it's coming from Dad in a weird way. Like she's a part of him and she's giving me that piece for a day. "It's perfect." I smile at her pulling her in for a hug, squishing the books in-between us.

When we pull away from each other I notice the few stray tears on her face and she must see the same thing on my face too. "Come on, no more tears today, those pancakes will go cold if you leave them."

We talk while we eat and Ella tells me about the birthdays Dad used to put together for her when she was kid. It's another little nugget of information I tuck away in my brain and it makes me feel like he's closer to me for a minute. I open the parcel and cards that have come from America. One from Mom, who called me last night because she knew the time difference would mean she wouldn't speak to me until the afternoon. She sent money to my bank account so I could get myself something. The parcel is from Nick and Bella, a care package full of all of my favourite snacks I've been missing, Cheetos, Reese's, a few different bars of Hershey's, Twinkies, etc. and a beautiful gold dress with a note attached.

I saw this in a store and couldn't not get it for you, make sure you make a reason to wear it - Bella xx

I'm not sure there would possibly be a reason for me to wear it here, but I love it anyway. It's gold satin, with spaghetti straps and a deep V neckline that pulls in at the waist and flows back out again touching just above my knees. My hair seems even brighter against the fabric. My face finally has a glow it only gets in the sun, my freckles seem to have multiplied. I look different on the outside from when I first arrived. Am I any different on the inside?

Ella left a little while ago for the shop and after thinking about it I put on a bikini, grabbed a wetsuit from the plethora that Ella owns, and headed to the beach.

The drive is quite and honestly probably one of the first times I've actually driven since I've been here. I can hear the waves draw closer and closer and it's like being called by a friend now. I never thought I'd find anything as calm as the hustle of the city, when you grow up somewhere like New York it becomes your norm. The quiet always used to get to me so much more, but now the sound of the wind coming through my windows and the crash of waves, feels like my new norm.

When I pull up to the shop I've got more than two hours before my shift. I've packed a backpack with clothes in it to get changed into later and considering James walks around the shop with wet hair every other day, I can't see why I can't do the same.

Damn it.

I'd been doing so well not thinking about him for the last couple of days, I finally thought I was over the whole thing. Any shift we've worked together, we've pretty much just pretended the other one didn't exist unless completely necessary, but it doesn't matter.

Anytime he's near me it comes back in flashes, his lips on mine, his hands on me, the feeling in my chest, the smell of him so close. It's like it happened yesterday regardless of it actually being three weeks ago. I don't know what to do about it. Ignoring him does nothing and talking to him about it can't help either of us surely. Being honest with myself hasn't gotten me very far either because I *honestly* don't know what I think or feel.

The *feeling* of kissing him was a feeling I've never had before, like my chest was light and my head was foggy, I feel like I could kiss him again.

I *think* he's an arrogant pig who hates me. I think he kissed me as a joke or just to mess with my head, because I can't think of a single moment when he was actually nice to me.

Apart from when Neil was being a dick, I guess.

It almost doesn't even matter what I think or feel anyway, I know what he thinks. He thinks I'm a total moron who believes in soulmates and will do anything to find mine, he thinks I'm the devil, the enemy. So my feelings are irrelevant, whatever it is I'm feeling.

    I can't control him or what happens, but I can go surfing.

Chapter 16

James

"What the fuck is she doing?" I mutter to myself as I stand in the shop watching Katherine take a surfboard off the rack outside and start marching down to the beach. She's got a wetsuit on and her hair's pulled back away from her face.

Looking at her it's like there's something different about her, she doesn't seem like my Katherine.

But she's not mine.

She doesn't look like her but like new, refreshed; something has changed.

It is her birthday, maybe it's that another year thing, or whatever. I've never liked birthdays. After Mum left everything was just weird and painful.

She would still send cards every year and it ended up being another stab in my chest. Reminding me how much things had changed. How it would never be the same because her card was coming in the mail and not being handed to me in the living room with her and Dad's handwriting together.

Dad's drinking didn't make it any easier, every birthday he'd promise he'd stop, that he'd get help, that was his birthday promise to me. He'd say *just you watch you won't recognise me next year.* He'd be sober for maybe three - four days and every year I'd think maybe, maybe this year, maybe I'd finally be enough for him to get better but before I could eat all the cake in the fridge we'd be back to the beginning again.

So to say I think birthdays are a bit overrated would be an understatement.

Katherine's gone by the time my brain catches up with my eyes, I move closer to the window to see her standing by the waters edge. I know Ella said she's been giving her a few lessons but I still feel this pit inside my stomach open up. And I know for a fact I don't like the feeling because it means only one thing and I'm not happy feeling that about her.

I lean in the window frame as I watch her and I slip my hands into my short pockets. The small gift box sitting in my pocket starts to burn a hole in my hand reminding me, deep down I know what the pit feeling is for. That only makes me feel sick because I don't want it to be true, I don't want to feel anything at all, least of all this.

None of this would be happening if she wasn't here, if she'd never turned up on that sunny day in August. The day has been stuck in my head since and nothing I've done has made any difference. I think somehow I knew she'd do this, that she'd fuck everything up the minute I laid eyes on her in this shop. Except I thought it'd be in a different way.

"Penny for your thoughts?" Ella asks, sneaking up behind me. Katherine's in the water now paddling out and she looks like a natural now. The hand wrapped around the box in my pocket stills as if she'll know it's here.

Ella's not stupid, in fact I think she's one of the smartest people I know, but as far as I know, I've still got her convinced the only feelings I have towards Katherine are those of hate and I'm sure as shit Katherine hasn't told her about the kiss.

"Just one of those days," I tell her, taking one final look out the window before walking away. "You sure Katherine won't kill herself out there?" I ask her as she stares out the window with a smile on her face.

"I think I'm a pretty good teacher, actually," she says with a chuckle. "Are *you* okay?" Her playful tone completely gone and replaced with a tone she hasn't used in years, not since I was a teen. It's not a passing *hope you're good*. It's a *tell me your deep dark secrets*. Two months ago, I would have, but now I don't even know my deep dark secrets well enough to tell her.

"Yeah, of course." I smile at her from behind the counter busying myself with the paperwork sat at the till, an order form I completed hours ago.

But I know it's not believable, I know I'm terrible at lying to her.

"You know you can talk to me if you need to." She stills my jittering hands by placing hers on top of mine. I know I can. The nights I've spent talking to her about Dad or Mum, or just everything. The times she's been the parent figure for me when no one else was are too many to count.

So instead, I come up with a very believable lie about my dad and some fight we've had because that's easy to think about. What's not easy is Katherine, she's like a tsunami that just keeps knocking me over again and again and I don't understand, maybe never will, maybe not till she's gone.

"I'm so proud of you, sweetheart," Ella gushes, pulling out of a hug with Katherine once she comes into the shop.

She's changed now into a pair of denim shorts and a white 'Ella's surf shop' vest top that just about hits the top of her shorts, she's never looked more like a local before. I guess I hadn't wanted to notice because all I wanted was her out of here, I still do, but her skin has tanned now and her face glows like someone who's finally seeing the right amount of sun. Her wet hair hangs around her shoulders, the red in her hair lighter now, you'd almost miss her walking down the street if it wasn't for the fact she was one the most beautiful girls I'd ever seen.

Man, you're losing it.

The box in my pocket bounces as I move.

"Thanks, Aunt Ella, but I wiped out like half the time," she tells her with a laugh and it's the first time I really see the fact that they are related. They looked so different when she first got here and now she seems to reflect all the safe things I see in Ella.

You've completely lost it.

My hands get sweaty thinking about it. Thinking about the fact I'm feeling all these things. Thinking about the god damn gift in my pocket. I make the quick decision while they're both distracted to put it in the back room where she normally puts her bag, so she'll find it, but also so I don't have to give it to her.

I didn't mean to buy the necklace. I just saw it in one of the gift shops in town and I walked past it at first not thinking too much of it but then I found myself being pulled back to the shop the next day too, and the next until I just brought the fucking thing. It had sat in the box on my dresser for a week, laughing at me every time my eyes caught it. Mocking me, because only a true idiot would buy her a birthday gift, especially if that idiot knew she hated him.

"Now are you sure you want to work?" I hear Ella's voice cutting through my own thoughts, I walk out the back room and bring a box of t-shirts as I do to not look too suspicious.

"Yeah, of course, you know me and birthdays," she tells Ella, the smile on her face not even the slightest bit believable. I don't know why but people like Katherine, all rainbows, sunshine and floral prints, give off the vibe they love birthdays. A whole day about them.

Maybe she's more like me than I thought.

Ella hands me the keys to lock up. "Try not to kill her on her birthday," she tells me as Katherine walks past us into the back room trying everything in her power to not make eye contact with me at all.

"I guess if it's her birthday, I'll try my best," I joke as she walks out of the shop, her steps only a little hesitant before disappearing from the store completely.

All of a sudden it feels like all the air in the room has gone, leaving behind my hot breaths anticipating Katherine's re-entrance into the room. The shop's empty and I'd never wished for the opposite.

"Do you know who left this?" Her quiet voice, piercing through me like a knife, brings me back into the room.

I turn in her direction, she's not even looking at me just down at the little box in her hands, like she's hypnotised by it.

"What is it?" I ask as casually as humanly possible, my sweating palms and hoarse voice giving me away if she was paying more attention to me.

"A necklace," she says as if she's looking at a puzzle. I didn't want her to know I got it for her which just sounds even weirder when I think about it more but lets face it she wouldn't want it if I did tell her I got it and I just want her to have it. I don't know why.

"That was very helpful, Katherine, how am I supposed to know." Reverting back to being a dick is the easiest thing I can do, it's easy and simple and it works. It lets my brain remember the truth about everything, it reminds me why I'm like this, why my life fell apart and why this girl is not my friend.

"Well someone left it in the back room, are you just letting anyone back there now?" Her snarly tone seeps into her words, her sunshine and rainbows falling for only a minute to let me see her and we finally seem to be reverting back to the easy hate we had for each other.

It seems odd that that's the safe space, the easy path, to just hate each other but god I'm happy for it. The awkward air that's been hanging over the two of us since the kiss has been suffocating.

"Obviously not," I say, taking it out of her hands examining it as if I hadn't been doing the same thing for a week. "What is it anyway?"

"A whale, you giant idiot," she tells me snatching it out of my hands, without thinking my fingers brush hers and she looks me dead in the eyes and it's enough to set my whole body on fire, my veins completely igniting inside me, I'm not sure I'm even breathing.

We both seem to need to take a deep breath when I finally pull away from her and I'm so out of breath I feel like I've been on the water for hours. I want to tell her it's actually a humpback whale, her favourite, but I hold myself back from it knowing the questions I'll get after.

I could hear it all too well in my head already. *How would you know?* As if she hasn't been talking about going on a whale watching tour since she got here, but I guess maybe I wasn't meant to notice that, I wasn't meant to remember all the conversations we've had or all the other conversations I've overheard her having. But my brain seems to store it all away in a little Katherine sized box in a corner. I've tried emptying it out, recycling the files, but still when I go to bed and close my eyes it's all here, being replayed right in front of me.

A haunting thought comes to mind as she stands there smiling down at her hands, examining the little silver pendant more. She looks up and she smiles at me, the first one I'm sure I've ever gotten, maybe the only one I'll ever get, and I melt. Seeing her like this, real. This is something else, not her trying to be anyone, or trying to be what she thinks other people want. Just her. Right in front of me, wet hair and denim shorts.

Look what she's done to me.

The thought doesn't go anywhere as a sharp pain in my chest takes over, maybe not painful but noticeable. I'm not sure I mind what I'm feeling as much as I don't recognise it. But the thought persists, even when she's put the necklace on and stopped looking at me, and when we've fallen into our regular routine of work.

I'm sure in all those moments, I will do anything in my power just to get her to smile at me like that again.

Chapter 17

Katherine

It's been almost three months.

It's gone by so quickly I think I blinked and missed it.

I have however managed to see all the landmarks I wanted to that were on my bucket list thanks to Ella. She took a couple days off last week and made sure to schedule other people in for my normal shifts now that she has some more seasonal staff in and we did all the tourist sightseeing.

"Kat, hunny, you know you saw this place when you were like twelve, right?" Ella shouts to me as I pose in front of the Sydney Opera House. She's been my Instagram boyfriend for the day, and she's surprisingly good at it.

"Yes, but I had braces and the worst hair cut of my life. I need new pictures," I tell her as I run down the stairs and take my phone from her. And I'm not kidding about the hair cut, I'm pretty sure I wore a hat for like two years straight until it grew out.

She does the same even when I pull her around Sydney's Walsh Bay looking for all the places Dance Academy was filmed, making her take pictures nearly every twenty seconds, she's a good sport indulging me like this. Spending this time with her is priceless.

Running around the city with her has to be the highlight for my time here so far.

Apart from that kiss.

That kiss is but a blip in my Australia timeline, nothing but a very small pebble in my shoe, a little pot hole on my road to my soulmate. So insignificant it's like it never happened.

Not even remotely believable.

James is back to acting like I'm the worst thing to happen since they cancelled The Ghost Whisper and I'm back to pretending he doesn't even exist.

Does it sting a little? Of course, but the same amount as being stung by a hundred bees. But what's that really? Nothing, that's what.

I've been on another five dates or so, two of them even kissed me and it was... fine. They were all... okay. We talked and laughed and only one of them was a total disaster. But I haven't seen any of them again, I just can't quite bring myself to and I don't know why.

Bella says it's because deep down I know they're not right. But how can I possibly know? I'm not sure I know anything right now. I'm starting to think maybe this whole trip was just a fantasy, a fairy tale I was telling myself about finding my one. I had hoped if I put myself in the right place, the right country, then maybe the universe would do the rest, and help me out a little. I'm not sure what I thought truly, so I've told myself I'm staying till the end of the year. Ella says I'm doing great in the store and she's definitely happy for the extra help over the summer, or maybe it's winter? Either way she's told me I can stay as long as I want, but I'm not sure I can stay forever, so I'm giving the universe until the end of December to bring my soulmate to me and if not I'll head back home and think of a new strategy.

It's the end of October now and I haven't had a single hot pumpkin flavoured coffee, or a single jump-in-a-pile-of-leaves moment.

Halloween is tomorrow and it all seems... weird. There are pumpkins and plastic skeletons in shop windows but the sea breeze is warm and I'm wearing a little floral dress.

Weird.

Bella's sending me pictures of the leaves in Central Park all on the ground and of all the new winter coats she's found.

Also, I think I've come to realise that Halloween might not be as big of a deal anywhere else but America. It's almost impossible to find Halloween related things in the shops. Home decorations, like cute ones, not the plastic ones, are non-existent. Halloween, my favourite holiday, by the way, seems forgotten while Christmas is plastered everywhere.

Not a single thick knitted scarf has touched my neck, not that I actually packed one of those. Surprising, I know.

I planned the time of this trip for this exact reason but trying to make your brain understand that you've gone from spring to summer to spring again is hard. It's like jet lag but for the weather.

I'm going to a Halloween party tonight with Maddie and that's also weird for a few reasons. This is the first Halloween I've spent without Bella since well, forever. Trying to find a costume appropriate for this weather is hard. I never leave my costume until this last minute but in some way I had been hoping to come up with a reason not to go.

Actually that last one isn't that weird for me.

Normally my biggest problem is finding a coat to go with my outfit and how much leg do I want to freeze off, now it's what character has a spring costume?

As I'm staring at my overflowing wardrobe I get a text from Maddie.

> **Our ginger dropped out, fancy being Blossom?**

> **If you don't have a costume already, that is.**

With an attached image for a pink skirt and a big pink hair bow sitting on her bed.

The Powerpuff Girls could be fun, I wouldn't have to do it on my own so I would feel like more of a group and it's extremely weather appropriate. From the corner of my eye, I see a mesh red cardigan that I can wear over it.

I reply with an *okay*, and she tells me I should come over now to check the outfit fits and so I can get ready with them instead of her picking me up from Ella's like we'd planned before. My heart slows at such a little text but to me, to my anxiety, that's actually everything.

As I grab all my stuff, I pick up a pair of red heeled sandals I thrifted in Sydney the other week. I wasn't sure I really liked them but for seven dollars who could argue with that. I gather all of my makeup, then jump in the car as soon as she sends me her address, but it's not until then I realise I've never actually been to her house before. Come to think about it, she's never actually talked about her family either.

As I pull up, to what I can only describe as a mansion, I'm sure I've gotten the wrong address. My phone must've gotten the wrong place, because oh my god. The house, mansion, in front of me is nothing like I've seen before, ever. You don't see a lot of mansions in New York, it's all about beautiful apartments and artist townhouses but no mansions, those are all reserved for LA.

There are gates and a giant wall surrounding the place, like who the hell is she?!

I call her, because there's no way she hasn't mentioned this before. Not that it would matter, I don't think I've ever met a more genuinely kind and good person like Maddie, but what is happening!?

"Hey, Maddie, I think I've got the wrong house."

"Oh really? I'm sure I sent the right address, wait a second." I hear a shuffling on her end of the phone and I hold my breath as I wait for her to tell me she accidentally sent me the address of a famous person who she was internet stalking. "No, I can see your car, just roll up to the gate and say your name into the telecom thing, Lee will let you in." She says it so casually as if I'm not at Buckingham Palace. Okay that's a little bit of an exaggeration, but I'm in shock.

As I roll the car forward, cringing at how much it sticks out against its surroundings, I hear a voice coming from the little box next to the gate. "Name?" the said box requests when I come to a stop.

"Katherine Miller," I stutter. This is insane, but it doesn't make me look at Maddie any differently when I pull up to the front of the house and get out finding her on the steps leading to the front door.

"If you leave the keys in the car, I'll get Lee to move it," she tells me, pulling me in for a hug, taking one of my bags from me. She pulls me inside, into what I can only assume is the lobby. There are doorways everywhere leading to what I can only assume are even more beautiful rooms. A fucking chandelier hangs above me as I turn my head in every direct to take it all in. "It can be a bit much," she tells me, laughing to herself. I'm sure I look like I've just seen a unicorn for the first time.

"Maddie, Maddie... What? Who?" I can't get out a whole sentence as I look at the staircase of dreams. If only Bella could see this, she's always dreamed of descending from a grand staircase in a beautiful vintage dress. Hell, I'm even dreaming of it now.

Maddie takes my hand and brings me back to earth and only then when I'm looking at her in the eyes do I realise that I'm reacting in the exact way she *didn't* want me to. I'm gawking at her home, her life like it's a zoo.

"I'm sorry."

"It's okay," she tells me, only now looking nervous for the first time since I met her. "Okay, quick run down. My dad, he's the owner of the biggest hotel chain in Australia." My eyes widen, but I don't say anything. "So, yes, he is very rich and this house is insane. I work at the shop because I don't like taking his money. It doesn't feel right, I didn't earn it and I don't deserve it. I didn't say anything cause people get weird."

I let out a long breath. "Okay." She smiles at me for not saying more, a real Maddie smile. I'm not, from this moment onwards, going to make this weird.

She grabs my hand pulling me up the staircase. "Come on, let's get ready."

"So how long have you been in Australia, Katherine?" Maddie's friend asks. She's Buttercup and she's very Buttercup before she even puts her costume on.

She's got crazy long dark hair that she's put up in a high ponytail. Her name is actually Ava, and just like Maddie, she's beautiful. A different kind of beautiful, she doesn't have the surfer girl kind of look like Maddie and her other friends I've met, she's got the 'nose ring, tattoos up her arm' kind of beautiful going on and I wonder how they became friends and how I've never met her before.

"Oh, call me Kat, and just under three months, I got here in mid August," I tell her as I sit close to a mirror on the floor doing my eyeliner, a task I have not skillfully mastered still, despite Bella's best efforts.

"Wow, what a whirlwind, Maddie told me about why you're here. Girl, you are fucking brave, I could never." The way she says it, with actual excitement, has me thinking she actually means it. I've never seen myself as brave, it takes me a minute to recover.

Or she thinks I'm a joke.

"I got you a drink, I only really have spirits, is vodka and coke okay?" Maddie asks as she walks back in the room and sets a drink down on the floor for me. I nod my head slowly to try not throw myself off, I'm almost worried the eyeliner knows I'm scared.

Maddie's room is just as beautiful as the rest of the house, or what I've seen of it. She's got a 'what dreams are made of' four post bed and a balcony built for Paris. It's pretty muted colours on the walls and floor which just makes all her colourful stuff stand out even more. When I asked why there were no surfboards, she said they have their own room and she doesn't want to carry them up that, in her words, *stupidly pretentious staircase.* Makes sense, but still the bikinis hanging over multiple chairs makes it actually feel like it's *her* room.

Ava turns her attention back to me. "I don't know why you'd want to leave New York, I've always wanted to visit," she says wishfully as she adds more blush to her cheeks.

This is nice. I didn't realise how much I missed getting ready with friends until I hadn't done it for so long.

I take a drink knowing I'm going to need all the liquid courage to get through the night. "Well, you can come and visit once I go back." I smile at her. I've only told Ella about my plan to go back in January, I would have only been here for six months, I just feel like maybe people will think I've given up. My old therapist would say I'm projecting because truly I'm the only one who's going to think that.

"Really?" Maddie asks from the corner where she's wrestling with a blue bodysuit.

"Yeah, of course." I haven't known Maddie for that long but I do feel close to her in a weird way. Maybe it's the way we've been thrown together, but I'd love to show her around New York and any other state she wants, like she's done with me here.

Ava sighs lightly from her spot on the bed. "Don't get her started on that."

SOUL BELIEFS

"On what?"

"Maddie's dream is to travel," she says it in a way like it's impossible, but I don't quite understand why.

"I want to leave this place," Maddie tells me in an almost whisper.

I've never seen her like that, as if she can't tell me something, and it's then that I'm reminded that we really haven't known each other for that long and that she doesn't need to tell me anything about her life. It also makes me realise why she was probably so reluctant to show me her house, I mentally slap myself again for the way I reacted.

But she continues, "I want to see things, feel things, I've been in one place my whole life and I love it, don't get me wrong. I love the people and the surf and my job, but there's got to be something else out there for me, surely?" she says it so quickly I can hardly take in what she's saying, but boy, do I get it. I get all the words she's saying and all the ones she's not. "Not that my dad would ever let me." She sinks into herself, and I dread to think about the many conversations she must have had with him for her to lose her smile that quickly.

I've never seen the look in her eyes before, almost sad, but more of a wanting and it's hard to know what to say to her. "Maddie, if you want the whole world, you should take it," I tell her and I don't know if it's the right thing or a weird thing to say but she deserves the world, I know that much.

She sends me a bright smile and I know if anything I haven't said the wrong thing at least. "Changing the subject. It'll be quite busy at Izzy's, she throws this party every year but I promise I won't leave you." I don't think she realises how much that means to me. It's probably a throw away comment, because she knows I'm new, but it helps me calm down a little and take a drink.

Maddie pauses and looks at me in the mirror, she wants to say something else I can tell, and then she finally does.

"James will be there too." Her face twists as she tells me. I get why she's telling me, the hope in her eyes tells me she's hoping we've maybe put things behind us.

I've been trying my best to get along with him after *the kiss*, for Ella's sake and for my own sanity. But it's safe to say it isn't working.

We're just not people who were meant to be friends, we're so different, we think different, we believe in different things and that's fine. Not everyone is meant to like everyone and I'm not crazy enough to think everyone likes me.

I was stupid to think that after what happened we could maybe laugh it off, shake hands and move on. My current strategy is avoidance, but that's easier said than done when every time I go to sleep, I dream of that kiss and of how it made me feel.

Ella tells me he's been through some stuff with his family and that he's a good guy. That maybe we just got off on the wrong foot.

I think I could have taken my feet completely off and it wouldn't have made a difference. He made up his mind about me before I'd even stepped a foot on this continent.

The other day he not so subtly told me I was throwing my life away in a 'I could be doing so much more with my life' kind of way. It's the way teachers used to tell me, it's the disappointment in the voices that catches me. I don't care if he's disappointed or not, so his argument is irrelevant to me.

I don't decide this much but I've decided I hate him. I hate his cocky smile, his weird sense of importance in my life, that I-know-better look I get from him. I hate that he kissed me and then acted like it was nothing to him. I hate that I feel like he did that to mess with my head and that it's working. I hate how everyone else seems to like him, and I hate that he hates me too.

"I can't believe you get to work with him everyday, that guy is gorgeous," Ava tells Maddie as she curls the ends of her ponytail, I let out a scoff as I finish my face and stand up to look myself over. I'm glad I picked up the cardigan, no matter how many times they both told me I looked great and could do without it, I couldn't.

It's a red crop top and a very short, very tight, red checkered mini skirt.

I needed the cardigan.

Ava gives Maddie a look. "Kat and James don't get along," she tells her bluntly, and then Ava gives me a look, a look like I'm crazy.

"I just don't like him." I sit on the bed to pull on my heels.

I pull my hair into a half up, half down look and attach the big pink bow to the hairband. We take a few pictures all together, and for a super last minute put together look, we turned out pretty good. And I like when people are able to tell what you're dressed up as so you don't have to explain it to everyone you see at a party.

Ava's boyfriend comes to pick us up at ten o'clock to take us. His name's Sam and he's a beautiful man. You know when some men aren't hot but actually pretty, that's this guy. I have to stop myself from staring.

I'm also happy to know someone else, even if I've only just met him in a twenty five minute car ride. It's good enough. The knot in my stomach is mostly gone when we get there and then we pull into the driveway or should I say the street, it's busy.

Then as I get out of the car, my hands start to sweat and my throat goes dry.

The thought of all those eyes on me or entering a house I don't know sets me on edge before I can catch a breath. The churn in my stomach hits me like a stormy ocean wave, I physically take a step back.

Anxiety is like having a friend with you all the time that you'd like to leave you alone. It's like having someone in your ear constantly telling you everyone will hate you a hundred times, it's someone telling you that you look so terrible and you should just leave and go home because no one wants you there. It's telling you all the worst case scenarios and never the best.

Losing Dad only made these thoughts a thousand times louder, not that I'd tell anyone. It's my silent thing, the thing I deal with on my own. I have ways of working around it and nine times out of ten, it doesn't stop me from going out or going to a party. I just have little things to help me.

Normally these 'things' are Bella and Nick.

Maddie links her arm into mine when she sees me standing still by the car and pulls me to the house. Sometimes having a different friend around helps, too.

Chapter 18
James

The music is loud.

So loud I can barely think straight. Not that I partially want to right now. Dad has been a dick and I walked out tonight after an argument. Sometimes I really think he does hate me. I sometimes think he thinks this is all my fault.

It's times like these I wish I drank. It's stupid probably and Maddie has told me more than once that drinking now and again won't make me like my dad but some deep part of my brain tells me that it will. Some part of me seems to think that if I start I'll never be able to stop, I won't be able to control myself like him. He's not drunk all the time, he's not a "wake up with a beer in his hand" kind of alcoholic. He's the type that once he's had one it can never just be one, or two, it has to be twenty. And I guess I'm scared I'll be just like him, angry, bitter and lonely.

The other bad thing is, I'm the first of my actual friends to get here. The guys are running late and I'm never surprised when Maddie's late.

I heard her saying something about inviting Katherine and I honestly can only hope that Maddie decided not to or that Katherine chose to stay home tonight. I'm in a mood and if I'm not careful, I'll end up taking it out on her or breaking my own promise of not kissing her again. Honestly it's a coin toss.

Because I want a distraction, I want something else to think about right now and she's the thing that seems to do that. When we kissed, everything else seemed to fall away.

She's gotten under my skin far more than I care to let on or admit.

Do I think she's beautiful? Yes. Do I look at her too much when we have to work together? Also yes. Do I want to kiss her again? God, yes.

But there's so much I just don't understand about her. The look she gets in her eyes sometimes, like panic passing through them. I'll never understand why she's so determined to find her soulmate now. I can't understand the way she looks at me or the way she kissed me back.

But what I truly don't understand is why I want to understand all of that, I need to understand it. What I should want is to forget all about the little airy breaths she takes when I get too close or forget the way her nails dug into my hair when we kissed. The only thing I do know is that I can't work any of it out.

We won't even talk about the date incidents, even with me trying to rationalise. I'm completely sure I was having a stroke through the whole thinking process of that. Date one was a coincidence I just happened to be in the same coffee shop that day but the next one was not. I can't say what came over me when I drove there after I heard her talking to Maddie about it.

I managed to make sure I was working on the third. She was stood up. What an idiot. God, I wish I'd been there to rescue her again.

The fourth was me looking out for her. Dom is a friend—and I use that term loosely—from school, and when I saw him talking to Katherine on the beach, I knew I had to step in. He's a total player and I didn't want her to have to deal with that. So I conveniently happened to be in the bar with some other friends.

Someone tell me what's wrong with me.

It's because you like her, my internal voice tells me and if it was possible to slap it I would. I don't, just to make that clear, I one hundred percent do not like her in that way. I just think about her a lot, and look at her a lot and wonder what it would be like to have her in my arms again. But I don't like her.

It's infuriating and I need to get a grip of myself. She's here for that bloody soulmate shit and it makes me angry. Not that she cares about me or what I think about it, she's made that clear and I guess I'm not surprised. I guess I shouldn't actually be angry at her, it's my mum I'm angry at. She's the one who ruined the whole soulmate thing for me, long before I even had a chance to decide if it was something I wanted or not. A long time before I knew a girl like Katherine even existed.

There's just this feeling I get when I'm with her where a part of me wants to *not* hate her but then something happens and I do. I want to be near her and also a million miles away. I want to talk to her and I also want to never see her again.

God, I sound like a bloody idiot.

As I make my way back through the kitchen, I catch the front door opening again from the corner of my eye. I smile and wave as I see Ava and Sam walk through the door happy to finally have someone worth talking to here and then Maddie following close behind them and then I see it. Someone linked to her arm and as my eyes travel up they lock with hers.

There she is.

Dressed in all red, in something that doesn't seem like her at all, it seems odd. Her cheeks are as red as the top she's wearing and her eyes don't stay on mine for long before they start darting around the room. It's like she's scooping the place out or assessing the situations like she's walked into somewhere dangerous.

I've never seen her react like that to a situation before. My eye brows knit together as I wonder why she feels like that. I wonder if it has something to do with the way her eyes look every time she's thinking something over a thousand times.

I try not to look at her too much as they all walk towards where I am, but god she makes it hard. She's wearing more makeup than usual but she's beautiful all the same; her hair is bright and half is down in curls and they bounce as she moves towards me with the group. Jesus, who let her wear those shoes? Her legs look so long and sexy, it's not as if I haven't seen her legs before of course, but what is it about her in this moment?

Parts of me come alive that I would much rather stay very dead, and those very parts think about her legs wrapped around my waist as I push her up against the wall with her lips on mine.

"Hey!" Maddie says dropping Katherine's arm and bringing me in for a hug, she doesn't stay there long as she spots the beer behind me. "Oh, thank god. Kat, beer?" Katherine nods her head but says nothing.

I'm confused and a little shocked, she never misses an opportunity to throw something my way. It makes me feel weird, almost hurt, like maybe she can't be bothered with me anymore. It definitely shouldn't bother me, I should be happy about it because finally we'll have the distance we so desperately need, or I need, and yet, it does. It bothers me in a way I don't like.

In a house with like fifty people in it, the place feels quiet; because she's being quiet. Even with Ava, Maddie and Sam talking around me as they get drinks, I can't look away from her. I'm waiting for her to say something to add to our never ending battle of words.

But she doesn't.

She doesn't even look up at me.

And I feel tiny. Unseen and unimportant to her all of a sudden. Like she's bored with all of this now. Why is this more annoying than when we're talking?

An uncomfortable feeling crawls up my throat, one I haven't felt in years, one I try not to think about for too long.

"James, it's been forever. What you been up to?" Sam asks as he claps a hand on my shoulder coming back around to stand in front of me.

I watch from the corner of my eye as Maddie hands Katherine a drink, she eyes it suspiciously but drinks from it anyway.

"You know, this and that."

"A man of many words, as always. Maddie, how do you get a word in with this chatterbox?" Ava jokes as she wraps an arm around Sam.

Then another weird feeling is in the pit of my stomach, and somehow I'm jealous. Jealous of the way they are together, the way they look at each other, the way he makes her laugh as he whispers something to her. My eyes shift to Katherine, and my eyes travel down to her month.

Her eyes snap to mine and she frowns at me. "Should we move this party to the lounge?" Sam asks, nodding his head behind him, he turns Ava and they move ahead of me, Maddie behind them.

But I pause catching Katherine's hand before she can follow them. We look over each other's faces, I notice how her freckles seem to have multiplied since I was this close to her last time, and I watch as her eyes flow along the line of my lips. "Are you okay?" I ask, her eyes move to meet mine and just for a second like we've done before I seem to forget everything, because those eyes are sad.

"What?" she says, but hasn't pulled away from me yet, and I like a little too much how well her hand fits in mine.

"You're just quieter than you normally are."

And just like that it's gone, her eyes realise mine and she pulls her hand from mine taking a whole step back. "I'm fine." She says it with all the believability of most women who say that. "And even if I wasn't, it wouldn't be you who I'd talk to."

I let out a sigh because I'm just not up for this tonight, whatever this is. "Fine," I say walking away from her.

Chapter 19
Katherine

I am now reminded of why I don't go to parties without Bella or Nick. They're like a comfort blanket, a buffer, they know how I am with people and these situations.

New people, they don't. They don't know or get it, and it's hard. Harder than I thought it would be. Could I have told Maddie about my anxiety before leaving for the party? Yes, but I had anxiety about that too, so that was a no go. And I'm always so scared of how people will react; will they treat me like I'll break? Or like I'm a loser?

People are talking around me, laughing about things I don't know and then there's me, and unfortunately for me, I am myself. I'm not anyone else, I'm not Maddie who's telling a funny story having everyone around her hang on her every word and I'm not Ava who's sitting in her boyfriend's lap in the chair next to me looking more in love than I think I'll even understand and I'm most certainly not James who hasn't stopped looking at me since I walked in the door.

As a group, we've managed to take up most of the living room, apart from the part of the floor where some people are dancing.

More of Maddie's friends arrived not long after us and I was thankful for it. More people meant it was easier for me to slip into the background. People pay less attention to you when there's more people.

I'm perched on the arm chair that is occupied by one of the guys that Maddie called Steve when we came in and he's talking with some guy sitting next to him.

In all honesty I'm a people watcher. My personality really is made up of people I've met in passing and people I've seen on the streets in New York. People watching is my favourite pastime, you learn so much by just taking people in. I've noticed this is a weird mix of people. No one really looks like they all know each other and yet every time a new person comes into the room everyone greets them like their all best friends. Normally, I'd be able to adapt better but I'm like a fish out of water right now.

I feel very out of place and so out of my comfort zone. I want to crawl out of my own skin.

Normally, Bella would have been talking to me or would have noticed by this point that I'm not engaging and given me a look. But she's not here, so I'm looking around the room—and then there it is again.

James eyes. On me. *Again*.

He's sitting in a chair somewhat across from me and some girl is talking to him, he's not paying attention which annoys me. I can't hear what she's saying over the music but nevertheless he's being rude. Yeah I'm sure that's what I'm feeling, annoyance at him, not her. Not this random girl I don't know with her hand on his arm and her face near his, her lips so close to his ear.

Yep, definitely him.

Even with me looking right over at him, he hasn't looked away and it's unnerving at this point. Maybe it's the three beers I've had before this, but I manage to bring myself to my feet.

His eyes widen but only for a moment when he realises I'm moving towards him, and then just as I'm in front of him, he stands.

I decide this is a threat or maybe a declaration of war because when he was sat, we were maybe at the same kind of height, now he towers over me. Looking down at me, he blinks a few times, one eyebrow raised like he's waiting for me to speak first and I'm surprised when words actually do come out of my mouth.

"It's rude to stare," I tell him, his eyes are dark and I can't tell if it's the lighting or maybe what he's drinking. I try to look in his cup but he moves it before I can and then I find myself wishing I knew what he was thinking.

I almost don't notice the girl next to him looking at me. Almost.

I watch as his throat moves, visibly swallowing. "I wasn't staring." His face hasn't changed and I hate that when I know my face gives me away every time it's like a painting of emotions.

"Oh, really?" I ask sarcastically. "What do you call it here then, 'cause in America, not taking your eyes off another person is called staring." This has to be the most words I've said all evening, I'm pretty sure given the looks I'm getting, some people here thought I couldn't speak.

I try not to notice that more heads have turned towards us now. Even Ava, whose face has been attached to Sam's for at least twenty minutes, is now looking at us both, with a little half smirk.

The feeling of retreat is strong. The pit of anxiety is growing in my stomach, I don't like people looking at me. But as much as I try, my feet don't move; they are solidly glued to the floor. Or maybe it's my eyes because for some reason I can't look away from him either.

He doesn't say anything else and I think this might be the end of it. I can go get a drink, pretend I didn't just try to start a fight, but my mouth is moving again before I can stop myself.

"Why don't you stop skating around it and just fucking say it to my face?"

"Say what?"

"That you hate me. All your snide little comments and all the weird shit you've been doing for weeks but you won't just say it." I almost shout. I lower my voice when I notice how close we are now and how hot my face feels. "God, it's so obvious, you have a huge problem with me."

"Well I guess I have a problem with you right now, yeah." He's staying too calm and I either don't like it because I seem to be a lot angrier than him, or because I'm causing a scene. I don't like either of these things. Yet here I am making this whole thing one hundred percent worse and not being able to stop it.

Also he still won't say it! I don't know why I want him to, I don't know why that'll make me feel better.

It'll make me forget the kiss.

"Look, Katherine." I hate the way my name sounds coming from him. The feeling shoots up my spine. "It's nothing personal." *That means it is.* "But I think you already know my problem."

A laugh slips from my lips. "Well, why don't you spell it out for me. I've always wanted someone who's not doing anything with their life to explain mine to me." My ability to play word chess with him right now is gone, I'm far too angry right now to think properly. And I don't know why.

He scoffs out a laugh and I want to disappear. He doesn't even blink, like what I've said doesn't even touch him. Yet I feel like he's all over me. The look in his eyes is dark and I feel like for the first time this won't end nicely.

"Of course, Katherine." He takes a step forward moving closer to me. Our faces are too close.

I hate that I don't know how to control this situation. In the private confines of the shop, I'll give it as good as I get it, but in front of this many people, this many people I don't know, I'm lost. I want to say something about how I was good enough to kiss a few weeks ago, but

I don't want everyone to know that. Not when it still feels too fresh, too confusing.

The anger that was fuelling me at the start has slipped away, and is now replaced with embarrassment.

My hands are getting sweaty as he gets even closer to me, so close I can smell the salt ingrained into his skin. "You're not doing any more with your life than me, you just want to be in love." He almost whispers it, but he's so close, I can hear it plain as day. I know that *everyone* hears him.

Everyone is watching. I feel like we're some kind of side show. I feel like all the air has been sucked out of the room the way he's looking at me, the monologue I want to tell him that's running through my head is screaming to be let out. But I can barely make out a whole sentence. "And tell me what's wrong with wanting to be in love?"

His classic smirk pulls itself across his face. "I don't know, being co-dependent for one. You're addicted to it, Katherine, the idea of being in love," he tells me. "You moved your whole life, not for a job or an actual *tangible* person, but the idea of a person. If either of us is throwing their life away, it's you... Sunshine."

We stare at each other for a minute. I feel like if I move, I might fall and I'm taking this minute to regain use for my own body before I can decide what to do.

I want to leave.

I want to run out of here.

But I don't.

I've had dirty and confused looks from people back home who I had told about my plans but no one had ever said it to me like that.

I feel stupid, like maybe for a minute he's right. Maybe I'm wasting my time. I can feel my eyes start to water but I don't give him the satisfaction of letting them spill over my eyes.

No one has ever actually made me completely question everything I had been working towards. I'd quite frankly like to get on a plane and go home in this moment. I'm sensitive, sue me.

Instead, I say, with my teeth gritted and my jaw tight, "You've got your entire life to be a prick, how about you take the night off."

No one makes a sound. I'm worried that if it weren't for the noise in the other rooms, they might be able to hear my heart pounding out of my chest.

Maddie stands there like she might sink into the floor, I don't expect her to say anything to him or to defend me. She's known him longer and I'm happy she's even bothered to include me. Well, I was happy up until this point anyway.

It doesn't stop me from thinking about what Bella or Nick might do in this moment. Bella has the classic drink in the face move. I have seen this be performed a couple times in the course of our college time, but I don't think I can bring myself to ruin someone else's carpet. I'm not sure if it makes me sad or want to laugh that Nick would try to punch him. Nick's shorter than James, and even though well built, I hate to say not as much as James—but he'd try none the less. I don't like my chances at even reaching his face now he's stood up completely again.

Eventually the urge to fall or punch him leaves my body and I down the rest of my drink, looking at him and then turn and walk into the kitchen and get myself another.

I down that too. Cheap beer tastes the same all over the world I decide. Not great.

I down another beer.

"I've never seen anyone get under James' skin quite like you before." A voice comes from behind me. A voice with a smirk attached, I can hear it.

I don't turn or look up from the drink I'm pouring myself again. My skin is warming and tingling, my head is light and I want to laugh but keep a tight voice as I talk.

"I don't think anyone's dared to disagree with him before." I'm drunk, I know, even I cringe a little at my own voice.

A laugh comes from behind me regardless, and I finally turn around.

The guy stood behind me easily stands a foot above me and he's close enough that I have to lean back on the counter to look up at his face. His hair is so dark I think it might be black and it's styled in what I think is a mullet. I've never seen a guy in New York with one but I've seen plenty here in Australia.

I decide he doesn't remind me at all of James and I like that.

"Pretty big mouth for such a little thing." He smiles at me. I'm not completely oblivious to the fact he's flirting, it's weird but I know it's happening. So I do the most un-Katherine thing, I flirt back—or try to.

"What's it they say? 'Great things in small packages.'" I move closer to him and look him up and down as he does the same. I can't say what I said was very clever but he doesn't seem to mind all that much as his eyes rack up from my bare legs to my chest and then hover at my lips for a while before coming back to my eyes.

The sensation of having his eyes all over me and the alcohol in my veins, makes my feet wobble as I move closer. I only stumble slightly, my hand landing on his chest. The feeling of his warm skin under his t-shirt heats my hand and I can't help feeling the way his muscles tense as my hand moves down a little and I look up at him through my lashes.

Is this what everyone was meaning when they said *have fun* or *live a little*?

He's looking down at me with a cocky smile, the kind I see everyday in the shop from James but I like his a little more, mostly because of the alcohol, mostly because he's not *him*.

"Well, you definitely are a great package." He laughs, taking my hand from his chest and holding it in his own. His words make me cringe but I'm concentrating on his face. Did I mention he doesn't remind me of James? "Do you want to get some air?" he says, turning his head towards the back sliding doors leading into the garden.

I'm angry, and on my way to being too drunk, so it seems like a good idea.

If only Bella could see me now.

I nod my head and he leads me through the house. We pass the living room on the way, the group still sat laughing and I catch eyes with him.

James' eyes flicker from me, to my hand, to the boy holding it. I see this nameless boy make eye contact with him, too and a muscle in James jaw jumps. Something I've never seen. I can't work out the emotion but he looks back at me and then back down at his drink. If this was all it took to really piss him off I would have done it sooner.

We reach the back porch and the warm night air hits my bar legs. No ones really out here considering this is Australia and even at midnight it's still really nice out. I see boys move near the end of the garden and smoke hover above their heads.

"I'm Kath—" But before I can finish, I'm being turned around and pushed up against the back wall of the house.

Now I really notice how tall he is, he towers over me, with his arm resting on the wall next to my head. I'm not entirely sure how comfortable I feel now.

"Dylan," he says, his eyes are attached to my lips and he licks his own before crushing his lips to mine.

It's warm and wet and sloppy and maybe a little gross.

That's all I can use to describe the way he's kissing me. It's not special or great and it doesn't make me feel any of the things I felt kissing James but it's not terrible. And I still snake my hands around the back of his neck and into his hair out of instinct.

I don't have to think while I'm doing this. This doesn't matter, this boy isn't going to be my soulmate and I'm not thinking about it for once.

My mind swirls as he nips my bottom lip and I let my mouth fall open letting his tongue swirl with mine in the same way. I scrap my fingers across his scalp tugging lightly on his hair, earning myself a moan from him that disappears in my mouth.

A cold wind whips around my ankles and it seems to wake my brain up a little, I decide I kinda don't want to do this any more. I feel kinda sick and I'm not sure if it's the beer or the way Dylan's hand slides up my thigh under my skirt.

"I think maybe we should stop," I tell him, pulling away from his face as best I can as my head hits the wall behind me and my vision blurs a little more. My feet are planted firmly on the floor and I feel like I'm not in my own body as he pushes his body onto me.

"Don't do that, Kat, we're just having a good time," he tells me like if he says it I'll believe him, and then my next protest is lost in his lips as he smacks them back on me again. I push at his chest but it seems to do nothing. He's like a statue, definitely stronger than I gave him credit for.

I can't think.

I can't get my mind to do anything.

I can't get my body to move again.

I can't breathe.

I squeeze my eyes shut and push him again and he finally falls off me.

I'm frozen, completely unable to move for what feels like hours, but after only a minute or so, I manage to open my eyes again and there Dylan is. On the floor with James hovering over him. "The fuck do you think you're doing?" James snarls at him.

He looks like he might combust. I don't think I've ever seen him this angry, this truly angry. I realise that the whole time we've been arguing and hating each other, it's been nothing compared to what he's really capable of.

Dylan scrambles to his feet, but even then he still doesn't quite hit the same height as James. He goes to step back towards me and I feel myself shrink away, trying so desperately to get even closer to the wall if that was at all possible. But James is quicker and puts his body between us, shielding me.

"James, we were just having some fun."

"Didn't fucking look like she was having fun," he bites back, and I never thought I'd say this, but I feel safe. I feel like nothing can get to me with him right there.

"And what's it to you? From what I saw, it didn't exactly look like you two cared about each other." The way he talks literally makes me want to throw up, or wash my mouth out. Easily both. I look around James' body to see that once again I have managed to gather a crowd, people that were at the bottom of the garden are now standing behind Dylan. And people are now huddled at the door leading back into the house. "Or is that it, do you care about that little bitch behind you?" Dylan's words sink into me like a sunburn.

"Watch your fucking mouth." The heat radiating from James' back does nothing to calm me or make me feel safe. I feel something take over my body.

It comes thick and fast and it's oh so familiar to me. I need to move, I need to get away from everyone. I can't do this in front of him. Or all these people.

"What are you going to do, James?"

My fight or flight kicks in like clockwork and my legs are pulling me away from the garden. The last thing I see before taking flight from the situation is James' fist coming down on Dylan's jaw, the sound of cracking bones filling the whole garden.

"Katherine!" I hear someone shout as I shoot through the house and up the stairs.

Quiet.

I need quiet.

I find the restroom and close the door behind me and I sink to the floor by the bath. The tiles are cold under me but it's not enough. I know there's nothing I can do and I just have to ride out the storm. Make it to the other side, I can do this, this isn't new, I know it won't kill me.

Won't it?

It feels like it will.

Tears stream down my face.

And then it feels like I can't breathe.

Like someone's taking the air right out of me and standing on my chest.

In.

Out.

In.

Out.

Breathe.

My heart's pounding so hard it's going to jump right out of me.

Where am I? What can I feel and smell?

Nothing.

My hands are shaking so much, I clench them together against my chest but it only makes the rest of me shiver.

"Katherine, breathe for me." That's not my voice and I'm not initially sure it's even real, because it sounds like my dad. Or I think it does.

I honestly don't care, I haven't had a panic attack like this in years and it hurts.

Mentally.

Physically.

Emotionally.

It hurts.

"You can do it." My dads right, it's a basic human action, something you're born already knowing how to do.

My dad takes my hand and places it on his chest. I feel his heart beating at a normal, non-panicked rate and it reminds me what mine should be doing.

"Do it with me, Katherine." He takes a big breath in, so deep I can feel the air fill his lungs as he does. "And out."

I follow suit and regain some kind of control of my own body but the panic is still seething through me. "Good." The voice reaches up, wiping the tears from my eyes. His thumb wipes over my cheek and then rests on my face for a moment.

The warmth of it seeps into my cool damp skin and it's nice, calming. I lean into it not even thinking, my eyes closing ever so slightly. The panic floats out my body like a storm being moved on by the wind. The only person who was able to bring me down that quickly was Dad.

"I can't do this, Dad." Fifteen year old me cries, it's like my chest is going to explode and cave in all at the same time. There is so much panic running through me. I don't know where it started or how I can stop it.

Why?

I can't even remember what I was thinking about two minutes ago.

"Yes you can, Katherine." Dad takes my hands in his, he's sitting in front of me in my bedroom. It's dark and I suddenly remember I'm keeping him from getting rest after this night shift and that only makes me feel worse.

"Do it with me, Kat." He takes a breath in and so do I and then he lets it out and so do I. "And another." I breathe with him again and again until I remember what's going on again. "See, I told you you could do it."

"That's it Sunshine, in and out, like me." My eyes fly open when the voice speaks again.

I focus on his voice, I focus on the way his face looks when he's looking at me right now and I hold on to the way he just called me Sunshine like a life line and I don't like it.

"James." The adrenaline from the panic attack is still working its way out of my body and that mixed with the alcohol I was drinking all of ten minutes ago, I'm lucky if I'm able to have a whole conversation.

"Let's just sit here for a minute," he says and he does, he sits crossed legged in front of me like a three year old waiting for a story to be read to him and holds my hands.

As we just sit in the silence with each other, I notice his knuckles as he runs his thumb over mine, red and raw. That's my fault. "I'm so sorry," I whisper to him as if we're hiding from something.

And I am, because the minute we're out that door, he'll go back to being an ass and I'll go back to hating him. And for some reason, that I'm sure is panic attack induced, I don't want that.

The confusion on his face washes away when I glance down at our entwined hands, he doesn't make an effort to move them or untangle himself from me. "Never apologise for someone else's actions Katherine. He's the one who should be sorry, not you." The look on his face is so new I don't know what to make of it. This is new for us, too new for me to work it out, too new for me to know what's going on and I'm too tired to play anything with him.

"Okay, then. I'm sorry to ruining your night," I say, trying to pull one of my hands free from his grip to wipe my still leaking eyes, but he stops me. Reaching up to my face and wiping them for me.

He watches me closely as he does, and I feel far too exposed. Not in a physical way, although maybe that too, but in an emotional way. The only people who have seen me have a panic attack have been Dad, Mom, Bella and Nick. And now James. He's seen me at my weakest, my true lowest point. I can't even begin to think about how this might shift us even more. Am I a real person to him now? Is he to me?

"Parties aren't really my thing, anyway," he says, a smile peeking through his words. The air is knocked out of me again as I see it happen.

We just sit there again in our own strange comfortable silence and then I yawn. The after effect of an earth shattering panic attack. My limbs feel heavy and I think if I closed my eyes right now, they wouldn't open again.

"I'll drive you home," he tells me, not as a question but as a statement. I could argue, I really could just because it's him, I could tell him a number of things to be mad and a bitch. But arguing would take so much more effort than I currently have. As he stands, one of my hands still in his, he pulls me up once I give him the other, and I don't fight it.

It's only when we exit the bathroom after I've made myself not look like I haven't just had a panic attack, something comes back to me. "You can't drive, you've been drinking," I tell him, pulling him back using the one hand he's entwined with his own again. The feeling warms my whole body again.

He stands so close to me. "Water, Katherine. I don't drink," he explains, his face completely flat. I know that he's telling me the truth. I had just assumed he was drinking too, I didn't even consider anything else. The concept of a twenty-five year old guy not drinking hadn't even crossed my mind.

So much so that I'm not too sure how to answer him. "Okay," is all I manage to say, not that I'm sure it's really a response.

After that I let him lead me down the stairs, through the house, out the front door and the whole two minutes down the street to his truck. Not once does he let go of my hand. I don't like the way I feel about it, I don't like the lighting bolt that goes up my arm every time he rubs his thumb over mine. I don't like the way that when he's leading me I don't have to think, I'm not worried where I'm going.

I'm tired and kind of done with this evening now, and I can't help but wonder what Bella and Nick are up to now.

I don't say a word as I get into the truck, or as he drives off towards Ella's. I don't ask why he doesn't drink or why he's helping me.

I trust him. I think that's my only option right now.

We're both completely silent as he drives, the only noise that passes through the car is the crashing waves around us seeping through my open window.

I trust that feeling I got when I touched him was thanks to the alcohol, and the feeling I get when he's near me was a product of a late night.

When he pulls into the driveway, I can't help myself from breaking the silence, a small part of me still drunk and feeling exposed already.

My body falls against the seat, only my head turning toward him. "Why are you helping me? Why not just leave me to deal with that on my own?" I'm so tired of being confused, and if he won't say it, I will.

He keeps his eyes fixed on the house in front of us, his hands so firm on the steering wheel even his bloody knuckles turn white. "Katherine, I don't think you really want an answer to that. This isn't the time." His words are so sure and steady.

I'm no less confused than I was before. "What do you mean? That's not—" I stop and start again. "I do want an answer." I'm sure I do. "I'm really tired of being confused all the time when it comes to you."

He finally turns towards me, his own eyes glassy and I want to lean forward and touch his face.

No I don't.

"I never *hated* you." The way he says it, it's almost like a confession to himself, as if he hadn't realised it until he said it to me. He leans forward and I think he's going to touch me again, I don't know if I want him to.

I do.

"You're exhausting, you know that right?" Even as I say it, I know my face gives away what I really want, that I want him to hold me. Kiss me.

But he reaches past me to open the door. "Go to bed, Katherine."

I can't even look at him as I unbuckle myself and get out. I feel embarrassed and like he still holds all the cards, while I'm left empty handed and exposed.

I grab a glass of water when I get in and watch out the kitchen window as he pulls out of the driveway. His eyes locked with mine through the glass.

When I get in bed I don't fall asleep for hours.

I watch Bella's Instagram story.

I catch a glimpse of Nick in one of them—he's not dressed up, of course.

I text my mom about nothing in particular, just that I miss her.

I watch an old video of Dad, I cry.

Then eventually sleep washes over me, but I don't think about why I felt so warm with him or about the words he said.

I'll never think about that again.

Chapter 20
Katherine

"Hey, sweetie. How was the party?" Ella asks me as I walk into the kitchen the next morning.

"Yeah, it was good." I lie, I don't want to tell her I had a panic attack and I don't want to tell her that James calmed me down like Dad used to do and then drove me home. So, it's better to lie.

"I saw James' truck pull out of the driveway in the early hours."

She lifts her eyebrows as she looks at me this time and I give myself an extra minute by biting into an apple in front of me. How does this woman know everything?

She's not giving up and stares at me like she might burn right through me. "He drove me home, that's all," I tell her, and it's not a total lie this time. My voice is much calmer than I thought possible, all things considered.

Her eyes squint together for another second and then she lets it go. "Well, I guess I need to go relieve James from the shop."

I think for a minute whether to offer to go instead.

Not because I want to see him or anything like that. Not because I woke up in a cold sweat last night after reliving every interaction we've had the whole time I've been here. Thinking over the words he told me last night.

I never hated *you.*

But because I feel bad about it all and ruining his night. And maybe I think I should go say thank you or something to him before it gets weird between us again, but who am I kidding? It was never not weird between us.

I try to rationalise a lot about last night. I tell myself the only reason he helped me is because he knew if he didn't, Ella would be mad at him. I tell myself it was all the alcohol in my system that made me think he was looking at me in the way I thought he was. A way that told me he wanted me in the same way I did him.

Maybe an extra day will mean it's not awkward tomorrow? I have to hope that's the case.

"Oh, darling, there's a parcel for you as well," Ella shouts from the front door and I run to grab it from her before waving her off as she pulls out of the driveway.

I go back to the kitchen, grab a pair of scissors and jump up on one of the chairs around the island. The box isn't that big and Mom didn't say she was sending anything and I definitely didn't order anything, or did I? No, there's a postage stamp from the U.S. on it, must be Mom.

As I open it there's a letter lying on the top in a blue envelope. I open it and it's not Mom's handwriting, it's Nick's.

Hey Katy,

How are you? Now don't laugh at the fact I'm writing to you, Bella already did that for like an hour. I know I could just send an email but this seemed better. Something you could keep in that little box under your bed you have (we all know it exists).

I miss you. That's probably obvious, I thought it was easy. You know, we did the whole me going to collage thing and it was okay. I missed you, but it was okay. Maybe it's because I knew you were still in the city and that made it okay cause you were home even if I wasn't but this is different. This is harder.

I'm sorry, I don't want to make you feel bad or sad or worry, or anything. I just wanted you to know I'm thinking of you.

I hope everything's going alright, you've only been gone two months when I sent this, so by the time you get it, I'll miss you even more.

I'm good. I've been applying to a few video game design jobs and programs, some here, some in Spain, guess it's best to keep my options open, you know?

Me, Bella, Mom, Dad and your mom went for dinner the other day. Don't worry about her too much, she's got us until you come back.

Anyway, I saw this the other day in the thrift store you like and I thought of you, I hope you like it.

Love, Nick x

It's handwritten and you can see where he's scribbled over things, and I hug it to my chest for what I'm certain is a whole minute. I didn't keep up my promise.

I haven't been in touch with him as much as I should be. At first, I didn't have anything to say to him, and now, I don't know.

The whole thing about wanting him to be my soulmate wasn't a lie. So, it's hard when I'm out here looking for mine and he's back home. If I didn't feel the need to be with my soulmate so much, like I *had* to find them, maybe I'd just go home and learn to love him in a different way than I do now. But I'd always be wondering 'what if' and that's not fair to him.

Or me either, I guess.

I never knew if he felt the same when we were younger but we've always had this... thing. The way we'd hold hands on the subway, or the way I'd lean into him when we sat on the couch together and the way his hand would rest on my knee. Just this *thing*. I think Dad hoped we'd be together in a way; Nick is safe, he's home. But he's not at the same time. And I think it's only now that I'm here that I realize that.

Once I stop wanting to cry, I finally lift the brown paper out of the box and then I start laughing.

It's not what I had expected, maybe a bag, some kind of jewellery, but I did not expect this.

It's a Taylor Swift Fearless Tour t-shirt from 2009, the tour we went to. The top I got then, when I was eleven, stopped fitting when I was like fifteen and I got rid of it. I hug the shirt for a moment, too.

Then I hurry to get dressed and take it with me. I pull it on with a pair of jean shorts. I take a picture making sure to get the top in it the most and send it to him with a message saying 'I love it!! Thank you so much.'

I want to say more, I want to tell him so much, but I don't want to put it in a text. I want to put it in a letter, too. I want him to have something to put in his metaphorical box under the bed. So I send another. 'Look out for a letter coming your way.' I don't want him to think I'm dismissing the letter either.

The next day rolls around and after popping to the post office to send Nick a letter that I wrote last night, along with some of my new favourite Australian snacks, Tim Tams, I walk into the shop. I'm totally fine and calm about seeing James today.

Not.

I gave myself a pep talk before I left the house and while in the car. I also thought over every scenario with everything he might say to me today.

I lock eyes with Maddie at the register and she smiles but it's a little hollow and I hope to god she's not mad at me. She has every right to be, I caused a scene in front of her friends and probably embarrassed her.

"Where's James?" I ask her. I'm not sure if I want to say thank you, or sorry, or what, but I know I'm meant to work with him today. I spent a lot of this morning thinking of a hundred things to say depending on what he was going to say or not say.

"Another personal day," she tells me, not looking up as she logs off ready for me to take over for the day.

I watch Gregg talk with some parents at the front of the shop as I walk over to her lowering my voice. "Another?" I question. Ella hadn't said anything about him not being there yesterday when she got back, I guess why would she.

Now, I'm starting to question why I care and why I'm bothered. I like working with Gregg, he's about the same age as Ella and it's nice to hear stories of Ella from when she first got to Australia and the customers love him, so normally my shifts are pretty chill with him.

But I'm bothered.

I'm bothered why he's not here.

Maddie doesn't make eye contact with me as she speaks, literally looking anywhere but me. I hope it's not because of the other night, I hope I haven't ruined our friendship, but I feel as though I might have.

I feel even more deflated thinking that I've ruined all of that because I was angry at James, because I overreacted. Because I made James leave early.

"Yeah he had to take yesterday off too, he's fine just...family stuff." She keeps it short but her voice is off.

"Maddie are we...are we okay?" I feel small and like a child again and what I really want to ask is *Do you hate me?* Because that's what my brain is telling me.

"Us? Oh, Kat, yeah of course we're fine." She runs a hand through her hair before pulling me in for a hug and all the air leaves my body at once, knowing I haven't ruined this. She pulls back smiling at me again. "I promise we're good, if you're asking about the party, it's honestly not a big deal, don't worry about it. I've just been up early, nothing to do with you, promise."

James obviously didn't tell her about anything after I left the living room, which I'm glad for. "Okay, okay good. I'll see you soon."

She smiles at me again and then waves to me as she leaves.

But the strange feeling doesn't leave my stomach for most of the day. I find it hard to concentrate and find myself refolding a towel about twenty times.

Not even the cute puppy that comes in with a woman picking out a new wetsuit picks up my mood.

"Desperate times call for desperate measures," I tell myself.

I go into autopilot as I search through the employee records on the computer. I'm sure searching for his address is all kinds of wrong, an evasion of his privacy that I'm sure he'll remind me about later. But right now I don't seem to care, the rational side of my brain is checked out and I can't go another day not knowing what he's going to say to me. It's driving me insane, the uncertainty of it all. There's no talking myself out of it.

I text Ella that I'll be home a bit late as I lock up the shop and wave Gregg off as he jumps in his car.

I look down at my phone's maps and think about it for the whole of two more minutes and then get into my car and head off.

I've been sitting in my car for maybe twenty minutes thinking over what a bad idea this is. The last time I saw James, he was driving me home after our weirdest interaction ever. Was he incredibly sweet and kind? Yes. I don't know if that changes anything between us, but it changed something in me. I know that.

I can't sit here and lie that much, I can't hate him any more, not after what he did for me. He could have left me to sit and cry and panic but he didn't. After everything I've said to him he sat there with me, held my hand and took me home. Not after what he said. I promised myself I wouldn't think about it but I can't help it.

I never hated you.

I can't get that out of my head.

A man staggers as he opens the door. He's old but the kind of old that comes from experience and not time. He's probably only in his fifties but wrinkles and dark circles around his eyes make him seem so much older.

"Hello, Sir." Looking at this man I actually have no idea what I'm doing here, why I've gone here or what I'm going to say when I actually see him. "I've come to see James, I'm a... we-we work together."

I couldn't call us friends, could I?

Definitely not. Even if I don't hate him any more.

Me falling over my own words doesn't seem to bother the man who's using the door frame to keep himself up. It's not until then that I notice the beer bottle in his hand.

He's looking me over as I stand there awkwardly wiping my hands over my shorts repeatedly, the thought of getting back in the car and leaving crosses my mind several times.

"James, someone here for you," he shouts back into the house, a smile on his face now. The kind I've only seen on James a handful of times, the kind that reaches his eyes, making the wrinkles around his eyes more prominent.

I can feel my heart start to slow back to a normal pace again when I see James appear in the doorway, it's a strange feeling that concerns me. The same I had last night when he was with me in the bathroom. Almost like when he's around, I feel calmer, safer. I like it.

Jesus.

"What is it, Dad?" James asks as he comes up behind, his height even more noticeable as he towers over him.

"A girl here for you," he says, the smile still plastered on his face.

James finally turns his attention towards me and I watch as his eyes grow wide, surprised, but he regains his usual flat face from seeing me. He doesn't say anything to me, just turns back to his dad.

"Dad, why don't you go back inside, I'll be back in a minute," he says patting his own dad on the shoulder, the parent child dynamic here seems to be backwards and some pieces fall into place.

"It was nice to meet you—" he stammers.

"Katherine," I answer him back.

"It was nice to meet you, Katherine," he says moving back into the house, unsteady on his feet as he goes.

"What are you doing here, Katherine?" James asks me through gritted teeth once his dad is out of ear shot, leaning up against the door frame, arms crossed over his chest.

Hostile, okay, good start. It's as if the guy who drove me home and told me he didn't hate me doesn't exist at all.

I plaster a smile on my face. "Don't you mean 'It's lovely to see you, Katherine,'" I say back, trying to lighten the mood.

"I don't have time for this." He goes to grab the door and go back inside. But then I do the one thing I know I shouldn't. I grab his wrist, turning him back around before he can leave.

And then there it is. The burn, I'm not drunk now so I know it's not a product of alcohol—and it's killing me. Killing me not knowing why. God, I hate things I don't know, and from the look on his face as he looks up from my hand to my face, he feels it too.

"I wanted to see if you were okay. You'd been gone for a couple of days, and I just," I don't know what I'm trying to say. Words are something I'm not lost for often, if ever, but he's making my head foggy. Like a tide coming in and I'm drowning in it. I don't like it. I don't like this feeling, whatever it is.

We stand there for a moment, my hand around his wrist. He's looking me over like he's done a hundred times before, but this time, it feels like his eyes are burning into me. I wondered how long I can take it, how long I can take being burnt alive by his stare.

Not long.

I feel my hand start to get clammy under the end of day heat, his body heat and whatever this burning feeling is. I slip my hand from around his wrist and take a step back putting distance between us again. Like a smart Katherine should do.

"And you just care?" he asks so matter of factly with his ever present cocky smirk on his face. Now, I just kinda want to slap him. How does he do this? Make my feelings towards him flip flop so quickly. I don't know what I was thinking, maybe that after the other night we could just be okay, that maybe I was a person to him, and not a silly girl looking for her soulmate.

The feeling spreading from my hand to my chest disappears. "Wow, here I was thinking maybe I did after the other night. I knew I'd regret this. Nothings changed." I turn to walk back to my car. This was a mistake. The guy who sat on the floor the other night clearly wasn't really him, he was an imposter, a nice twin, the evil ones back in play and I'm making a fool of myself.

I don't know why I came and I knew I shouldn't have. I don't care, and I couldn't possibly have been worried about him.

Or maybe I did care and that only makes me feel worse.

"Wait," he calls out and now he's the one with his hand around my wrist. His hand engulfs it. "I'm sorry." He pauses like it actually pains him to say this to me, I can't help but smile, James being uncomfortable is something I can deal with. "Thank you for checking in on me." For once the look in his eyes seems sincere even if the words seem foreign coming from his month. "Sit?" he asks, gesturing to the bench on the porch.

I look over his face again before his hand slips down my arm grazing my hand before falling to his side. I walk over to the bench and sit down ever so reluctantly.

He doesn't sit but leans on the railing of the porch across from me, hands either side of him on the bar running across. The early evening sun slips over his face making him almost look golden, like a beautiful statue I shouldn't be allowed so close to. I sit with my hands in my lap looking down at them, I feel like I've been looking at him too much.

When I finally look up he's already looking at me, boring into me with his eyes, the flames in my chest that extinguished themselves a minute ago fan back to life. "So, are you okay?" I finally ask, the silence eating at me a bit too much.

"Yeah." He looks toward his front door before looking back at me. "Just had to take a couple of days to help my dad." He pauses again also like he's thinking over what he should say, wondering whether to say it or not. I'm surprised when he continues. "He's... my dad. He's had a lot of drinking problems since my mum left eight years ago."

SOUL BELIEFS

I feel like I've just seen him for the first time. Like the James I've seen this whole time wasn't really him in any way. I wonder if his mum left his dad for her soulmate and god my heart hurts for him. Any pieces of the puzzle in front of me that had been lost or couldn't find their place slide into view and I feel like maybe I never had the whole picture.

"He's been on and off the wagon for the last four years but I got an invite to my mum's wedding a couple months ago. I hid it from him but he found it before the party the other night." His voice trails off like he thinks he doesn't really need to say any more and the last words come out slow like he's still processing it all.

The last bit makes me feel like shit. I went after him the other night for no good reason and that was definitely the last thing he needed considering everything he was dealing with.

I'm lost for words for the second time that day. I can't even imagine having to look after a parent like that. When Dad died, Mom was devastated but we looked after each other and we had my nan and uncle to help. I wonder if he has any other family. I don't say anything and I think he can tell I don't want to say the wrong thing.

He pushes himself off the railing and sits down next to me. Not looking at me though just looking ahead, he runs his hand through his hair.

"I'm sorry," is all I know to say. This whole thing feels weird, seeing him as an actual human not a constant annoyance. Why do I feel like sharing with him right now?

There's a moment of silence between us and I can feel he wants to say more, tell me something else so I stay quiet and give him the chance to. I'm not ready or really willing to share with him.

"Mum left when I was seventeen." He's still not looking at me and I don't push for him to. This is the most real moment I think we've ever had. I don't want to burst that bubble. "She met her soulmate." It comes out his mouth like venom, like it's poison on his lips, but it confirms my suspicions. "I haven't seen her since, I didn't want to and after a couple of years of her trying to get in contact, she gave up. Dad, well he fell apart, and I don't blame him but it was hard for me too, you know? I was only a kid really."

He looks up from his lap and sits back against the bench letting out a long heavy breath.

"I don't know what I'm meant to do, you know? Like, do I go?" He's talking into the air and I'm not sure if he wants me to answer.

"What?"

"I'm sorry, it's just…" He stops himself before he says anything more. I can tell he's finding this as strange as I am.

"There's no one else to ask and you know I'll tell you what I really think?"

"Yeah, pretty much."

We both let out a little laugh. "Honestly?" He looks at me like he might just regret asking me. "If I had the chance to see my dad one last time, I'd do anything. The other night, at the party, you're the first person to calm me like that since him." A sad smile tugs on my lips, I have no idea why I told him that last bit, it's like I feel the need to be as open with him as he is with me right now. "You never know when you'll lose someone."

He doesn't say anything but the look of his face is the same as Halloween, the part when we weren't trying to kill each other. His eyes are soft, the same as his lazy smile.

After a short minute, I remember something my dad would tell me when my anxiety was bad, not that I always listened. "Never let your fear make you miss out on the joy," I say ever so slightly under my breath trying to think of the right thing to say to him.

"What?" he asks me, confused.

It's a rare occasion that I can talk about my dad without crying and I'm happy this is one of them. As much as this is a nice moment we're having, I can't know he won't use this against me at some point. "My dad used to say you should never let your fear of something keep you from experiencing the joy in things," I tell him, turning my body slightly to face him more.

"Again, what?" he says, laughing slightly, turning towards me and all I want is to move closer. I can feel the heat from his chest radiating from him.

I let out a sigh, shaking my head but with a smile on my face. "Basically, you don't want to not go because you're scared of seeing your mom or worried about what might happen when you do. The worst that can happen is you have a terrible time and you can leave when you want and never see her again." The look on his face does not fill me with hope that I am saying the right thing, but I continue anyway. "But if you don't go, the worst that can happen is you'll regret not going, maybe for the rest of your life. Wondering 'what if'... You know?"

Silence surrounds us for a minute and I just look at him the same way he's looking at me. A small smile finally starts to grow on his face and I feel my body relax at the sight.

I can't even help myself as I smile at him. "And why don't you take someone with you like a buffer?" My question lingers in the air as I can see him thinking over my words. My words meant maybe a friend like Maddie or one of the many girls he must be talking to. My words didn't not mean what he asks me next.

"Would you go with me?"

"Me?" I echo. His smile fades a little and it breaks my heart in a way I don't understand. He's opened up to me more than I thought he would ever. "I'll think about it," I say finally because looking at his sad face now just makes me feel like I kicked a puppy. Standing from the bench I say, "I should get going."

He lets me, only standing himself when I've walked down the small steps leading back to the driveway. "Katherine," he calls and I turn to see him leaning on the railing again looking at me with some stupid handsome smile on his face. "You know it's not true right?"

"What?"

"That nothing has changed. It has, and you know it."

Almost as if on cue, I get a call the minute I walk back in the house. I wave to Ella as I pass the kitchen, answering the call as I step into my room.

"Isabella, what are you doing up at 2 a.m?" I question before I say anything else.

I haven't spoken to her since the quick texts we sent at Halloween and I haven't wanted to text any of the things that happened, it seemed too long to type out and now I don't know if half of it is even relevant after going to see James today.

"Well the other night, or day, you said you had so much to catch me up on and I can't sleep so it seemed like the perfect time, what's up?" There's concern in her voice. I can hear it even though I think she's also whispering a bit.

I give her a quick run down of Halloween night, trying to not make myself sound like a lunatic but she already knows that. I hear her take a big breath in when I tell her about Dylan. Then another when I tell her about James stepping in; I'm sure she holds her breath when I tell her about the panic attack.

I don't tell her about the way I felt around him or the burning feeling I get when we touch. I'm not sure I can bring myself to say any of that out loud or try to explain it to her or myself.

Then I shift to what happened after work. She's a little too quiet when I finish and I wonder if she's fallen asleep or if we've been disconnected.

"You still there Bella?" I ask, ready to hang up and have to do this another time.

"I have so many questions and things to say." She is no longer keeping herself quiet. I wait in silence as she gathers her thoughts. "Okay, so one, I'm proud of you for going to a party. Two, he was so jealous. I mean thank god he came and found you but like why did he go looking in the first place?" I'm prepared to jump in and tell her that's ridiculous, but she continues. "And three, what did you say to the wedding invite?"

"That I'd think about it." I hear a laugh come from her. "What? What was I meant to say?" I say, flinging myself down on my bed staring up at the ceiling.

"Oh, I don't know, maybe, 'yes gorgeous muscular Australian man, I'd love to spend the whole day with you while you're in a suit.' Maybe something like that would have been better," she explains, doing her best impression of me, and it's terrifyingly good. "God, he'll look so good in a suit."

God he will.

I let out a long sigh. "I never said I thought he was gorgeous," I tell her knowing that she knows she's right and I hate it just a little.

"Are we forgetting the part where I already found his Instagram?" We both laugh before she gets all serious on me again. "Katherine, you are going to call him and say yes, you're going have a great time, and look hot in that dress I got you."

I don't say anything. She's right, I know she is, I know I'd probably have a good time now that we seem to have some kind of truce and it's sweet that he asked me to go with him. I shouldn't be thinking so much into it because I know he's not going to be the one so what's the harm in going.

Except I think I might know the harm.

The feeling I've been getting in my chest when I'm around him, the tight knot like I might choke, is the harm. The feeling that maybe, just maybe, I might like him, just a little, is the harm. The fact that I know it won't end well for me, like at all, is the harm. The fact that I know that there is no way on this earth after what he told me about his mom he'll ever feel that back is the harm.

The feeling I have right now, thinking about going to this wedding with him, the giddy nervous sensation, is the harm.

My inability to be able to tell myself any of this and believe it is the harm.

I don't know when it happened, probably when he was telling me everything today, or when he said things had changed and my heart leaped in my chest. When he was opening up to me, being a real person with me, it was probably then. But I won't acknowledge it, it'll go away if I do that.

Bella doesn't take me going silent all that well. "You better not be talking yourself out of it, or I'll fly out and make you go, because—"

"Fine," I cut her off. "I'll call him tomorrow, but I can't promise I'll look hot, you're not here to help me."

"Good girl, and I can still help you from a million miles away, don't you worry your pretty little mind. Send me some pictures and I'll tell you what will go with it, can't have you looking like a grandma."

"And here I was about to ask you how the internship was going."

"Oh, well since you asked and I'm so awake now, let me fill you in on everything."

SOUL BELIEFS

"I'd love that," I say, smiling, while she starts to talk.

Chapter 21

James

The sun setting casts all kinds of shadows over the front garden. I feel like I've been in a weird state since she left yesterday like a tidal wave. Pulling in, saying shit I didn't want to hear, and leaving the wreckage of me behind.

Why would I do that?

I bury my head in my hands.

God, why would I ask her to go with me to my mum's wedding, I don't even want to go.

But she was sitting here looking at me with these eyes that I'm sure could cut right through me and she was talking about her dad with me. It's like she trusted me, maybe, just a little. As if I wasn't some sort of monster she'd built up in her head. I don't know why that means something to me, why it means so much to me that she'd talk to me like that, but I know I liked it. And I'm starting to realise that there's a lot about my feelings towards Katherine that I don't and won't ever understand.

But it felt like we were real people for a change, not the people we both put out into the world. Not the people we let other people see but the real thing; the real people that we see when we look in the mirror. And I liked what I saw of her today, and it kills me that I can't know if she thought the same.

She was saying all that stuff about regrets and it just slipped out. After seeing her the way I did the other night, even after everything, even the kiss, that was the first time I really knew I couldn't hate her. I couldn't possibly. I wasn't lying when I told her I never did, seeing her like that made me realise I'd just been lying to myself.

I'm such an idiot, my inner voice reminds me, and for once I can't really disagree.

Went I back into the house yesterday after she left and Dad threw about a hundred questions at me. *Who's she? She's pretty, James, do you like her? She came to check on you.* I wanted to scream a little.

She didn't even say yes, it's been just over twenty four hours and you'd think it'd been weeks the way my brain is making me spiral. Which should definitely not bother me as much as it does. To make matters worse, Ella gave me another day off and I know Katherine would have been working today. I can't help thinking of wanting to see her. Just to be near her again, to smell her personal mix of sweet vanilla and flowers.

Actually maybe it's better to not see her until she tells me a definite no. Then I'll know, I'll have my answer when it comes to her.

Sitting on the porch, on the bench—I can't stop my mind from thinking about how it felt to see her standing there in my doorway. I thought I was imagining it. I thought the stress had finally gotten to me and I was hallucinating a beautiful woman standing at my door.

God, she looked stunning. I haven't been able to have an intelligent thought since she left. I'm waiting for someone to come wake me up. She was in her work top and a pair of shorts. Dear lord, what if she says yes and I have to see her all dressed up? I'll go into cardiac arrest.

The question I keep coming back to is why would she want to check on me? I'd like to think I know the answer, that maybe it's the same reason I would go and check on her, but it won't be.

It can't be because her chest gets tight when she's around me like mine does, or because she can't stop but wonder about me when I'm not around like I do with her. And it can't be because she cares no matter what she said when she was here, and I don't like the way that stings.

I'm not like this, I'm not. I don't get hung up on girls like this, ever. Since my mum left, I just decided that love wasn't worth it, because god forbid the person you love finds their soulmate and runs off into the sunset like you never existed. I can't even tell you where my soul stone is. I packed it away somewhere the second mum was out of the house, swearing off the whole thing for the rest of my life.

Why I'm thinking about it now, I honestly don't even know, because it truly doesn't matter. Because I'll never be in love, never give myself over to another person, never give them so much power over me like that.

But then in comes little Miss American Sunshine and all of my sanity seems to have disappeared. I must be having some kind of quarter life crisis.

I can hear the TV inside through the window next to me, Dad shouting at some show he's too drunk to understand, or remember. This is my life, and she is meant for so much more. Katherine is beautiful and smart and like a soul out of time. There's so much more to her, parts I'm not sure I'll ever get to see or know.

And I am, me. I'm a closed off asshole because I don't want anyone else to have to deal with this and that's my choice, my decision. I don't need a soulmate like she does. She needs it like she needs air or water. She needs to believe in something bigger and better than what she sees and I don't. I know what the world has in store for me.

I know the world, and I know how real it is and can be. I can't let myself fall into the fantasy of her, it's not fair.

Because she'll find her soulmate, I know she will. She's determined and stubborn. Nothing will stand in her way, no one would change her mind.

I have no doubt that girl will find what she's looking for, I just know it's not me. No matter how much I might want or like it to be.

Okay, too far!

Just as I've decided I need to call her and say I take it back, that she doesn't have to come with me, because I'm not going to go and taking her will just complicate everything even more by it basically being a date, my phone rings. The screen lights up and her name is right there in black and white.

"Hey." I'm trying to sound as casual as possible, it's actually painful.

"Hey, I'm sorry I didn't call sooner," she pauses and I suck in all of the air left in my body, anticipating what she has to say. "I'll come with you to the wedding." Another pause. "If you still want me to, of course?"

No, is what I should say, it's the smart thing to do, but as we've found out lately I've not been very smart since she came along. Instead, I finally let myself breathe and respond with, "Of course, Katherine. It's only a week away though?" I actually almost want her to change her mind because then it wasn't me, it was her, I'm not sure if I can actually keep it together going with her.

"Yeah, that'll be fine, I'll talk to Ella tonight. Text me the details and stuff," she says, like she doesn't see the danger in the agreement she's walking into. Or am I the only one with these feelings? Am I the only one who can't keep my mind off her? Does the idea of dancing with me not fill her with dread and also set every nerve on fire?

I feel like the path I'm letting myself walk down is only going to lead to some kind of hurt and yet I think I might be too far down it to turn back.

Chapter 22

Katherine

P osted 11th November 2024 08:23

Weddings.

They can be a celebration of all things love, life and happy endings. They can also be stressful, scary and sad.

I have every expectation that this one will be the latter. Because weddings aren't just about the bride and groom they are also about all the family that comes along with them.

Nevertheless, I've always looked forward to going to my first wedding; amazing food, dancing until your feet fall off, the love from everyone swirling in the air. But the best part is that at the end of the day, you get to bask in the love the two people getting married have for each other.

But they don't always last, and I think that's inevitable. As a soulmate believer, I couldn't imagine marrying someone who isn't my soulmate but plenty of people do and plenty of people live long happy lives with people who aren't.

My heart hurts a little for James and his dad, and on one hand I kinda understand if his mom found her soulmate, but I can't understand how she could just leave him like that. To walk out of your son's life for someone at that point she barely knew.

And especially not James.

A soulmate love—or so I've heard—feels like something you'll never know until it happens. Something you've never felt before, and I can imagine that feeling is intoxicating. Makes your head swim and your skin burn. But a love a parent has for their child I had always assumed was even more.

Maybe I'm wrong, I haven't found my soulmate and I'm also not a parent, but I don't think I can be on anyone else's side besides James.

Today is going to be stressful, I can feel it

My eyes drift over to the gold dress hung up in front of my wardrobe and the heels sitting under it. Bella and I FaceTimed yesterday so she could see it on and help me with the rest, telling me explicitly I had to have my hair up to show off my back; I've opted for a butterfly clip from the '90s.

My focus is brought back to my laptop when it lets out a ding alerting me to an email. The address is unknown to me but the name Thomas Mitchel sitting before the email handle makes my heart skip, *literally*.

Thomas Mitchel <thomas.mitchel@soulmatechronicles.com>
To Katherine Miller
Subject: Your soulmate adventure

Dear Miss Miller,
My name is Tommy Mitchel and I'm emailing you from the offices of Soulmate Chronicles.

I had the pleasure of meeting your friend Isabella Sainz at a photo shoot the other day and we got to talking, about you mostly.

She told me all about your soulmate adventure and I just couldn't pass up the opportunity to speak to you, hence this email. She also mentioned that you graduated from NYU currently for journalism, and she gave me the address for your blog so I could see some of what you'd written about your personal soulmate experience.

I would love to have a chat with you about what we at Soulmate Chronicles might be able to do in terms of collaborating with you.

I look forward to hearing from you soon.

Kind regards,
Tommy Mitchel
Editor in Chief at Soulmate Chronicles.

I reread the email at least twenty times before I determine that there is in fact really an email from Soulmate Chronicles sitting in my inbox, and not just any email. One from the man I'd been reading articles from since I could buy magazines.

This isn't happening!

Surely, Bella would have told me she talked to him, or that she's told him all about me!

I check the time again and decide it is far too early to be calling her to make sure this isn't a scam, I put that on my list of to-do's for tomorrow.

Leaning back in my chair, I can't quite decide if I'm crazy-excited or crazy-nervous or crazy-anxious, or just maybe crazy. I still get up and jump around my room like said crazy person, because *OMG!*

If this is real, and a big *if*, then I could very well be talking to Tommy Mitchel and not just talking, but collaborating. That wasn't a job offer but I'm delusional enough to tell myself that maybe it could be.

I've been reading Soulmate Chronicles since before I could afford to buy it for myself. There are plenty of soulmate related blogs online, people just talking about their experiences, but Soulmate Chronicles is the only physical magazine to be successful. I learnt almost everything that I didn't learn from my nan about soulmates from this magazine. It always made me feel more connected to a community I didn't have in real life.

The crushing feeling of the realisation that I'm still in Australia hits me like a ton of bricks. Soulmate Chronicles are in New York, back home. I mean I haven't even talked to the guy, but I have a feeling if anything is to happen, I need to be back there. But what does that mean for my soulmate?

I know I said I'd be gone by the end of the year but what if I *do* find my soulmate? What if he wants to stay here?

I can't do this right now. I have two hours until James picks me up and I can't be having a crisis when I need to do my makeup, and also keep myself from having a *different* crisis about having to meet James' family when I don't even know where we stand.

What am I even talking about, we're not anything. We just kissed once, and he helped me with a panic attack, and we just look at each other like we've never seen each other before and like we'll never get enough of looking. But yes, we aren't anything, so that shouldn't be something I'm worrying about. I sit completely still for another five minutes, collecting myself before I push everything I'm now panicking about to the very back of my brain. They are things that Tomorrow Katherine will have to think about, not Today Katherine, not the Katherine who has to go to a wedding.

What if James was my soulmate? If I could know, maybe it will make all of this easier.

If he is, then it would make sense why I feel the need to be near him, even if it is to torment and tease each other. If he isn't, then I can tell myself to stop and this is all a trick my mind is playing on me.

I don't think I've ever thought something so ridiculous in my life. James: my soulmate. It's almost laughable. It's in fact so laughable that I do laugh.

But then again, I've never denied how stupidly attracted to him I am. And then there was that time in the store a few weeks ago when I was ignoring him, we brushed arms while trying to both come out of the back room at the same time, and it stopped me in my tracks. So simple, so small and yet it felt like all of the earth's electricity surged through my body from the smallest touch. And that's not the only time it's happened, sometimes I feel it just when he's a little *too* close to me, not even touching me, it makes me feel like a wire coiled too tight.

I feel like I'm watching a tennis match between the two different sides of my brain, and I'm getting dizzy.

I know there is only one way to solve this but I promised myself, Ella, Mom, and Bella I wouldn't do it. I know what they all said, that I need to let life happen, that I shouldn't put so much pressure on it, that I should just live—but I can't. Did I really think I ever could? I don't know if I can let myself think about anyone else until I know for sure.

I think about it the whole time I do my make up, my hair and put on my dress. Only once I'm ready do I take a deep breath and make up my mind.

Ella's working all day at the shop and she only left an hour ago so there's no chance of her coming back and catching me.

I walk into Ella's room, deciding that's got to be where she put it. It feels wrong being in here like this, it feels like I'm breaking her trust but I just don't think I'll be able to calm down till I have it back again.

I'm pulling drawers open and looking in shoe boxes. Under the bed, and inside her desk.

Nothing.

I turn towards the door again and my eyes catch her bedside table, I walk towards it and pull open the drawer. There it is. It's almost like reuniting with an old friend. An old friend who I feel like I've abandoned.

Although I'm sure my soul stone doesn't have actual feelings, I still feel bad that it's been here this whole time. I just look at it for a moment and I think over whether to actually pick it up or not. It's honestly not until this moment, when I'm willing to break my promise to everyone, that's when I realise I do like him.

I like his ridiculous blue eyes and blonde hair. I like how passionate he is about surfing and about the kids he gets to teach. I like how he gets under my skin in every way, the best way and the worst. I like how I feel when he touches me and how I feel safe when he's near.

God, this is terrible. I came here to find my soulmate, not to get rejected by the one guy I told myself was the total opposite of what I wanted. And even if he does by some kind of miracle feel the same, it won't matter, he won't be my soulmate. I let out a watery laugh at the thought. I blink up at the ceiling a few times to stop the tears I know are building.

Wiping my increasingly sweaty hands over my dress, I need to make this decision quickly because James will be here soon.

And then I'm thinking about what if he *is* my soulmate and I never let myself get any closer to him because I'm so sure that he's not.

Before I know it, my hand is around the stone taking it out of the drawer. I roll it around in my hand, it's cold and that just reminds me of how long I've not had it on.

I close the drawer and debate whether or not to actually wear it. I can't actually hide it under my dress, the neckline is too low. I think if he sees it on me we might go back to square one with the whole thing and I'm not sure if I can really take that or not.

I shove it in my purse, surely it'll still work even if I'm not wearing it. Most people don't wear theirs.

I play with the whale around my neck for a minute, giving myself time to change my mind and then there's a knock at the door. I brush my dress off and go answer it.

I open the door and he's standing there looking as unbelievably handsome as ever. I try to take a breath in but it doesn't seem to happen. I feel more lightheaded than I did a minute ago and I know it's because he's looking at me with that boyish grin, his blue eyes sparkling in the way they only do when I know his smile is real.

And I'm left only feeling more confused than I was seconds ago because all of a sudden, I'm wishing he was and wasn't my soulmate all at the same time.

Chapter 23
James

I'm not sure what I'm more nervous about.

If it's seeing my mum for the first time in so long, or having to spend the whole day with Katherine.

It must be the former.

Because I think if it's the latter, I might be in trouble. I spend the day with her all the time at the shop, this shouldn't be any different.

It shouldn't. But it is, because this time, we've chosen to spend time together. There's no obligation on either side. Neither of us have to be here but we are.

I've spent most of the morning thinking over when it all changed, when I changed because I have. More than I think I realised, none of that would have happened if she hadn't been here in the first place.

But the more I think about it, I take notice that no one has ever pushed me back when I push the way she does. Someone making me look at things and myself a little different, I've never had to question the beliefs I had about the world. The beliefs I had about certain people. But Katherine she's not what I thought, not what I'd told myself people like her were like. Kinda made me start thinking I'd had some of this all wrong. It scares me and also kinda excites me. She makes me think I don't have to play life with the cards I was dealt, I can make new rules.

Maybe I'm getting ahead of myself. I'm not her soulmate but maybe I can show her why she might not need that anymore. I'm almost determined to show her a bit more of myself today, show her the pieces I've had in the shadows for so long. Because I think she has some beliefs about who I am too, about the kind of person I am. But I don't think that is the picture I want her to have anymore.

As I knock on the front door for Ella's house, I find my hands sweating. I'm thinking about what we'll talk about, and if we'll be able to keep up with this non-friendship friendship we have going on at the moment. Because I want to push it, I want to see how far I can push her until we fall off the cliff completely. I want to see how far I can take this until she sees it could be more. Because I can't and won't do anything until I know, until I see it in her eyes that she wants more from me.

I'm thinking about whether we'll dance together if the day goes well and if we'll laugh about things once she's had a drink, god I'd pay to hear her laugh at something I've said.

Yeah, I'm in trouble.

Then she opens the door and I think I forget to breathe.

Come on. Keep it together.

She's beautiful.

She's always beautiful, but right now in this doorway, she looks even more breathtaking. I'm not sure I'll even be able to take it all in, I need to be able to stop time completely just so I can look at her and memorise the way she's looking at me. As much as I want her to want this, I can't be sure she will, so I make note to remember everything from today, so I can pretend that I am the only guy she'll ever want.

Her hair is pulled up off her shoulders and neck, with some strands that fall around her face. The gold dress she's wearing makes her skin glow under the sunlight. And I can't help but notice she's still wearing the whale necklace.

That warms up my heart more than anything, the fact she's wearing something I got her. Sure, she doesn't know I got it but I like it all the same. It's like a little secret I'm carrying around with me. One I'm dying to tell her, maybe she'd hate me a little less if I did.

Maybe she'd believe me when I tell her I don't hate her. But we're in a good rhythm right now. I can't deny that. I don't think she'd be doing this for me, coming to the wedding, if she didn't like me just a little.

"You look..." I'm blank, there aren't enough words in the English language to try and explain how she looks. She looks surprised and almost shocked, does she think I'm having trouble thinking because she looks bad? Surely she knows how amazing she looks?

She plays with the hem of the dress as she looks me over too, and then her face finally snaps back to a small smile. "I'm going to come up with my own complaint in my head if you can't string a sentence together." She teases me and it actually makes me feel more normal when she does, like this is the thing that's totally normal to us.

"Make it a good one. Something about the sun not shining as bright as you." Her cheeks go red and I think that might be my favourite thing. No matter how much of our back and forth we have and everything we say, every now and then I'll say something that manages to embarrass her.

"Got it, sun, me better. Thank you."

I like catching her off guard, making her cheeks flush and her eyes twinkle in a way only the stars could try and compete with.

"Should we go?" she finally says, tipping her head towards my truck parked behind her car, popping the bubble around us.

I put my hand out for her, wondering how well she'll walk in those heels and honestly because I just want to hold it again. I could have let go of her a million times at that Halloween party, but I didn't want to.

She looks at it for a second, chewing at her bottom lip before taking my hand in hers.

The spark from feeling her touch runs up my arm and goes right to my head. Making me feel light, a bit like I've had my oxygen restricted.

I watch her face from the side as we walk to my truck, she's concentrating far too much on walking over the uneven surface to notice. I have to mentally slap myself a little. I'm being an idiot, I'm letting myself think like there's anyway, any chance in this world, that in any universe we exist in, she would look at me the way I'm looking at her.

I have to be imagining it.

Because there isn't a universe where a guy like me deserves a girl like her and definitely not when her heart is set on her soulmate. I can't blame her, I'm not even sure I can be mad about it anymore, I just wish she didn't. I wish I could put into words the way I feel, the way I can feel literal electricity when I touch her, the way I would protect her from all the evil, all the pain she's ever felt.

Christ.

Yeah, you and me both, brain.

I like her a lot, and there's not a single thing I can do about it.

Chapter 24
Katherine

Has there ever been such a beautiful man in a suit before?
No, the answer is no, there hasn't been.

I don't think there ever will be. This will go down in history as the day the most beautiful man in the world wore the best suit in the world.

I'm looking down, watching my step but it's just to distract myself from looking at him more. The way he looked at me made my insides melt and I feel like I'm trying to scoop them back in to no avail.

As we approach his truck, the hand he has in mine lets go, moving to the small of my back and the touch almost burns through my dress. He looks at me like he's worried I'm going to pass out. I just about manage a smile as he unlocks the door and opens it for me as I shuffle out of the way avoiding his hand so I don't catch fire.

I slide in and watch as he closes the door for me.

The urge to run while he's not in the truck is huge, massive, but my legs couldn't move if I tried. I know that much, they are jelly at this point.

In the midst of all this I also forget about the stone neatly tucked into my purse, burning its own hole in my heart. I have five seconds to check it and I don't hesitate to take a look at it.

The thing is I want to live in this world where he calls me beautiful and opens car doors for me. Where I can look at him in that suit and we smile at each other and I can pretend. But I can't. I can want something so much but deep down I know myself.

I pop open my bag and there it is, sitting in between a lipstick and my phone.

Not glowing.

Disappointment sits heavy in my stomach. It's not until then, looking at it dull and misty, that I know how much I really wanted it. How much I had wanted him to be it and for us to finally put every little bit of bullshit behind us.

A feeling I hadn't expected creeps up my throat.

Anger.

I'm mad at the universe for doing this to me, for putting him in front of me and still keeping him three steps away from me. Mad at myself for being stupid and developing feelings for someone I knew deep down wasn't going to be my soulmate. Just mad, not really at anyone and also everyone all at once.

Frustration tears threaten to spill over my lids, I fight them off just as he gets in the truck, controlling my emotions has never been something I've been great at but I guess no time like the present. I have five seconds to pat down every emotion raging in me, sadness, anger, disappointment, before he speaks.

"You ready?"

No, I don't think I am.

The drive goes by quickly. Quietly—but quickly. Neither one of us quite knowing how to break the silence, I have no idea what he's thinking but my brain won't stop yelling at me. It's too loud for me to even think of a conversation.

I can't piece a word together to even understand what it's screaming about, what things I should be stressing or sad most about.

I take a breath and look out my window. You'd think when you've been living near the beach for a few months that a new beach wouldn't take your breath away but you'd be wrong.

We drive in the opposite direction to Sydney along the coastline and the sun high in the sky streams through the window and warms my face. I take a deep breath taking in the salty air clearing my head a little.

Even with what I now know in the forefront of my brain, I can't help but catch glimpses of him as we drive. He's concentrating on the road and I hope he can't see me looking at him but I'm not being subtle, it's hard to be in a truck where you're sitting so close to the driver.

He throw his jacket on the seat between us before we set off and his shirt clings to every muscle on his arms and shoulders. Some of his tattoos are so dark, I can see outlines though the thin white material. It's like I've never seen him without a shirt on which is ridiculous, topless if basically his uniform. But something about him in a shirt is even better, somehow him with clothes on for a change is even more attractive to me.

"It's not that far out of town." Hearing him finally speak makes me jump. It's been twenty minutes since we got in the truck and it's the first thing either of us has said, the distance to the wedding hadn't been the most pressing matter on my mind.

"I don't mind too much, I like long drives when the view is this nice." I'm still looking at him when I say it but he knows I mean the beach, right? Do I mean the beach?

The twinkle in his eyes catches the sunlight when he looks over at me. "Yeah it is, isn't it?" I feel the heat creep up my cheeks at his words, ones I try not to take to heart too much. But I smile at him. I smile like a real smile, I think it's the first one I've actually given him. The first one I really mean, he catches a look at me and smiles too as he looks back at the road. It's the first time I catch the faintness of a dimple on his cheek as the sun hits his face.

I speak again. "So, any chance you want to give me a run down of the day?"

He takes his eyes off the open road for the whole of two seconds to give me a confused look.

"Okay, so like, who do we not make small talk with? Who do we like?"

"*We?*" I can tell he's smiling even if I can't see his face completely. It makes my heart too warm for my liking as I remember the not-glowing stone in my bag.

I dampen down the feeling long enough to continue. "Yes, I'm your moral support, am I not? I need to know who I might need to fight." I try to put on some kind of mean face, it makes us both laugh and the sound is so foreign for the both of us. I think about it for a minute. "I'm on your side today."

If I've read this all wrong and he actually really hates me and is just using me to get through today then I've just made this all weird and I can't be doing a whole day with him if it's going to be weird and awkward. Especially when I've had a revelation about my feelings for him, for them to be crushed in the space of about five minutes.

It feels like forever before he speaks again.

"My nan." He pauses and I see him check his mirrors before taking an exit to a smaller road. "She's great, I still see her, talk to her on the phone, get a birthday card every year, and all that jazz. My uncle is a sexist piece of shit, so if he's there, I'll steer you away from him, or I'll let you deck him." He stops and I don't press. This doesn't seem like the day to be prodding for information about people he's not comfortable telling me about.

"Well I guess for once you'll be pleased that I'm a ray of sunshine." He scoffs, and I ignore him. "You always say how annoying it is I'm so good at being nice to people, but today I'll use it for the greater good." He thinks I'm joking but for some reason my stomach is only in a small knot, I feel pretty calm all things considered. Which doesn't really make much sense.

"Are you saying you'll do all the talking?" He cocks a brow at me but doesn't turn.

"If you want me to."

His hand slides from the gear stick to my knee, sending goosebumps all up my leg. I restrain myself from wanting to squeeze my thighs together at the feeling of his thumb drawing little circles. "Katherine, my very own knight in shining armour, we'll finally put you running your mouth to good use."

Dear lord.

He says it so quietly like someone might hear him. Before I can say anything, he's stopping the truck and pulling up in front of a cute looking inn.

The building is rustic, all white wooden panels and a porch that looks like it wraps around most of the house, like something out of a hallmark movie. Before I can blink, his hand moves off of my knee and he's opening his door. I watch him as he rounds the hood and opens my door, giving me his hand to help me out.

As we walk towards the front door, I feel him tense up and his strides slow down until he stops completely, only looking forward.

There's a chalkboard on an easel with white and orange flowers around it that says 'Welcome to the Wedding of Christina and Lee' in fancy handwriting.

I squeeze his hand that is still in mine and bring his attention back to me. "It'll be okay, I'm here." I could say so much more than that like *I want to be here with you* or *I'll stay with you like this for as long as you need* but I'm not sure I would be able to. "If all else fails, it's an open bar, isn't it? That'll help me at least," I tell him with a smile, one I hope is reassuring.

He finally gives me a small smile and squeezes my hand back.

It seems that they've rented out the whole place for the wedding and I can't help but look in every room we pass as we make our way to the back garden. James doesn't stop to talk to a single person as we do, like he wouldn't be able to breathe until we're back outside and he can see the sea again. He's like a bullet train until an old lady stops him just on the back porch.

She's an elegant woman, maybe in her late seventies. Her beautiful grey curly hair is pinned back from her face with flower clips. Her face is warm and soft just like my nan's and when he drops my hand and wraps her in a hug, I assume she is his. He's so much taller than her he has to duck down so much to hold her, her head on his shoulder turns to me and her smile eases a small bit of my nerves in my stomach.

"James, don't be rude, introduce me to this beautiful girl you've brought with you," she tells him, pulling out of his grip but linking her arm in his. The sight makes something in her glow, seeing him smile at her like he means it. It's a strange feeling.

"This is Katherine, we're..." He looks at me and his unsure tone seems to make me happy and I know that's not good, I don't want him to be confused about what we are.

"Friends," I say, jumping in. "I'm Ella's niece. I've been visiting for a couple of months." I put my hand out to her. "It's nice to meet you."

She looks it over for a second before pulling away from her grandson and pulls me in for a hug. "It's so nice to meet you, dear."

"You, too," I tell her when she pulls away from me. James just watches us, when I catch his eyes over her shoulder he smiles at me, it's a smile I've never seen before and my heart skips. It's warm and easy, the kind of smile you get when you're daydreaming about something.

"You're right James, she is pretty." She smiles in that eye twinkling way, mischief radiates off her.

"Nan!"

"Well, I best take a seat, I'll see you in a bit." She pats James on arm, smiles at me again, and then she's gone and we're by ourselves again.

"Sh-she doesn't know what she's talking about, old age." I see what he's doing, and I'll play along just to make him feel better for today.

"I wouldn't let her hear you say that."

My eyes dart around the room for a second and I can't help but feel like everyone is staring at us—at me.

"They aren't looking at you, although they should be," James says, bending down to be closer to my ear. "Relax, Sunshine, I can practically hear your mind running away from here," he tells me standing up, putting his hand out for me again. I hesitate taking it for the whole of two seconds before I decide today is not the day to make him feel pushed away.

"I'm pretty sure I'm meant to be telling you to relax." My voice comes out shakier than I would have liked as we finally step out into the garden.

Chapter 25

James

There are a few things I wish I'd said to Katherine inside but didn't, two of them being: *Yes, I did tell my nan about you when she called me this morning to check up on me, more specifically I described you as the prettiest girl I'd ever seen.* And *what I meant was, they should all be looking at you because you are the most beautiful person they'll ever get to lay their eyes on.*

I did not say any of these things because I would like to save myself the embarrassment of her laughing in my face.

I spot familiar faces as we make our way into the garden.

Mum's friends I remember who used to come round for dinner and parties, relatives who took Mum's side who I haven't really spoken to since she left, people who I imagine are Lee's family and friends.

I don't even know him and I know that I don't like him. That's probably a basic response from me but I can't help it, just seeing his name everywhere irritates me. It doesn't feel surprising that I don't like him, he's the man my mum decided to replace my dad with, I've been so protective of my dad since it all happened. I feel guilty that I'm even here.

"You know we could still make a getaway," I say to Katherine as she stands next to me unsurprisingly taking her surroundings in. That's her baseline—surveying her surroundings—I've noticed it more and more since the party, thought back to past interactions and realised the signs of her anxiety were always there, I just wasn't paying enough attention.

She looks up at me all doe-eyed, her skin glowing. "James, if you pull me away from this before I've had a chance to eat any of that cake, I will never speak to you again," she explains pointing to the cake sat over in the corner of the garden with other people looking over it. It's a tall simple cake covered with autumn orange and forest green flowers. It reminds me of my mum in a way I'm not sure about.

A few weeks ago the promise of Katherine never speaking to me again was my dream, now as she speaks it into existence my heart squeezes. Looking at her like this, with me, she smiles up at me and I nearly fall over right there and then. What wouldn't I do for her?

An usher approaches us and asks us to take our seats. I hesitate for a moment knowing this is it. I'll see her again after almost ten years. It seems surreal, like a nightmare I'm sure I've had before. Katherine leads the way, and if she didn't, I'm certain I'd stand here forever, letting the grass and weeds grow over my shoes.

She starts to walk up the rows, but I tug her back, pulling her to the last row. I need to be as far away as humanly possible, I need to put a barrier between me and my mum. If she can't make eye contact with me, maybe she won't notice I'm here and I can just disappear when this is all done with.

I wasn't totally aware of it, but I was staring at *him*. The man that was deemed so much better than my father simply because the universe said so. He doesn't look all that much different than Dad, maybe a bit fuller in the face and with less grey hair, and yet a glowing rock pushed him and my mum together while pulling my whole world apart.

His eyes take a minute and then it's like his whole world has fallen in on itself too, nice to know I'm not the only one. My eyes shift towards Katherine before I can burn a hole through him. "This really is a beautiful wedding," she tells me, and it's then that I think she might be trying to distract me because then I notice how I'm squeezing her hand. The poor girl looks like she's had a run in with a boa constrictor but she tries not to show it in her eyes.

"Sorry." I pull my hand from hers only to wipe it down my trouser leg and then something I hadn't been ready for happens and she grabs it again. The surprise on my face would be obvious if she was even looking at me. Her eyes float around the garden but my hand is firmly grasped in hers. The sunlight catches her jawline just perfectly and makes her freckles that are splattered across her face stick out even more. She looks like a sun-kissed goddess and I can't believe she's here with me.

The rows of chairs around us start to fill and then the music picks up and I know it's time. I'm not sure if I'm ready, I don't think I'll ever be ready to see her again, not today, not in a week or in a month's time. But Katherine was right, annoyingly. Deep down, the idea of something happening to my mum, and me never getting to talk to her, hurts more than the pain of having to see her today ever would.

We stand and everyone turns to see her walk out of the house behind us, but I don't. I look at him. If he really loves her, I'll be able to see it on his face when he looks at her. If he was worth leaving my dad for, I think I'll be able to see it in his eyes.

As my mum comes into view as she passes me, my heart stops. She looks the same, ten years older, but her eyes are still the same ones that always matched mine and her blonde hair still flows down her back. Her face is still warm and tanned. She walks herself down the aisle holding a beautiful bouquet of orange and cream coloured flowers. She looks beautiful.

"Please, everyone be seated," the woman officiant says from up front, and Katherine has to basically pull me down to my seat but not before Mum sees me. Her eyes catch mine for a second before I force myself to look away.

"You okay?" Katherine whispers to me, leaning in close. Her scent flows up to me as a breeze passes by. I can barely look at her, I'm not sure if I am okay. I think I'm going to be sick. My heart feels too many things all at once. Some kind of affection and comfort for the girl next to me, sad and hurt for my dad sitting back home, and all of the above and more for the woman standing ahead of me in a white dress.

I'm having to confront far too many of my feelings today. Too many things I was content never dealing with. I never felt the need to, never felt like it was necessary, and why would I?

Why would I ever want to deal with being abandoned, left to be raised by an alcoholic?

Why would I want to deal with how that's made it completely impossible for me to have a normal relationship with Katherine?

Why would I want to deal with it when it never affected how I lived my life? I was fine, totally fine, and now I feel like I have to deal with them just to move forward. Just to keep going.

It never felt like they were holding me back, they were just protecting me, protecting these feelings. Now, it feels like they're holding me under the water, content to drown me.

The ceremony goes by quickly and somewhat pain free if you don't count the hand cramp both Katherine and I get from holding hands.

We stand on the side of the garden near a little bar handing out 'reception drinks' whatever that's meant to mean, all I know is Katherine got two, and when I reminded her I don't drink, she said, "Oh, I know, they're both for me." I laughed at her and she smiled at me and for that minute it felt so normal.

Mum and Lee went down to the beach that runs along the end of the garden down a few steps to take some pictures. The staff are currently running around, moving chairs and bringing tables in.

Weddings seem far too stressful and I don't think I ever want to do this myself. I mean I'll never have to, another thing I've sworn off.

"You know this is the first wedding I've been to," she says, taking a sip from the second glass in her hand; it's some pink and fruity looking thing and it coats her lips with sugar every time she takes a sip of it. I want to know what she tastes like with it on her.

I take a drink from my soda. "And you chose to pop your wedding cherry by coming to my estranged mother's wedding? Bold choice." I smile down at her as she looks over the garden again.

"Well 'choice' wouldn't be the word I'd use."

"I didn't make you come." I feel my tone shift as I say it. I don't like the idea of me making her do anything.

She must notice my shift in mood because she places her hand on my arm making me look down at her, a mocking smile on her face. "It was the puppy dog eyes." Her smile only grows bigger. "I couldn't help but save you."

Suddenly, a cloud of a white dress appears by the stairs. I watch as my mum starts walking towards me, us, and I'm stuck. Katherine squeezes my arm, I'm not sure she knows she's doing it, but I do know that I can't move.

I'm too busy having what I can only assume is some form of panic attack. I had come to the conclusion I would never see my mum again. I accepted that my memory of her walking out the door would be my last. She would forever be frozen in time. In my sixteen year old mind. As I'm standing there that's who I am, sixteen year old James. That version of me feels like it's only been five minutes since he saw his mum instead of the ten years it's actually been.

"I was only joking about the cake." My brows knit together even if I'm not looking at Katherine. "We can run if you want, but if you want to stay, I'm right here with you." We still don't look at each other, still focused right ahead of us but I understand what she's saying and it goes right to the organ I wasn't aware still beat in that way. If my heart hadn't already been in my throat it was now.

This girl.

This girl.

The girl I swore would be the end of me, very well might still be, but for a very different reason. This girl who seems to have seen every bad and broken part of me, and is still right here. With me. It seems like something we'll need to circle back to at a better time, but as my mum approaches us, that time is not right now.

"James," my mum breathes out as if she's been holding her breath the entire time she was walking over here. She looks over my face as if maybe I'm not real, at least that's how I feel.

It can't be real. She left, she was gone and now my brain can't understand how she's really here.

So much for who I am as a person is because of her. She bought me my first board, she showed me all the surfing basics and she's the one who took me to my first lesson. I don't think I'd be who I am today without surfing, I certainly wouldn't have gotten through the hard times without it. I wouldn't have the family I have now without it.

It always hurts my heart that even though my mum caused the destruction of everything, she was also the one who gave me the one thing that kept me together through it all. Dad never understood surfing but Mum, she did. She understood its power.

"I... I wasn't sure you'd really come." There's something in her voice I don't like, like sadness, I'm not a heartless guy and as much as I'd like to think I'm totally done with her, if she were to cry right now, I'm not sure I could stop myself from hugging her. She's the villain in my story but I'm not sure if it's all as black and white as it used to be, the red head next to me is all the proof that I need.

I don't even know how to respond to her now. Over the years, I thought of everything I'd say to her if I had the chance. Ranging from *Why* to *Do you understand what you did?* But none of that seems right in this moment. "I did RSVP."

"I know, I—" She takes a breath and her hands glide down the front of her dress. "I'm so happy to see you." Her eyes are glossy and her smile wavers but she holds back from crying, so that helps a little.

I feel Katherine shift next to me and I had almost forgotten about her hand in mine. "This is Katherine." My mum's eyes shift to the girl next to me and go a little wide but she catches herself quick enough. "We - umm we work together." I sound even less believable than when we talked to my nan.

My stutter seems to bring a smile to Katherine's face as I glance at her. She's tucked herself in my side, and I'm gone.

Dead. Done. Deceased.

Because, god, how can one girl be so hot and cute all at once. I want to scoop her up and carry her out of here.

She extends her hand out for my mum to shake. "Congratulations. You look beautiful, and this whole wedding is amazing, thank you for having me," Katherine tells her, and even though there's warmth to her voice, and sincerity in her words, I have no doubt she's still on my side, if taking sides were needed.

"It's lovely to meet you, Katherine. That's an American accent if my ears don't deceive me. What brings you to Australia?" my mum asks, and I'm not sure what's happening, if she thinks that Katherine's my girlfriend and that's why she's asking, or if she's stalling?

This is the most awkward situation I've ever been in, and Katherine has completely frozen.

And my brain spins into a frenzy. She wouldn't possibly tell my mum why she's really here, would she? She's standing like a statue next to me. I put my hand on the small of her back, because I'm here for her, too, and it may be too much to ask for, but I'm sure I can feel her relax into my touch.

"I'm visiting family, my aunt owns the store James works in, or I guess the store *we* work in." Relief fills my body, because any other answer could lead my mum to think I've forgiven the whole soulmate community. I have not, and I don't want her to think I will just forgive her and that's the reason why I'm here.

Her eyes float up to mine and the look she gives me says *thank you* but also *I'm sorry* and I don't have enough time to catch on to what's happening until it's happening. "I'm just going to pop to the restroom, give you guys a minute to talk." She's goes to walk away but I have a grip on her waist and I don't want her to go, I don't want to be alone or at least without her.

"You'll be fine, you've got to do this. I believe in you," she whispers to me as I let my hand fall and she slips back into the house. Just like that, my mum and I are alone.

"James." Hearing my mum's voice brings me back to the whole situation from years ago. I start to feel the panic again. The truth is I don't have to forgive her, I don't even have to hear her out. I learned a long time ago that family isn't always the people you're related to, it's the people who are always here for you, who show up, who you choose to spend your time with; I have that with Maddie, Ella, Willie, and maybe even now Katherine. They are my family, and that's okay,

I'm okay with that but I can't help but keep Katherine's words in my head: *You don't want to regret missing out.*

Katherine's kind of right I guess. If my mum was gone tomorrow, how would I feel? Would I be glad I didn't give her a chance to make up for the lost years, or would I wish we'd had a second chance? I don't know.

"I know that you hate me, I know I made so many mistakes and I know I've missed out on so much. I'm not sure I'll ever be able to tell you how sorry I am, but god, I'd love to try." Yeah she's definitely crying a little, I don't even want to look her in the eyes now, because no matter what, there's still a little part of me that will always love her. That'll always want to share my thoughts and feelings with her, to have her in my life. I think I'd just been burying that want so far down because it felt wrong. Like I shouldn't want that, I shouldn't even think about forgiving her. And not seeing her for so many years made that easy, easy to not miss what I didn't think about. But now, now we're face to face. I'm face to face with the life I think I could have again. "James, I don't expect you to ever forgive me but you showed up today and that gives me some hope." Her wavering smile tells me she means it and maybe this is it, maybe I can give her a chance.

"Yeah, well you can thank Katherine for that. Not sure I would have turned up if it weren't for her," I tell her, my tone light in hopes of easing the worry on her face.

Her smile grows brighter. "Is she someone special?" Her eyes shift toward something behind me, I look over my shoulder to see Katherine leaning on the door frame leading into the garden with a shit eating grin on her face looking at us. She tries to look away when I catch her but it's almost as if she can't, like she's locked into my gaze, and I like it.

I pull my eyes from her reluctantly to look back at Mum. "Yeah, I think she is, she's—it's hard to explain. She's special to me." It feels crazy to be sharing any of this with my mum, but the smile on her face tells me I'm making the right decision. "Are you guys going away for a honeymoon?" I ask her.

She nods. "A couple of weeks near the Gold Coast, why?"

I swallow down the lump that's formed again in my throat. "Maybe when you get back, we can meet up or something." I try to act as casual as possible when in fact my heart is beating so fast I'm sure it's a heart attack.

"I would love that."

"Okay." We stand there for a minute not sure whether to hug each other or not, it feels too soon. I'm not sure if I'm really okay or over anything right now. She seems to sense it too and just takes ahold of my hand, squeezes it and smiles.

I watch as she makes her way back over to the head table making some kind of hand signal to her new husband, he gives her a bright smile and two thumbs up, hugging her when she reaches him. He holds her like he never wants to let go of her ever, and she looks at him like he's hung the moon for her. They seem happy, and my heart breaks for a minute thinking I wish Dad could be just as happy.

"See, that wasn't so bad," Katherine says as she makes her way in front of me again.

And when I look down at her I'm not sure she knows she's doing it but she's looking at me the way my mum just looked at Lee. And I feel like maybe if I get the chance to hold her again, I won't ever want to let go.

I take her hand in mine again and pull her closer to me, her hand lands on my chest, our faces inches away from each other. I can feel her jagged breaths on my skin and I can see the way her eyes float down to my lips before looking me in the eyes again, and fuck me, if that doesn't make me groan at the thought of leaving with her right now...

"You leave me alone like that again, and I can't be held responsible for my actions, okay?" She just nods at me. I pull back slightly from her, not really wanting to. I want to kiss her while she looks at me like she's out of breath from just being near me, I want to hold her close to me for as long as I possibly can but I don't, even if she looks like she wants me to. "I guess we should go eat."

Chapter 26
Katherine

Sat around one of the round tables at the edge of the dance floor, I watch as the two little flower girls hold each other's hands as they spin around the floor. Careless and totally free.

The rest of the reception went by pretty seamlessly with Christina and Lee sitting at the head table by themselves. James didn't have to speak to his mom again which I think he was happy about. I'm not sorry for leaving him alone with her. The only way he was ever going to know if he could talk to her was to just do it.

He didn't seem to hate me after, apart from the kinda threatening me part. But then he looked at me like he wanted to make out—but then didn't. And I totally haven't been thinking about it since.

Okay, that's a lie. I can't stop looking at his mouth every time he talks. It's awful.

We sat at the table with his nan, which I was definitely happy about, as she told stories about James when he was a kid, information I would not have gotten otherwise.

"Oh, when James was a kid we could never get him out the sea, I was sure he was going to sprout a tail and swim away. That boy was made for the water the minute he met it." Her eyes all glassy and full of the past, I can't even begin to imagine what all of this has been like for her, loving her daughter and her grandson but also understanding the hurt one brought to the other.

It feels like only now, being around James and his mom, that I'm realizing the hurt and pain that soulmates can also bring, not just the love aspect of it all. I just always thought that much love could never bring any bad with it, I'd only seen the happiness it brought people. I'd seen how happy my mom and dad made each other. But as I sit there looking at him, my thoughts float back to the stone in my purse and how it not glowing is bringing me pain even if I don't completely understand it. I don't understand why I'm so angry or upset but I am, and I never thought my soul stone could make me feel like this. Even when I learned that Nick and I weren't soulmates, I didn't feel this way.

This was not what I had expected, any of it. I don't know what I thought would happen but none of this was even in my wildest dreams.

My mind snaps back to the present when he turns and smiles at me.

James has taken his jacket off now and I'm reminded once again of how the size of his arms makes me feel. The fabric of his shirt wraps tightly around his biceps and it looks like it might rip as he brings his glass up to his lips. His sleeves rolled up show off his tan, tattooed forearms, I can't help looking at them.

My eyes travel up his arm to the glass he's holding and then where it connects to his lips. It's actually criminal how many times a day I remember our kiss. I wish I didn't, it would be easier, but every time I look at him I see his hands on me and his lips locked to mine.

I have to stop myself from looking before I get lost in the sight of him, or before he notices I'm looking, but it's too late.

"Eyes up here, Katherine," he tells me, putting a finger under my chin and lifting my head up to look at his face. What a face it is and when did he get so close?

The fairy lights hanging in the trees behind him make him look like he's glowing, like some godly present sent down to grace me with his chiselled cheek bones, full lips, and muscular body.

Someone needs to cut me off, or I'm about to kiss him.

The first one seems like a better idea even if the latter is what I really want, but it's too dangerous.

"What is it?" he asks and I realise we're literally sitting so close with his hand under my chin. The skin where he's touching me feels warmer than it should, like my body is actively telling me I should want this. It doesn't need to remind me, my mind is doing a pretty good job of that all on its own. Painting a picture of what it would be like to kiss him here, his lips crushing down on mine, my hands back in his hair. The way he'd sigh when my body was finally pressed to his.

My eyes shift over to the people on the other side of the table and the ladies smiling at us.

We look like a couple.

My heart literally stops knowing that will never be possible.

"Dance with me?" I ask only to get out of this current situation. His eyebrows knit together before he stands and extends his hand to me. I take it and he leads me to the dance floor, only for me to finally see I've gone from the kiddie pool to the literal shark tank. And also the fact that I'm a lot more unstable on my feet than I thought I'd be.

Dancing together... who thought that was a good idea?

The DJ's been playing upbeat songs for the last twenty minutes only for him to change his mind the minute I step a toe on the dance floor.

I see you, Universe. I see you.

There is absolutely nothing I can do now as he snakes his arm around my waist, resting his hand on my hip, and his other hand still holding mine. This much contact should be setting me on fire, literally, and I'm not sure if it's because of the amount we've touched today but it's down to a nice warm feeling rather than a skin melting feeling. It's comforting and makes my stomach churn all at the same time.

I know he's not my soulmate, and yet today has me even more confused than before I knew that fact. The way he's found any excuse to hold my hand, and the way I keep catching him looking at me. Everything tells me I could do this again, spend time with him. It makes my soul happy in a way I'm not sure I've experienced before. Just being around him makes me feel happy, safe, calm. I like it, I like the feeling. I'm not sure I've felt all those things at the same time in a long while.

He looks down at my neck, then back at me again, smiling. It's not the same cocky grin he sports so much, but a real smile. He opens his mouth like he's going to say something but then closes it again. We sway to the music and he spins me around, bringing me back by putting both his hands on my hips leaving me no where to put my arms but around his neck. Our bodies touch at every point possible. Mine melts into every crevice of his muscles.

He smells incredible this close up, intoxicating, like sea salt and honey. I close my eyes for a second just to let myself pretend, just for tonight. Tomorrow I'll go back to sanity and I'll forget about this, whatever this is. But tonight I want to pretend, to live in this world, in this moment where we can do this without everything else getting in the way of us.

I don't think I've done that in such a long time, I almost forgot what it felt like to just be. I slowly open my eyes to find him already looking at me. "What?" My voice comes out cracked, I'm afraid it gives me away.

If it does, he doesn't say anything about it. He looks at me like he's finally seeing me in a new light.

"I haven't seen you without that necklace since I gave it to you," he tells me, but I don't register a single thing he says because for a minute I feel like all the characters I read about. It's something about the look on his face, the way he looks at me like I really am his sunshine, and for this moment I feel like I could be. I never felt so important to someone just from one look.

The twinkling lights behind him, the other couples dancing around us fade away. His hand squeezes my hip lightly as if just to remind me it's really him, that he is in fact standing, swaying, with me. It's all too much and I'm sure my legs are going to give up on me, all my senses are over loading.

"Thank you," I say just to try and get something out so he doesn't think I've lost all my brain cells. Then, as I look at him, it clicks together and he just smiles at me. "Wait, you got me this?"

He simply nods his head, a small bit of his hair falling from behind his ear tickles my face, I move it out of his face running my fingers through his hair. Then I'm thinking about how different this all feels. This doesn't feel like when we kissed and his hands were on me, this feels different. This time I have time to take in the way his breath on my face makes my mind foggy and the way I can see tiny specks of green in his eyes.

It takes me a minute before I can think again.

"I had no idea. I've—I've been trying to work out who got it for me for weeks." My brain stalls trying to think back to my birthday. "Why didn't you say anything?"

He lets out a small laugh. "I didn't think you'd want it if I told you I got it for you," he tells me truthfully.

Then we're doing it again. We're just looking at each other and I don't think I know what else to do.

I can't imagine ever feeling this way again. But he's not my soulmate, the fact that I can feel this way with someone and them not be 'the one' makes me a little sick.

Just for tonight, pretend it's okay.

My brain goes into full dumb mode and I say the first thing that comes to mind. "Humpback whales are my favourite."

"I know." He doesn't even miss a beat, doesn't even stutter as he totally confesses to paying far too much attention to the things I've said.

"Right. It's beautiful, I'm happy I can finally thank someone for it, so thank you." My instinct is to touch it like I would with my stone, but I don't want to break the bubble. I don't want to move. I'm scared once he lets go of me that'll be the end of it, that I'll sink away from him, never to come back up for air.

I don't know why but I rest my head on his chest. It's the most bizarre and most natural thing I've ever done. James' body goes stiff for a split second and I want to lift it again but then he relaxes. I swear I hear his heartbeat pick up.

I move my hand up into his hair and twist my fingers in the strands, and in response, he rests his chin on my head. It's the smallest gesture but it makes me feel safe in a way I'm not sure I've ever felt.

What am I doing?!

This is dangerous territory. I'm in danger. I can pretend as much as I want with my brain but I can't let my heart start to pretend as well. I can make my brain understand that this isn't real, but my heart? That's tricky, I don't think I can rewire it the same way I can my mind.

I don't budge from his grip, not that I'm sure he'd let me at this point.

As the song comes to an end and more people walk on to the make-shift dance floor in the middle of the grass. I drop my hands, then his fall from my hips, only to grab one of my hands hanging at my side.

"Do you want to go for a walk?" he asks, tilting his head towards the steps down to the beach.

I nod at him. I'm not sure why, this seems like a bad idea. That's a lie, I totally know why.

Why do I keep doing this?

As he leads me down the wooden steps, I don't look where I'm going, though I should. Instead, I just watch the way he walks while he keeps my hand in his. We hit sand, still warm beneath my feet, but then I feel sick. It's not my usual brand of anxiety I'm feeling.

I've been alone with him before, in the shop, outside his house. Hell, I was just dancing with him, but only now does it hit me.

I feel nervous being alone with him. The feeling in my stomach is a 'worried you're going to say something wrong' kind of sickness. When you like someone so much and don't want to fuck it up.

As if he can read my thoughts, he says, "I've never known you to be so quiet."

"Sorry." I finally slip my hand from his, big mistake, because I wobble on the uneven sand and rocks. I don't take his hand again though and it makes me feel cold. But it does unfog my brain. "It's just a beautiful night, I don't think I've been to the beach at night since I got here. I want to see the sunset from Stargaze Perch Lighthouse. It's on my list."

"You have a list? Why am I not surprised." He lets out a little laugh before his face turns back to mine. "Well maybe we could do that. Together, I mean." He scratches the back on his neck looking away from me, I can only imagine he's realised how that sounds.

"Yeah, maybe." I smile to myself, it's a weird mix of feelings thinking about it. We're making new plans with each other before tonight is even over, like he can't wait to spend more time with me. I'd be excited if today hadn't shown me that it's a bad idea to even consider getting closer to him.

"It's my favourite time," he tells me, bringing me back to the moment. "The beach at night. When I was a kid and things weren't great, I'd go down and walk along the beach just to clear my head." He looks at me like he's just spilled the codes to some secret detonation, but regardless, it's nice having an actual conversation.

The more I know about him, the more he seems like a real person. A real person you would like and could maybe even love.

Then I find myself spilling my own secret codes. "I get that. When I lost my dad at first, I'd get the boat to the Statue of Liberty and just stay there all day. Looking at the city from the outside, looking at tourists who had come from all over the place, it let me stop feeling like myself for a minute, like I could pretend to be one of those tourists, it sounds silly, but…"

"No, it doesn't," he interrupts me and I can see his smile even in the dim light. It sounds weird but I know that he actually gets it in a way, maybe not the same way but in his own way he does. "When your…" he starts and stops himself. We've walked a ways down the beach without me even realising and he stops completely.

He looks up over the hill back to the house, and when he looks back at me, it's like his eyes are asking me to leave with him. Then it's gone and it's replaced by something I'm familiar with, something I don't want to see from him, pity. And I'm worried he's about to ask me something about my dad, so I jump ahead of it before his question can catch me off guard.

"He was the best man I knew," I start taking his hand back in mine, swinging it a little for no reason. "My dad was." I let out a sigh looking at the sea behind James. "He would have loved this, he loved an adventure. Running off to places he'd never been. Ella was the wild child, he said, but I think he had a bit of that in him too. Sadly he didn't give me any of that," I finish and look back up at him and he's already looking at me.

"I don't know about that, you don't think he would have called what you're doing an adventure?" he asks and it's the first time he's talking about me coming to Australia without insulting me at the same time.

"Honestly?" He looks at me like *obviously*. "I think he'd actually be kinda disappointed." He slides his hand up my arm but doesn't say anything. "He wasn't really into the whole soulmate thing, that all comes from my mom's side of the family. I guess he was kinda like your mom, he was married when he met my mom. His marriage broke down on its own, my mom stayed far away from him until he was divorced. Depending what side of the story you're on, it wasn't a fairytale."

"Is that why you're so determined to find yours?" he asks slowly like he's just worked something out.

"What do you mean?" I ask, just wondering if he will, even with everything, get it.

"Well... I guess it's just if he didn't meet your mum till late, and then, well, five years ago..." The carefulness in his voice almost brings tears to my eyes. "I'm just saying it makes sense if that's why you want to find yours so much, have more time with them."

He's right. So right it hurts my insides, because if he didn't just hit the nail on the head, I'd do this 'thing' between us for longer. I'd stay and spend time with him, if that's what he wanted and find my soulmate later whenever this thing stopped working but I just can't. I can't bring myself to do that to myself, not when I know time is fleeting and special. "We never know how much time we'll get," is all I say.

It dawns on me that no one has even understood that before, no one has ever got why I want this so early. Everyone thinks I'm stupid and too young but he might just actually get it. He might actually understand me.

"There's something else." He looks at me so hard I think he can see right into my soul.

"There is?" I play with the silver ring he's wearing on his middle finger.

"Yeah, I don't know but there's something else in your eyes when you say that. Like that's not the whole story." He waits a second when I don't answer because that is it, the whole story.

"I... That's... shit." I feel my heart become heavy in my chest. "I guess... I'm kinda scared that if someone's not cosmically forced to be with me then they'll leave." I haven't thought that in such a long time, not since my lowest points. "I don't know if you've noticed, but I can be a lot." I laugh, but it's that laugh you do when it's not funny and you actually want to cry.

"Yeah, you're a lot." My eyebrows rise. "A lot of everything, you're the kind of person who puts a lot into everything, you're not a half in, half out person, Katherine. You give everyone everything. If anyone ever makes you feel like you're too much, they're not worth your everything, because your everything makes people feel special." I'd kiss him if I wasn't in shock. He looks over my face and I watch as his cheeks go red. "Do you think he'd like me?" he asks and it catches me off guard.

I can't even address everything else he's just said. "Oh, absolutely not," I say sarcastically, laughing, and he laughs with me. "Yes, annoyingly so. I think he would have liked you. My mom on the other hand, I'm more like her, so she'll hate you." I laugh again but he's not, I don't know why I said that, like he's going to meet her, why would he? My mouth moves before my brain thinks and I say, "However I turned out liking you a lot more than I originally planned." It's the only kind of confession I'm able to give and I don't know why I feel the overwhelming need to tell him something.

We're just looking at each other again. It's a game I'm not sure how to play, or win or lose. Then in a second it's like he remembers who we are. Where he is. Who I am and who he is and why he shouldn't be looking at me the way he is. The way I'm looking at him.

"We should probably go back," he says, and he's right but I don't want him to be.

I want to stay here on this beach and pretend nothing else exists. If the rest of the world didn't have a say, I'd probably live right here if I could, in this moment. If not with him, then just in this feeling I have, as if for the first time in a long time someone sees me.

I nod and turn, walking back up towards the wooden stairs. His hand is still intertwined with mine as we walk.

James' fingers brush against mine, then slip away completely. A shiver races down my spine, throwing me out of kilter completely.

Reaching for the first step, my foot snags on something hidden in the dark. The world tilts sideways and a yelp escapes me before I can stop it. In a blur of movement, James' hand shoots out to catch me, so strong and warm. But it's not enough. I crash down on the wooden steps, the force sending a shot of pain up my legs.

I see it all happen like I'm watching it from above my own body. James kneels beside me, his face creased with worry. "Jesus, Katherine, are you okay?" he asks, his voice tight with concern.

My breath is lodged in my throat. Embarrassment burns in my cheeks, hotter than the pain searing my palms. Slowly, my limbs start to feel like my own again, the throbbing in my legs very real but not nearly as bad as my initial panic has me thinking.

"You're bleeding," he tells me as if I can't already tell. He also sounds shocked, and he looks it too which seems somewhat out of character for him. There's also something in his eyes, worry maybe?

I let myself think for a second it's not there but it is. "Are you okay?" he asks again, because I realize I haven't said anything. I nod my head, giving him a smile. His hand is on my bare shoulder looking over my face, and the way he rubs his thumb back and forth, I almost forget about the stinging in my knees.

"I don't think I can climb the stairs." I laugh a little. He doesn't say anything but he links his arm under my knees and the other round my back. I have to fight myself to put my arms around his neck as much as I want to, and god I want to, but we're already teetering on the edge of danger. And I don't know if I'm trying to fall over that edge yet.

I realise he's heading towards the kitchen when we enter the house and a small amount of staff that are left are mingling in the corridor.

"First aid box?" he asks when we reach them. I realise that's how rude he used to sound when talking to me. For the first time, I start to feel stupid. I look like a little twelve year old being carried and I want nothing more than to be put down as they look at me.

"Under the sink." A tall slim man with blonde ageing hair says pointing into the grand sized room.

He sets me down on a kitchen counter and turns to look for the kit.

I watch him from my vantage point. The fabric of his shirt stretches more over his back and he rolls his sleeves up more as he digs into the back of the cupboard. He runs a hand through his hair as he walks to me and when it falls back in his face, I smile at him. Because I kinda love how he's always doing that, like he can't stop himself. I see him do it all the time in the store, when he's teaching, I feel like I need to teach him how to put it in a ponytail.

He sets the box down next to me and opens it, looking for something. "This is going to sting," he tells me, then he rips open a packet of what I can only assume is some kind of antibacterial wipe. I don't say anything but bite down on my bottom lip as he brings it to my skin.

Chapter 27
James

I look back up at her before I do anything but she's looking down at my hands biting her lip, which she must absolutely stop doing right this minute.

Blood on her knees, dirt on her hands and still the most beautiful thing I've seen. I remind myself what I'm doing and start to wipe her knees gently.

She lets out a hissing noise and lunges forward grabbing my shoulder with one of her hands as the other braces her on the counter top. Her nails dig in a little.

"Sorry," she says sheepishly and removes her hand. I wish she wouldn't. With her at this height, we're pretty much face-to-face and it's unbearable. "I'll stop being a baby," she tells me, smiling, and I go back to her knees trying my absolute best to not be distracted by my hands on her bare thigh.

I can feel her eyes on me and I'm not so worried about what her eyes will tell me but what mine will show her. The last hour or so with her have been painful in a totally new way, in a way I don't want to stop being with her. In a way that makes me want to stop whatever this thing is we're doing. Because we're doing something, even if I'm not too sure what it is.

Dancing with her might have been the breaking point, her hands in my hair and my hands on her, I thought I was going to drop dead right there but hearing her speak about her dad the way she did on the beach, that was something else.

She trusted me.

Knowing that, knowing that she trusts me, even just a bit, that did something to me. I know people trust me; Ella trusts me with her business, Maddie trusts me with literally everything, but this is just further proof to me that Katherine is different. Because when she trusts me, I get a light and dizzy feeling like nothing I've felt before.

Knowing she was being real, completely real with me, that was something else. Because I get the feeling she doesn't do that often. I'm only guessing from the way I've seen her with other people, it's in the way she smiles. When she smiled at me today, it was the kind that reached her eyes, that had her glowing even more. That's how she looks when she's being honest, too.

I wasn't lying about her giving her everything to everyone, but I don't know how other people feel about it. I only know how I feel, I meant me, she makes me feel special like I matter. To her. And I'm scared to think about why that matters so much to me.

"Will I survive, doctor?" she asks me and I can only guess she's looking at my hands that have stopped moving. Her voice is light and soft and not a shred of the hate I thought she felt towards me.

But I can't move, I can't physically get myself to move my head and it's like she's reading my mind, because the next second, her hand is under my chin. She tilts my head up until my eyes catch hers.

She looks back at me like she's letting me see all of her in that moment and I have no doubt I'm looking back at her in the same way.

She's here.

Here with me.

Everything today would have been far too much if it hadn't been for her. Keeping me calm and keeping me in one piece. I could have so easily fallen apart a million times today but I didn't.

Because of her.

Now as my chest constricts, I know it's because I feel like I'm falling apart but in a completely different way. Because of her. I can't tell if I like it, hate it or want to run like the real coward I am.

And then all at once I forget everything else as I move her hand from my chin back to the counter top, and straighten myself.

"What are you thinking about?" she asks me, her voice quiet, matching the silence in the room that's threatening to swallow us up.

God, I want to think of something smart to say to her but I can't.

"Kissing you." It just comes out, it just falls out of my mouth.

Her lips part slightly like she's going to say something but doesn't and I want to crawl out of my own skin. It's like a disaster you can't look away from no matter how much you wish you could. I wish I hadn't said it. Because this is so much worse than just wanting her, knowing she doesn't want me to hurts.

The noise from outside seeps into the room and my head moves towards the window knowing full well I have to go back out there.

Her fingers make contact with my cheek moving my head back to face her. If her hands don't feel like pure lightning, pure electricity on my skin, I don't know what will. Her eyes tell me she feels it too but she doesn't voice it.

I can see it in her eyes, the cogs turning, she's calculating everything in that perfect head of hers but I wish she wouldn't. I wish she would just do whatever she was feeling in that moment, let her heart guide her for a moment. One moment would be all I'd need from her.

Because I know I'm not the one for her, not her true love, her soulmate. But I could be just for a moment.

"Tell me what you want," I plead.

"You."

I don't waste a second because I know her and I know she'll think of a million cons why to take it back. But I want to show her why we should give this a shot.

My lips crash onto hers, and holding the counter is all I can do to not fall totally over. I kiss her softly and gently as if we have all the time in the world, even if we don't, but she makes me feel like the rest of the world slips away.

The way she kisses me back makes my head foggy. I've thought about our first kiss more times then I care to admit, practically memorising the way she felt on my lips. And kissing her now feels like a homecoming, like that first kiss was just a taste of what life with her could feel like.

She moves her legs, letting me stand in-between them to be closer to her. Once I am, she cups my face with her hands and rubs my cheeks with her thumbs, and my god, I don't want to do this with anyone else.

It's an alarming thought.

My fingers dig into her hips slightly but the touch makes her gasp giving me the perfect moment to get acquainted with her tongue and she doesn't fight me for long, and the soft sigh she lets out makes me think she's thinking all the same things as I am.

That maybe I'm the best kiss she's ever had too, that maybe she could do this forever with me too.

The hand on the back of her neck keeps her there like I'm worried she might run away from me any second. But as my hand moves from her hip to her thigh, she pulls me closer to her with her foot and I know she doesn't want me to go anywhere. And neither do I.

The waistband of my slacks begin to get tighter and tighter the longer her hands are on me and I'm trying my best to be controlled with her, to hold back. To treat her the way she should be treated, to touch her delicate skin with all the care it deserves.

But when we're this close, I can feel the points of her nipples rub against my shirt and she lets out a moan, deep in her throat and it travels down my whole body. Then another moan when I shift and they rub against me again and I know the sound is just for me. Only for me, it eats at me. The last few threads of my sanity snapping one by one.

My fingers inch their way up under her dress, landing on the soft skin on her hip. I can feel the deep breath she takes while my mouth is still attached to hers, the goosebumps rising on her back where my other hand is trailing down and it turns parts of me inside out. The hold I have on myself starts slipping through my fingers.

But this feels good. Too good.

I only pull away when I think the both of us might suffocate and lean my forehead on hers. Our heavy breathing is the only noise through the silent house, with the soft sound of music and laughter leaking through the window behind her.

"Wow." I don't have the capacity to make a whole sentence. She's stolen every word I know with that kiss.

"Right," she says back laughing a little at our current state. I lift my head so I can look at her properly again, to check that she's real. I don't know what's going on in her head and I hate that. I don't know if she's thinking the same as me, that was the best kiss I've ever had in my life.

I was quite content pretending with her tonight, to have her for just tonight. And then tomorrow, I'd wake up and we'd go back to what we were before and I'd forget everything I felt and thought about her. I'd go back to remembering why she's here and that would be enough for me.

That will not happen now.

I need her like I need air and water and surfing. What do I do now?
I can't do this to her.
But I want to, I want to be selfish with her.

"We should—"

"Do that again?" I cut her off, because kissing her again would at least calm me down, stop my brain from spinning out.

"Not what I was going to say." But as she says it, she looks at my lips and her hands find their way back into my hair.

I hear the shuffling of feet from outside the kitchen, I'd most completely forgotten anyone else was even here. My mum's head appears around the door as I look over my shoulder.

"Hey, Lee is going to make a speech, will you guys come back outside?" She's gone before either of us can respond, like she was never here. But our bubbles burst. The moment is gone.

Our moment, and before I can even blink her hands are back in her lap, the feeling of her hands in my hair a ghost of the memory. She slides off the countertop and moves around me toward the door.

"Come on," she tells me, holding a hand out for me as I look at the countertop, hating the space she's left behind. Wishing she was still here. Still with all the possibilities of us.

Chapter 28
Katherine

"And then what?" Bella was the first person I thought of when I got back from the wedding. She's been saying 'and then what?' for what feels like the whole conversation and my social battery is about to run out at this point.

"And then we kissed." It comes out so fast I'm almost hoping she didn't hear it, because seriously, what am I meant to do?

"WHAT?!" she screeches and I pull the phone away from me to try and save my poor ear drums. "You saved that for the end! You should have started with that."

"Yeah, well..."

"Tell me everything." God, I wish I was with her right now; we'd be sitting on my bedroom floor with a glass of wine and pizza laughing and crying about the whole thing. Like we've always done—like we've done for every crush, every school drama, every time we needed each other we'd be here in a second. Granted, in high school, it was Gatorade.

It's not the same without her, and it makes my heart hurt.

"Nothing to say, it was a kiss." I don't know why I'm playing it so cool with her, I know my tone gives me away before I have a chance to catch it. I guess maybe I'm just embarrassed of how much I'm screwing this whole thing up, of how my feelings have changed so much. But still, she knows even if I don't tell her every little bit.

"Bullshit. Katherine, I'm not sure who you think I am, but I'm your best friend."

"Yes, Bella, I am very aware." I let out a long sigh. God, I'm exhausted, physically and mentally, and maybe a little emotionally.

I hear a scoff at the end of her line and my ability to read her hasn't wavered since moving. I'm in for what I fear is a lecture or some truth I don't want to hear. "That kiss meant something, and you know it." She pauses and I hold my breath. "You like him, don't you?"

I'm especially exhausted of this question. Because I know the answer. But I can't even admit the truth to myself let alone to Bella. Not right now, not when I'm still trying to wind my brain down from today.

My best bet is to lie, and sleep on it.

"No! That would be ridiculous, it's obviously just some kind of physical thing. He doesn't even believe and I don't think he's the kinda person who'd be my soulmate." I know it for a fact because of the stone. But I can't let her know I took the stone back.

Did I honestly think I liked him enough to check with my stone? Did I really think the physical feeling I'd been having towards him was really enough? Enough for me to think we could really put everything aside, that this could be anything more than it is right now? The thought makes my stomach twist and I think I might be sick, or maybe cry, I don't know.

My heart squeezes when I think of it. When I finally find my soulmate, will I forget how I felt with him today? Will all these feelings simply disappear and I'll forget how painful they feel right now. I'll forget how I felt when he opened up and told me things about himself, I hope in a way I won't, how messed up is that. That I want to remember my time spent with him even if he's not the one.

I've spent all this time here thinking I'd just fall upon my soulmate or they'd just walk into the shop one day. I let myself get too close to someone I knew deep down wouldn't be my soulmate, I'm not even sure he'd want to be mine. I let myself get attached to him and start to think of him in a way I shouldn't have and now I know it's not real. How sad that my heart felt like it was. Do I even know what I want, or what I need? Because for a minute tonight, it felt like I needed him, I felt safe with him in a way I haven't in years.

I'll think about it in years to come and probably cry at the thought.

"I don't think that's how it works, Katherine. I don't think you know what kind of person is meant to be your soulmate. I think the universe decides that for you."

The words she says makes me think I've just said all that out loud because they hit me harder than I think she meant. I fall down on my bed kicking my shoes off.

The silence stretches longer than I intend it to because I have no response to that at all.

"Have you answered Tommy's email?" she asks, changing the subject to something just as confusing.

If I had gotten that email a few months ago back when I was in New York I wouldn't have even thought twice about it. I would have been knocking on his office door in a heartbeat, but now, now I'm here and my heart and head are so confused that I'm not sure what's the best choice any more.

I hate not knowing and I hate surprises. I hate not knowing the path I'm meant to take. I like lists and planning and knowing. I was a curious kid, always wanting answers. Never settling for a simple 'because I said so' from my parents or teachers. Journalism was such an easy career choice; digging for things, understanding the things that have happened, the reason people have chosen to do things.

I also know from years of therapy that it's a side effect of my anxiety. You can't be anxious about events if you know what's going to happen. If you know the outcome of everything happening to you. I can control the outcome if I know all the angles. The problem usually stands with the emotions that follow, and other people don't always play along with that.

My biggest fear is and has always been making the wrong choice, I always think I'll make the wrong decision. It's another reason why my soulmate is so important to me, not just the legacy I feel I have to keep up or just the love I know I'll get from that person, but because it takes the decision away from me completely. The right choice has always been made for me.

"No, I will tomorrow. Thank you again." I try to make my voice sound as happy as I should be. She stuck her neck out for me, and I should be over the moon about it and yet something inside me feels so sad.

"Kat?"

"Yeah?"

"Did you want it to be more than a kiss?"

God, I wish I knew the answer to that.

Chapter 29
James

"And then what?" I've been standing waiting to walk into my bedroom for twenty minutes and my dad is acting like a teenage girl at a sleepover.

I've been reliving my day at the wedding with my dad since I got in, minus the kiss of course. I managed to get into the house and to my bedroom door, and then I was trapped. He's like a dog, and worryingly, I'm the bone.

The most surprising thing about it all is that not a single one of the questions has been about Mum. Every one of them has been about Katherine.

I can't tell if I should be worried or not.

"And then I drove her home." I've managed to get my jacket, tie and shoes off during this interrogation. While being very careful with my words to not give too much away.

"Oh, son." I can't tell if it's the alcohol in his system or if it's actual concern in his eyes; I haven't seen that in a while, normally it's the other way around. I finally scan the living room only just registering the rest of the house.

It's tidy.

I don't see a single beer bottle or box of pizza. Now, I'm glad I'm leaning on my door frame or I might fall over. I think about asking him about it and then I decide against it. I don't want to push him one way or the other. I've learned over the years that with him it's best not to acknowledge these kinds of things because it'll only last a few days. Also like if I bring it up it ends up pushing him further the other way, if that is even possible. Like if I voice it, out loud, not in my head, the universe just wants to laugh even harder at me.

"James, do you like this girl?" Yeah, that one does knock me back a little.

I blink at him like I've misunderstood what he's said. "What?"

My dad's not a tall man, I got my height from my grandad, not my parents. I passed my mum in height when I was about eleven, and then my dad when I was fourteen; I pretty much stopped looking up to him in more ways than one because I had to become the adult in the house. But the way he's looking at me now, it's the most fatherly look I've gotten in years, I feel like I'm a preteen all over again.

"Do you like her?" He's sat back down again now, his arms crossed in a 'don't lie to me' kind of way.

I guess the truth is my only option in this one, something that's not easy for me. Not when it comes to feelings, anyway.

A long sigh leaves my mouth. "Yeah I do. I don't get it at all but it doesn't matter. She's here for her soulmate, I'd just be a placeholder regardless." I blink again at him, shocked at my own total honesty about it. I don't think I've admitted to myself that I do like her, or how I feel about the way I know we'll have to leave things. Do I really think that these physical feelings we clearly have towards each other are really enough for her? Are they enough for me to put aside everything I think about people like her? People who put all their faith into something I think only ruins things.

Will I ruin her? Her well laid out plans, her goal...

My hands slide into my pockets as I think about the way she looked at me tonight. Like maybe all of this could be enough for her. The way we danced together, the way our lips moulded together.

His eyes linger on my face for a minute. "And you know for a fact you're not hers?" he questions.

I let out a dry laugh. It's not like the idea hadn't crossed my mind before but considering my feelings about soul stones compared to hers how could we be. Soulmates are meant to be people who are compatible, not people who almost tore each other's heads off the first time they met. "Her soulmate? I don't think the mysterious universe wants me and her together."

The universe hates you, the little voice in my head tells me, I'm not sure it's wrong. How cruel of it to put this girl in front of me and yet so far away at the same time. To once again put someone in my life who'll walk away from me in the end.

"And you've had a conversation with this mysterious universe, I'm assuming, because in my mind that would be the only thing that would stop my determined son from going after what he wants." He's right, because in any other situation, I'd be putting everything in it. Ready to prove everyone wrong but this is different, this isn't a job or an accomplishment. Those things, I worked for them. I hold onto these things and work, and work, until I've made it. Prove I deserve them to people who've been questioning me the whole time. That's what it was like when we got to town. People talking about the drunk and his no good teen boy who moved to town. That we'd only bring down the town's vault. My dad, maybe he played right into their hands, but me, I stood tall. I worked hard and I made them eat their words.

I teach most of their kids how to surf now.

But this is Katherine.

She's not something I can just take, or train for. People like Katherine, if I believe there's anyone else out there like her, you can't prepare for them. You can't be ready for the whirlwind that they are. They stir you up in ways you've never known, leave you questioning every belief you've taught yourself, and then leave again. Maybe I could work for her too, prove to her I'm worth more than what she thinks.

"She doesn't want me." I spit it out like the words might eat me alive if I keep them in my mouth too long. There's so much self-pity strung through the words it feels pathetic but I can't help but think it.

Why would she?

"And I'm also assuming you've had a conversation with her about this then? Or are you just taking a guess?" His eyebrows go up and I shake my head at him. "Because Kat, she's changed you, you seem different somehow. You've been changing since she got here and I don't think that's a coincidence. I can't think of a single reason why you wouldn't be good enough for her."

I have nothing more to say. It'll just be a back and forth with him, I can tell. He's been thinking about this for longer than I thought.

"Your mum and I, we—we made a lot of mistakes," he admits and I feel like all the air has been sucked out of the room, and knocked out of my chest too. "I made a lot of mistakes. You, all on your own, made yourself the hard working, accomplished, handsome young man you are today."

It's hard to tell who might cry first, me or him.

"James, tell the girl you like her." And that's all he says before he gets up, pats me on the shoulder, and walks off to his room.

I stand in that doorway for at least another ten minutes, staring at the spot he was sitting. Even after everything he's been through with Mum it seems mad for him to be pushing this. My head is swimming too much for me to think about how this makes me feel about maybe having a relationship with my mum.

My father has always been a man of few words, always saving them up for important moments like these. Giving the truth, advice, you don't want but know is right. Saying things you didn't even know you already knew, it makes me frustrated that I can't have him like this all the time. I shake my head not wanting to speak him drinking again into the universe.

Maybe he's right.
Maybe I'll fall flat on my face.
Maybe it's worth it.

The last time I had a sleepless night like this, my mum was still here.

When I couldn't sleep, she would open the curtains in my room, the room in the house she was part of, and we'd stare out the window at the sea and I'd watch the waves until I fell asleep in her arms.

I can't stop thinking about all the things she did. Maybe I do believe she did love me or still loves me, but I'm still not sure I can fully forgive her—at least I can't for a while.

Given everything, *that* should be what's keeping me up, seeing my mum today, but it's not.

It's Katherine.

I haven't stopped thinking about her since I dropped her off at Ella's hours ago. It's almost 2 a.m. now and I can't do this. I can't sleep or really breathe until I talk to her.

Talk to her about what this means now, how she feels about it all. I need to know if it's just me staying awake at night thinking about the way her soft skin feels against my callused fingers. Talk to her about what I meant the other night about not hating her. Talk to her about how it made me feel to see her like that, broken and falling apart and how I just wanted to scoop her up and hold her till she felt whole again.

Talk to her about how fucking scared I am by these feelings and how I'll feel when she leaves with another guy.

Will he understand her? Will he believe in the things she does? Will that make her happy?

How am I meant to leave things like this when she kissed me that way. What are we meant to do? Pretend it never happened like we did last time? I can't do that, I could barely do that last time. Not this time, not when it's all I can think about, consuming my brain, and my dick, too, apparently as it twitches at the thought of her on that countertop.

I need to talk to her. Not tomorrow, or the next time she'll let me, because god knows she'll be avoiding me for days.

Now. I have to see her now.

Sitting up from my bed, I get dressed and leave.

Chapter 30
Katherine

As if I thought I'd be able to sleep after a night like that, it was like something out of a movie or romance book. I touch my fingers to my lips remembering the way he kissed me only hours ago and my mind goes blank at the thought.

How am I meant to ever function again after that? It was passionate and sweet and soft and furious all at the same time and I feel my body buzz at the memory. I squeeze my thighs together as the images of him standing in between my thighs flash through my mind.

Sitting with my laptop in my lap, I stare out my French doors into the dark garden as I sit on the floor. The air is still warm even though the sun disappeared hours again, the thick air doesn't help the tight knot in my throat.

A knot only made bigger by the soul stone now in my bed side table drawer. God, I couldn't tell Ella I had taken it when I got back, I felt too awful about going through her room. After everything she's done for me, it feels like I've betrayed her.

Yet I couldn't bring myself to actually put my necklace back on, not after tonight, I feel betrayed by it. I can't look at it without feeling like it's been lying to me all these years, like it was always telling me how happy it would make me, just to rip my heart out of my chest instead. So now it's burning a hole in my drawer.

I stare at the blinking cursor on my screen, thinking about how Tommy Mitchel might very well see this blog post and it's the mad ramblings of a confused sleepless girl but I still haven't replied to his email or thought about what to do.

But right now, I seem to have too much to think about and this is the only thing that helps. This is the only thing, short of spilling my guts to a real person, that helps. That lets me sort my thoughts in front of me, lets me see the things that are swirling around.

When I was little, my nan used to tell me a story about a man. A man who travelled the world in search of his one true love. The woman who would make him happy like no other, someone to share his dreams and hopes with. This man sailed from country to country looking for her, but he had no luck.

She told me that one day he woke up in a country he'd forgotten the name of with a tight feeling in his chest. He was worried he was dying, so the man stepped out of the house he was staying in to find a woman all of ten feet away from him with a basket of flowers and crystals. They took one look at each other and knew.

Love at first sight.

Right there in a little village in a country he couldn't remember the name of, he had finally found her. Nan said they fell in love instantly and that they were the first soulmates, as legend goes anyway.

I like that story, I like that two people who never would have found each other, against all odds, did. Now the likelihood of that being the real start of soul stones and soulmates is thin but it gives me hope. They didn't have a stone helping them and yet they found each other anyway. He didn't have an old lady in DC telling him what country to look in or a glowing stone to tell him when he had it right. He only had himself and a belief that he would find the one.

I'm not sure if I have that belief. I have it for soul stones, I've seen first hand the kind of love they bring together, in my nan and grandad, and in my mom and dad but I don't know if I have that belief in myself. I don't know if I'll know when I find them. I don't know if I'll trust myself to believe it might be real without that stone.

I never thought I'd wish this in a million years, it's all I've ever known, but right now I kinda wish none of it existed. I wish that I could fall in love again and again and believe it was true love. Wish that I'd have to put myself back together again and feel that pain. I've only ever felt that once, when I lost Dad, the feeling that someone had physically ripped my heart out and stomped on it, it was the most real thing I've ever felt in my life.

That thought scares me.

I save the blog post and watch as it loads onto my front page. The feeling of tears rolling down my cheeks reminds me that this is all so real and not a legend or campfire story told to children about love and faith.

My heart speeds up as I hear a rustle coming from the back gate round the corner of the house.

I hear the back-gate open and then footsteps. "Shit." The voice is quiet as I hear a low grumble like they tripped on the decking.

Then James in full view of me squinting at the light.

My heart stops and then speeds up again. I have to stop myself from just throwing myself at him and asking him to hold me.

"Katherine," he whispers again and I don't know when it happened or when it changed, but listening to him say my name is something different. It lights something in me. It's like he's singing a song just for me and it's intoxicating. I think about all the times he said my name before and how irritated I was, how insufferable I thought he was, and now here I am practically swooning over him saying it.

"Katherine?" he says again, bringing me back to the place I actually am.

I close my laptop, lifting it off my legs and place it on the floor as I stand. "What are you doing here?" I ask, trying my best to lace it with some anger or irritation to make all this go back to how it was but I'm too happy to see him.

He just looks at me with a small smile on his face as I step out onto the porch right outside my door, he stays on the grass just in front keeping some distance between us, that I'm both happy for and sad about. "Nice pjs," he tells me and my cheeks flush knowing I'm wearing the Taylor Swift t-shirt Nick got me and a pair of shorts. He only smiles more as my cheeks glow. God, that smile.

I try to keep my lips thin as I take a step closer to him. I'm very aware that Ella is only a few rooms over from me and I'd never hear the end of it if she saw him here like this. "What are you doing here?" I ask again, hoping to get a response this time.

His eyes linger on my lips for a second before he speaks. "I just..." He runs a hand through his hair, the curls fall all over the place and all I can think is how I want my fingers in it. "I couldn't sleep," is all he says. I know what he means, I know how to read the words in-between what he's saying. It doesn't make me understand the situation any more but at least I know he's in the same boat as me.

"Me, either." My arms come up and cross over my chest, like it's the only defence I have, the only kind of barrier I have. The truth is admitting that to him makes me nervous.

It's only then I notice I've made my way over to him. The porch giving me a little bit of extra height but not enough for me to be the same height as him.

The way the light hits his face only makes him more beautiful, his jaw looks even sharper and his cheek bones even higher and his blue eyes sparkle with something I'm sure is not good for me as he looks down at me.

"I can't stop thinking about you," he tells me and I think my heart melts right there on that back porch and if not my heart, then my legs definitely do. I know deep down it's probably just a line he tells girls but it sure does work on this girl right now.

I can't stop thinking about him either or at least that kiss, or any of our kisses, but I can't tell him that I can't be that open with him because I only see it ending with me broken into pieces. "James."

"Katherine."

"I'm not sure what you want me to say." My arms fall back to my sides.

He doesn't say anything back and all words in the English language seem to leave me as he moves his hand around to the back of my neck.

"Tell me you want me to kiss you again. Tell me you want to feel my hands on your skin as much as I do. Tell me this isn't all in my head, that it's not totally one sided. Tell me I've not completely lost my mind showing up here cause it kinda feels like I have." His face is so close to mine but I see it, he's being honest. There's not a hint of confidence, he's nervous, too. I don't know what I'm meant to do, I could tell him 'no' and he'd let me go and leave.

The words are at the tip of my tongue, they're right here. I'm basically playing with my own heart. If we do this again, I know it's not just going to be a kiss, I know it's going to be so much harder to walk away, because we'll have to.

Maybe just try and let life happen for a change.

Ella's words ring in my head as I go back and forth with mine. Is this what she meant?

"I think losing your mind might be contagious." I look over at his face. My ears ring and I can feel my heart beating in my head as he watches me. The ball is in my sweaty hands and I don't want to drop it. "Kiss me, James." His eyes light up before his face is too close for me to see them and his lips are on mine again and it's like the world goes quiet around me.

It's not like last time, it doesn't take my brain a whole minute to click in gear. I'm ready this time. He kisses me like he's been starved for weeks and I'm the only thing that he wants. It feels different to be wanted like that, wanted in a way that feels like a need.

His hand near my neck loses itself in my hair, pulling my head back lightly so he can kiss me deeper and his other arm wraps around my waist, basically keeping me from falling over. He's in control here and I love it, it's like he's taken all the worry about me doing the wrong thing away from me. My hands go straight to his hair so desperately, wanting to know what his hands feel all the time when he's nervous or stressed.

I stumble back pulling him closer to the doors and I can't help but moan as he runs his tongue along my lips biting so I'll let him in.

My brain doesn't think as I pull apart from him and I just look at his face for a second making sure I'm not imagining it all. "What are you thinking Katherine?" he asks, his voice heavy and his lips wet, but his eyes are soft.

My lips find their way back to his as I kiss him with more urgency than I've ever had before. It's easier to go back to kissing him then telling him what I'm really thinking. I want to know what it feels like to have his hands on my bare skin when we're alone. I don't want to think about how temporary this all is when it feels like the most solid thing in the world right now, I want to fossilise this moment to have it forever.

Finding the bottom hem of his top, my hand slides under it, pausing when they touch his skin for the first time. As if he's reading my mind, he breaks our kiss, leaving me to mourn the loss of his lips on mine. All so he can lift his sweater and t-shirt off over his head in one swift movement.

I just look at him and a smile warms my face, the humour in the moment is not lost on me after telling myself there was nothing between the two of us, yet here we stand. I bite my lip so I don't laugh at how past us would be so pissed right now.

"Oh, so me being shirtless is funny, Katherine?" His voice is so thick from the kissing, my laugh is instantly lost in the intensity of his eyes and how the moonlight sharpens his features. He's like a Greek god and I'm suddenly so self conscious I can hardly breathe. I'm nothing compared to him, nothing compared to the guy he actually is under all of his layers.

My layers are so mixed up and ripped, I'm not sure I know how to organise them any more. I'm so confused by the girl I am right now, how can he possibly understand it?

He grabs my hands and lays them on his chest, my fingers instantly finding the octopus tattoo tracing the tentacles that spiral around the muscles—so many muscles—on his chest. "If you don't want to do this, Katherine, we—"

"No." It comes out so fast I can only guess it sounds desperate and I guess in a way maybe I am. "I mean, I want to," I say as my fingers run along the waistband of his shorts, only now noticing the bulge at the front of them. Any question over whether he wants me or not seems to answer itself.

I can feel him watching me and when I look back up at his face he doesn't even try to look away, his eyes are so dark I should be scared of what he's going to do next but as the warm feeling between my legs gets stronger and my breathing gets airier, I'm not scared. I'm excited to see what he'll do.

"I think we should make this even first." His hands go to my top, and I don't stop him. But before he does anything, he grabs me by the waist, lifting me and carrying me back into my room, shutting the doors behind me before pushing me up against them and kissing me again. Everything after that seems to happen so fast. His hands work quick as they get me out of my top and then his hands are on my chest the same way mine are on his. I want to be able to pause the scene to take everything in, knowing this is only a one time thing.

"Katherine, you look..."

"What?" Everything in me wants me to cover my chest with my arms but he stops me before I can do that.

"The things I want to do to you." The smile pulling on his lips is wild and untamed. When his lips find my nipple, it's already the best feeling before he's even got me out of my pants and I wonder if all the other times I've had sex, I'd been doing it wrong.

"Oh, god." My head falls back as he swirls it with his tongue biting lightly before pulling it with his teeth.

He lifts me again and I wrap my legs around him without even thinking, I feel his hard dick rub where I desperately want him the most. My arms go around his neck and I pull at his hair while he kisses me again just so I can feel him moan into my mouth.

Turning us around, he walks to the bed and lays me down on it, never stopping his assault on my lips, my legs still locked around him. That doesn't seem to stop him crawling on top of me, his forearms resting on either side of my head. The weight of him, even if not all of it should make me feel restricted but it lights something in me, a need I hadn't realised I had for him.

He pulls away from me when I think we might both need to take a breath. But I don't get a chance to catch mine when he works his way out of his pants. "I've wanted to do this since the first time I kissed you."

I watch as he slides his fingers into the waistband of my shorts, looking back up at me like he's asking permission. I nod my head at him and he pulls my shorts down, throwing them somewhere in the room. "That was two months ago?" I manage to say before he parts my legs, sliding two fingers up my slit; I let out a soft moan at the relief of him finally touching me where I want him, the idea of him thinking about me for that long confuses me and yet it makes me feel better about my thoughts of him.

He doesn't break eye contact with me as he finally plunges them into me, moving far too slowing for my liking. "Seven weeks to be precise."

"Oh." My brain stalls and the only thing I can see and feel is him lowering his face and those damn long fingers moving painfully slow. I'm not sure what I should be concentrating on more, that piece of information he just dropped, or the scene in front of me right now. Why has he kept track of that? And what does that even mean!?

"Seven weeks of pure torture. Thinking about you." Then he's not talking any more. His lips are wrapped around my clit while his fingers finally pick up speed and I need nothing but him in between my legs. I suppose we can circle back to that other stuff later.

My hand clings to his hair pushing him closer to me if that's humanly possible, but I can't stop looking at him. I'm not sure why watching him causes me so much bliss, it seems to turn me on even more. When he curls his fingers hitting a spot I'm sure only I have before the room goes white and I can't stop my head falling back on the pillow as I fall apart. I try to muffle my moans as much as possible but as I come down from my orgasm, he doesn't stop completely until my back is flat on the bed and I'm able to look at him.

He crawls back up my body as my brain tries to reconnect with my body. "So sweet, Katherine, just how I thought my Sunshine would taste." He rocks his hips, grinding on me as his mouth works its way along my jaw and down my neck, sucking on it, making every part of my body light up. I can't do this, I can't go slow and do all this foreplay. It seems like all the tension in my body from every fight I've had with him has nestled itself between my legs and I think if he doesn't finally get inside of me, I'm going to melt away.

"Can you just—"

"What?" He pulls his head up from where he was kissing my breast.

"Just—" I say gesturing down to where our hips are pushing into each other, I can see on his face how much he's restraining himself too and I don't know why. I just want him to take me in anyway he wants.

"Words, Katherine, use them. Tell me what you want." I stall, my mind having to catch up again, he just keeps saying things to me I'm not ready for. Things I don't expect from him, things that make me attracted to far more than just his body. My heart picks back up again and I dont think it's from the orgasm.

The lines are getting blurry, quicker than I can keep up with. Quicker than I can make clear again. I want to keep this just physical, I think. But when he looks at me the way he is, like I'm some magical being lying in front of him, I don't know if that is what I want. Because when I look at him with his hair falling around his face, he is. He's the elusive unicorn or merman. He's magical. "Fuck me anyway you want."

"Much better, Sunshine. Condom." He doesn't ask, he's telling me. He backs off the bed finding his shorts again, I watch him as his naked body stretches and flexes as he finds his wallet, opening it and pulling one out. Seeing him like this should be strange, it should feel crazy but it isn't. As I look over his body, every part of it, it's like seeing a piece of artwork. The kind they keep behind a velvet rope, one I shouldn't be this close to, one that's going to pull me in and transport me to somewhere beautiful. He's back again before I can wrap my mind around every thought I'm having about him.

I watch him sit on his heels as he rolls it on himself. "Just to be sure, this is a one time thing right? Just to get it out of our systems?" I want to take it back, it hasn't even happened yet and I know my body will want him again even if my brain knows better.

"Just once," he tells me moving back on top of me again, his face is so close to mine I can't read it and I think that might be a good thing, I don't want to know if he really means it or not. I'm not sure if I want him to. The pain in my chest tells me I don't.

He lines himself up with me and rubs the tip over where I'm most sensitive, gaining a moan from me I can't help let slip. "Tell me you want it Katherine, tell me you want me," he whispers into my neck he's kissing, as he lets his tip slide into me.

I'd tell him just about anything to get him to fill me but as the words leave my lips I know I'm not lying. "I want you, James."

That's enough for him; he thrusts the rest of him into me letting out an animal-like groan. I feel full, all over, in every way I've never felt before. Stretched and yet fitting him perfectly all at the same time. He doesn't move for a minute, his breathing is heavy on top of my head and I assume he's giving me a second to adjust.

I let out a breath now needing him to move more than anything, I circle my hip against him giving myself some relief. But he grips my hips stopping me. "You need to give me like a second."

"If you've changed your mind—" I start to move away from him.

"No." He stops me. "Katherine... you feel so good that I'm worried the minute I move, I'm going to explode like a real dickhead, and considering I'm only getting one chance at this, I'd rather that not happen."

My heart is beating faster than I think is humanly possible, I look up at him, bring his face down to mine and I kiss him like the world around us is burning down and this is the last moment we'll have on earth, cause that's how it kinda feels all of a sudden.

He kisses me back harder and I feel as he starts moving his hips against me. Pulling out slowly and pushing back in fast. His muscles flex under my fingertips as he pushes into me harder and harder.

"James... oh, god." Nothing I say is fully audible in-between our moaning and heavy breathing.

That way he groans my name and runs his hands over my body, makes me feel desired. Makes me feel brave.

I push his body over, laying him on his back with me on top of him. His dick still inside of me, and when I throw my head back rocking my hips on him at a speed I didn't think I could muster, I somehow feel even fuller.

He reaches forward, pitching my nipple in-between his fingers, gaining another moan from me. "If I'd realised you'd look this good on top, I would have started with it."

"Shut up," I say laughing and I wonder when the last time was I felt free enough to laugh while being completely naked with a guy. I lean my hands onto his chest, lowering my head enough to kiss him deep, his tongue getting lost in my mouth. I try to fight him back but I'm completely lost in the feeling of my hips swirling down onto him.

I pull away from his mouth, bending my back as he grips on to my hips moving me faster and my hands fully back landing on his thighs.

The familiar sensation starts to build in my stomach and I know I'm close and from the look on his face I think he is too.

Moving forward, I place my hands on the head board, my breast inches from his face, which he takes full advantage of taking one in his mouth. God, that feels so good. He lifts his knees giving himself the right angles to buck into me at a focus that makes my eyes water in the best way.

My nipple comes out his mouth. "Does my Sunshine want to come?" he asks gripping onto my waist giving himself all the leverage to fuck me at speeds that should be killing me. Placing my forearms either side of his head, I can't help kissing him to muffle my moans in his mouth.

"Please, James." I'm not able to say much else as he grunts and moans into the space between our faces.

"Come for me, Sunshine, come on my cock." I'm very happy to follow his commands. Pushing down on him even more, hitting all the right places as one of his hands travels pulling at the hair at the nape of my neck. Moving my head back so he can kiss and bite at my sweet spot.

Then the room goes white and I'm sure I'm moaning his name, who really knows considering I can't really hear anything except for the ecstasy that rushes through my body—into my veins, clouding my brain. When I'm coming down, his thrusts get erratic and his eyes are watching every part of me. I get closer to his ear, kissing his neck.

"Come for me, James, show me how good I make you feel." As the words leave my lips, his grip on my hips gets tighter and he moans my name as I feel him finish into the condom, his dick twitching inside me, his thrusts getting sloppy and unrhythmic.

"Shit," we say together as we both stop moving.

Now that the pleasure, the passion and the moment is over, I'm not sure how to be with him.

I roll off of him and onto my back on the bed. Already cold, not having his hands on me. I'm too tired to even think about what this means now. I feel the weight shift on the bed, I don't watch as he gets up and moves towards the bin in my room. A tight feeling in my chest now, one I've not felt before, one I don't know how to describe.

When he comes back, he's got his boxers back on and is holding my t-shirt for me. He lays back down on the bed and I feel like he doesn't know what to do with himself as much as I don't know what to do with myself.

"Well…" he says like he's going to get up and leave but he doesn't.

"You don't—I mean, you can stay if you want," I almost whisper as I lay next to him. It's strange now it's all over. I don't know how to touch him. I want to feel his hot skin against mine and I want to run my hands across his face while I just look at him. But I don't know how, like if I do, he'll burn me alive.

He lets a soft sigh out and once again I think he's going to climb out of the bed. But as he turns towards my bedside table, he flicks the lamp off and rolls back into bed, curling an arm under my back and pulling me toward him, while he fishes around the bottom on the bed pulling the cover up over us.

My hand settles on his chest and my head seems to tuck perfectly into the crook under his chin, while his arm lifts wrapping itself around my shoulder pulling me flush to him. My breathing turns into something that would resemble normal now that I can smell him again, a normal mix of salt and sunshine.

"Night, Katherine." He places a gentle kiss onto my forehead and my heart melts right here, the way he holds me like I'm going to float away or disappear and the way I run a lazy hand up and down his side like I'll never get the chance to again.

"Night, James."

Chapter 31
Katherine

When I wake in the morning, everything south of my waist feels like I've been running a marathon.

And yet even with the soreness, I feel the best I have in a while. My chest feels warm and happy. My brain is quiet, and I just had the best night sleep I've had in years. Last night was the most connected to another person in that way I've ever felt. I'm confused as to why I'm not panicking, why I'm not stressed about it. For some reason, I'm not scared by it.

The confusion I had for him last night is gone and I feel lighter as the clarity sinks into me. I like him. And the only thing I can really think about is when I'll get to see him again, or when I'll get to feel his lips on mine, or the next time he'll make me feel like the only person in the world.

As I roll over into the middle of the bed it's only then I realise I'm alone.

I'm not surprised he's gone, but fuck I sure am disappointed.

The things he said to me, the way he looked at me. It was enough to make every part of me come undone under him.

What was I expecting? For him to stay, make breakfast and cuddle in the morning? I'm the one that said it should be a one time thing.

I feel stupid, and then the "non-glowing" stone in my bedside table rolls back into my mind. I need to be smarter, I need to get a grip of these feelings and get back to the reason I'm here. The reason that'll keep James as far away as humanly possible, even if that's not what I want. Because I can't let myself get hurt by him.

Pulling myself from bed, my legs only wobble once as I find my discarded shorts from last night, pulling on a sweatshirt just for good measure. The fact that his clothes are gone from my room doesn't even in the slightest bother me. Not even when I notice the sweatshirt I've pulled on is in fact his, I don't even stand and smell it for a minute.

Walking down the corridor to the kitchen I hear a noise coming from it before I reach it and it's not Ella, although her voice is mixed in with it too.

There is no way.

Not a chance because if he came out of my room and straight into the kitchen with Ella, I'd kill him. I'll never stop hearing it from her and I'll die.

Simply die.

As I round the corner my heart seems to stop and start again, and then stop. All the feelings of being sad that he left seem to wash away as I look at him because the truth is I'm just happy he's back.

He's got different clothes on from last night.

The thought of talking to him, even looking at him, makes a lump form in my throat, threatening to choke me.

I must start actually choking cause next thing I know, Ella is rounding the corner towards me.

"Kat, you okay?" Ella asks, coming up to me, hand on my back patting me as she guides me to a stool at the island. It's so much worse with the way he's looking at me.

He's leaning against the island, all gorgeous looking with his elbows on the counter while he holds a mug of what I assume is coffee. God, I need some of that. He turns his head looking me up and down as Ella grabs me a mug too, and his smart-ass smirk only grows bigger and smugger when his gaze lingers on the sweatshirt I have on.

"It was on my floor, don't look at me like that," I whisper at him as Ella comes back over.

"James was just telling me about last night," Ella says. I choke on my coffee, spluttering a little.

I don't miss his laugh before he talks. "Yeah, just saying what a help you were with my mum and stuff." His face goes sheepish and he tries to hide it behind his coffee mug but I see it, written all over his beautiful perfect face. My mind shifts to the places he touched last night like I'm watching a movie over in my head. His fingers digging into my hips, his lips wrapped around my nipples, my skin burns everywhere. I feel guilty for thinking about it but I don't feel guilty that we did it.

I do feel guilty about how I don't think anyone will be able to read my body like he can, I don't think I'll ever have better sex than last night, and that seems like the most bizarre thing in the world. I feel guilty about the fact that I want to change my mind about the whole one time thing. I feel guilty because this isn't why I'm here, somehow I feel like I'm letting everyone down.

"So, why did you come by?" I ask him, the warm feeling spreading through my body just from being near him wants it to be for me but the smart part of my brain hopes he never looks at me like he did last night again.

"Oh, I asked him over, need his set of keys for Maddie this afternoon." I'm sure sometimes in the middle of a conversation she leaves and comes back without me noticing. She's gone again before I can even say anything.

"Right." It shouldn't sting at all, yet it does. I'm the one who made it obvious this wasn't a thing, how hypocritical of me to feel a physical pain in my chest at the thought. "Let me give you this back," I say to him motioning to his sweatshirt I'm wearing. My tone is much harsher than I want, I can't be angry at him and after all this at least we can be friends. I don't have it in me to fight with him any more.

"I could take it back," he pauses, taking a proper look at me for the first time since I got in the room, "but I'm not sure that's actually what you want, and it definitely looks better on you." He finishes his coffee and turns his whole body towards me, pulling my stool so I'm facing him, too. The move is way sexier than it should be. I cross my legs just at the thought of him between them again. The way he looks at me, his eyes now dark, his hair falling around his face, makes me think that he's ready to ruin me again, and it has my blood running hot.

"Was that some kind of pick up line?" I ask, busying my hands with my mug so I don't do something stupid with them, like slide them up his t-shirt and touch his chest again. I completely ignore everything else he's said, because yes, I do want to keep it.

"Nope." His face shifts a little like he's thinking about what he wants to say or if he wants to say it or not so I stay silent until he makes up his mind. "You free today?"

"That depends on who's asking," I tease, enjoying this moment more than I should.

He moves closer to me, placing a hand on my knee, drawing little circles with his thumb on it. "A yes or no will do, Sunshine."

"Oh, that is so not becoming a thing, you can't call me that anywhere else—"

"Except your bedroom, Kat. Got it."

My eyes widen with surprise and he looks at me weird. "Wait, did you just call me Kat?" I question trying to distract myself from him mentioning any part of last night.

"Yeah, it's your name, isn't it?" He laughs a little watching behind me checking that we're still alone, sliding his hand up my thigh a little more.

It takes my brain a minute to think with his hands on me in this way. "Yeah, but you never call me Kat, only ever Katherine." I completely ignore the new nickname he seems to have placed on me, even if it's my new favourite.

"Well, it didn't seem right." The tips of his fingers brush under my shorts a little and my brain fogs at the feeling. I told him it was a one time thing but I'm not sure my body was paying attention as I let out an airy sigh.

I grab the front of his t-shirt pulling him down to me a little. "Please elaborate?"

"It's a nickname right?" I nod my head at him and he brings his lips closer to mine, brushing the corner of my mouth with his. "Well I just feel like they're kinda something people call you when they know you, care about you." He pulls away from me enough to look over my face completely.

"And you just care?" I ask the way he did outside his house what feels like forever ago now, that seemed to be the start of all this. I shouldn't be poking the bear, especially when all I really want to do is drag him back to my room.

"Yeah I do, and even though you didn't ask, I think I know you pretty well, too." He's so sure, so steady when he says it, like I shouldn't question him. My skin heats at the way he looks at me, he doesn't look away from my eyes like he can make me believe it if he looks long enough. I'm not sure how well I'm going to do at staying away from him if he's going to look at me like that now. "Also, I could tell how much it pissed you off," he says, smirking at me.

"Fuck you," I say with a smile.

There's been a shift in the universe. I think I'm only just now noticing it, the air seems thinner and the sun a bit brighter and I feel lighter. It could be the way he's looking at me like I'm the only person in the world or the way I know I'm looking back at him but it's here, a shift. One I don't think we'll be able to undo.

"Fine, yes, I'm free," I finally tell him, leaning back on the stool a little just to put a little more space between the two of us. The space I'm going to have to fight to keep there, when his body seems to pull me to him without trying.

He stands up fully and takes a few steps back away from me. "Great, it's a date," he says with a smirk. "I'll be back at five thirty for you." Then he walks towards the front door.

"It is not a date!" I shout out after him.

It is *not*.

I'm not sure how or when this all got so fucking complicated but I need to make it uncomplicated. Boundaries need to be set and lines need to be drawn, to keep this all in one piece. Or maybe to keep *me* in one piece.

"A date, hey?" Ella says walking back into the kitchen with an arm full of papers and a smug looking smile on her face.

"No," I tell her, picking up my coffee mug and taking a drink. "Definitely not, we're just going to hang out," I tell her, I don't even know what he has in mind, I should have asked.

"What? Even after he spent the night here?"

I stop moving and breathing altogether. Losing all ability to even think at the knowledge she knows he was here.

"It... He didn't... It's definitely not what you think." All the words seem to fall out of my mouth at the same time and I'm not sure what lie I'm trying to come up with or tell and I'm not sure why.

James is a great guy, I've even witnessed it for myself. Ella loves him like a literal son, so I'm not sure why I don't want her to know. Maybe it's because if she knows, then it's real. And if it's real I fear I may already know how it's going to end.

SOUL BELIEFS

"It's okay, Kat, I was your age once too, you know." She says it like it's not still the most embarrassing thing.

Maybe it's because I don't want her to think I've given up on the reason I came here in the first place and I don't want her to think I'm messing around with him and that I'm just going to leave him in the dust once I find what I'm looking for.

He knows what this is, he knows why I'm here. He won't get his feelings hurt. The boy doesn't believe in soulmates and from what I've seen, he doesn't even believe in relationships. I can't hurt him if he's not open enough to hurt, right?

"It's still not like that, I promise." I get up from the stool taking the rest of my coffee with me, but I stop in the hallway when I hear her follow me.

"Katherine." I'm not sure she's even looked at me like this before, a strange mix between sadness, disappointment and something else that makes my heart squeeze. "I know, Katherine. I should have put it somewhere better, but..."

My stone. The feeling I had at the beginning of yesterday comes rushing back.

"Yeah," is all I can say over the lump in my throat threatening to choke me. "I guess, I thought maybe—"

She pulls me into an unexpected hug and I feel my eyes start to sting at the feeling. I shouldn't be this upset over it, I shouldn't be this disappointed. When he's near it makes it kinda okay, like even though he's not really mine, he doesn't seem to mind playing pretend with me.

Pulling away from me, she puts her hands on my shoulders. "Katherine, I'm going to say something now and just listen to me." I nod my head. "He is a great guy, a guy who's been through a lot of shit when it comes to love, or anything for that matter, but I have a feeling he's already told you all that. I don't mean this in any particular way but you'd be happy with him, I think." She sucks in a deep breath like she's been thinking about this maybe as much as I have. "Soulmates aren't always what you think they are, but James, he's exactly what he says he is and I think when you're around each other, he's more himself then I've seen in a while. And you, well, you're the best thing to show up for him in a long time. As much as you don't want to admit it, he is for you, too." She lets go of me and walks back into the kitchen. I'm too confused and stunned to move.

My heart is in my throat and tears threaten to run down my face, but she's right—I think. I'm not the same person I was when I got here and he's not the same person I met on that first day. But I didn't think for a second that those two things were connected.

I've been trying to hide it from her this whole time, and it seems like she's seen more of what's going on than I have.

She's seen the bigger picture, better than I have, stepped a few steps out of the spotlight enough to see the two of us. To see what's really been happening. To see me falling for him before I could see it, and my breath gets stuck as I think maybe she's seen him falling for me, too.

It's the first time that I think maybe everyone else has had it right this whole time, that maybe there was someone else out there for me this whole time.

Someone who isn't my soulmate.

Someone who could be James.

Chapter 32
Katherine

Katherine Miller <katherine.miller@gmail.com>
To Thomas Mitchel
Subject: Re: Your soulmate adventure

Dear Mr. Mitchel,
Thank you so much for your email.
I don't mean for this to sound at all crazy, but I've been reading Soulmate Chronicles since I was a kid, this almost feels like a dream to be receiving an email from you.
I'm sure Bella informed you that I am currently in Australia, so I'm not sure what we would be able to do at this moment in time, with me being in a very different time zone from yourself. I am planning to come back to New York in the new year if that is better.
I'm also very sorry if you have read some of my blog posts. They do tend to be ramblings that probably make me sound a bit crazy.
Once again, thank you so much for your email and I hope to hear from you soon.

Kind regards,
Katherine Miller

Thomas Mitchel <thomas.mitchel@soulmatechronicles.com>
To Katherine Miller
Subject: Re: Your soulmate adventure

Hi Katherine,

Please call me Tom or Tommy from now on, Mr. Mitchel is my father and makes me feel much older than I'd like.

Thank you so much. It's so nice to know the magazine has been in your life for so long, as it has been mine.

I completely understand the difficulty with the current time differences, so if it's okay with you, I'd love to get my assistant to look at the hours and arrange a call with you in a few days?

And never apologise for ramblings, you'd be surprised at the gold you can get from just letting yourself write freely.

I hope to speak to you soon. Look out for an email from my assistant.

Kind regards,
Tommy Mitchel
Editor in Chief of Soulmate Chronicles

Natasha Davies <natasha.davies@soulmatechronicles.com>
To Katherine Miller
Subject: Schedule meeting with Mr.Mitchel

Dear Miss Miller,
My name is Natasha, Mr. Mitchel's assistant.
I'd like to confirm a call with Mr. Mitchel and yourself on the 14th November at 10 a.m. your time.
If this is okay for you, please let me know by replying to this email.

Kind regards,
Natasha Davies
Assistant to Tommy Mitchel

Katherine Miller <katherine.miller@gmail.com>
To Natasha Davies
Subject: Re: Schedule meeting with Mr.Mitchel

Dear Natasha,
Thank you for your email, 10 a.m. works perfectly for me. Thank you so much.

Kind regards,
Katherine Miller

Chapter 33
James

I should *not* be doing this.

I should be trying to stay as far away from her as possible.

Just to get it out of our system.

God, why did hearing her say that hurt so much?

That should have gotten it out of my system, but now she seems to be in my system more than ever before. She's in every vein and nerve, and when I close my eyes, she's there too.

To put it lightly, seeing her in this new light isn't something I'm ever going to forget, and I think I'll dream about her every night for the rest of my life. My memories of her are something I'll hold on to long after she's gone from Gull's Bay. That's it she's etched into every corner of my brain and soul, and I'll never be able to buff it out.

That's putting it lightly.

I can't not think of her, I see her in everything. I'm consumed by her. To say I like her would be like saying the sky likes the sun.

I should not be picking her up and taking her out like we're dating.

Her telling me I could stay last night almost sent me into a tailspin, I was so ready for her to kick me out the minute it was over. Then I pulled her into my body and it's like she melted into me; any last bits of mistrust or hate or even dislike was gone like it was never there in the first place. I can't believe I'm the only one feeling this, because she looks at me the way I do her, like I'm safe with her.

In the morning, she looked so at peace and calm, I don't think I've seen it on her before. She's always so wound up, always walking this thin line no one else can see, always trying so hard to keep that smile on her face. But the one she had this morning, that one was real, that one was calm and really happy. I felt like the grinch when his heart finally grew ten sizes bigger, felt my own smile grow just by looking at her. Felt those dark parts of my heart start to fill with something—with sunshine. It was the first time I felt like maybe I had been wrong this whole time, maybe I was wrong about never letting anyone in.

And I never expected that, the thought that Kat of all people would be able to change how I see things.

I never expected to spend so much time with her, never expected to sleep with her, but the most surprising thing was I never expected her to be such a cuddler. I didn't want to get out of bed with her.

I could have very happily stayed in bed with her for the whole day and repeated the night before, but I didn't want to have Ella walk in and find me there. I don't think her walking in would be the greatest start to whatever is happening between us.

Trying to pry myself out of Katherine's iron grip was a mean feat. Somehow in the night we had to become even more entangled with each other, her legs wrapped around mine. Like some little koala. Leaving her was physically painful. I have truly fallen so deep down the rabbit hole when it comes to her.

I don't think she's going to give up on her soulmate search, even if I want her to, but I understand her more now and I can't be mad at her anymore. But the idea of her packing up and leaving still burns me from the inside.

I don't know if I'm ready for a real relationship with her, I've never had the chance to prove to myself I can, and she deserves nothing but the best. I want to be that person. I don't think anyone else will be good enough for her. But I'm not even sure I am.

But my mind is clear for once, and if I have any hope of getting her to forget about her goal of finding her soulmate, I've got to show her it's worth trying with someone else.

My hands are sweating when the door swings open. She's in a white flowy dress that I've seen her wear before, but it's like I'm seeing it for the first time now. She gestures for me to come in as she holds her phone to her ear.

"I know, Mom, I'm excited too, but can't get my hopes up. You know, expect the worst," I hear her say as she leads me into her room, where she proceeds to fish around for a pair of shoes.

An uncomfortable stabbing pain stirs in my chest at that, that she expects the worst from things so she's not disappointed. I know the feeling all too well and I hate that she feels that too. I want her to always expect the best. To always shoot for the best case scenario because that's what she deserves.

I lean on the door frame as I watch. "Okay, Mom, I'll speak to you later, I love you lots."

I expect her to hang up, but she seems to wait for a minute.

"Bella, if you scream down the phone one more time, I'm hanging up." It's kinda odd in a way to think of her having another life, other people, another place. It seems like she's been here for so long this is her place but it's not and that thought seems to send a kinda new pain into my chest. "Yes, he's here." She tries to whisper but I'm in her room now and too close to not hear it, a smile pulls on my face knowing she's told her other life about me, although I hate to think what she said about me before a few days ago. I try to squash it before she sees it, but I'm too late.

It gives me another moment to cast my eyes over her surroundings, my quick assessment is that she's not a minimalist. Souvenirs scattered over her dresser, books piled up on her desk spilling onto the floor in more piles, clothes are hung up over the wardrobe door but not inside and more on the floor and it's just so contrasting to the way she is outwardly. But now that I know her, it actually seems very her.

She turns towards me as she lifts up my sweatshirt, handing it back to me as she grabs her bag. "Yes, I'll talk to you tomorrow." She makes a face at me like something between a smile and a 'I'm sorry.' "I will if you let me go." She points out her room, shuffling me out, turning her light off and walking ahead of me towards the door. "Okay, I love and miss you."

She finally hangs up and lets out a little sigh turning to me before we get to the front door.

"I'm sorry about that, the time difference is hard sometimes, sometimes it's like a whole village thing when my friends are at my mom's, do I need a jacket?" she says a little frazzled, like maybe that phone call had caught her off guard.

I hold onto her arm, making her stop and really look at me, she takes a breath with me. "It's okay, and no it's still pretty warm but you can always keep hold of this," I say letting go of her and handing her back the sweatshirt she's just returned.

It's a little weird, a little primitive of me but seeing her in it this morning did things to me in so many ways. In that moment, I wanted everyone to know who's clothes she was wearing, and I wanted to run my hands under it while she sat on my lap, naked in every way besides my jumper.

She takes it back, smiling at me as she does, almost like she can't help it and I love it a little more than I should. Because when Katherine smiles, it's like the whole world opens up in front of me just because I've made her smile for a minute.

"Where are we going?" she asks for the tenth time since we left Ella's.

I was a little worried it was going to be awkward between us on the drive. But we've just been talking like two very normal people would. Like two people who do this all the time, go out together, do things together.

"The concept of a surprise really is lost on you Katherine isn't it?" I ask her not taking my eyes off the road but I can feel her smiling at me.

"Alright, well are we nearly there?" she asks, shifting in the seat of my truck.

"We are not starting that," I laugh knowing just what she's doing. "It's only like ten more minutes, but we have to walk the rest." Pulling into a road and parking, I stop my truck steps away from a small beach.

"Walk? Where are we? Are you finally going to kill me?" she jokes, I watch her face still as I reach into the back seat not taking my eyes off her until I pass her a blanket.

"You carry this, I got the food." We both jump out the truck and I lock up as she meets me on the footpath.

"This is starting to definitely look like a date," she huffs, folding her arms over the blanket looking like a sulking child, but the way she pushes her lips out while she does, does nothing to stop me wanting to kiss her.

It would be so easy, just lean down and do it, but I think if I start I won't stop. So I suppress it by leaning down and kissing her forehead. Which feels far too much like what a boyfriend would do but I try to move past it. "Come on, just up the little hill," I say walking away from her. I hear her footsteps catch up with me.

We walk up what Kat decides as a *damn mountain* for a few minutes before we hit the flat path again and her hand brushes with mine as she talks. I don't think she realises until I link my pinky with hers. She stops talking only for a second to look at them, she smiles to herself and then keeps going. She's so busy looking around she totally misses the building right in front of her, until I stop moving and she walks into the side of me.

My hand goes to her waist stopping her from tripping in the dimming light, I pause for a beat knowing that touching her like this is a step too far for my self control. I let go of her slowly and point at the reason I've brought her out here.

"Oh my god, you didn't," she says, not breaking eye contact with the tall structure.

"I did." We look up at the Stargaze Perch Lighthouse together for a moment before she walks away towards it more, I follow after her. It's an old lighthouse, the red and white paint flaking all over, the door that used to lead into the base is sealed off now.

I honestly didn't even know it was here until she mentioned it, I spent all day working out how to get here. Having to ask Maddie in the most discreet way possible to see if she'd ever been up here before. But now that we are, I can see why people come up here, the view.

And I'm not meaning Kat, although watching her as she stands near the cliff edge looking out over to the cities across the water strikes me with something. A feeling I don't think I've ever felt before and one I can only describe as longing. A longing to do this all the time, to surprise her and take her places she wants to go. To hold her hand as we walk and kiss her just because. It takes my breath away.

I try to cough it down as I walk over to join her. "Why did you want to come here, anyway?"

"I don't really know," she says truthfully; that's something I like about her the most. I never think she's lying to me, even when we were fighting I still think she was telling me the truth. Even if some of the things were mean, god I'd rather that than her lying to me. "I think maybe I saw it on some tourist website when I first found out my soulmate was in Sydney."

There it is again.

The unmistakable truth. The reason she's here. I notice her still a little, like she wishes she hadn't said it.

No matter how much I wish she'd lie to me about that one thing, I know she never will and I'm turning into someone I don't recognise. I'm not even sure if that's a bad thing, I haven't been this open with someone other than Maddie and Ella in years and it's a little scary I guess.

"We have about an hour until sunset, so I packed some food."

"You're telling me your favourite sandwich is peanut butter and jelly?" She laughs at me as the sun starts moving down the sky, moving the most beautiful light across the sea. She's watching the sunset, but I'm watching her.

The way the light moves over her shows freckles I've never seen before, making me see colours in her hair I don't think have even been discovered and somehow making her laugh sound even more like a song written by the angels.

"Excuse you, it's called jam here," I tease, popping another grape in my mouth. The laugh she gives me makes my insides melt.

God, it's so peaceful here. We haven't seen a single other person since we got here. The waves crashing on the rocks below the cliff are the only sound, apart from the occasional Cockatoo.

"Can I ask you something?" I look at her, one eyebrow cocked from where I'm sitting, because I know she'll ask even if I say no anyway.

Her eyes dart away like she's not sure why she wants to ask but it's playing on her mind, and then the words just seem to fall out of her like she can't help it. "You see, my best friend Bella, back in New York who I was on the phone to earlier, well she knows everything, more than me anyway and I was talking to her and she seems to think that maybe, you know, possibly..."

"Kat, what do you want to ask?" I ask knowing this babbling could go on until the sun goes down.

"Well, were you jealous at the Halloween party? Is that why you came looking for me?" she asks, playing with the fringe of the blanket next to her. I don't get a chance to say anything when she starts again. "I mean I'm glad you did, you know find me and then again in the bathroom, I was just..."

"Wondering?" I cut her off as the memories of that night come back thick and fast. I was ready to completely rearrange Dylan's face then, and I'm not saying I haven't thought about it since. But when I saw her run off like that, I couldn't help but forget about him entirely and only think of her and I'm glad I did. Seeing her so helpless and vulnerable kinda broke my heart. I'm not sure I'd see her the way I do now if I hadn't seen her like that, like the curtain was pulled back and there stood this girl. Just a girl with all this stuff going on, not this enemy who stood for everything I was against. I didn't care about any of that then I just cared about her, about helping her and getting her home.

"Yeah." She's sheepish now, a shy version of Kat I've never really gotten to see, apart from that first day in the shop.

If I'm going to have to be honest, then so does she. "Okay, how about a game of twenty questions then?"

She only nods her head at me like she's not too sure how to feel about having to answer my questions.

I take a breath. "Yes." I don't elaborate on the answer in any way, even if I think she might want me to. If I'm honest, I'm too scared to, too afraid of what she'll say if I even try and explain my feelings for her right now.

"Oh, okay this is a 'yes or no' game? I see... Okay, well, ask your question." She pokes at my ribs making me finally look at her and I want to grab hold of her hand and pull her to me and kiss her until she forgets who she's kissing and why we shouldn't be.

But instead, I ask the question I'm sure will give me away, the one I'm sure will tell her everything she needs to know about my feelings. "Do you regret sleeping together last night?"

"No." She doesn't think about it, she's so sure. "Do you?" she asks back.

"No." A grin pulls on my lips only just visible by the lowering sun. Let's be honest, this is a pretty damn good date-not-date. I shouldn't want this to be a date, because that means it's not just a physical thing and that's dangerous.

I brought her here to see the sun set, and yet we seem to be looking at each other more than the sky.

My next question sits on the tip of my tongue waiting for its turn ready to leap off. "Do you think we'd be together if all this soulmate stuff didn't exist?" If she didn't know how I felt before, she does now. But I'm kinda tired of pretending it's not what we're both wondering.

"No." She laughs a little at the blank expression on my face as what I assume shows all my blood leaving it. "I come from a very long line of soulmates, I don't think I'd be alive if soulmates didn't exist." I shake my head at her avoiding my question. "But I do think everyone who was meant to find each other, still would." I don't know if she means that we still would have found each other, but I like to think that's what she means.

I watch as she stretches her legs out in front of her, hanging her head back letting her hair flow down her back. "Okay, do you really not want to be in love?" She doesn't look at me as she asks and I have to hope she doesn't either as I answer.

"I've spent most of my life alone." I move closer to her, copying her position, facing towards the darkening sky. "Not always in the physical sense but in every way that mattered. I could be surrounded by people and still feel utterly alone. When Mum left, I spiralled. I thought—still think sometimes—that people are just going to leave." She's looking at me now, I can feel her eyes bore into my cheek. I can only assume the look on her face is pity or sadness. "It just felt safer to be on my own, but every now and again I wonder what it would be like to have that person. So to answer your very much not a yes or no question, no, I want to be in love. I'm just not sure I'd know how to, or that I'd be very good at it."

The planets must have stopped spinning and pigs are now flying because I have somehow managed to stun Katherine Miller into silence. I sneak a look at her while I'm sure she's not looking and she's so still, it's almost unsettling.

"That panic attack I had the other night wasn't my first," she says, breaking her own silence, a breeze blows through her hair, moving it out of her face, showing me the glassy look in her eyes. "That's kinda been my life since I can remember, worry, panic, anxiety." My hand slides to hers, my pinky wrapping around hers. Just to remind her I'm here, here for her. "My mind is so busy and loud I'm not sure how I can possibly have space for other people. I feel like such a burden sometimes, that I need so many people helping me but I'm not able to do the same because of my mental health."

My brows pull together, does she not know how she's helped me? How she could never be a burden to me? How strong and brave she really is.

She's been fighting so much, with herself, with the demons that I only got a small glimpse of the other night. I can't beat them for her but I want to be holding her hand while we work through it together and I want to be the one to hold her when the day's been long and hard. To cheer her on while she wins one battle after another. I want to be the one she turns to when she needs someone, when she just wants to talk things though.

She surprises me when she continues. "Sometimes I don't think it'll ever be quiet in here, it's like having a hundred mini-mes telling me so many different things, it's hard to know who's telling the truth, and some of them are mean. The only time it seems to go quiet is when..."

She pauses and my heart is in my throat because I know what I want her to say. "When?" I push because I have to know?

She finally turns to me, our eyes connecting and hers holding mine like she's searching for something. "When—when I'm around you." She moves closer to me. "I take up far too much space. I'm not sure I'm going to be very good at being in love either." When her eyes hit mine, there's a glint in them like she might cry.

And she might not be the only one. This amazing, beautiful, kind, full of warmth, ball of sunshine—my Sunshine. How can she think that? How can I convince her all the things she's built in her mind aren't true? I'm stuck, I don't know what to tell her and I'm not sure anything I do say will be enough.

We're still just watching each other's faces, she just laid her soul out in front of me and it's beautiful, a little broken but not beyond repair. "Kat, I—" What's the right thing to say? Maybe it's not about saying the right thing, maybe it's just about saying something true? How do I tell her I *want* her to take up all of my space? I take a breath.

"You know you're the first person in a long time to make me feel seen and supported. That's what you do, Kat. You literally make everyone you meet feel happy and safe to just be around you. People can be themselves with you, I think you already know how to love. I think you just need to learn to accept the love other people are trying to give you, too."

She finally looks away from me, she lets go of my little finger and pushes her hand through her hair. The way it falls back down around her face has me wanting to tuck it behind her ear, but I don't. "I like the view from up here. It's peaceful and still. It makes me feel like I'm alone for a while. The city back home is so busy, you're never really alone," she tells me, avoiding everything I just told her, which is fine. I just hope she listens to it at some point.

"Do you want to be alone?"

"Yes... No." She stops and looks at me. "I want to be alone, but with you."

This right here, this is peace, this is calm and quiet. It's all I could want and yet I feel like I'm stealing it all from someone else because someone else should be feeling this with her. Taking her calm and imprinting it into their skin for hard days. Someone else should be stealing looks at her while the sun goes down and the air cools.

But it's me, I'm the one looking at her right now, taking in every part of her. Soaking up every ray for later when it's dark. "The suns almost set," I tell her, my voice sounding foreign to me, shaky and unsure. Nothing like the me that wound up in her room last night, trying to take every bit, any bit of her she'd give me.

"I know." She watches as the sky becomes a mix of oranges and pinks, and I watch her as her face takes it all in. The sun moves below the ocean and disappears into the watery grave for the evening, the sky engulfing into an almost darkness and only lights coming from the town across from the hill we're on.

Neither of us make a move, instead she turns to look at me. "Thank you." She sounds small and shy, equally just as much not the her from last night.

I move closer to her knowing I don't have many more of these moments left. Even if she doesn't find her soulmate, she'll soon realise whatever we're doing is a lost cause. I'm selfish, and I'm going to steal as many moments with her that I can get before the truth sinks into her bones.

My hand brushes against hers on the blanket and I feel like a teenager again. The electric feeling that runs up my arm and straight to my chest. I'm somehow more nervous than I was last night, in these simple moments with her my mind races.

I tilt my head back to fill my lungs as much as possible. The sky above us is littered with the stars you wouldn't see in the city. She follows my gaze up to the sky and I look back down at her. "It's beautiful," she tells me, unaware of my gaze on her.

"You're beautiful, Sunshine."

She lowers her head slowly to look at me again, our faces so close I can feel every uneven breath she lets out hit my face and it goes right through me. "We should head back." But she doesn't move, like she's stuck there just like me.

"Is that what you want Kat?" If it were me though, I'd live in this darkness with her forever if she asked.

"I don't know what I want," she responds with a bit of frustration and sadness in her voice. "Just sitting here, with you, everything just feels so—"

"Small?"

"Yeah, like everything I'm always worrying about has just kinda stopped." A tear rolls down her cheek and my heart cracks in two.

I was so wrong, so incredibly wrong, about her it hurts.

I'll take her back home in a minute. We'll stop and get ice cream from that place near the store I heard her say she likes and I'll let her play Taylor Swift all the way home. I'm going to make her smile again. But right now, I need to hold her.

She moves with ease as I pull her into my lap, her head tucking under my chin perfectly. And I just hold her. I just need to feel her steady heart beat against my chest and smell the vanilla scent she wears so well.

A shaky breath leaves her as she relaxes into me, her hands hold on to the arm wrapped around her. She shifts, wrapping her arms around me, and I hold her.

I hold her until I'm sure she's not going to cry again. I hold her until the sun has truly been drowned by the sea. I hold her until she kisses me lightly on the cheek.

I hold her until it feels like it's holding me together too.

Chapter 34
Katherine

Not having Bella right here to talk to about all this has been hard, to say the least, the time difference, the not being able to read each other's faces. We never had to do anything but look at each other to know exactly what the other was thinking. I didn't think it would be this hard. I mean I knew it would be hard, but I never imagined I'd feel this far from her.

So I caved and called Maddie this morning asking her to come over. I then proceeded to spill everything, every detail from start to finish. In my defence, I was very sleep deprived from the lack of sleep I got after James dropped me home last night.

I don't know what last night was, but if that wasn't a date then I'm not sure I really know what one is.

I have never spilled my guts so easily to a guy before, besides Nick. He's just so easy to be around and he makes it so easy to let your guard down. The way he held me when I started to cry, embarrassing I know, it felt like he was holding all of me together. Like he was trying to keep all my pieces together.

And I'm back to feeling even more confused about what to do than I was before. I had expected him to come in and maybe have a repeat of the other night. But he dropped me off and kissed me good night like I'd held him together too.

"You really thought I was that clueless?" Maddie tells me as she drives us into Sydney. She said we'd do one of the things on my list to take my mind off everything but then didn't tell me what we're going to do, so I'm twirling my hair and picking my fingers while my stomach churns in the passenger seat.

"I didn't even know I liked him until like three days ago, how could you have known?" I ask, trying my best to not sound as pathetic as I feel.

"Oh, come on, all the fighting, the longing looks, and the fact you two look like the perfect couple. It was going to happen at some point. I just can't believe it took you guys this long to work it out." She takes the right turn as we come off the bridge then five minutes later we park up and start walking in whatever direction she's leading me.

I can't help thinking maybe she's right, a lot of passion goes into hating a person, and when you see a different side to that person where do you put all those feelings? Did he and his mum break my heart? Yes. Did seeing him open and vulnerable make me feel things for him? Also yes.

Is that all it was? A weird mix of my brain trying to make sense of me not hating him any more. It would be nice if it was that simple but I don't think I would have let him into my room the other night if that was all it was. He brought down walls I didn't ever know I had up. That's no mean feat, a girl as anxious as me wears so many masks I'm never too sure which one I've got on, but when I'm with him I know I'm not wearing a single one. I'm me and I kinda think he likes that.

Maddie stops and I fall into her side. "We're here!" she says in a sing-song voice that she does that reminds me of Jessica Day from New Girl.

I look at the little shop tucked away between a coffee place and a vintage store, its windows are big and open, letting me see right into it.

A tattoo shop.

Maddie has a few from what I've seen and James is covered so I'm not surprised. But I'm scared as shit.

"Oh come on you'll be fine, just something small," she tells me grabbing my hand and pulling me through the door, the bell above the door chirps alerting the girl behind the desk to our arrival. She looks like she belongs here, her dark hair is pulled back in a high, very sleek ponytail showing off all her piercings and neck tattoos. Her grey tank top shows off all the tattoos she has down her arms, and she looks like she's drawing something as we get closer.

I look down at my green floral shorts and white tank top; I do not look like I should be here.

"I don't even know what I want," I whisper to Maddie as she waves to the girl pulling me down the long corridor past doors and cubicles. The place is the closest thing I've ever seen to a Tardis, bigger on the inside than it looks on the outside.

"Think of something to do with this trip, something you don't want to ever forget." I know the first thing that comes to mind but it seems too final, too much like it might mean something it shouldn't.

Like I'm putting too much pressure on a situation I shouldn't be, but it's the first thing I think of and something I never want to forget. No matter who my soulmate ends up being.

Maddie knocks on the door at the end of the corridor and it swings open revealing a guy I've met before but I can't quite remember when.

"Thanks for doing this, Willie," Maddie says smiling up at the wall of dark muscles holding the door open, he smiles down at her in a way I'm sure she doesn't see or notice.

"Anything for you Mads." After she walks in he looks back at me lingering in the doorway. "Kat, right?" He moves out of the way but I stay rooted to my spot unsure if I'm actually ready to do this or not. "I promise they don't hurt as much as you think, and we can stop as many times as you want."

"Wait, you're doing it? I thought you were a surfer?" I stutter out, my brain finally catching up with my surroundings.

"Surfer, tattoo artist, male model."

"And apparently real modest, too," Maddie calls from her seat in the room, where she flicks through some portfolio but when she smiles up at him when he looks over at her, it's not quite her normal smile, not one that reaches her eyes.

Note to self: ask her about that when we're alone again.

I finally walk into the room and it's just like I'd expected. Art on the white walls, stickers on every surface, an adjustable chair bed thing in the centre that Willie gestures for me to sit in.

When I do, he sits in the chair next to me. He sticks a hand out to me. "Willie Lewis, I'm James and Maddie's friend, we met very briefly at the bar a few weeks ago." I take his hand and shake it, which feels far too formal for our current setting.

"Katherine Miller, I'm sorry if I was drunk the last time we met."

"She is also my new best friend, you and James have been replaced," Maddie tells him, smiling at me. My heart squeezes with a sensation like I might cry.

My eyes glance down at what I assume is the tattoo gun on a rolling table next to me. Willie's eyes follow mine and then he looks up at my face. "I promise I know what I'm doing. I trained here while I was trying to get on the competition circuit, and I always come back for a guest spot while I'm home," he reassures me with his calm tone and explanation. "Who do you think did all James' ink? I made that guy hotter than he should be," he laughs, grabbing an iPad off one counter.

The mere mention of his inked arms and torso seems to light my skin on fire and make my palms sweat. I try to take a deep breath while Maddie pulls a chair up next to me. "So, what are you thinking?" she asks and Willie looks at me.

"Okay maybe I have an idea, but you can't say anything," I say pointing a finger at Maddie and she holds her hands up in defence.

Someone should've told me that once you get one tattoo you'll want more because as I stare at the new permanent addition to my body I know it won't be the last I get.

"It looks so good," Maddie says, coming up to stand next to me in the mirror.

My eyes water a little looking at the fine lines and text swirling on the back of my arm.

"Okay, so remember not to swim for at least four weeks, sorry. And keep it wrapped for a few hours then wash with warm water and put this cream on every few hours. Not too much, but don't let it get dry," he says, pulling off his gloves and handing me a bottle of cream.

"Thank you so much for this." I turn towards him, wiping my eyes as subtly as I can. "How much do I owe you?"

"Oh, no it's cool, on the house," he smiles at Maddie in a knowing way.

"No, no way you're not paying for me, Maddie." I turn back to her again.

"Think of it as a Christmas present."

"It's November."

"Maybe you girls could take this somewhere else, I have another client in thirty minutes," Willie says to both of us but mostly to Maddie, once again reminding me to try to get some insight into that relationship. "I think some of us are going out later, you coming?"

I'm not invited and once again, I'm reminded I'm just a droplet in the ocean for these guys. In months to come, I won't even be a blip on their radar and I know why that hurts so much because I care about them.

It hurts because I don't want that. I don't want to leave and be nothing to them.

Nothing to James.

For once me and my brain agree with each other, I don't want him to forget about me which is selfish and mean, and probably a bunch of other stuff I will feel bad about later, but that's the truth.

I just feel like a filler in their lives and my heart tells me I don't want to be that with these people. They are important and so beautiful on the inside. It makes me happy I've had the chance to even be around them.

Maybe that's it. I should just be happy I got the chance to see them, to be in their orbit for a while. Happy that I got to be Pluto in their solar system.

I still want to find my soulmate but I'm not sure this is the best way anymore, I can't force it like I thought I could. I think I'm starting to realise that now.

"Yeah of course we will." Maddie's voice brings me out of my mind palace.

"What?"

"I texted you about it the other day." My mind wanders back to a very long text she sent the other day and so much was in it I totally missed the part about going out. "You kinda ignored that part so I just took it as a yes."

"Oh." I'm not sure what to say as all my own thoughts come to a crashing stop.

"We'll see you later," Maddie calls to Willie as she pulls me out of the room.

She did invite me.

Thought of me.

All of a sudden this feeling comes over me and Maddie's arm linked through mine is the only thing keeping me up. It's like I'm having this crazy realisation that I've been trying to read everyone's minds my whole life, assuming I knew what they were really thinking. Also assuming that I was just tagging along but never really wanted.

Bella was the popular one through high school, and I was just her best friend. I always kinda felt like an accessory, like people felt like they had to invite me to parties, sleepovers and hang outs because they knew Bella wouldn't come if I was left out.

"You okay?" Maddie asks, and I realise I've stopped moving.

"Yeah."

"You sure, you kinda look like you're going to throw up or cry? Is it your blood sugar? Do I need to get you chocolate?"

"No, I'm actually really good." I smile at her, my chest feeling a weird lightness, something I don't think I've had since I was in therapy as a kid. "So, what's the plan for tonight?"

I convince Maddie to get ready with me at Ella's. I decided it's time I try to be around the people I like more, that it feels good to be with people who want to be around me. And I won't let myself feel weird about it.

"Hey, Bella." I wave at my laptop screen as I FaceTime while she's still in bed.

"HEY! Oh my god I need an update!" I'm sure I see a bit of coffee fly out her mug as she sits up.

"Okay, first I want you to meet someone. Bella this is Maddie, Maddie this is Bella." I angle my screen just right on my desk and let Maddie move more into the frame.

"Hi! It's so good to meet you. Kat talks about you all the time," Maddie says waving at the camera giving Bella her signature smile. I've felt bad for not keeping Bella in the loop about my feelings for James as much as I would have liked and I feel like it's time to be completely open with how I'm feeling now.

"So good to meet you too! You are so much more beautiful than your Instagram gives you credit for." Bella gushes and we spend the next hour chatting just like friends do. Bella tells us everything going on with her and I feel bad that I didn't realise how hard things had been at her job but she tells me she thinks it's going to get better now that she's applied for a full time job there.

I tell her about everything with me and James that I haven't had a chance to tell her yet. Queue lots of squealing from her. Having to go into detail about my feelings is probably the hardest thing but also crazy therapeutic. Sometimes it's hard for me to keep my own thoughts in order in my head, that's why I have a lot of word vomit moments on my blog, so talking it through with two people really helps.

"So, just to clarify, you do like, like like him?" Bella asks me as she sips her second cup of coffee.

"Yeah, I think so." I fiddle with a thread on my sock, as I sit cross legged on the floor.

"Okay, so what's the problem? He obviously likes you too, and don't even think about fighting me about that. The date he took you on yesterday proves it and don't even get me started on the mind blowing sex you had." Bella does not mince her words with me when she truly thinks I'm being an idiot about something, which is fair.

"Yeah, but he's not my soulmate." I almost whisper as if me not saying it loud enough for the world to hear it won't be true.

"Oh, hunny," Maddie says from behind me where she's pulling my hair into two French braids. "But what if you guys could be really happy together?"

"And what if we end up hating each other in a few years and I've wasted all that time or what if we don't actually have anything in common and it's just this crazy passion physical thing, or he ends up loving someone more than me, or—"

"Maddie, stop her before she spirals," Bella says, Maddie hands me the glass of vodka and lemonade next to her and I take a long drink. "What did your dad used to say to us? *You never want to miss out on something because of fear or what ifs.* What if it works out and you're really happy, what if he's the one for you just not your soulmate? Come on, Kat, I know how important it is to you and I get it, but if you like him at least give the poor guy a chance."

Bella's right. I know she is. "Fine, but can we change the subject to Maddie and Willie now?"

And we do, Maddie tells us about him. How he was James first friend when he moved here, how they'd known each other for most of their lives, practically growing up together but it wasn't till she and James started to work together that they all started to hang out. Their whole friendship group is a weird mix of people they seemed to have picked up along the way but it used to be the three of them.

"Me and James have always been a brother/sister thing. I can not stress that enough, but me and Willie... I don't know. For a minute I thought maybe it would be more, you know?" she tells me as she shifts through my wardrobe like she needs to be doing something to be able to tell us this and we let her.

"Just the way we were. I don't know, it's hard to explain, in the way he'd hold me sometimes, the way he was always here making me feel safe, he was the first person I'd call when I needed someone and he'd be there without a doubt. He'd look at me sometimes like I was something special," her voice cracks but she continues.

"But when he got picked up for the circuit, to go all over and do competitions something changed, he changed. He wasn't the same guy any more, I couldn't depend on him or trust him and I just kinda stopped wanting anything from him, cause I knew he couldn't give me that. Watching him have girls all over him is enough to put anyone off." I've never heard her sound so sad before. She takes a deep breath before pulling a dress out of my wardrobe and holding it out in front of herself in the mirror.

I give her a thumbs up from where I'm still sat on the floor and angle my laptop so Bella can see it too.

"Oh yes, love! With the red shoes Kat has too." Bella's right again, of course. It's a black little dress I've owned for like five years but it's always a good choice.

"Anyway, we're still friends and everything, but it's not the same and sometimes I actually kinda hate him a little for it. To almost give me something like that and then just kinda disappearing. Even now sometimes he looks at me in a way and just for a second I wonder what it might have been like. If we actually had been together, if one of us had been brave enough." She has a wishful look on her face I've never seen on her before but it's gone in a second.

We talk a little more as Maddie and I get dressed.

"This has been truly amazing, and Maddie, I can't wait for you to come to New York, dates pending but I should get dressed, our moms and I are doing some early Christmas shopping."

"Don't tell me that," I groan, the thought of New York right now makes my heart sink, it would be the perfect amount of cold right now, that nip in the air, maybe even a bit of snow.

"It was lovely getting to meet you too, Bella." Maddie waves to her as she sits at my desk and does the buckle up on the red shoes.

"Let me know what happens tonight and how the meeting with Tommy goes. Love you," Bella says as I lean forward on my desk to blow her a kiss.

"I will, can you give my mom a big hug from me? Love you too."

"Of course, Kat."

Chapter 35
James

I hadn't planned on being out tonight, Willie had texted me the other day about coming out and I'd said no. That was a week ago before Katherine turned up on my front pouch, before I'd been to my mum's wedding, and before I'd been on the best date of my life.

So when Willie called me earlier to ask again, and told me he knew for sure Maddie and Katherine were coming, I said yes.

That led to me being back in The Sydney Siren, images of my first kiss with Kat flash in my mind. I know I need to tell her how I really feel, I need to give her a reason to stay here, to want to try us, whatever this is or could be but she needs to know how I feel about her.

Willie's been telling me how he got a call from Maddie this morning about giving Katherine her first tattoo. He said that he's been sworn to not say what she got, which is a weird thing when she's going to have it on her body forever. "Yeah, she sat like a trooper."

I laugh knowing she would have wanted to seem as cool as humanly possible, would have wanted him to think she was cool. "That girl is stronger than she looks."

He smiles at me for a moment like he can read in my eyes how much I like her, then his face shifts. "Dude, weird question?" Most of Willie's questions are.

"Shoot." I turn my head back towards the door as we talk, wanting to see her the minute she enters the room. Wanting to see her eyes search the room for her nearest exits and then me.

"Do you know if Maddie's seeing anyone?" I have to physically turn to look at him to be sure I've heard him right, because what? Not in the nearly ten years that I've known Willie has he ever made any indication he was interested in Maddie. Jesus, I don't think I'd let him date her, anyway. I'd never stop Maddie if she really wanted to, but I'd also kill him if he hurt her.

"Not that I know of, why?" I say at such a slow pace I think he's about to burst into flames but he recovers quickly as he always does.

He leans forward on the railing in front of us and I follow his action, setting my sight back in front of me again. "Oh, no reason."

Yep, definitely need to keep an eye on him, but right now my eyes are on the red head who's just walked in laughing with my best friend on her arm. She looks beautiful, of course; her hair is pulled back into a hair style I've seen on Maddie before, she can't hide behind it like she likes to do. The dress she's wearing isn't one I think I've seen before, or it's not one I've noticed before. It's green and silky, hugging her in every place I'd like to put my hands.

"So you and Kat then? Saw that coming from a mile away," he tells me, I don't need to be looking at him to see the cocky grin he's got on his face.

"Fuck off," I tell him with no real threat, the smile on my face is enough for him to know I don't mean it.

I watch as she and Maddie get their bearings but she doesn't do her usual sweep of the place, not checking every corner or looking for the exits. Maybe it's because she's been here before but something pulls at my chest seeing her as comfortable as she is.

"Oh, come on, this is the first girl you've even considered dating ever, it's big." He doesn't sound like he's taking the piss, he sounds proud. I look at him and he's got a real smile, one I don't see very often. "I'm proud of you, man."

"Thanks, but don't get all emotional on me, it's weird." We don't do emotional conversations, maybe that's why I've never noticed anything with him and Maddie, or maybe I wasn't paying enough attention.

I look back at Katherine as she grabs her phone out of her bag and then brings it to her face as she and Maddie start to weave through the crowd in front of us.

My phone vibrates in my pocket and when I pull it on it's her name on the screen.

"You know you kinda look like a creep watching the crowd like that?" she tells me over the noise on both ends of the call.

I raise my voice a little. "Maybe I was looking for someone."

"Your next victim?" Somehow I can tell she's closer just by the way the crowd sounds on the phone.

"No, I've already got one." I look for her again but she's nowhere in front of me. "But she's a bit slippery."

"You make me sound like a fish." I can feel her behind me, hanging up the phone in the process.

I turn to look at her, the look on her face light and soft something I don't see much, also catching Maddie and Willie at the bar behind her. I'm so close to her, I can smell her signature of sunshine and vanilla. I grab onto her waist and pull her back towards me until my back hits the railing behind me, my hands don't leave her sides as my finger draws little circles on her right side.

"Who said I was talking about you?" I whisper into her ear, I'm so closer to her, my lips touch the lobe of her ear as I pull back.

She doesn't let me get very far, she pulls me down to kiss her with her hand on the back of my neck. I'm a little shocked and it takes me a second to kiss her back. She's never this forward but it looks good on her. It makes a nice change to me kissing her all the time, I guess it's a little boost to me knowing she does actually want to kiss me.

We sink into a rhythm we're both used to at this point, her biting at my bottom lip, my tongue winning the war with hers. It's comfortable, and warm—it feels like home, and I don't want to let her go. Even when she pulls away from me. My hands don't slip from her and she doesn't make a move to get out of my grip. Instead her hands rest on my chest like that's where they belong.

My mind slips to the places I've tried my best to not let it. The place where this is it, just us. We do this kinda thing all the time, at weekends, at parties, around Ella. I hold her hand and kiss her forehead and it's not the craziest thing in the world. As much as I have to lose, she has so much more.

"Hey," Willie says, coming back to us with a fruity looking drink in his hand that he hands Kat once I let her go, reluctantly. "How's the arm?"

"Oh, yeah, this secret tattoo, let's see." I want to know what this thing is that she wants to have for her for the rest of her life. Is it unbelievably sad that I'm jealous of that tattoo?

"Okay, fine, but you can't laugh or make it a thing," she tells me, only me. I look at Maddie who's trying so desperately to hide her smile behind the straw in her drink, Willie looking at her just as confused as me. I'm guessing he doesn't understand the context of what he's put on her.

Kat turns to the side slightly, showing me the back of her arm and I finally get why she was being weird about it. The back of her bicep now has the delicate swirls of a lighthouse, not exactly the one we went to but I think it's implied by the text under that reads 'the joy'. A somewhat quote of what she told me her dad used to say.

When she turns back around, the pink on her cheeks is bright enough for me to see in the dim light of the bar. "It's beautiful," I tell her because my heart is literally in my throat.

I wanted to talk to her, tell her what I'm feeling, and finally find out how she feels too.

Now I'm not sure I'm in any state to be doing that now, I'm not sure I'll get a sentence out at this rate.

"Hey, Willie, you fancy a dance?" I hear Maddie ask to the side of me but I don't turn. I have my hand on Kat's elbow like she might float away from me at any moment. They walk away and it's just us in our little bubble looking at each other in the way we do.

"Maybe we should talk?" she says, pulling me towards a fire exit I'm sure we're not meant to go through.

When we're outside the warm air hits my bare arms, but when she stops walking, she shivers. I run a hand down her arm making sure not it's not the arm with the tattoo.

She looks me over like she needs time, I can see the little cogs in her mind going, the soft and light version of Katherine gone. Taking a long drink, she goes to run a hand through her hair and falters when she remembers it's braided back.

"What did you want to talk about Katherine?" I ask her, feeling like I might have to kick this into gear.

"You know..." She barely looks at me as she scans the alley way, anywhere but my face.

I grab hold of her chin tilting her head so she looks at me again. "I want you to tell me."

"You're not going to make this easy, are you?" She tries to shake me off but I don't let my hand move from her.

"Me? Easy? Never." I tease.

"You, me, we need to decide what this is, what's going on." She sounds as frazzled as I feel. But I'm impressed, a little shocked at how direct that really was. I'd like to think for a second that maybe I have rubbed off on her.

It takes me a second to say. "What do you want to be going on?"

"This isn't just about me," she fires back, still trying to make me make the decision.

"True, but I have a feeling what you want isn't always what you do, so I *want* to know what you actually *want*. Do you understand?"

I watch her swallow and I let go of her taking a step back like we'll need the space to fit this conversation between us.

"I want this to not be so hard," she says mostly under her breath and I don't make like I heard her. "You and me, I can't pretend I don't like you anymore, it's too hard now." *There it is*, I'm not on my own in this. "And I get it, everything with your mom makes it hard for you to want anything but I can't just be some girl you have sex with. I'm a sensitive person, as much as I tried not to be."

And I'm lost again.

"Just some girl I have sex with, is that how you see this?" I skip over the line about my mum because I know she's right, she knows she's right. I know that's why I haven't had a serious relationship ever but this isn't about that. "Katherine, you know I haven't slept with another girl since our first kiss. That's not because I just didn't have time, that's because I physically couldn't want anyone else. You're all I've been able to think about, I think feelings have been involved in this for longer than either of us realise." It seems obvious to me, and apparently everyone else around us, but not to her. Has she honestly been thinking I've been thinking about her non-stop just because I want to have sex with her?

The look on her face tells me she did in fact think that.

"Well." She's gone so pale I'm surprised she's able to speak really. "I feel kinda out of my depth now, I had this whole thing worked out in my mind of what to say when you told me it's hard for you to commit to one girl," she half laughs, at herself more than me.

I just want to hold her. "If anyone was going to get me to commit to one girl, it was you, Sunshine."

Her face does this light and airy thing I love so much and her eyes are soft when she looks at me like no one's ever really talked to her all that before. "Are you sure? I don't want to pressure you or make you do anything you don't want to, but honestly, which is kinda hard for me, I can't seem to think about anything else other than you either."

I step closer to her. "Why does it kinda sound like you're trying to talk me out of this? Katherine, I'm not saying that I'll be perfect or that this will work straight away, but I think we should at least give ourselves the chance to find out." I'm not sure who's more shocked by my words, her or me, but I don't stop. "I think we both know I'm not going to be your soulmate and I can't ask you to give up on that but I am asking if you'll give me a shot to at least try and show you what we could have."

She falters for a second like she wants to answer right away but holds herself back, but she takes a step towards me anyway. "Okay, but you have to understand my brain's not going to make it easy on us. I'll think everything through three hundred times and I'll be anxious I'm doing everything wrong all the time." She smiles at me a little the way she does when she's told me something so honest it worries her.

"I wouldn't expect anything less but I'll be there when the dark clouds roll in and I'll find all your emergency exits for you," I laugh, linking my arms around her waist pulling her closer to me. Something on her face tells me no one has ever noticed that before. "Slow and steady wins the race, Kat."

"Are you calling me a turtle now?" she asks, leaning back in my arms so she can look up at me.

"No, I'm saying we'll be slow and steady, no rushing, no expectations, we'll just see what happens, no pressure," I tell her because I think that's what we both need to know. That neither one of us is pressured into anything here, that we can just tread along the beach and see what happens.

"No pressure," she repeats back like a little promise to ourselves.

Chapter 36
Katherine

I promise myself then and there that no matter what Tommy says to me tomorrow morning, I'll be staying in Australia. I owe it to James and to myself to see where this might go.

"Katherine, I'm going to cut to the chase," Tommy says through the screen on my laptop. His office in New York has the most amazing view, I can see skyscrapers and the glow of city lights behind him through his window making my heart feel weird. He's also saying "cut to it" as if he wants to get this over and done with quickly, but we have in fact been talking for like an hour, he's on his second glass of whiskey, and I'm on my second cup of coffee; it's weird alright.

I almost feel like I've known him forever the way we talk about soulmates and journalism.

"I want you to work for me." I'm sure he thinks my end of the call has frozen because everything around me stops including my breathing.

"Excuse me?" There is no way he just said what I think he did, not a chance. There must be bad Wi-Fi somewhere on this link.

"I know it may be a bit forward but it's kinda how I am, my wife says it's something I need to work on." He takes another drink from his glass. "Katherine, you've got something about you that I just feel will work so well here; you believe."

"I'm not sure what to say." I nervously pick at my fingers in my lap.

"Say you'll at least think about it, you'd be the youngest writer I've ever hired but that's what we need. Someone to give a new fresh voice to a media that seems to be on the edge of extinction." I see his face get visibly more excited as he continues to talk. "I have big ideas to push us more into the online space and that's what I want from you, your blog is so real and exposed, that's what I want." He's basically saying he wants to pay me to do what I do already.

I might combust right now in front of him, this is everything I wanted, the opportunity I wanted the minute I stepped out of my graduation ceremony but I stopped myself from applying for any of them because of this trip. I said I would go home at Christmas if I hadn't gotten very far with the search.

I also said I'd try with James.

"I guess I'll think about it then." I can't just say no to him, I can't shut him down right now when I can't even quite wrap my head around what's even happened.

"Perfect, I'd obviously need you to come back here to start if you did take it."

Obviously.

A feeling in my chest starts pulling at me and it moves to my fingers. Panic. This is big, real big, life changing, career starting stuff. Am I really in a position to turn that down because of a boy?

He's not just a boy.

My brain starts to move faster than I can keep up with and before Tommy says goodbye I've already got thirty terrible scenarios going in my mind.

"Well, I'll get Natasha to send over an offer, just so you can see what we'd be expecting. It was wonderful getting to talk to you Katherine. I hope to speak to you soon."

"Thank you so much, speak soon," I say, closing my laptop and leaning back in my chair staring up at the ceiling of my room.

My room.

OH.

Ella.

MY.

Maddie.

GOD.

James.

"So, how did it go?" Ella says bursting into my room. She's still got her wetsuit on and her hair is sticking up in every direction.

"Did you just run back here after your class?" I ask as she drips water where she stands.

"Yes, but please just tell me what he said!"

"I guess really well, he offered me a job." I should be saying that in a way that sounds far more excited and yet I sound about as flat as I feel.

"Oh, my god, that's amazing! Well done, sweetie," she says pulling me into a big hug lifting me out of the chair. Hearing someone else being excited about it kinda makes me more proud about it if that's really possible, like pride is contagious.

"Yeah it is, but I'd have to go home," I tell her pulling away so I can see her face again. I watch the light in her eyes drop just a little but it happens.

"You've got to do what's best for you Katherine, whatever feels right in here." She points her fingers into my chest where I can feel my heart beating a mile a minute.

"And what would that be?" I ask her, feeling like a little kid that wants to be told what to do.

"I can't tell you that, Kat, but you'll know. Whatever you choose, I am so proud of you."

When she says it, it's so similar to the tone my dad used to use that I feel my eyes sting. I've been so worried about letting him down, not doing what he wanted me to. Would he be proud of me? Is this the universe's way of setting me back to the path he wanted for me?

And as if I don't already have enough voices in my head, my dad's comes to the front, soft and gentle the way he was.

Make sure you have your own life.

I was never too sure what he really meant, and I never got to ask more questions, but I think this is what he wanted. Wanted me to make the decisions for myself, for me to guide myself and not my soul stone.

And for the first time my soul stone is actually the last of my worries.

The days after my call with Tommy are hard and confusing and everything else I could possibly feel. I can't make a decision for the life of me, and every time I think I know what I want, something else seems to pull me the other way.

James doesn't miss a beat with this whole new relationship we have going on and takes me out for dinner the night after. I want to tell him, I have this urge to tell him everything, every thought I've ever had, I want him to know.

"Okay, what's my favourite colour?" I ask as I lean back in my chair. The candle on the table makes his face glow and I like the way his eyes sparkle at me.

"Oh, easy, it's green." Somehow we've managed to get to twelve of twenty questions without getting a single one wrong. I'm not sure how we started, something about us not knowing each other enough, and him telling me he has in fact been paying a lot of attention. Apparently I was paying a lot more attention than I thought. "What's mine?"

"Okay, one, not fair you know green looks great against my hair, and two, blue, obviously," I finish by stabbing the last carrots on my plate and stuffing them in my mouth.

"Every colour looks great on you, Sunshine," he smiles at me; he's got that whole surfer boy charm really going for him tonight and my heart has been melting since he picked me up. The shirt he's wearing is unbuttoned so far I can see chest tattoos peeking through and I kinda just want him to take it off.

"You've got to stop with all these compliments or I'm going to get a big head," I smile at him. I like this, this easy conversation. It feels nice, good, like I could do this for a long time.

Forever.

"Oh, well we can't have that can we?" A wicked grin pulls on his face and I feel my skin get hot. "All your clothes are terrible and I think you should be naked all the time instead," he says, all calm and cool as our waiter comes back to our table. But his eyes are dark as he looks over the bare skin on my shoulders and collar bone.

"Can I get you guys everything else?" he asks as he picks our plates up and I feel my cheeks heat even more.

"Yeah, can we get a dessert menu, please?" James asks, moving to hold my hand across the table.

"Of course, I'll be right back."

"You can't say that shit outside," I say with a pointed look "And you're not a dessert guy." He's playing with my hand in his but I just watch his face.

My heart squeezes as I watch him take a drink from his water, and god what I wouldn't give to be that glass. To have his mouth on mine again.

He smirks at me and he puts his glass down. "Oh, I'm not, but you are. Cheesecake, I'm guessing. I'll have my dessert later." Want drips from every word, so much so my breath stops. He seems to take great pleasure in reminding me how much he wants me every opportunity he gets. "Next question," he asks while I squirm in my seat, heat starting to spread from between my legs and up my chest.

It doesn't take long for him to notice, flagging down our waiter and we order dessert to go. Cheesecake, of course.

He takes my hand as we head back to his truck and we laugh the whole way back to my place, and for a minute I forget. Forget that I need to make a choice between here and going back home, because in moments like these with him, the choice is obvious and easy to make.

I want to be where he is. And I want to be his and I want him to be mine.

"You read a lot." I watch him pick up several of my books, his arms hanging over the edge of the end of my bed.

"Yeah, I guess. I feel calm when I read," I say bringing myself down to the end of the bed laying down next to him, my arm brushes his and I get goosebumps. I've never had this, being with another person and not worrying for a minute. He calms me. He makes me feel happy and I'm not nervous at all because I know he'll never judge me.

"What are they about?" he asks, flicking the pages of one. His face is confused and almost amused.

"They're romance," I tell him, tracing my fingers down his side not looking at what his hands are doing but watching the way his muscles flex on his back, the way his tattoos move.

"All of them? I guess I shouldn't be surprised, you romantics." He turns to look at me more using one of his hands to move my sex hair out of my face. "So, they're all the same?" That one gets my attention.

"All the same?" I roll over and grab two different books. "Of course not. This one," I lift a blue one with white flowers and cartoon characters on the front to his face, "is about a small town cowboy who's grumpy for no good reason and a sunshine city woman who comes to town to help said cowboy's family with PR for the ranch, it's very forced proximity."

"It's very *what*?"

"And this one," I show him another, with pink flowers and gold lettering, "is about a grumpy CEO who is far too busy for anyone, except the woman who lives next door who he's been in love with for years. This one's fake dating."

"Faking dating? What does that mean?" He looks almost as confused as I guessed he would be.

"They're tropes, it's like a theme I guess. We have a lot of them in romance books—one bed, single dad, marriage of convenience, and my personal favourite, enemies to lovers." He's right, I am a romantic and I could read the same tropes over and over again set in different small towns and big cities and still squeal when the slow burn finally starts to *burn*.

"Enemies to lovers is your favourite?" He's close to laughing. I can see it in his eyes.

"The idea that someone can see all the bad things in you, see you at your literal worst but still learn to love you anyway. Yeah, it's my favourite."

He kisses me gently on my forehead, telling me he's heard me even if he has nothing to add, then he grabs them out of my hands, putting them back down on the floor. "Sunshine, I think we should take the books away. They're rotting your brain."

"Never!" I shout as he starts to tickle at my ribs. "That's not fair," I say in between laughs and wheezes.

He rolls me over still tickling at my sides and in one swift motion has me straddling him, with his hands tight on my hips. I feel his dick twitch behind me hitting my arse. I like this position. I have power this way. I lower my head down so I'm closer to him. "You seem to like the grumpy ones, too." He's cocky smirk on his face.

"Well I like you, don't I?"

"Oh, I see. So you've been picturing me this whole time as these grumpy CEOs or cowboys?" He's confident, and before I would have wanted to slap him, now it makes me want to push my hips back teasing him a little, so I do. I've never been very confident with this kinda thing, being sexy, but with him I'm not embarrassed to show him what I want or show him I want him.

"The whole time? No, I've been picturing Henry Cavill, actually." I pull back from his face a little but his hands on hips don't let me go too far.

"And what's he got on me?" His smug smile doesn't budge one inch, if I could I'd be squeezing my legs together but they're pushed tight to him, and I'm sure he can feel my heat pooling in-between my legs. I feel his dick harden more, he can definitely feel it.

"I mean, what doesn't he have?" I squeal at the end as he flips us both over me now pinned under him, his hands either side my head holding my hands there and my legs splayed open for him to put himself between.

"You want to try that again?" he mocks, he's cock rubbing at my clit as he moves himself. "Cat got your tongue, Sunshine? Or would you like to tell me who you really think about," he tells me as he grabs himself rubbing his cocks head over my clit and then lining himself up with my entrance teasing me with the first two inches of him.

"Oh, god."

"No, still not right. One last chance, Kat."

"You," I'll tell him anything just to get him inside of me again. Apparently the two orgasms after dinner were not enough for me. "You, James, please."

"Since you asked so nicely." He pulls out, rolling on a condom from the box next to him on the bed and then he smiles down at me sliding himself in me. "Jesus, still so tight." Once he's filled me, his hands come back down to the bed and his face lines back up with mine and I grab it so I can taste him again.

He still tastes like the cheesecake we shared after orgasm number one and I now know that every time I eat it from here on out, I'm going to be turned on.

He leans back on his heels and shifts so my legs are over his shoulders, and the angle he hits, it's almost otherworldly. "Fuck." He thrusts into me hard and fast and I have no idea until having sex with him that this was what I liked. That I like being fucked and not soft and gentle sex. It's new and liberating in a way to know myself better because of him.

"Sorry, did that hurt?" And yet, when he is sweet, it's still sexy.

"God, no, don't stop," I beg, feeling my insides clench around him.

"You keep clenching like that, I won't last long." He nips at my ankle next to his head and leans his body forward, bending me in a way I was unaware I could do.

The build up in my body is so intense, I have no idea what to do with my hands but grip my sheets. The noises I make I'm sure are either inaudible or pure gibberish.

"That's it, Sunshine. God, you take it so well." The praise for being fucked by him grows the knot in my belly, new turn on unlocked. I watch in pure awe as his hips slap against mine and I no longer have control of my body but he holds tight to my thighs stopping my body from falling apart.

"Yes, fuck, right here."

I lift my head in time to see him lick his thumb and bring it down to my clit, rubbing at it. "How'd I get so lucky?" I have no idea how he's still talking while blowing my brain from my body but it's completely impossible for me to respond to him. Honestly, I think I'm the lucky one in this, the man literally gets pleasure from getting me off, like who is he? I feel it and then it's taking over my whole body and mind and I'm not sure if I say anything other than his name. "That's it, Sunshine, come for me."

"Come with me," I manage to get out while so close to the edge, I grip around him as tight as I can to bring him over with me.

"Fuck, Kat." His thrusts get sloppy and his thumb works circles on my clit and I feel myself lose all control and the room goes white. I can't hear anything I might be saying but I can feel him lose control too.

He lets go of my legs and lets me flop on my side, I'm still spaced out as he pulls out of me.

"Is death by orgasm a thing?" I ask laughing as we lay next to each other, chests heaving and breaths uneven. I like this bit too, the after, the talking we do. He slides an arm under me and pulls me back to his chest, my head under his chin, he lifts his head and kisses the top of mine.

"I don't know, but I'm up for trying."

Chapter 37
Katherine

I'm in the shop for like five minutes before a sea of kids come walking in for a surf lesson which means James will be kept out of the shop for the rest of the day.

Giving me time to finally work out what I want to say. I need to tell him what's going on. I can't keep going on dates with him that end with us in bed together without telling him, it feels so wrong.

I haven't really decided if I am going or not, but when I think of it in a logical way I don't see how I can't go back.

Dad said I shouldn't put my soulmate search ahead of everything else and I almost feel like I'll be letting him down somehow if I don't go back and take the job. I know if he was still here that's what he'd be telling me to do.

But I'm not on my soulmate search anymore. I'm with James, I'm with someone who I love.

Wait.

I've never loved another person, I don't even know what it should feel like.

This is new and fresh. But that's what it feels like, it's exciting and I just love the way he makes me feel when he's around. I want to spend all my time with him, around him, just near him. And it feels like every nerve in my body is on fire when his hands are on me, like nothing I've ever felt before in my life. And when he looks at me, sometimes it's like being hit by a truck, my chest hurts and my legs wobble and I can't look away from it.

I'm not in love, but maybe I'm falling.

As five o'clock rolls around, I turn the sign over on the door saying we're closed and then go back to the counter and start to cash out.

As I turn back towards the cash register, there he is standing in front of me. Only the counter separates us.

I can't help but take him in, the skin on his arms is sun-kissed making the black swirls of his tattoos stand out more. His hair is still damp from the day in the sea. I wonder what it would be like to run my fingers through it like this and then I wish I hadn't thought that at all.

I see his eyes move over me too, and then meet my own. "Good day?" he asks, his brows raised, reminding me I was just checking him out shamelessly, which of course he loves. I shake my head slightly to get the thought out.

"Yeah, good takings. Ella will be happy it was busy."

Small talk, this is horrible, we are never this awkward, not even when we were hating on each other. Will the world open up and swallow me whole, please?

"Feel like I haven't seen you at all today." He runs his hand through his hair, and I watch as little droplets fall from it.

"That would be because you haven't," I retort as I step out from behind the counter about to slide past him to tidy the wetsuits when he stops me with a big hand on my bare forearm.

"What's wrong? Are you avoiding me?" he quizzes. Not even twenty words from me and he knows something's up. And yes, I am trying my best to avoid him until I can get my head around a hundred different emotions and scenarios.

"Nothing, I'm fine." *Yeah, that'll really convince him, good one, Kat.*

"Yeah, sorry, I think I know you enough to know that's not true," he says, suspicious of me. He looks over my face for a moment, I'm glad he can't read my mind. Cause right now, I'm thinking about how I'm contemplating throwing away my career, my future, to stay here with him. If it wasn't for the job, I would stay and see what we could make but I have to take it, I know.

That's what my head thinks, at least. My heart tells me none of it makes sense that I feel any of the things I do for him, and yet I do.

I wonder if I'd left my stone in that drawer, maybe this would be easier. Maybe I'd let myself make up my own mind about him, but it's too late now. I know it's not him and it hurts. It did then, but even more now. Now I've seen who he really is.

Then his hands are on my face and I melt under his touch. I can't move. I think he's going to say something, or maybe I'm going to say something, but then he's rubbing his hand over my cheek and his thumb over my lower lip as I look up at him. I don't feel the need to stop him.

"Katherine." My breath hitches in my throat as his other hand comes up to cup my other cheek. "I can see those cogs going and I'm not sure what's going on but I'm going to kiss you now." His breath hits my face as he speaks and my brain turns to liquid.

"Please," I tell him, almost whispering.

His eyes shift for a second and something flashes over them and I think he's thinking he regrets everything he said to me the other night. But that's clearly not what he's thinking, because a second later, his lips are on mine.

My mind is finally quiet for the first time in two days. His lips are soft and perfect like the rest of him and I kick myself for this because I don't think I'll ever want to kiss anyone else, ever. Nothing feels like this, as his hands slide from my face into my hair I know no one will touch me the way he does.

SOUL BELIEFS

It's like all my doubts and worries take a vacation whenever he's in the room because I don't think anything bad will happen when he's with me and I feel safe and at home in his arms. My heart races and my palms sweat as I wrap my hands about the back on his neck, entwining my fingers, pulling him closer to me.

I was wrong, I've fallen. I was already there. I just don't think I knew how badly until right now how much he'd really pulled me under. The second I was debating staying for him I should have known.

I can feel it taking over me like a perfect morning wave crushing me under the water, completely engulfing me.

Fuck.

His mouth moves across mine like nothing I've ever experienced before. It's like I'm melting into him, like our mouths are made to be doing this. But they aren't, I remind myself.

And yet when his tongue swipes over my lower lip, I don't hesitate to open my mouth and let him in. At the same time, his arm that's been holding onto my hip moves around my back and pulls me even closer to him which I didn't think was possible.

"The fuck is that," James says, pulling away from me a little, looking down at the pocket of my shorts.

A bright glow is showing through the fabric, I untangle myself from him and fish around until my hand makes contact with it. My hand shakes as I pull it out, my hand laying out in front of us and there in my palm is my soul stone, glowing.

His eyes go as wide as mine do.

"I didn't put it in there," I tell him, I was sure it had been sitting in my bedside drawer since the night of the wedding and I have no idea how it ended up in my pocket. "Why is it only glowing now? This doesn't make sense," I say to myself more than to James. This really doesn't make any sense, everything I thought I knew about the stones made me think it would just glow right away, so why didn't mine?

What if it's broken?

When I look back up at James, he's just looking at me, but not in the usual way. I'm not even sure if he's breathing, he's just staring. He's still mere millimetres away from my face. I'd love to know what he's thinking because he's not looking at me like he did at the wedding when I was sitting on that kitchen counter or at the lighthouse or even in my bedroom or like he was a few minutes ago before he kissed me. He's looking at me like it's that first day I stepped foot in this store.

He doesn't look like he's feeling what I'm feeling, or maybe he is and that's what the problem is, maybe he doesn't want to feel this.

I wish I knew what he was thinking, because my thoughts won't slow down.

"I can't believe you have that," he practically growls, he looks angry but he also looks so sad. I close my hand around it hoping to hide it. "What happened to seeing how things went?" I've only really ever seen him truly angry once, the night of the Halloween party and I was not on the receiving end of it then.

"James." This is not what should be happening. "It... I... it wasn't supposed to be this way—"

"Could you not have just let yourself fall? Let yourself feel what I felt? Did you have to have that thing glow to tell you?" His words sting, sting like falling on to those rocks the other night, my knees ache thinking about it, or maybe it's the sick feeling filling my stomach making me feel weak.

"James..." He cuts me off, taking a few steps away from me. I instantly feel cold with him so far away.

"I felt it the minute I looked into your eyes the other night at the wedding. I felt the tight squeeze around my heart. Every minute I've spent with you since, I only felt it more," he confesses, looking down at his hands, anywhere but at me. "I'd hoped you felt it too but all that matters is that thing!"

My brain has completely fogged and the feeling of being whole is replaced by the feeling I'm all too familiar with, anxiety. I'm so worried I can't reel this back or say the right thing, my mouth goes so dry that I don't think I can open it at all.

I had not planned for this, I have nothing in place to help me. "Why didn't you tell me?" is all I'm able to muster. His voice and words swirled in my head and I can't possibly say something back to what he's saying.

I know what he said the other night about giving it a go but he made it sound so casual, like he didn't want to jump in. Like while I was here we'd go out but he didn't word it like he loves me.

"Because I know you Katherine, I know if I had, you would have ran to get that thing and test it and I didn't want that. I wanted you to understand your own feelings but I know you." Katherine, not Sunshine or Kat, just Katherine. The last bit comes out dripped in disappointment, it's the only time his disappointment has affected me.

I don't dare tell him I got it out for the wedding.

"No, you don't." This was the moment I had been waiting for since I stepped foot in this city. I knew that, he knew that. "If you did, then you would have known I'd test it at some point. Even if I had listened to the feeling in my heart, even if I told you I'd fallen. I—" We stand inches apart from each other again like we can't help but be close. I'm starting to worry that if my heart beats any harder my chest will hit his.

"You what?" I can hear the anger in his voice creep out, the tone I'd heard plenty of times before but it's different, mixed with other things. It's like all the versions of himself are fighting with each other. I imagine all the little James' in his head, like my little Katherine's, fighting over what to feel and say.

I don't want him to see me cry right now, I blink to keep my tears back. "I couldn't let myself truly believe I had." I'd never let myself fall apart for someone no matter how much I told myself I would. It's too scary, too much risk, too much like losing more of myself.

"So, it wouldn't have mattered. I could have done anything and it wouldn't have mattered unless you checked, unless you knew for sure?" His voice is so cold it cuts right through me and I'm stuck again.

"James."

"Any feelings you had for me, you would just swept them under the carpet when you met your real soulmate, is that it? In twenty years time you wouldn't even give a thought to me because at least you had your soulmate. Right? You're just like her."

I flinch like I've been hit, I can't believe he compared me to his mom. "But—" I'm not even sure I can say it out loud. "James, you are my soulmate." Considering he just confessed his feelings to me, I'd think this would be a good thing. But I can see the way his face twists and I know how he feels now.

"Don't do that, Katherine." He puts a hand through his hair like I've watched him do a thousand times before taking a few steps back until he hits the counter, putting his hands on it and leaning back. I don't think he can decide if he wants to be close or a thousand miles away.

I watch his chest rise and fall as mine does the same. I feel like I've just ran a marathon; out of breath, sweating, feeling like I might throw up at any moment.

"Fine," I say, making him look up from his feet, time to be brave Katherine. "I don't know what I'm doing, James." I look away from him so I can actually think without having his eyes bore into me. "You think I have any clue about any of this? I don't. I don't know how any of this works." I don't know where any of this is coming from, what part of my brain these feelings are pouring from.

The truthful part.

"The truth is, I'm so lost, I don't know what I'm doing. When we just kissed," I pause, I don't know what I'm trying to tell him or say or explain. I just wanted to run, that's always been my default.

The cowards way out.

"What are you scared of, Katherine?" His voice is soft now, but it's too late my perfect moment is gone. The moment I'd dreamt of since I was a kid, since the day I was told the stories of soulmates, since I got my stone, is gone. I'll never get it back.

"What am I scared of?" I can feel the angry build in myself now, growing like an untamed rose bush, climbing up the side of a house, covering the windows, blocking out the light.

I take a step towards him.

"I'm scared of everything!" I shout. "I'm scared I'll make the wrong decision. I'm scared I can't make a decision! I'm scared that I... that I don't actually know what I want anymore. I was willing to throw it away to stay here with you. But you'll never get past how I believe, will you?" I can feel the words flow like a river now, I can't stop them even if I wanted to.

I take another step.

"You walked into my life as the complete opposite of what I thought I wanted, and now look at me. Look at this." I thrust the stone, still in my hand, closer to him. I stare at it to make sure it is still glowing and I'm not losing my mind. I take a breath, my heart still pounding hard in my chest but I don't want to shout anymore.

I take one more step.

"I'm scared that regardless of this stone, I'll never actually let myself love anyone. Because loving someone is like losing a part of yourself, and I've lost such a big part, I'm not sure how much I have left to lose." I finally let the tears roll from my eyes. I'm inches from him now and I can hear him breathing.

He's so close, I want to hold him, for him to hold me and tell me this will be okay, that we'll work through this together but I don't and neither does he. But I can't stop myself from looking at him.

"Katherine."

"You know I could have let myself love you, I could." He puts his hand on my cheek again and I lean into it. "I could have done it maybe without the stone but I think I need it because I never trust myself, never know if I'm making the right decision. But you are so sure of things, and I thought I was sure about you and somehow convinced myself I *was* making the right decision. Maybe my stone's broken because I am."

I take a long breath in and then exhale before stepping out of his touch. "Katherine." His eyes are a little pleading, like maybe he wants to continue this conversation but I feel like it'll go nowhere.

"I got offered a job at a magazine in New York, that's why I was avoiding you. Because I couldn't decide if I should take it and move back home, or to stay here with you." Somehow that seems like the easiest thing to say now. Hours ago, I was sweaty and panicked about it but now it's like nothing.

"Katherine, that's... that's amazing. You shouldn't give up that opportunity." I know he's right but he's also breaking my heart and I think maybe his own.

"I've been panicking for days, I think I didn't want to disappoint you or let you down. But I think you just made up my mind for me." The choice couldn't be clearer. "You should go." I don't really want him to, but I'm not sure what else we have left to say to each other, I'm exhausted.

He stalls for a moment, pushing himself off the counter top just to linger in front of me. I manage to not cry while he looks at me one last time in a way that tells me he never will again. "Bye, Kat," he says holding my cheek as he kisses my forehead and then with one last look he's gone.

Kat.

One last reminder that he really did know me, truly. The fact I'll never hear it from his lips again starts the wave of sadness and then I don't think it'll ever stop.

I sit in the darkness of the shop on the floor and cry. My chest hurts in so many ways and I forget how to breathe properly for a few minutes and then I feel it.

I feel it.

I feel a small crack and then another and another until it feels like it's fallen apart completely. I've only ever known a complete heartbreak once before.

And I'd never wanted that again, never wanted to lose someone again who meant that much to me and yet here I am, on my own, in an empty shop falling completely and utterly apart. Because the one thing I thought I could do, the one thing I thought would make me whole again, was gone, and I don't think I'll ever get it back again.

Ella tries to call, or maybe it's Mom checking in, I feel my phone vibrate in my pocket but I don't touch it. I can't, I don't think I would make an audible word if I tried.

Eventually, Ella comes to the shop when I'm an hour late home. I feel even worse when I realise how much she was probably worrying, and that makes me cry more. She doesn't ask me what happened, I'm sure she can work it out from the now clear stone on the floor next to me. She just hugs me until I stand myself up.

When we get home, I just take myself to my room, pulling myself under my covers and crying some more. I'm not sure I know what I'm crying for anymore. I don't think I'll ever stop. The worst part is that I know it's all my fault.

If I'd just let myself feel what I was feeling, trusted myself for a change, if I'd not been so stubborn, if I'd just left the stone in the drawer, it still would have glowed. But I wouldn't have known, maybe I could have just fallen for him and we could have worked out the whole job thing together.

I cry myself to sleep.

Chapter 38
James

I don't really know how I manage to get in my truck and start driving but I do it with a numb feeling spreading through me.

But I keep moving.

I have to; if I stop, then I don't know what I'll start to feel.

Rage builds inside of me, and my hands grip the steering wheel to the point of pain.

I'm like a shark. I feel like if I stop moving, I'll suffocate. I'm completely on autopilot, just going through the motions.

My view starts to get blurry and I squint out into the sky to check for rain, wondering if the sky feels the same way I do but there's none and then I realise it's me.

Tears sting my face as they fall from my eyes and an unfamiliar sound leaks from my throat and then another, I can feel my hands shake. I pull over to the side of the road and bury my head in my hands.

Pain grips my chest and my throat goes dry. My body shakes in my seat, my chest burning.

What the fuck?

What on earth just happened and why am I crying?

I can't even remember the last time I cried in a way that made my body shake and my head hurt.

I do.

I haven't since she left. Since Mum walked out, that was the last time I lost it. This feels like that, this feels like losing someone I should never have to let go of. Someone who's just meant to be there forever, meant to be with me for my lifetime. This feels like my heart is breaking, or maybe I'm dying.

I manage to pull myself together long enough to drive home, I sit in my truck long enough to make sure I'm not going to cry again. I pull myself from my truck, but before I get to the door, Dad is already outside almost like he's been waiting for me, already knowing.

"Dad, I really fucked up," I tell him when I reach him and there I am, crying again. For too many reasons to count and for the fact he's here for me right now. I don't even get a whiff of beer as he pulls me down into a hug.

I haven't felt comfort from him in years. I can't even remember the last time I actually wanted it from him, it breaks my heart even more that it took all of this for it to happen.

Feeling close to him vanished years ago, replaced by the fear I would end up just like him instead. But now I just need my dad, I need him to hold me like he did years ago.

"It's going to be okay," he tells me and I'm not sure I believe him.

I'm not sure it ever will be again because I don't know how it can be, I don't know how I'm meant to be okay if she's not here. If she's not by my side.

How am I meant to be okay knowing the only girl I've ever fallen for will now hate me forever?

Chapter 39

Katherine

I haven't come out of my room in three days.

That's a little lie, I've been to the kitchen to get very nutritious meals that consist of ice cream and Twinkies, and to go to the restroom.

Other than that, I have wallowed.

I've come to the conclusion I'm going home because even looking at my bed makes me cry.

Emailing Tommy was actually the easiest part of this whole thing, giving me something else to think about.

Not that it stopped my brain for too long.

How pathetic do you have to be for your soulmate to not even want you?

Ella's stopped trying to talk to me about it, and it's not that I don't want to talk to her, but it's hard. She knows every reason why this is hard for him, too, but right now I'd like a little bias on my side. Really, though, I'm a little girl who would really like her mom right now.

I haven't even called her because I just know I'll be worrying her for no reason. I'll be home soon and I'll curl up with her and she'll make it okay right from our couch in New York.

Home.

Bella texted about a hundred times but I don't physically have the energy to cry on the phone to her right now because I know that's all I'll do. I had to give her a very brief summary over text with the promise I'd be home in less then a week and asked if we could eat enough chinese food to die when I do.

"Honey?" Ella says from my bedroom door.

"I'm outside," I call.

"There's someone here to see you." Her voice is unsure.

My heart jumps for a second wondering if it's him, the same way it has every time I've heard the doorbell ring. But any hope for that went in the first two days I spent lying in my bed.

"No, Ella, please," I start to say standing and turning to see her standing in the middle of my room with someone I hadn't thought in a million years would be here. "Mom?"

"Hey, honey," she says, opening her arms that I don't hesitate running right into, burying my face into her neck. I can still smell the city on her, my clothes smell like sunscreen and fresh air. Hers smell like smoke and traffic and everything I can't wait to be around again.

I can't stop myself from crying again.

"But how did you get here?" I think I'm still in shock seeing my mom here, it's like seeing snow settle on the ocean. Out of place but exactly what I needed.

Ella comes back outside with a tray of iced tea and sets it down on the table between all of us.

"Thank you, El," Mom says, her cheeks are flush and she picks up a glass pressing it to her face, her favourite winter coat left on my bed now. I laugh a little and it feels like the first time in forever. "Hey, no laughing at your mother, it was like 40°F in New York when I left yesterday, or was that the day before that? Anyway it's hotter here than I remember." She takes a long sip before placing it back down again. "Well when El called me the other day telling me everything, I couldn't not, honey." She leans across, taking my hand in hers.

"I'm sorry I know you didn't want to worry your mom but I just didn't know what to do, I had to talk to her," Ella says from her seat and I don't blame her. It's not exactly like I've been easy to deal with the last couple of days.

"I understand, Ella, thank you," I tell her, gripping on to her hand with the one Mom's not holding, we look like some kind of weird support group, or a witch coven. Truly this is exactly what I needed, and Ella knew that even if I didn't.

"Well, I've got to get to the shop, I'll leave you two to it." She gives us both a hug before leaving us to look out into her garden, the flowers that were barely blooming when I arrived are in full force now.

"So," Mom finally breaks the silence knowing I won't. "Tell me about him."

"Mom, I don't think I can without crying again," I half laugh, half sniffle knowing I'm right.

"And you don't think I've seen you cry before? Honey, cry and talk, it's good for the soul." There is no point fighting it.

So I tell her everything, from start to finish. The fighting, the wedding, the lighthouse, my new tattoo—which she loves—everything.

She's moved her chair closer by the time I've finished, me leaning my head onto her shoulder as we both stare out into the garden. The sun is much lower in the sky now than when she first got here.

"Did I ever tell you about the time I first met your dad?" she asks, still not moving. We don't talk about Dad a lot, just in passing, here and there, but big stories are saved for times like these.

"Well, yeah, you met at the hospital."

"And did I tell you how much it broke my heart when he ran away from me?" I don't say a word. "When I first saw him in that corridor, I'd just lost a patient, a car crash, it was my first. Then there was your dad, his first shift and the first thing he sees is me crying my eyes out."

Her voice shifts only a little but as I look at her face, her eyes are misted in a way I haven't seen in years.

"I'd barely said five words to him before my stone started to glow and his face, god his face... I might as well have slapped him, but then he just ran. It felt like I'd been hit by a truck." I can't look away from her. "I finished my shift and went home to Nan and cried as much as you, I imagine. I didn't know him, I didn't know anything he was going through.

"We avoided each other like the plague but no matter what, we'd end up running into each other all the time. It was awful, I debated leaving the hospital but I just couldn't. So after a year—"

"A year?" I say, cutting her off. How did I have no idea about all this? I had made Mom and Dad's story some kind of fairytale in my head, about how everything had come together perfectly.

I felt like I'd be a failure if my story wasn't as perfect as theirs. I feel something in me change, like it all clicks into place. Maybe that's what Dad was talking about. Maybe he knew even if I didn't go looking for my soulmate they would still find me at the right time. That I shouldn't waste so much time searching and looking. I don't know how but it kinda makes me feel better?

"Yeah, a year later, he turned up at Nan's with a bunch of flowers. We sat out on her porch for like two hours while he told me everything, that he'd just started his divorce when he ran into me that day and he just couldn't do it until he knew he was properly outside of that relationship. I think I fell in love with him right then. That even though he wanted nothing more than to get to know me, he didn't, because he was worried about someone else. That's who he was.

"Anyway, the rest is history, I guess, but what I'm trying to say, Katherine is that it's okay that it's not perfect right now, or tomorrow or next week. Because it will be, if not with James, then with someone else. You're going to be okay, Kat, I promise." She pulls me more into her and hugs me again and I believe her.

Something pulls at me when she lets go of me and looks back out into the garden.

"I feel at home here, Mom," I tell her and I hate myself a little for saying it. Like I'm betraying her in some way, and I don't know why I need to say it, but I do.

"Then why are you leaving? You can stay." And every bone in my body believes that she would be okay with that, every part tells me she'd be happy for me if I did, but...

"I can't be here while he is too. My heart hurts just being on the same planet as him, the least I can do is put a few thousand miles between us." It hurts to even say it out loud. To admit this is the end of something before I feel like it's even started. To admit he's done this to me, that he's broken my heart, that maybe I've broken his too. I can't know that last bit but I feel it.

"Oh, sweetie." She pulls me into a tight hug and I tell myself I won't cry again, I won't. I've cried enough and I won't.

I do feel at home here, I love it here, but New York is my home too, and if I stay here, I don't think I'll ever heal. I need to go back, I need to take this job and focus my energy on something else. Then I'll come back, maybe in a year or two, and when I come back, I'll face it.

I've spent all this time trying to find him and now I have. He doesn't want me and now I guess it's time I had a new dream.

Posted 22nd November 2024 21:46

I've been filling a void.

A big, very deep void that my dad left behind.

I'll never know how I didn't see it or realise it, but I thought if I found my soulmate that void would be filled. The love I had and got from my dad would be replaced by someone new, by my soulmate.

I've only now realised that's not how love works. You can always make more love, always let more people into your heart. But the people that were there before, they don't lose their space. They always have a hold on that little corner of your heart, and the more people you love, the more you let in, that'll never fill that corner.

I was stupid to ever think it would.

Stupid to ever think this quest or adventure, however I dressed it up, wasn't just a distraction. Something else to fill my head so I didn't have to deal with it. So I could keep pretending for a bit longer.

Soulmates aren't a fix all. They aren't super glue, they are people. I've put mine on a pedestal for so long that I forgot that when I found them, they would just be a person with their own problems and baggage just like me.

I think maybe we shouldn't put so much weight on our soulmates. Coming from me, that's almost funny.

I should feel deflated, so much more disappointed, but really I'm relieved. I found my soulmate, I reached my goal and okay yeah he doesn't want me, but there's nothing I can do about that. I can't make him love me if he doesn't want to. But I can control how I move forward from this though.

SOUL BELIEFS

This is maybe the most free I've ever felt.

Chapter 40
James

I made a mistake.

I'm not too sure what else I'm meant to say.

The numb feeling that's been eating away at my insides for the last five days is a constant reminder for that very fact.

I don't know how to make it right or to make it work.

This place should make me feel better but it doesn't; the beach just seems to remind me of her now and it's awful, quite frankly. I stare out to the ocean from where I'm sitting on the sand, the waves crashing do their best to try and drown out the sound of her voice in my head but she's still there.

She managed to get into every corner of my life and there was a moment in time when I hated that and now I know it's the only way I'll get to see her again; only in my head and when I walk around this town and remember every place she's been.

You're just like her.

My own voice rings through the noise. I can't believe I said that to her.

I think you just made up my mind for me. You should go.

The pain in her voice gets me every time I relive it. I shouldn't have left. I shouldn't have let go of her. I should have said more, said something but I couldn't, I didn't.

SOUL BELIEFS

I now have to live with the fact that the rest of my life is known as After Katherine. I will never know what it's like to not know her, to not of had her in my hands, to not of had her, even if just for a little while. I'll never be able to go back to what I was like before her but I don't know how to be after her. I don't know who I am now.

The sound of footsteps travelling towards me brings me back to the real world and for a second, half a second, I think, I hope, it's her. I don't dare look, I don't want to know; it'll only break my heart more when it's not.

"Hey," Maddie says sitting down next to me. I can't even look at her, I can just picture the look in her eyes, pity, anger. I've been avoiding her just the same as I have everyone else. God knows how I've managed to teach classes this week.

"Hey." My voice sounds hoarse, a dead give away that the night it happened was not the last time I cried.

She throws an arm around my shoulder and has to practically pull me to get me to fall onto her shoulder. "Will you just let me comfort you for like two seconds please?" A small laugh slips from my lips and I think it's the first time since that night. "How are you?"

I can't even begin to try and explain how I am. Angry. Sad. Happy that the universe thought I was the perfect fit for someone like Katherine. Someone so kind and loving, someone who made me better without really trying.

But I don't really care about how I am to think about it enough, I'm worried about how Kat is. "That's not important, I'm more worried about her." I can't deny that I'm pretty sure I'm the villain in this. She should be with her, she should be plotting ways to make me feel worse, if that was at all possible.

I hurt, but Kat feels everything so much more, so I want her to be okay. And it hurts more that I'm not the one to make her feel better, that I'm not the one with her, holding her. Making her feel strong enough to get through it.

"Well I happen to know from a reliable source that one, you're my best friend and even when I think maybe you've fucked up, I still love you and will *always* be by your side, and two, Kat's mum is here so I think she has that side covered." Have I said I love Maddie? No, I don't think I've said it enough. I'm so unbelievably lucky to have her in my life.

"I love you too, Mads." I don't miss the way she looks at me like maybe I've never actually said that out loud to her before, maybe it wasn't just romantic love I'd been hiding away from this whole time. "Her mum is here?"

"Yeah, she—she's here to help Kat go back to New York." Maddie's voice goes small, like she knows how much my heart is breaking right now.

"So, she's really going?" I'm not sure what else could be worse but she can't miss out on this opportunity, it's everything she wants in a career. She deserves it, I guess I just thought maybe I'd be part of that conversation and from the sounds of it maybe I would have been if it wasn't for that stone.

"She came to see me earlier to say goodbye and stuff, they're going in a few days." She falls silent and I feel her body shift her eyes darting in a million directions but not my face.

"What is it? What aren't you saying?"

"You could stop her if you wanted to, if you talked to her."

Maybe I could, I could talk to her and stop her. I want to. But I can't.

"I can't, she deserves this job and I belong here." I lift my head up so I can look at her properly. "Maddie, some things are just too hard to get past."

"Respectfully, bull-fucking-shit."

"Excuse me?"

"You heard me, bullshit." A fire lights in her eyes and I brace myself for the burn I'm eventually going to get from her. "James, I get it and I've never pushed you as much as I wanted to because I love you and I didn't want to hurt you, but this shit has gone too far." I can literally feel my palms start to sweat from the tone of her voice. "The stuff with your mum can't control the rest of your life. Kat is not her, and you are not your dad... that last bit is important. You have literally never had a drink because you think somehow it'll make you him. You love her, and you're going to regret it for the rest of your life if you let her go, for the love of god you should be shouting from the hills because she's actually your soulmate."

I blink are her because I'm scared to say anything. Maddie's tough, she's pushed me to do things and be things when everyone else was happy to let a sixteen year old depressed boy fall apart. But truthfully I had a feeling she was always holding back a little. There was always more she wanted to say but she always just said enough to get me back on my feet every time.

"Wow."

"Well, someone had to say it."

"I'm just glad it was you." She smiles at me but it's sad, and I try to give her one back but I know it doesn't come out how I want it too but it's the best I've got right now. "She's like the light in the darkness, all consuming and kinda life changing and I don't feel like—"

"Like you deserve it?"

I run a shaky hand through my hair. "She deserves the best of everything and I don't think that's me, I'm the dark cloud rolling in, ruining a perfect surf."

"You think that's how she sees it? You think she spent all that time with you because that's how she saw you? Ever thought maybe she sees you the way you see her?"

"She only wanted her soulmate. You really think if that thing hadn't glowed it would have been hard for her to leave?"

She pauses for a minute and I know it's because she knows I'm right, but she looks at me like I'm the one that's grown an extra head. "Yes."

The fact I've still driven here under current circumstances can only tell me I have truly lost my mind. As I look up at the house my feet plant themselves very firmly into the driveway.

My mum's house looks back at me, feeling much more like a haunted house than it should.

"I can do this," I tell myself but when I made these plans, I thought Kat would be by my side when the time came.

I didn't think I'd come. Kat got me to make these plans with Mum the day after our lighthouse trip. Without her, it feels like I'm falling. Falling into a darkness that I have no way of getting out of and torturing myself with a trip to my mum's seemed fitting.

The door flies open and a black Labrador comes running out at top speed flying at me. If I wasn't the height I am, or had the muscles I have, I'd definitely be on my ass right now.

"Harvey, no!" Lee shouts as he comes running after him, but the dog's sat at my feet now looking up at me like I'm his new best friend as I scratch behind his ear. "Sorry, James he's, well, a little crazy." Lee looks at me like I might very well punch him in the face and maybe a few months ago I would have, but honestly I don't have the emotional energy to hate him right now.

"Harvey, in!" My mum shouts from the doorway and he gets up and legs it back into the house. "Are you coming in?" she asks, walking a little closer slowly like I'm some wild animal that might bolt at any second.

"Yeah." I follow her and Lee into the house slowly. The house is, well it's a house. It doesn't conjure up any kind of emotion from me. It's not like our old one, it's not like the one she talked about owning, it's just a house. Living room to the right, kitchen to the left, with stairs even further than that. It's nice, not like her but also just like her. Like I said, it's just a house.

We walk out to the back patio, Harvey weaving though my legs as we do. Mum and I sit on two garden chairs facing out into her garden which in fact does look like our old one. The ocean is in view and that makes my shoulders drop at least three inches.

"I'll be in the office," Lee says, excusing himself, kissing my mum before going inside. Harvey nestles himself at my feet, guess I won't be making a quick getaway at any point then.

"I won't lie, I didn't think you'd come," she says not quite looking at me but in my direction. It's good to know this is awkward for her, too.

"I said I would." It comes out angrier than I would have liked but it's my default with her.

This would be easier with Katherine.

She softens all my jagged edges and smoothing out my wrinkles. I've tried to stop thinking about it but after my conversation with Maddie yesterday I didn't sleep much and my comfort place is somewhere between Kat's kisses and her smile. Maddie's words haven't stopped spinning yet either.

"When your dad called to say what happened, I just thought—"

"Dad called?" I interrupt her as my brain clicks back into the present. This is clearly a week of bat-shit crazy stuff happening because what?

"Yeah, the other day. Sometimes loving someone will make you do crazy things and your dad loves you like nothing else." She says it like there's something more she wants to say but doesn't. I'm not even sure what we're meant to say or talk about but I guess this breaks the ice.

"So he called?" I'm still kinda stuck on that really, the man hasn't uttered her name in ten years and lost his shit when he found her wedding invitation.

"Yep, but I want to ask if you're okay?" she asks, and then I realise we're looking at each other, like really looking at each other. In the kind of way we used to, in a way that truly makes me feel comforted by her.

Just be honest with her, talk to her. Remember no what ifs.

So, honesty... Let's try it. "No."

"I know I'm maybe the last person you want to talk to about this, but if we're here anyway, maybe you might want to?" Her voice is hopeful and light, the look in her eyes reminds me of when I was younger. "I will stay quiet and you can just vent all your feelings at me if that helps. Sometimes it helps to talk it out loud rather than in your head." This won't fix everything but I guess what have I got to lose.

So I go from the start, the moment I met Katherine until the moment I walked away from her. She doesn't say a thing and lets me get everything out. I don't think I realised how much I was holding on to until I finish and look back over to the sea and the sun is lower in the sky.

"Do you want my opinion? Or are you just happy to have got it out?" she asks, treading so carefully with her words.

I just nod at her as I think about everything I've just told her, it's not like it can get any worse.

"I think you should tell her you love her and then let her make up her mind about what to do with that information."

"I didn't say I was in love."

"You didn't have to."

"I've barely known her four months, and half of that time we spent arguing," I remind her. I wish I hadn't wasted so much time telling myself I hated her.

She smiles at me. "Yeah, that's kinda not how it works, love isn't about time, you can know someone for five minutes and know you're going to love them. I think the moment you met her, you knew you'd love her and that scared you." I guess honesty is working both ways today, will anyone just tell me I'm right and let me be?

"Can you blame me?" I retort back because let's face it, who made me afraid of love? Who set me on this path?

"No, it's my fault." I'm a little thrown off by her just saying it. "I made you think that love was the enemy, that love was the thing that ruined things. That's on me and I'm so sorry James. But my point is, loving her isn't going to ruin you and it won't fix you either, but god, will it help you find the pieces again. It'll help you realise the life you haven't been living because you've been closed off to such a big part for so long. James, being loved and loving someone else is like holding real magic, whether that's a soulmate or not."

She's right. When I was with Katherine, it was the most whole I've felt in so long, like the missing piece of me was there again, she made me feel alive even if it was because I was angry at her. But when we were on the other side, when she let me hold her, that's what living was meant to feel like. I could breathe when she was around.

Fuck, I love her.

I love her.

"Are you staying for dinner?" Lee asks, sticking his head though the sliding door, he looks hesitant, I don't blame him. I haven't exactly given him any reason to think I like him, I don't know him, maybe I should.

Harvey gets up wagging his tail at me, before running though Lee's legs back inside.

"Yeah, that would be great."

Chapter 41
Katherine

Leaving wasn't easy in any description of the word.

It wasn't like I was just leaving behind Ella, Maddie and James. It was like I was leaving behind a new part of myself, like something in me had grown while I was there. A free part and a part of me that wasn't stressed and anxious.

And I don't know how to be that me without this place. How to take everything I've learnt with me, because it all just seems so entangled with Gull's Bay.

But truthfully I know it's not the place that changed me, he did.

"I'm going to miss you so much," Ella told me as she practically squeezed every morsel of oxygen out of my body. "But I'll see you soon, I'll come to the States, I promise," she said, pulling back, holding my face in her hands like I was six again.

"You know you don't have to do that." The whole reason it had been so long was because of losing Dad, she couldn't deal with being in the city he lived in without all the pain coming back, I guess that's the reason we didn't come to visit either. No one ever said it, but everyone knew.

"I think it's time we all decided to not let the bad times take away for the good ones, I think Ben would be kicking all of us if he knew how bad we'd let things get." She's right, Dad was all about staying connected as much as we could and I think we all thought the space would be good but it's done the opposite.

"Aunt Ella is right, we're family and we need each other," Mom says, rolling the last suitcase out of my room.

Ella drives us to the airport and it's like a scene out of a movie, hugging and crying at the check-in desk like we'll never see each other again.

When we touch down at JFK, I expect to feel this overwhelming sense of relief or maybe regret but I don't. Nothing that strong hits me until we walk through the doors of the airport and Bella and Nick are waiting at the taxi stand. I don't even think as I run to them.

I've missed this more than I thought I would.

We don't move from our group hug until Mom catches up, and it's like I never left.

When we get back to the apartment, Mom says she's in need of a very long nap. I am too but I'm hyped up on adrenaline, so the three of us order the greasiest, most New York pizza from a shop a few blocks away. We stay up for most of the night talking and me crying.

Nick hugs me in the way he always has, strong and sturdy. I'd missed these, needed them more than I thought I did. But I don't get any of the feelings I used to. No longing or wishing for him in the way I used to. He's just my best friend hugging life back into me because I'm heartbroken.

I wanted easy, I wanted familiar and safe, and I thought that was Nick for years. But the universe gave me difficult, frustrating and yet the safest I've ever felt. It gave me James and now that I've known the feeling of being with him, I'm not sure I can ever forget it. Not sure how I am meant to feel whole ever again.

When I wake in the morning, I have that moment where I completely forget who I am, where I am, and what I'm doing. It's nice for a minute, to forget I ran away. I reach for my phone off the nightstand just to remember it's not where it was at Ella's. I root around under my pillow, finally finding it. I have a text from Maddie saying she hopes we got back safe and sound, and I feel a tear roll down my face. I wipe it away quickly when I feel Bella stir next to me.

I'd also forgotten they were both here, Nick curled up on a futon on the floor. His legs hang off the end but he looks peaceful.

Bella sits up more and pulls me into the side of her, my head resting on her shoulder. "It'll be okay. You'll get through this," Bella tells me as I feel more tears fall down my face.

"Will I? Because I feel like there's this hole in my chest now." I know I made the right decision, I needed to come home. It was time even if I didn't know it.

That's a lie.

He said to me the last time I saw him, *Any feelings you had for me, you would have just swept them under the carpet when you met your real soulmate, is that it? In twenty years time you wouldn't even give a thought to me because at least you had your soulmate.* Well I guess truly it's the opposite way round, I'll have to forget about my soulmate. Have to pretend with someone else the way I wanted to, was going to do, with him.

"You're stronger than you think, Kat."

I just have to believe it's true. I'm surrounded by so much love in the city and with a new job days away to take up all my attention, I can do this.

In the ever wise words of Taylor Swift, "*I wanna be defined by the things that I love. Not the things I hate. Not the things that I'm afraid of. Not the things that haunt me in the middle of the night. I just think that you are what you love.*"

And I love the people around me, I love New York, I love my family, I love writing, I love grabbing a coffee and listening to music while I get lost in the city, I love the smell and feel of a new book, I love little knick-knacks from travels and trips—and I love James.

He's a part of me now, he changed me more than I ever thought was possible. And he'll be one of those things that defines the rest of my life, even if he's not in it. He'll always be there, in a corner of my heart but I'll be okay and I hope he is too.

I think growing up might mean not hating people for breaking your heart when they were probably breaking their own too.

Chapter 42
James

Two weeks without Katherine feels like a lifetime.

Now that she's been part of it, it feels like she was always here, like she's always been irritating me and by my side. I can't imagine doing this for much longer, I don't know how I'm meant to pretend that she hasn't clawed her way into my soul and put a part of herself there.

How do people do this? Let someone go but keep loving them. I'm trying to do the right thing, be the better person. I don't even think she'd want me now anyway, not after I ruined her soulmate moment. I ruined that, I exploded and over-reacted. Not because I was actually mad but because I didn't know how to deal with it and my best option seemed to be anger.

And the thing I can't stop thinking about was how she said, *I didn't put it in there.* And, *why is it only glowing now?* I didn't register any of that at the time but she did. Like she was confused, like it wasn't the first time she had it around me, but that doesn't make sense. We always both said I'd never be her soulmate.

That almost feels like a joke now.

"Wow, I'm so impressed, you've managed to fold one t-shirt in the last half an hour," Ella says, coming into the back room looking at the delivery that would normally take me twenty minutes to put away.

"Yeah, well, perfection takes time." I offer her the best smile I've got in my arsenal but it does little to move the frown from her face. It's sad how I used to see a little of Ella in Kat, in the caring sunshine kind of way, and now whenever I look at Ella that doesn't comfort me.

"Yeah, or you're distracted." She steps closer to me. "James, you can always tell me the truth."

I look away from her, unable to look at her eyes any longer. "I know," I say, trying with all of my strength to literally not think about how Katherine has been all over this stockroom.

She sighs, leaning on the table next to her. "How was seeing your mum?" she asks.

The flip in conversation almost gives me whiplash. "Is this ask James hard questions hour?" My joke doesn't make either of us laugh. "Hard. I thought—I thought Kat would be here to help me. But good, I guess."

"Good."

Ella and I have never been like this, never tiptoed around the real questions, never avoided everything with each other. She's like a mum I didn't have, a bit like the dad I didn't have either.

"I'm sorry, Ella, I just don't know what to do anymore." I know she'll tell me it'll take time, that I'll be okay soon. That this will hurt a little less in a few weeks or months. That one day I'll wake up and it'll just stop being painful.

"I do. Fly to New York and tell my niece exactly how you feel. Because honestly you're bringing us all down and I can't cope knowing she's probably acting the exact same way a thousand miles away." She crosses her arms over her chest and I feel about sixteen again.

"Ella." I let out a shaky breath cause honestly going and seeing her is all I want to do. "I can't, she's starting a new job, and my life is here, and as I'm sure she's already told you I fucked up."

"She may have mentioned it, she also mentioned how she understood your reaction even if she wasn't happy about it. Look, I can't tell you what she's thinking any more than I can tell her what you're thinking but you can."

"But Dad..."

"Will be happy you found someone you love," she says, interjecting. "James, we don't choose where we grow up but we can choose where we make our home. I wasn't born here but I'd call Gull's Bay home before I would California. Much as I imagine you would call Kat home before this place. A person can be home just as much as a house. Where you live isn't as important as the people you have with you. I don't know where you and Kat will end up but as long as you're together it doesn't matter."

"How long have you had that one brewing away?" I smile for the first time in what feels like forever.

"Oh, at least a week. I was just waiting for the right time." She stands up fully again. "I've got enough air miles to get you there, and you'll just have to hope she forgives you cause I don't have enough to get you back."

My brain swirls for a moment, I could do this, go running after her. I could have my standing at her window with a boombox moment, I could but I shouldn't.

"She's probably settled by now."

"Then go unsettle her. That's what you two have been doing for each other since she got here."

Ella's words linger in my mind as I finish my shift early, per her request, apparently I'm not much help at the moment anyway. I drive home and Dad's car is parked in the driveway, in the middle of the day, which is normally a bad sign.

Lately he's actually been holding it together pretty well. He hasn't really talked about Mum, or why he called her or how he feels about it, but he is going to meetings again. He's told me this is the time it's going to stick and I'd normally roll my eyes and wait the week out until he's back down the pub, but I think maybe this is it.

It feels weird to have a feeling of hope when it comes to my dad but this time I do. It feels about the only thing in my life right now that I actually think will work out. I know not to put too much on it or him so I've kept my optimism to myself.

There's a bag packed by the door when I get in, it's his.

"Dad?" I call out into the house and his head pops out from his bedroom.

"Hey, kid." He walks towards me like a man who's been sober for more than a few days. "We need to talk."

"Yeah, I can see that, where are you going?" I ask moving into the living room following after him. He sits in his normal recliner, I sit on the arm of the sofa across from him. "What's going on?"

His eyes are full of something I'm not sure I can put my finger on, almost regretful. Wistful I think the word is.

"Well, you know that rehab I mentioned a week ago? Well, a space opened up." He looks over my face for a second. "It's mine if I want it, but I have to go today," he tells me, his hand shaking a little. I reach across to hold them.

"I didn't even think—today? This seems a bit soon." What I really mean is I didn't think he'd really go, didn't think he'd have to leave so soon after her.

"I've been holding on to too much. I think it's time I let some of it go." Every time he's been sober for a while it's just been a cold turkey and willpower situation, which he never had a lot of. He never talked about actually talking to someone, a therapist, to help with the brain part of it. To talk through the reason he actually drinks.

"I'm not sure what to say."

"Well, I imagine it's something along the lines of 'about damn time' because we both know that I've put this off long enough, Son. I was so sure I could do it myself, I guess I was too scared to admit I couldn't." He lets out a breath and it seems to deflate his whole body but he's got this light in his eyes I haven't seen in years and for the first time, I believe him. And it's not about me or anyone else, just him, and I don't think he's going to let me or himself down this time.

"Now I'm really not sure what to say. I'm proud of you." I pull him off the chair and bring him in for a hug and my chest feels full and a little like I might cry. All I can think about is the life he might have after this and the extra time I'll get to have with him. Because years ago, I had come to the conclusion that I'd have no parents before I was thirty. That Mum was gone and Dad would get so ill from the alcohol that I wouldn't be able to do anything and he'd be gone too.

"I wouldn't be doing this if it wasn't for you. Seeing how you managed to work though your own demons, seeing how happy you were with Katherine. How you're working things out with your mum, you're an inspiration."

My next breath gets stuck in my throat. Have I really worked through anything? Have I really changed that much to affect him to this point?

"And since I'll be gone for a while, there's no excuse not to go and get your girl back." His eyes light up even more, a little more air in him, this has Ella written all over it. Maybe not the rehab but the rest has her finger prints embedded in it.

"This isn't about me, Dad, it's about you. I'll be right here when you get back. I'm not running off to New York."

Even if I really want to.

Even if I can't help feeling this pulling on my chest every other minute, even if my mind wanders to her all the time, even if I wonder what it might be like to actually be with her. To hold her hand when

I want to, to kiss her until I forget who I am, to plan the future with her.

"No, Son, it's about us. About us finally taking control of our lives again. I've let my drinking get in the way of so many things, so many good things, I've let it ruin so many good things with you. So I'm taking back control for me and for you and you are going to do the same." His face is like stone, like he's so set on this, so sure about what he's saying it's not an opinion it's fact and I almost believe him, in the way you believe your parents when they tell you Santa Claus is real. "You've been writing off love for years, you've put it down as something evil, something to be warded off. And god it might have ended so badly, but the years I had with your mum, I wouldn't trade for the world.

"Love is like holding real magic in your hands, it's everything you think it's going to be and so much more, and I want you to have that. To get to experience that. You wanted her to like you, love you, because she wanted to, not because of the stone. How about loving her because of it? Why don't we both try something different for a change?"

Maybe I really do believe him. Maybe this many people telling me it's time to leap into something I'm scared of means they're right.

Maybe it's time to take control of my life again.

Chapter 43

Katherine

I stare at the blinking cursor on the screen in front of me, willing words to write themselves, hoping if I stare at it enough, it'll just happen on its own.

I came to meet Tommy the day after I got back two weeks ago and then started work the day after that. He told me to take a few days, start in a few weeks but I just wanted to get to it. I needed this, I needed to start immediately. To have something to focus on.

My mom says I'm looking for a distraction, and she's definitely right, I'm not denying that. I had one therapist at one point who said it was good for my anxiety to have something to look forward to, to keep myself going. He meant like a vacation or a shopping trip or a theatre show. I took it one step further and now I need a constant thing in life that's going to push me, that's going to help "future" me.

Working on myself is a constant job. I've got an appointment with a new therapist in a week, I've decided that even if I don't think I need therapy maybe I do, because let's face it I never worked through anything when I lost dad. I kinda hope James thinks about seeing someone, god I hope he went to see his mom, just to talk, see if maybe that was a relationship he could get back.

Fuck.

There I go again. Even when I think I'm not thinking about him, I am.

I close my eyes and let my head fall back against my chair. It doesn't entirely help that my first assignment is a five part article about my trip and my experience. It'll be part of the relaunch of the magazine's website.

That's right I will be one of the first writers to be posted on the website, for the most famous soulmate magazine in history.

No pressure, Katherine.

Don't get me wrong, I'm flattered and honoured and excited but I'm literally sitting here reliving the last four months of my life, and some would say they were a pretty life changing four months. But it's totally fine, I don't mind thinking about James from nine until five.

Totally fine.

The blinking cursor and blank page in front of me laugh back at me.

I have a week to get the first draft to Tommy, and honestly it shouldn't even be this hard but I just don't know how to start. Do people care about the why or do they just want to get to know how I packed up my life in two suitcases and ran half away around the world to find my soulmate?

I try to focus back on my computer. My eyes wander over my screen into the office in front of me.

Everyone has been crazy friendly since I started, not a single upturned nose or people whispering in the corner while looking over at me, like I imagined, like my anxious brain told me would happen.

A loud *bing* brings my eyes over the elevator, I thank my lucky stars we have one that goes right into the office. We're so high up, sometimes I just go and stand by one of the million windows and look out at the city. I've really appreciated getting that perspective the last couple of weeks.

It gives me the same feeling as being at the lighthouse again, I feel alone again just for a minute. And if I close my eyes, I can smell the salt in the air and feel his hand in mine and I'm at peace again. At peace with my situation, with the way things have to be. Me, here, and him, there, but sometimes it feels like he is here with me.

"Your final contract, Kat. Sorry it took a couple weeks, I didn't expect you to want to start so soon and there were a few changes I wanted to make after our last chat," Tommy says, laying down an at least thirty page content in front of me. I don't think I've ever had to sign one before. "Take it home, read over it a few times to make sure everything is okay, then just sign if you're happy and give it to HR on the thirty-second floor."

I feel him linger at my desk as I just kinda stare at it for a minute. "Yeah sure, thank you so much." My eyes get stuck on the job title part, 'Junior Writer'. That's me, that's the first stepping stone, this is the step I need. Yet I'm not sure how I feel about it, happy for sure.

"You alright?" he asks when I don't say what he had been expecting or at last my face doesn't match my words.

He's been great since I started, maybe he'll be more of a boss type once I've been here for a while, shouting about deadlines and bad ideas. But I don't think he will, I think he wants everyone here to be happy and work well because they want to, not because he's scaring them into it. No one has said a bad word about him and that's probably why I say what I say. "What if I'm not good enough?"

That's honestly what I've been worried about the most, not living up to what he thinks, or what anyone thinks. Studying for this and writing my blog are one thing, but actually doing it, it's like being thrown into a shark tank and not knowing how to swim.

"Oh, Katherine." He moves around to the side of my desk resting his hip on it so he can look at me better. "One, I wouldn't have hired you in the first place if I didn't think you were good enough. Two, if you're not ready to write these articles we can think of something else for you to have ready for the website. Three, I kinda think this has more to do with you having to relive it all then if you can actually write it."

"I think you might be right."

"Of course I am, I'm the boss, I'm always right." A slow smile creeps across his face turning into one that takes up his whole face. "Katherine, I'd understand if you didn't want to but I think a lot of people would be interested in what you have to say about what you went through."

"I guess it's just having to think about him." That's it, that's all it is, all the moments we had, they come rushing back the minute I think of him. His face stuck in my mind for hours. But that's just what I'll have to get used to because no matter what he'll always be a part of my story even if he didn't want to be.

"Is that him?" Tommy says standing up fully and turning his body away from me, and I'm not sure what he means until I follow his line of sight towards the elevator in front.

"James?" I almost don't recognise him in jeans, a sweater and a coat. The guy looks like he's going to catch hypothermia any second.

"I'm taking that as a yes," he says, practically pulling me from my chair and pushing me out from behind my desk.

How is he here?

Why is he here?

I trip over my own feet while I move around my cubicle, playing with my hair, flattening it down at my roots.

I feel my heart pick up, I was never nervous around him like this. Seeing him here right now it's like a dream, one I've had most nights since being back. I wait for my alarm to wake me up, throwing me back into the nightmare that is my life without him.

But as I get closer to him and the smell of sunshine and sea waves hit me and I know this is real. "What are you doing here?"

Chapter 44

James

She looks about as shocked as I thought she would be and yet the look still catches me off guard. Even in her turtle-neck jumper and jeans, she's still the most beautiful person I've ever seen; even in the dreary background of an office and grey clouds showing through the big windows behind her.

It's so out of place for me to see her like this, she's almost not My Katherine but when she looks at me, everything is the same, as if we're standing on the sandy beach in Gull's Bay again.

"What are you doing here?" she asks, still at least a foot away from me, like if she gets any closer, we'll combust, which I think I just might if I can't hold her in some way.

"I missed you." Before she replies to me, she grabs my hand leading to me to an empty office room, pulling me in the room and then she lets go of my hand like I've burnt her and she moves so far away from me, I feel cold all over.

She leans on the big table in the middle of the room and runs a hand through her hair. "Don't say shit like that. I left because you didn't want this. Don't say things like *I missed you* when you're the one who didn't want me. You're not allowed to miss me." Her voice shakes at the end, and I just want to wrap her up in my arms and make it all okay. How could she ever think I don't want her?

"Katherine." I can do this, tell her how I feel, she hasn't run away yet, so that's a good sign. "When my mum left, I decided I didn't need to love anyone, ever. I decided it was too painful to ever give someone that kind of power over me and soulmates and stones were just another thing having a power over me. All I wanted was control over everything I possibly could. I wanted to control everything I felt."

She just looks at me, the look on her face unchanged, pained and angry.

"When you walked into the shop that day, you were just another reminder of everything wrong with my life and with me. You were so open to love and it just made me sick to look at you because of that reminder."

"Gee, thanks," she says half under her breath because I know she just can't help but say something back at me.

"Then I got to know you and you were just as much of a pain in the ass as I thought you'd be but I just couldn't stay away from you. Everything seemed to draw me to you in a way I just couldn't understand and no matter what I did, how much I tried I couldn't stop myself. I couldn't control it. I couldn't control my feelings around you."

I fumble around in my pocket, her eyes only shifting slightly when she sees it. I take a few steps closer to her.

It glows just like hers did, it glows so bright I can't quite look right at it, but she does. "This has been in a box under my bed since the day my mum left. I never wanted to think about it again but I never threw it out. It just sat there gathering dust, and maybe somewhere really deep down I just knew one day I'd meet someone who would change my mind. I met you. You've been like a fucking tornado in my life Katherine."

My fist tightens around the glowing stone in my hand and I slide it into my back pocket.

"I fucked it up, I over-reacted and blew up. I know I can't live without you. Not now—not now that you've been a part of it, I can't just forget about you. I'm so sorry I took that moment away from you, and I'll spend the rest of my life making it up to you if you'll let me. I'm sorry it wasn't what you deserved, I know how important to you it was and I guess I was just so angry and all the feelings about my mum came rushing back, so much so that I missed the part where the girl I love is my soulmate."

"James, what?" She's so close to me now that if I reached out I could touch her but I don't because the minute I do I'll forget everything I need to tell her.

"I love the ridiculous amount of sunshine you have inside of you and how you can make anyone feel like you're their best friend the second you meet them. I love the way you read a book and the way you smile while you do. I love how you make me feel when I'm around you, like I can do anything. I love how after everything you've been through, when you had every right to hate the world, you didn't. You just kept going, kept believing in love and magic. You're my magic, you're my Sunshine.

"I knew I would love you the moment I saw you and I was just too god damn scared and stupid to see it, it turns out that love and hate feel far too similar and I just wanted to believe I could keep controlling it."

It seems like once I start confessing my feelings I can't stop.

"If I could take it all back I would. Or maybe I wouldn't. Maybe this was meant to be our story." I reach for her, cupping her cheek in my hand. She doesn't move away from me but leans into my touch and I'm warm all over. "I remember everything, I remember the way you taste, the way you move. The way your breath catches before you bite your lip and the way your body moulds into mine so perfectly. I remember the feeling of kissing you for the first time and knowing I didn't want to kiss anyone else ever."

I watch her chew her bottom lip before she talks. "I missed you, too." She finally smiles at me and I know I would suffer flying for twenty four hours again just to have her smile at me. "I get why you were angry, you trusted me and I broke that by having my stone with me. I still don't understand how it got there, but that's not the point. All you wanted was for me to want you because I did and not because of my stone but that's the thing I did. I wanted to be allowed to fall for you so I tested to see if you were on the day of the wedding," she confesses and it's like all the air has been stuck out the room.

"What? So you... we did all that stuff after even though you thought we weren't?"

"It hurt every part of me knowing, or thinking, you weren't my soulmate. Because I didn't understand how I could feel that way for you without you being my soulmate and you could call me scared and stupid too."

I lock my fingers between hers and we just look at each other. I know what she's just said and what she meant by it even if she's not quite saying it in. Because I know her, I know every little thing she doesn't want to be known. The smell of her fills my head and I take a big breath in hoping that somehow this will all be enough, that I will be enough. That she won't want me to leave, that she'll let me stay.

With her.

I lean my forehead against hers and my other hand goes to her arm as I work my way up, up to her shoulder and then her face. Holding on to her cheek, I run my thumb over her bottom lip and she leans into my touch. If we weren't in an office, at her new job, I'd stay like this forever with her.

I watch as she opens her mouth and closes it again, and then she looks up at me. "I love you, James."

And that's it. That's all I need to press my lips to hers and it's like we're experts at it now, I don't even have to think about how our lips mould together.

And I don't need her to tell me why she loves me, I don't need a speech or a list because I just know she does because kissing her is like coming home.

Kissing her is the only thing I want to do for the rest of my life. She's the only person I want to do it with, forever. She pulls away from me after what feels like forever but even that will never be enough.

"Kat, I will love you for as long as I live, I don't ever want to know what a world without you in it is like." A tear rounds down her cheek and I wipe it away with my thumb. I never want to see her cry, but I'll be there every time she does. I'll piece it all back together again.

We both stand up properly again and she takes my hand in hers again leading me back to the desk she was sitting at when I arrived.

"Tommy, would it maybe be okay if I left early?" she asks the man sitting at what I assume is her desk, he leans back in the chair, the biggest smile spreading across his face as he looks at our hands.

"I'll see you on Monday. Don't forget to take this, make sure you read over page seven for me," he tells her, getting up from the chair and walking away.

She grabs her stuff and the pages he handed her and then we walk back to the elevator.

"Do you think everyone heard all that?" she whispers to me, and honestly yes probably. I look out of the door back towards the other desks, people smiling and chatting but I don't care if they did, I want to tell every stranger I see that I love her and she loves me too.

When we reach the street again we start walking, I don't know where we're going, I don't care as long as she's next to me. I turn to look at her as I walk next to her and she's already looking at me. "You know, flying all the way here to tell me you love me is pretty romantic," she states and that makes my cheeks warm thinking about how she's right. "This is so cliché, it's making you sick isn't it?" she asks.

"Just a little, but I'd do it a hundred more times just to have you next to me, Sunshine," I tell her and I don't think I've ever meant anything more in my life.

Truthfully, it's like a revolting romcom and yet I couldn't regret it if I tried. I'd do it all again if it meant she would be walking down a random street in New York with me. In that moment I realise I'd do it all again for her, for my soulmate.

No matter how reluctant I had been about falling in love, here I am walking into a completely unknown future with her.

Epilogue
Katherine

Two and half years later

I'm not sure how it's taken us this long to finally get a chance to surf in California but it has.

We're staying in Santa Monica where Dad and Ella grow up while I write a new article, but today, we got up early—stupid early—to catch the morning waves at a secret spot Ella told us about.

We're the only two people out on the water at the moment and for a second it feels like our first date all over again, yes I do count Stargaze Perch Lighthouse as our first date. Alone, but with each other. The sun's only been up for a few hours but it beats down on my face when I look up to the sky.

"It's still not as good as the waves in Gull's," James tells me from the board next to me, he grabs my calf under the water and pulls me closer to him.

My right leg wrapping around his left to keep me in place. "You've said that about everywhere we've been." He has.

Turns out the ocean is somehow magical in Gull's Bay because no surf has been as good since we started travelling. I mean he's not wrong there is something truly magical about that place. God I can't wait to be back there next year but right now we're State side and I've tried my best to guide my writing jobs to the coast.

I'm basically Tommy's travelling writer now. As per my contract anyway, I am allowed to work remotely and considering the kind of work I do for the website now, it makes complete sense.

After I published the first part of my story about James and I, I was inundated with emails and DMs from people all over the world telling me about their crazy soulmates stories. Because as it turns out, the world is just as crazy and unsettling as I'd always worried but now I get to share all those stories with millions of readers.

"Am I wrong?" he says, moving his hand in the water, watching the shoreline for our next wave.

God I love this.

I never thought one of my favourite things in the world would be surfing with him. Or really doing anything with him, truthfully I actually think one of my favourite things might be going to the grocery store with him past eleven. Not a single other soul, just us, singing to the music playing and picking snacks out for each other. But I'll tell him it's surfing.

"No, never." I mock leaning over to kiss his cheek, it's salty but I'm kinda used to that skin ingrained with salt thing now.

This wasn't how I pictured the first few years of our relationship going, long distance, talking on the phone more than face to face, flying to just see each other for a few weeks at a time. If I could have it my way I'd be living with him by now, I'd wake up everyday with his blonde hair over my pillow or the smell of his coffee coming from the kitchen of the house we have together. But nothing about our relationship has ever been easy. So why start now? But I'm hoping to change that soon.

I haven't told him yet but I've gotten enough stories lined up for next year in Australia for us to finally be in the same country for long enough for us to consider renting together. If he wants to of course, it's not something we've talked about a lot but this is for the long term, us, him and me. It's forever even if we haven't said so yet.

"How's your dad, by the way?" I honestly can't believe James' dad will be three years sober in a few months.

What a journey that one has been, James stayed in New York for two months after he came to *get his girl back* as he put it. Our first Christmas, our first New Year's. He really threw himself in the deep end with all that, meeting my mom, meeting Bella and Nick. I honestly thought Nick would be the one he'd have to win over the most but really it was Bella. Her job as my best friend, of course but I think deep down she loves him.

They both do and honestly that's all I could ask for, I'm hoping to plan a little holiday for all of us. Bella, Nick, Maddie, Willie, James and me. They've all met on different occasions, that's a long story for another time but I just feel like we're going to be each other's family for a long time, might as well make them all be friends now.

It's kind of crazy how the two of us have contacted four other people to each other, and sometimes I wonder how love will change and grow that one day.

"Yeah, good, he said things with his girlfriend Sally are going well." And honestly if Jame's dad can find love again after everything that happened, I truly believe there's something to be said for finally making the changes you need to.

That's one thing that therapy has helped me with, teaching me that it's never too late to make the change you need to. I think James and I both benefited from that lesson and despite the fact I love the man next to me like nothing else that didn't mean there weren't things we had to work through. Separately and together.

I learnt that not everything has to run on my timeline, that things will happen when they're meant to and I can't rush them. I feel like those realizations came from finally processing my grief over my dad passing. Which is a constraint work in progress, but I'm getting there.

James learnt that I wasn't going to leave, that one was hard, but he's better at trusting now. He learnt that loving people and being vulnerable didn't mean they were going to take that part of him and run. I think him working on his relationship with his mom helped with that too.

"Hey, here's one," I say pointing off into the distance, the wave too far away to actually start moving but I can see it now. I can feel the ocean change as the kinetic energy moves us.

"Sunshine, can I ask you something?" he asks, sheepish in a way he never is. But I feel my face burn at the nickname, something that has never gone away.

I smile at him, because he can ask me whatever he wants for the rest of my life. "Yeah, but make it quick." My attention moves from him to the sea back to him.

"Kat, will you keep spending every day with me?" My brows knit together, where is this going? "Spend every day making me happier than the last? Spend every day making me thankful you packed up everything to come find me?"

Is he asking me to live with him?

"James, what are you talking about?" I quiz, the movement of the water picking up as I unhook my leg from him getting ready to move.

He takes a deep breath. "Katherine Miller, will you marry me?"

What?

I didn't hear that right.

My eyes move from him back to the four hundred ton wave moving closer to us. "James, there is a massive wave coming!"

"Is that a yes?" A smirk pulls on his lips not taking his eyes off of me, the wave getting closer with every passing second.

But I can't look away from him either. There is no way he's doing this right now. I look into his eyes and everything in me tells me this is real. That he has chosen right now to propose to me.

"We don't even live together!" Yet.

"That's all just logistic, I want to know if one day you'll let me call you my wife."

He's proposing to me!

I want to leap at him and kiss him until I'm out of breath but that's not going to work right now. "YES!"

"Thank god because that wave's about to hit us," he laughs, smiling bigger than I think I've ever seen.

"You are crazy!"

"Only for you, Sunshine, always for you. I'd start paddling if I was you," he tells me smiling before turning and paddling back to the shore.

We paddle all the way until I beat him to the break and ride that wave like it's the last one I'll get. But it won't be, because he'll always let me have the wave, he'll let me beat him to it.

And when I run on to the beach and drop my board at my feet, there he is already on the sand. Down on one knee, a ring box in his hand and forever in his eyes. And I finally understand why he wouldn't let me pack the bag this morning.

And I cry as he puts the ring on my finger, I cry while I kiss him and then I cry when I call my mom. And then again when I call Ella and again when I call Bella.

And I cry while we sit on the beach together, watching as more people make their way into the water. And he holds me like he always has, he holds me like he promised he always would.

This is the forever I wanted, the forever I didn't know I needed but the one I get to have.

The one I was meant to have even if I didn't know it three years ago.

Extended Epilogue
James

<u>Ten years later</u>

"MUMMY! Did you see me!" I let go of Ben's hand when we reach the top of the stairs leading from the beach back to our house. I let him run away from me toward our house's backyard porch where Kat is sitting reading.

When I look up at the house, I can't quite believe we did it, we made a little place for us, for our family. Never did I think I'd have this, my own family; I didn't think I could possibly ever be this happy. But every day I wake up and I have to pinch myself because it kinda feels like a dream.

I may have had to twist Kat's arm a little to get her to agree to live right on the beach, but I think secretly she wanted it; she just wanted to make me work for it. God, did I.

That sounds like us.

Nothing has changed even after all these years together, we bicker like we love each other and we love like we'll never get tired of each other.

"I did, baby," she says, catching our mad four year old as he throws himself toward her. She spins him around as he laughs, her yellow sundress spinning around her knees as she does. He tells her about the wave he totally shredded.

Got to teach the kid the important things.

I can't help watching them, she's just as beautiful as the day she walked into my life. Her hair is still fiery red but now in a short bob to try and stop the kids from grabbing it. Her allover freckles paint the most beautiful picture across her skin, she's far more tanned now, our years of living in the sun showing on her.

"Daddy said I could give Uncle Willie a lesson," he tells her, the kid talks a lot. I'm not too sure who he got that one from, his red hair is from Kat, his blue eyes from me, his tanned skin from growing up in Australia. His personality is from spending too much time with his aunties. Maddie and Bella dote on him like he's the only kid to ever exist, now Bella's expecting her own. I can't wait to turn her kid into a menace too.

"Why don't you go get washed up from dinner," she tells him and he tornados into the house. "Don't wake your sister!" she shouts after him.

I walk up to her now and slip my hands around her waist. "You get her down?" Ellie is what I can only describe as a night owl and an early bird. She doesn't sleep. Ben was like a log for the first year. I guess we're paying for it now, but my precious daughter, not a wink and six months old, is starting to kill us both.

"Yes, are you sure we should inflict this on Willie and Maddie? I'm starting to feel bad," she asks, putting her hands around my neck.

"It's one night, one night for just us to be us for twenty-four hours. They'll survive. They owe us anyway." I treasure Ellie but I'm not sure they will. What are best friends for if not to babysit your kids?

I spin her around so her back is pressed into my chest and we both stare out to the ocean. "We could call your dad?" she asks.

I snort a laugh, my dad's been sober since the day he went into rehab and I can't believe he'll be ten years sober this year. Not that I didn't think he could do it, I guess I just wasn't sure after all this time, but he's impressed me everyday since and showed me that it's never too late to make a change if you want it bad enough for yourself. Him and Sally have been together for almost eight years now, she's great, I don't think I could have asked for a better match for my dad. Both my kids are lucky to have five grandparents all together.

"I'd be worried about his sobriety," I joke.

"James Buckley, you are terrible," she laughs too, swatting my arm wrapped around her. "Your daughter is an angel."

"My daughter?"

"Well yeah there's no way that wailing banshee is related to me." I can't see her face from here but I know my wife well enough, she has a big smile and creases in the corner of her eyes. Her face lit up like a Christmas tree. I kiss the top of her head. "God, I love it here," she says to no one in particular.

"Yeah." It was tough picking anywhere to settle down. We spent two whole years doing long distance, me joining her in the States for a few weeks here and there when she was working on stories. Then just after we got engaged we got to spend a whole two years living on the Gold Coast, it made it hard to pick one place but really it was no contest. But then just before we got married it was like we both knew where we needed to be.

I run a finger over her tattoo on her shoulder. She wasn't wrong about the whole getting addicted thing, she got the bug pretty quick. She has a few littered on her arms and legs, but the one on her shoulder is my second favourite, just after her lighthouse.

Soon after we got married seven years ago she came home with her shoulder wrapped. She started crying and when she pulled back the wrap, I saw it and even I wanted to cry a little. Willie gave her a more feminine version of the octopus I have on my shoulder. Hers is smaller, with thinner lines, more dainty details but the sentiment is all the same.

"Gull's Bay really is our home, isn't it?" It is in fact not, not really. She is. She's been my home since the day she promised to love me no matter what. The day she let me put a ring on her finger and called me husband for the first time.

When I come home, and she's sitting on the sofa with Ben in her lap and she's watching some sitcom on the TV, all the air leaves my body. Seeing her on a surfboard next to me in the ocean, seeing her smile at me like it's the first time again. That's when I'm home.

"It's where we met, it's where it all started and as much as I would have loved to have brought the kids up in New York, I don't think your heart could have taken it."

New York had been a discussion, for all of five minutes, but the idea of them not having the chance to be around all of this and being so crowded in the city seemed to suffocate the both of us. We're so used to having space, to being able to step out our door and not see another person but the ocean instead.

It's been so long since either of us have been in New York, Kat hasn't lived there since her first six months at Soulmate Chronicles. In the first few years of our relationship we used to go back all the time, visiting her family, showing me around the beautiful places she grew up. New York is something else, I don't think there's anywhere else in the world quite like it, but it wasn't the place for us to make our forever home.

The only thing holding Kat back from leaving the city was her mum. And when she retired a couple of years ago, Kat didn't know what she'd do with herself, she was worried about her. That she'd wallow in the apartment and just think about all the things her and Ben, Kat's dad, were going to do once they'd both retired but she did the opposite. She sold the apartment and then started visiting all the places they both wanted to see.

I think in the last two years she's seen more places than Kat and I have. She even came and stayed with us the first four months of Ben's life, helping us find our feet.

Bella's still in New York so we always have somewhere to be when we want to visit, but it's been a while with Ben being so young and with Kat being pregnant with Ellie. Bella and Kat are still joined at the hip even from a million miles away. They just added Maddie to the hip too. I'm not bitter, I just became great friends with Nick just to even it all out a little.

"Speaking of New York, Tommy called and said he hoped everything was going okay with Ellie, just checking in." There's an edge to her voice I've learned to read before she's even decided it's there. "Would you be mad if I went back to work early?"

Mad is not a word I use when describing any of my feelings toward Kat, ever. Slightly irritated, but never mad. "No," I smile into her hair. With me running Ella's Surf Shop now, Kat's work is the one we work around the most. Being in Gull's Bay means we have the best support system, my parents, Ella, Maddie and Willie. Neither of us had to be away from work for long. "How early is early?"

"Well I said I wouldn't until we get little miss vampire to sleep through the night. I gave him an estimate of like two months."

Kat's work is so important to her that I'd move heaven and earth to get her back to it as soon as she wants. The older Ben gets, the easier it is for him if she's gone and even if Ellie isn't sleeping, I've got back up even if she has to travel a little—not that she's ever gone for more than a few days. "Would you need to go back to New York?" I ask.

"Only for like a week just to touch bases, and it would be good to see Bella and Adam." I see what's going on, my wife is far less sneaky than she thinks she is. I spin her around so she's facing me again.

I look over her face and watch as she avoids my eyes. "Bella's due to have her girl in two months, those two things wouldn't happen to be connected would they?" Ever since we had Ben, Bella's had baby fever.

It wasn't easy for her to get pregnant on her own, Kat cried every time she got off the phone with her wishing there was something more she could do to help. It took Bella and Adam a little while but it seems to have worked out for them and they're expecting a little girl in a few months now. The fact that Ellie will only be eight months old when Bella gives birth means that the girls have been planning how they'll be best friends too.

The fact they'll live ten thousand miles away from each other doesn't seem to worry either of them.

"Yes." Her face is coy, after this long I'm always so surprised when she seems to think I can't read her like a book.

"If you just wanted to go to New York to see her and the baby you could have just said," I smile at her, if I thought it was at all possible to get Ellie on a plane we'd all make the trip but for right now I think it's safer if it's just her.

"Okay." The difference now is she doesn't fight me on it, doesn't pretend the way we used to, I like it. "I'd like to go to New York to see Bella and the baby when she's here."

"I guess we better get that darling daughter of yours into a sleep routine fast," I laugh.

We fall into the silence we always love, the one that's just the waves in the distance and her heart beating against my chest.

"I changed my mind," she tells me. I've learned a lot of things about Katherine in the twelve years we've been together. She has to have pancakes on her birthday, sometimes she just needs some time on her own but she'll still want me in the room. Those little tabs in her books were far more important than she initially let me think—I learned a lot from those pink ones. One of the best things is that she'll bring me into a conversation mid way through. I've learnt to roll with it and let her brain catch up with the fact she's been talking to herself.

"We can't get a divorce, I'm afraid I love you too much."

"Not that," she laughs. "I do think we would have found each other even if soulmates didn't exist."

"Yeah, I think we would have too. Some things in life are inevitable, and you and I, Sunshine, we're one of them."

I don't ever want to think about what my life would be like now if she hadn't turned up, I don't want to think about how lonely I'd probably be, how I'd still think love was the enemy and not the magic it really is.

I want to see everyday with her by my side. I meant it when I told her I wanted to grow with her, I want to be old in rocking chairs on this very back porch surrounded by our grandchildren and our crazy extended family made up of our friends.

"Daddy!" I'm brought back to the part of our life I'm privileged to be living now by Ben running back out to us.

I spin around and catch him by the waist before he runs head first into my legs, I pick him up and spin him in the air while he giggles at me, and when I catch Katherine's eyes, they are misted but her smile is all sunshine.

Always sunshine.

"Okay, dinner time," she says, clapping her hands and wiping her cheek.

Ben wiggles until I put him down and he follows his mum back into the house and catches her hand when he reaches her.

I watch them walk through the backdoor together and I realise I'm the luckiest man in the world.

I got her.

I got this.

I got to be happy.

The End.

Acknowledgements

I guess as this is my debut novel it should be obvious that this is the first time I'm writing an acknowledgment page, but I would just like to start with that, as much like this whole writing and publishing process I have absolutely no idea what I'm doing.

Theres probably a lot of people I could start this with but I feel like it's only right to start with *you*, wonderful reader, because you are the one who is making my dreams come true. And I know most people skip this bit so I want to make sure you see it. Without you picking up my book, reading it and (hopefully) loving it, I wouldn't get do the thing I love.

I hope that in one way or another you got something from this story, whether that be to never miss out on the joy in life because your scared, or that maybe you don't have to have control over everything happening in you life right now, or maybe it's that you don't have to live life with the cards you were dealt.

I truly hope you stick around for all of the other hundred of stories I have in my head (and in my notes app). I love you.

I guess next it's only right to thank the one person who's known about this story from the start, my amazing and supportive husband, Matt.

You have never made me feel like this dream couldn't be a reality or like this wasn't something I was capable of doing. Thank you for truly being my soulmate, for helping me rationalise every crazy thought I have. Thank you for never making me feel bad for taking time to write and thank you for making me believe in myself even when truly sometimes I never did.

I don't know who I have to thank for bringing you into my life, because we know it wasn't a soul stone, but I know I wouldn't be the girl sat here right now in our living room while you play Halo today if it wasn't for you, always being by my side, always holding my hand when I need it and always wiping my tears when I cry.

I love you infinity, and I can't wait to thank you in every book I release.

I want to thank the amazing Elaine from Ellie's Edits, I have said this to you before but I truly think this book would not be what it is today without your help. You helped me see things with in this book I never would have, you have made me a better author because of it and I'll be forever thankful for finding you. I hope you're ready for book two!

Thank you to the crazy talented Aida from Algart for my cover! You took the picture I had in my head and made it a reality, I will never know what kind of magic you used to do it but it turned out even better than I could have imagined. You truly brought this book it life.

A huge thank you to everyone over at Forever After PR for all your help and for helping me get my debut to more people than I could have dreamed. You guys are amazing.

To the wonderful authors in Chlo's Library Book Club, you know who you all are, everyday I am amazed by your talent and your kindness. Thank you for always being there when I needed someone to help. Thank you for all your support, I don't think you'll ever really know how much it meant to me.

To Noah Kahan and Taylor Swift for getting me out of every moment of writes block I ever had and because this is my acknowledgement page and I can thank whoever I want.

And lastly I guess I should thank myself, you have wanted to give up more times than I think we can count but you never did. You kept coming back to your laptop night after night wanting to tell this story. Wanting for other people to see themselves in these characters the way you see yourself in them. Your drive and determination to not let this story die pushed me everyday. I probably don't say this enough but I love you.

If you've made it to the end then just know Katherine and James will always be here when the world gets too loud or when you're questioning yourself. You can do literally anything you set your mind to, I believe in you. I love you. Keep going.

Penelope x

About the author

Penelope Coggins is a indie romance author, self-proclaimed Swiftie, who embraces all things considered "basic" from the South of England. But beneath the bubbly exterior lies a passion for tackling mental health in her stories. She sheds light on aspects she feels are sometimes over looked, hoping readers find comfort and connection in her relatable characters.

When not brainstorming in her notes app, Penelope's likely booking another adventure, engrossed in a hockey or cowboy romance, or cheering on her favourite Formula One drivers on a Sunday. When in doubt you'll find her curled up re-watching a Marvel movie.

Her novels consistently feature characters navigating their mental health journeys. Drawing from her own experiences, Penelope deals with these struggles with understanding and compassion.

Printed in Great Britain
by Amazon